LIGHTSOURCE

BARI WOOD
LIGHTSOURCE

9011046198

Macdonald

A Macdonald Book

Copyright © 1984 by Bari Wood

First published in Great Britain in 1985 by
Macdonald & Co (Publishers) Ltd
London & Sydney

British Library Cataloguing in Publication Data

Wood, Bari
  Lightsource.
  I. Title
  813'.54[F]   PS3573.0588

  ISBN 0-356-10664-0

Printed and bound in Great Britain by
Biddles Ltd, Guildford and King's Lynn

Macdonald & Co (Publishers) Ltd
Maxwell House
74 Worship Street
London EC2A 2EN

A BPCC plc Company

To my aunt, Susie Lewin Leonard

I would like to thank Joe Patrick
for trying to help me with the science,
and Connie Wood for good company on
some lonely autumn nights.

"Mr. Roark, we're alone here. Why don't you tell me what you think of me. In any words you wish. No one will hear us."

"But I don't think of you."

—Ayn Rand, *The Fountainhead*

PROLOGUE

RITA CALLED Nantucket Power and Light to turn on the lights in the Squam house, then called the phone company, and then she went back into her living room, sat down in front of the fireplace. She opened her book to pass the time. She didn't know what she was waiting for. Emily said they hadn't followed her, didn't know Rita Reed; they didn't know of any special connection between them. Rita was safe, Emily was sure of it. She wouldn't have come otherwise. And Rita believed her, but she waited anyway.

Everything was quiet; the clock in the hall chimed, the spring sun slanted and made shadows on the light green lawn. Rita read steadily, only half-concentrating . . . she was listening, even though she didn't think she'd hear anything.

Then the sound of a car came faintly through the windows, coming from the reservoir. Rita was sure that the sound would peak just outside the house, then die away as the car passed, heading for the Aldrich house or the Murphys' or down the road toward Route 57 and Redding. But the car slowed and stopped at her driveway, and she heard doors open and close.

Rita went to the window.

Two men got out of the car; a third stayed behind. The sun reflected on the car windows, and all she saw was the silhouette of a profile. She couldn't see it clearly, but it seemed familiar.

The other two men were strangers. They looked up at the house, then came up the path toward the door. One was very tall and hefty. His skin was ruddy, as if he worked outdoors, and from a distance he looked young. But as he got closer, she saw white creases around his eyes, and long indents that ran down his cheeks. He was rugged-looking, almost handsome, with thick blond hair and light eyes and lashes. He looked like an actor in the westerns she used to see when she was young. If they hurt her, and she had to describe them to the police, she'd have no trouble telling them what Number One looked like. Number Two was another matter. He was blond too, and he was losing his hair. Otherwise, there was nothing she could say about his face. He was the man who takes your ticket at the movies or your toll on the thruway. Mr. Nobody.

The emptiness of that face frightened her, and she backed away from the window.

The doorbell rang and Rita had a sudden impulse to run out of the house and across the back lawn. But that led to the Aldriches'. It was Friday; Margaret Aldrich was at the library until four, the children were still in school. The Aldrich house was empty. The other direction was no good; there were ten acres of woods between her and the next house. If they chased her, they'd catch her long before she could reach it.

The bell rang again.

She could run upstairs and lock herself in the attic. But Emily had said they were determined men. She'd said it wryly, as if it were an immense understatement. They could get into the house, break down the attic door, and find her cowering in the dust behind Grandma Parker's steamer trunk.

The bell again; she decided she was being an idiot. It was broad daylight, and they weren't wearing guns at their belts or rifles slung over their shoulders. This was Weston, Connecticut, not some town in Russia or Nazi Germany. She'd tell them she was busy, that it wasn't their business whom she knew or didn't know, and then she'd send them on their way.

The bell went again; that made four times, and she marched into the foyer to answer it. She put her hand on the knob, then looked back into the living room. Her book was open over the arm of the sofa; the fire was laid but unlit, the wide plank floor gleamed, and the house smelled of beeswax. She'd always lived here. Her great-great-great-grandfather had built this house, her children had been raised in it.

Sadness touched her like a premonition, but she quelled it, slipped the chain on, and opened the door a crack,

The handsome one was in front of it. He had his ID out, ready to show her.

"I'm sorry," she said, not looking at the card, "but I'm very busy now."

"Mrs. Reed, it's very important that we talk to you."

His voice was soft; he had a good accent.

She looked at the laminated card he held out in its case. His name was Kurt Gelb and he worked for a government agency with initials that she didn't recognize; it was part of the Department of Commerce, and the card was signed by Paul K. Stockton. She knew that name; he had something to do with conservation and environmental protection. According to the card, he was the director of this obscure agency.

"You know Dr. Emily Brand," he said.

"I'm sorry," she said, "I told you I'm busy," and she tried to shut the door, but he'd wedged his foot in the opening.

"We know she was here," he said, "we know you saw her . . ."

If they find you, Emily had said, *tell them what they want to know.*

"I don't know what Dr. Brand told you," he said.

"She didn't 'tell' me anything. She's an old friend, and she stopped to chat." He laughed, and the sound raised the hair on her arms. She shoved the door hard against his foot, and it must have hurt, even through the shoe, but he didn't move.

"No, Mrs. Reed," he said, still laughing. "Dr. Brand is wanted for murdering six people. She didn't stop by for a chat."

Rita's voice scaled up and out of control. "I tell you she did. We talked about the weather and movies and old friends . . ." She pushed the door with all her might, but Gelb grabbed the edge and shoved it so hard the chain housing ripped free of the wood and the door hit Rita and knocked her back into the foyer. She almost fell, but she kept her balance, and she slid, then ran back into the foyer to the phone table. She yanked up the receiver, punched 911, but he grabbed her wrist before it rang.

3

They were in the kitchen. Number Two leaned back against the counter, and Gelb sat across from her at the kitchen table.

"Now," Gelb said, "this is much better, isn't it?"

Rita didn't answer.

"About Dr. Brand."

"I told you—"

"Did you give her money, Mrs. Reed?"

No answer.

"Where was she headed when she left here?"

Still no answer.

"What did she tell you?"

No answer.

"It was a wild story, wasn't it?" Gelb asked softly. "All about people chasing her because of something she'd discovered. The government, the oil companies, she probably even threw in the Arabs and the Russians, and maybe the Chinese for good measure . . ."

"If it's so absurd," Rita said, "what are you doing here?"

A look went between the two men, and Rita wanted to call back her words. Gelb went on as gently as before, "Dr. Brand was part of a high-security project, she had a serious mental breakdown, and we believe she sabotaged a small plane. You may have read about it."

He stared earnestly at Rita. Maybe Emily's story *had* been wild, but Rita'd had to coax her, force her almost, to tell it, and the woman who'd just left her house—Rita looked at the clock—an hour and fifteen minutes ago and was now heading northeast on old Route 1 was just as she'd been when she was a little girl: intense . . . but certainly sane. Gelb and Number Two were lying. She felt sweat collect under her arms, trickle coolly down her ribs. She pushed her arms against her sides.

"Mrs. Reed?" Gelb asked.

"I have nothing to say." Rita didn't look at them. Gelb sighed and then he stood up and moved toward the door. They were leaving. They'd never meant to hurt her.

But if they were leaving, then Emily had made up the story, and to make up such things, Emily had to be crazy. Banked paranoia, Rita thought, blazing out after years, like the fire in the hold of a ship. She was sorry for Emily, sorry that she'd been wrong about her all of these years, but she was so relieved at the same time that she felt a little faint and, head

4

still down, she raised her hands and gripped the edge of the table. As soon as they left, she was going to have some ice cream. She'd driven up to Ridgefield yesterday and gotten a gallon of Heibeck's homemade. Her husband, Mayo, said the only place you could buy better ice cream was in Naples. Gelb was next to Number Two. They'd be gone any second, and all she had to do—she grinned to herself—was keep from fainting until they got out of the door and down the driveway to the other mysterious man.

God damn Emily, she thought furiously. How could she come here and frighten me like that? I'm not young . . . But then, Rita reminded herself, Emily had gone mad.

Just let them get out of here, she prayed, and then she'd sort it all out. She took a breath. They must be at the kitchen door by now; any second she'd hear it open and close behind them. She didn't hear anything, and she looked up. Mr. Gelb was in front of the door, Number Two was just to the side. Number Two was pointing a dull black gun with a long grip at her, and Mr. Gelb had a small leather case in his hand, like a case for manicuring tools. He started to unzip it.

She almost laughed out loud when she saw the hypo, because she'd expected torture, incredible, exquisite pain that she'd never imagined before: fingernails torn out . . . the soles of her feet burned . . . her teeth drilled to the root. But this way there'd be no blood, no screaming: she'd tell them everything without blame. Better this way, she thought.

Gelb grabbed her arm and shoved up the sleeve of her sweater. But there was no cotton in Gelb's other hand. She didn't smell alcohol. He wasn't going to swab her arm . . . he didn't care if her skin was clean, or the needle. He didn't care if the needle prick infected and she died of sepsis or hepatitis, because they were going to kill her anyway as soon as she'd told them where Emily was going.

She pulled back and almost got her arm away from Gelb, but Number Two raced across the kitchen and grabbed her. One hand was on her shoulder, the other on the back of her neck, and he must've pressed a nerve or something, because suddenly she couldn't move. The needle stabbed into her arm; the fluid burned as it went in.

Mr. Gelb, the handsome one, was watching her; his head

was to the side, his light blue eyes fixed on her with distant professional interest, as if they were doing some not-very-important research. He looked so reasonable that she was sure that she could explain to him that killing her was absurd. She wasn't the one that they wanted. It was Emily. She—Rita Benson Reed, of the Bensons who'd lived in Weston' for generations—was a minor character, almost an extra. She was only here because of an impulsive promise she'd made to a little girl almost thirty years ago. Not that she was sorry. Emily was worth dying for.

Still, she wanted Mr. Gelb to understand that killing so minor a character as Rita Reed was simply bad drama. She was ready to tell him this eloquently and persuasively, but suddenly she started to dream, and the brilliant exegesis that she'd composed went right out of her head. Mr. Gelb and the wall of cabinets behind him dwindled to a tiny point of light and disappeared.

In her dream, her ancestor Isaiah Benson had just landed at Plymouth; he was wearing a Pilgrim hat, and buckled shoes, and looked like a character in a school pageant, except that his clothes were tattered and he had her grandfather's face with its deep lines on either side of the mouth and the piercing deep-set eyes. He spoke to her in a gurgling distant dream voice. *You come from a good family*, he said. *We came through revolution, civil war, panic, and the great depression. These are rats with twitching tails in your kitchen; you can beat them.*

Under his voice, she knew that she was answering their questions. She'd known Emily since—when?—1962. Yes, 1962, and here it was 1990. Amazing. Yes, Emily'd come here . . . it must be an hour and forty minutes ago. Yes, she'd given her money. All she had in the house. About three hundred dollars. Her fuck-off fund, she called it. Now . . . now . . . Emily was on the run, on the road. Heading north by northeast . . . Rita felt herself giggle. Felt herself fight. North by northeast. She'd have passed Providence and be coming up hard on Fall River. Or maybe . . . No . . . just to Groton . . . coming up hard on Providence. Who knew how fast she'd drive? Maybe 55 . . . maybe . . .

Her head snapped and she knew that Gelb had slapped her, but she couldn't feel it.

The car? A Volvo. Time was, she told them, that a car was a car. Now, who knew?—there were so many kinds. GLE, GT, Turbo . . . 760 . . . 264 . . .

Gelb slapped her again.

No, she didn't know the license-plate number. She didn't know the state.

Where was Emily going?

Her ancestor's dream voice cleared and got louder. *Rats!* he yelled at her. *Swine. . . . Fight them.*

She made herself shake and moan, as if she were convulsing. Then she realized she couldn't stop shaking if she wanted to. She couldn't see, either, but she knew her kitchen. Just behind her to the right was the stainless-steel-fronted dishwasher they'd installed badly five years ago. One edge wasn't flush with the cabinets, and the corner of it stuck out, sharp and dangerous. She'd ripped stockings on it, torn a skirt.

"Where did she go?" Gelb asked. He slapped her again. The shakes got much worse; she felt the moans in her throat get louder, sharper.

"Island," she moaned, shaking harder. "Cape island . . ."

"Which cape island?"

She gasped.

"Goddammit . . . which island?"

She pushed her dead palms against the tabletop and felt herself getting up. Her moans got louder, hoarser, turned to shrieks, and she pitched sideways, past Gelb toward the sharp shiny steel edge of the dishwasher. She felt her head hit it, and she lost consciousness.

She woke up in the open air. The men were dragging her away from the car. Her arms were across their shoulders, and she managed to raise her head and look back. The third man was still in the car, as mysterious and familiar as before. Moving her head made her dizzy and sick to her stomach, and she turned front and let her head drop. They'd put her coat on her, and the front of it was covered with blood. She could feel it trickling down the side of her face from her head. Out of the corner of her eye she saw her purse dangling from one of their shoulders.

They dragged her past trees, along an invisible trail. Her

7

toes scraped through dead ferns and rotting leaves. Finally they got to a place that seemed to satisfy them. It was a sort of glade surrounded by thin maples. They must be near the reservoir; the ground was very damp and covered with moss and ground pine. She smelled mushrooms and bark, and that dank sweet-sour smell of spring.

The glade was lovely, the ground pine soft and dark green. Tree branches cast long shadows in the late-afternoon sun. They were gentle with her now. Together they eased her down so she was half-sitting, half-lying against one of the thin maples. Then Gelb squatted in front of her. She knew she could focus on him, but she kept her eyes glazed and distant.

"Cuttyhunk?" he said. "Elizabeth? Nantucket? . . ." It took her a second to realize that he was naming the cape islands. But now she didn't have to tell him anything.

"Tuckernuck?" he went on. "Martha's Vineyard?"

Her head rolled to the side. Number Two said, "Forget it," and then the third man got out of the car, and she saw it was David Lucci. She remembered the game she'd made them play twenty-eight years ago, and the night only four or five months ago when she'd seen him again for the first time since he was a little boy and she'd been his teacher. She remembered trying to see his eyes, that last night at George Talbot's mansion in Greenwich, but she couldn't because they'd been in shadow, and she remembered the pain in his voice when he'd said, "She won, didn't she? Emily Brand won. . . ."

Now everything made sense: David worked for Talbot, Talbot owned NARCON, and Emily was going to ruin NARCON. But Rita had the feeling that David wasn't just here to save NARCON, but because of the game too. Because Emily Brand hadn't played then and wouldn't play now. Maybe Rita was only a minor player, but she'd started it all with that game. The game had brought her to this sticky green place on a lovely spring day, to die. The game might kill Emily too. But Emily Brand was no second-stringer. Emily Brand was someone to be reckoned with, and Rita wasn't sure where she'd have put her money if she'd had the chance to bet. On David Lucci and these empty-eyed men, and all the power of NARCON; or on Emily Brand.

Gelb moved away, and Number Two faced her, his gun out and pointing at her forehead. She looked into the muzzle, then past it, and saw David turn his back. They were going to kill her, and he wasn't going to stop them. She wasn't surprised. He'd been her pet; but now she knew that there'd always been something a little wrong. . . .

A *little* wrong. If she hadn't been at the scene of her own assassination, she'd have laughed out loud at the understatement. She heard the hammer of the gun cock back, and she knew she had a second or two to live. She wanted to think of her Mayo one last time, or her children. But as she looked into the gun muzzle, so close now it blurred and made her eyes cross, she thought of Emily. Not the worn, almost middle-aged Emily who'd come to see her only this afternoon. But the little-girl Emily, the plain, brilliant, incredibly stubborn little girl who wouldn't play the game. Rita tried to remember the real woman for whom she was going to die in a second. The right picture came to her in time.

"Is it worth it?" she asked.

"Maybe," answered her vision. "If I get away . . . maybe."

Then get away, Rita thought fiercely as the gun muzzle touched her forehead. *Run, Emily. Run.*

PART
I

CHAPTER

1

EMILY LEFT Princeton in 1986, four years before Rita was murdered. Her boss, Herb Mendel, tried to stop her. He offered her more money, better housing, a better title. She said she wanted to leave anyway. He thought she'd change her mind, but she didn't. Then it was the afternoon of her last day and she came into his office to say good-bye. He was a proud man, but he had to try one more time.

"You can stay, Brand."

"I know," she said.

"Placid's good . . ." he said, tapping burned tobacco out of his pipe, "but it's not Princeton."

"I know," she said again.

He really hated her sometimes. He wondered why he was bothering, except that no one understood the machine the way she did. This morning he'd looked at the thing and had an insane moment of feeling sorry for a fusion reactor because it was going to lose its best friend.

"Then why the hell are you leaving?" he cried.

"Placid's in the mountains," she said. "I've never lived in the mountains."

Mountains! he wanted to scream at her. She was leaving the best plasma-physics lab in the world for a change of scenery. It was obscene . . . there had to be another reason. She had no important connections here, even after ten years. She could have had. She was pretty when you looked closely, she'd never showed temper or temperament, and men liked that. A few of them had fallen for her. Breemer was in love with her. He was young, decent-looking, and rich, and Mendel was sure that Emily slept with him. But she lived alone, and that, he told himself, was the real reason Emily Brand was leaving. She wanted the right man and he wasn't at Princeton, so she was going to Placid the way his daughters used to go to the Poconos for singles weekends. Only Emily never dissembled. If she were going to Placid to find a man, she'd say so. She was leaving him and his beautiful lab for exactly the reason she gave: she wanted to live in the mountains. He took a long trembling breath, relit his pipe, and tried another tack.

"You might make it work, Brand, have you thought of that?"

She didn't answer and he waved at the air. "Not that I'd put money on it, mind you, but you might do it. What then?"

No answer from her. He leaned over and tried to sound menacing. "It's no game, Em. If you *do* do it, a lot of very powerful people might get very cranky. Have you thought of that?"

"No," she answered.

"Think about it. They could make things hard for you at a dead-end hole like Placid. But this is Princeton! Mainstream celebrity science. We might as well have a direct line to the New York *Times*. You won't get that kind of protection at Placid."

She thought for a minute, and then she said, "I'm not afraid."

Mendel went home and drank a bottle of wine with dinner, and half of a second bottle while he and Ann watched TV. There was a nature special on, and he sat, woozy and sad, watching sharks glide across the screen.

"She should be frightened," he mumbled to himself. "She should be terrified." His wife looked in his direction for a second, then back at the screen. The narrator told them that sharks were the most competent animals on earth; they bred, ate, killed, and were so good at it that they hadn't had to evolve in over a million years. Like the industry men he had to deal with, Mendel thought, and the politicians, and some other scientists.

"Sharks," he muttered.

"What?" Ann asked.

"I said there're sharks out there, and Emily should be afraid."

She wasn't. He couldn't scare her with his vague threats, he couldn't change her mind, and finally there had been nothing left to do but hold out his hand to her and say good-bye. He looked blearily at his wife.

"She held my hand, Ann. Did I tell you that?"

"No," Ann said.

"She did. I meant to shake her hand, you know, but she just took my hand and held it."

It had been a gesture of affection, and when Mendel realized that, he had a moment of stunning exultation because this impossible genius of a woman liked him.

"I was so shocked," he told his wife, "that I forgot to wish her luck."

"Emily Brand doesn't need luck," Ann said, but Mendel didn't hear her. He got up, walked carefully across the room and up the stairs.

He took a shower and got into bed. He was drunk, all right, but he knew he would not sleep for a while. He'd lost her, and it ate at him. She might win the hardest, highest-stakes game since poor old Oppy Oppenheimer cajoled a fission bomb out of that bunch of maniacs in New Mexico. But if she did, it would be for Marvin Lipsky, not Herb Mendel, and she would do it in that dreary, lonely lab in the Adirondacks, not here, inside the safe circle of public attention. Mendel punched his pillow and tried to blank out his mind so he could fall asleep.

Downstairs, Ann Mendel turned off the TV, carried the glasses and ashtrays into the kitchen. She rinsed everything, put it in the dishwasher. She turned out the overhead light, but left the light on over the sink, then went to the kitchen table and poured herself a glass of wine. She was going to miss Emily too. She couldn't say that she liked Emily—it didn't apply, for some reason—but she had a mad impression that the furnace burned cleaner, the light bulbs lasted longer when Emily was in this house. She finished her wine, poured more, and drank it too. Her thoughts were getting away from her, but she let them go. Emily would never come here again, and Ann Mendel wanted her back with superstitious longing.

Maybe Emily was only a thin, outrageously shy woman who couldn't make conversation for three seconds, but to Ann she was a charm—the silver bullet in the werewolves' den . . . the cross of gold in the vampire's castle.

"Good-bye, Emily," she whispered, and then she added, just in case, "Good luck, dear."

Emily wrapped her mother's carriage clock to pack into one of the boxes. She remembered her mother's rosewood writing desk, where the clock had sat, and then she remembered her mother's room. It was big and dim; the draperies stayed closed after her mother got sick, but the sun came through the apertures, and lit the room in dusty stripes.

They sold the house right after Emily's mother died, and Emily never went back there. She never really lived anywhere after that, and when people asked her where she was from, she didn't know what to say.

Her great-great-grandfather had built the house in Wilton, Connecticut, in 1830, and it had stayed in the family until her mother died. It was huge and rambling and it must have been beautiful once, but by the time Emily was born the land was overgrown, the floors in the house sagged in places, and the facade had turned yellow with years of snow melt from rusty gutters. But Emily had loved it anyway.

She held the clock for a moment, then put it in the box. Her mother had died twenty-eight years ago, when Emily was nine, and all she had left was the clock, a leather-bound volume of *Sonnets from the Portuguese* with her mother's bookplate in the front, and the stuffed green plush brontosaurus that her mother had made for her. They were all in this last box, and she taped it up and carried it down to the car. She didn't have much, and between the trunk and the fold-down back seat she got it all in the car. The furniture stayed with the apartment; so did the pots and pans.

She went back upstairs for a last look. She had everything, the place was clean. She'd said her few good-byes, and she'd told Richard Breemer that she would write to him and he said that they might see each other again, but she knew that they wouldn't. She locked the door, dropped the key in the mailbox, and left the two-family house on Mercer Street, half a block from Einstein's house.

She liked night driving, the roads were good heading north, and she thought she'd be in Placid by one in the morning. She meant to go right to the turnpike, but when she got to the stop sign at the end of the street, she turned back toward the lab.

The building was closed and she'd turned in her ID, but the guard knew her and he let her in. Higgens and Span were on duty at the entrance to the reactor room. They were surprised to see her.

"Thought you were gone, Doc," Higgens said.

"I'm leaving now. I just wanted . . . a last look."

Higgens and Span looked at each other. Higgens shrugged, then let her in. He keyed her through the control room and out onto the balcony of the reactor room.

"Please, Doc," he said, "just a few minutes."

She nodded, and he left her. She leaned on the railing and looked down at the machine. She'd never been alone with it before, and she was surprised at how lost and ugly it looked; feelings that she didn't have words for came to her. The work lights reflected dully on the steel-and-molybdenum skin of the reactor; the air was dry and cold and smelled of metal. For five minutes she stood on the balcony watching the machine; then she whispered, "We'll see."

She nodded at the Tokamak fusion reactor and went back through the door to the control room.

The winter of 1990 was almost over, but the lakes in the Adirondacks were still frozen. The snow in the mountains packed down and turned solid, and when the night wind blew down the slopes and passes and across the valleys, the temperature went to twenty below. It was cold in the control room of the Placid facility, and the staff wore sweaters under their lab coats. Marvin Lipsky called out the numbers as they flashed on the screen, even though they could see them.

"Seventy-five," he called. The screen went blank; the same numbers flashed again. "Seventy-five."

Inside the reactor the temperature was at seventy-five million degrees centigrade: nuclei crashed into each other, grabbed on, fused, and blew off the orphan neutron that Lipsky said would light the world someday. But Emily knew it wouldn't be today.

Lipsky rocked in his chair; his lips moved.

The numbers flashed again, and Lipsky glared down at the machine.

"Do it," he whispered hoarsely. "Go, motherfucker!"

Sally Avery flinched and Miles Carver looked impassive. The laser would falter soon; they'd lose power and have to come up out of the lab like rats in the dark. Emily gently moved Lipsky's hand out of the way and keyed in for cool-down.

"What do you think you're doing?" he yelled at her.

She didn't answer and he threw himself back in his chair. "Oh, my God," he moaned. "Oh, Emily, what am I going to tell them?"

On Monday Lipsky had to make his annual trip to Washington to ask for money he wouldn't get. The directors of the labs at Princeton, Stanford, and Los Alamos hadn't gotten their money either. The reactors didn't work; newer ones just like them wouldn't work. They needed something they didn't have, and without it the machines were done for.

This year the President himself was going to see Lipsky. He'd seen Mendel and Crowder, and no one knew why. Maybe just to satisfy himself that controlled fusion energy was a dream that they all had to wake up from. And when he did, the funding would dry up, the lab would close down, and the helpless machine would be dismantled.

"Fuckers," Lipsky moaned. "They spend twice what we need on some shit bomber that'll be scrap in five years."

Emily stared down through the glass wall of the control room at the reactor and had a sudden thought of something silver. She couldn't tell what it was, but it had to do with the reactor. She stared down at the machine, trying to remember. The reactor was silver; . . . a tarnished silver, doughnut-shaped racetrack for the neuclei of tritium and deuterium atoms. Sleek and slick . . . a toboggan run. But not slick enough, not fast enough. Poor nuclei running and trying to keep polarized, to keep going and hang on at the same time. Charged by a billion volts, deflected by almost inconceivable magnetic force; turning back on each other, trying to grab, bind, build, like a billion-billion corals creating a continent in an instant. Adhesion and speed. Perpetual speed. Infinite speed. Infinity . . . it was here on earth. She knew where it was; everybody knew. It was silver . . . and it had to do with her new dress. The blue one with the high collar that she'd bought at Razook's last week for the party tonight. Mrs. Constanza, the saleswoman, said Emily looked elegant in it.

"Emily," a sharp voice intruded. She ignored it.

"Elegant," Mrs. Constanza had said. "Crap," said Mrs. Kaufman. "She looks skinny." Mrs. Kaufman was in the shop buying a purse. She owned the motel at the foot of White-face; she was wearing a flannel shirt and heavy pants.

"Elegant," Mrs. Constanza insisted. She moved the three-way mirror so Emily could see her back, and light erupted and spilled through the shop. It smashed through the windows across the snow, and Emily's reflection exploded into slices.

"Emily," Miles Carver cried. Emily came out of it and looked around. Carver stared at her with a scared look she didn't understand.

"Are you all right?" Lipsky asked.

"Fine," she said.

Sally had left the control room; Emily heard her heels clanging on the metal stairs to the reactor room. Then Sally reached the floor below, the clanging stopped, and the muffled voices of the technicians came up the stairs and through the open door. Carver kept staring at her.

"I was just thinking," she explained.

"Nu?" Lipsky said.

Carver inhaled sharply, and she wondered what was wrong with him.

"Nothing," she told Lipsky. "I can't think of it yet."

That night she put on the mascara that Sally told her to buy; it was hard getting it on without sticking the brush in her eye, but it made her eyes look enormous. She wished she didn't have to wear her glasses, but she couldn't see across the room without them. Then she put on the dress from Razook's and looked at herself in the mirror.

The bell rang, she started to move away from the mirror, then stopped. It was the mirror . . . not this one, but the mirror at Razook's. The bell rang again; it was a cold night, and she couldn't leave John standing outside while she contemplated mirrors.

She was spending the night with him; she'd spent almost

19

every Friday night with him for three years, and she picked up her overnight bag with clothes for tomorrow and ran downstairs to open the door.

The huge fieldstone fireplaces on either end of the living room were lit; music blasted out of built-in speakers, and everyone had to shout to be heard. Faith Lawrence never fed her guests before ten, and by then most of them were drunk. Emily ate peanuts to try to stay sober, but the heat and noise in the huge living room were oppressive and she wanted air. John was talking to cronies from the tissue-culture lab, and Emily moved away without his noticing. She eased her way through the crowd to the sliding glass doors at one end of the room. The terrace was empty and covered with snow, and she pulled one door open, slipped out into the fresh air. It was freezing; her shoes broke the crust on the snow and sank, but the cold felt good. She went to the railing and looked out at the lake. It was still frozen and covered with snow. Pale strips of gold slid across the surface from the lights behind her, but far out the lake was dark blue. The snow ate the light. Not like water in summer that shot it back, rippled it. The memory started to come and she tried to concentrate; but she was starving and a little drunk.

Wind blew across the lake and through the wool dress. The snow swirled and Emily wrapped her arms around herself. Mrs. Kaufman was right: she was skinny. Her sister, Susie, had said the same thing the last time Emily saw her. Their father had died last summer, and Emily drove down to Great Neck to pay her respects.

Susie must have been watching for her the way she did when they were kids, and she threw the door open before Emily could ring. She looked awful; her hair was lank and dark at the roots, and her eyes were swollen and red. She pulled Emily into the foyer under the pink Venetian chandelier and threw her arms around her. As usual, Emily didn't respond for a second; then she hugged her sister back and Susie kissed her on both cheeks.

"You missed the funeral," Susie cried.

Emily had missed her father's funeral on purpose. Her father had been a Jew, her mother a Quaker. Emily hated death, and religion confused her.

20

"It doesn't matter," Susie said, "you're here now. Oh, God, Emily, I miss you."

"I miss you too," Emily said.

"You're skinny, worse than last year. Come and see Mother, then we can eat."

Susie kept one arm around Emily and led her into the living room. The whole family was there: aunts, uncles, cousins whom Emily barely knew. They balanced plates of cold cuts on their knees and chatted softly. The room was huge, and all done in different shades of pink. The color and textures of the carpeting and upholstery seemed to trap the heat, and the room was stifling, in spite of the air conditioning.

Emily's stepmother sat on the big pink silk sofa. Her hair was freshly bleached and glowed in the soft light. She was wearing black silk and diamond earrings; her hair and makeup looked perfect. She saw Emily and stopped talking. Then everyone stopped and the Brands, the Roths, and the Cohens stared silently at the sisters in the middle of the room. Slowly, regally, the second Mrs. Brand inclined her head toward Emily.

"It was nice of you to make the trip," she said coldly.

Emily knew she should say that she was sorry, but that was a lie, so she kept quiet. Mrs. Brand stared hard at her for a moment; then her eyes flicked away and back to the old man—Uncle Simon, Emily thought—that she'd been talking to. The rest went back to their food and conversation and left Emily and Susie clinging together in the middle of the pink room.

Steven, Susie's husband, came from the dining room carrying a plate full of food. He'd gotten fatter and his hair was thinning. He stopped and glared at Emily; then he deliberately turned his back on her and left the room. Susie's arm tightened around Emily, and Emily hugged her back.

"It's the will," Susie whispered. Aloud she said, "You're a coathook, for God's sake . . . come and eat."

They ignored the buffet in the dining room and went to the kitchen. Susie filled their plates and they took them and a bottle of wine out to the garden. It was hot and still; yellow bug lights kept the insects away, but they could hear them whining out in the darkness. Susie opened the wine and poured it into plastic glasses.

"What about the will?" Emily asked.

"He left you a third of his money—as much as he left me and Mother. She's furious, so's Steven. They want to contest the will."

"I don't want his money," Emily said.

"The hell you don't. He meant you to have it. He told me he was going to do it when . . . when he knew he was dying."

Susie started to cry and Emily held her hand, but her eyes were dry. She hadn't loved her father. He had left her mother when Emily was two and she didn't see him again until he came to sell the house and take her away when her mother died.

He didn't like Emily either, apparently, but he did his duty. He paid for her schools, camps, college, graduate school. Four times a year, at Christmas, semester breaks, and in between summer camps, he let her come to Great Neck for a week or two at a time. He ignored her when she was in the house, but her stepmother tried to be kind. She took Emily and Susie shopping and to the country club to swim. All Emily remembered of those excursions was the poisonous blue of the pool, and the long glass stores that smelled of heavy perfumes.

When the visit was over, the limousine came around the drive to the double front doors and Emily's bag and books were stashed in the trunk. Her father hid in the study, Susie stayed in her room sobbing her heart out because Emily was leaving, and poor Mrs. Brand was left to say good-bye alone. The good-bye was always correct—a handshake and a dry kiss on the cheek. . . .

Susie wiped her eyes and looked at Emily. "Oh, Em. Not a tear for him?"

Emily didn't say anything. Susie raised Emily's hand and held it against her cheek. "He loved you, Em. He never showed it, but he did. He loved you as much as he loved me, maybe more."

Everybody talked about love. John said he loved her, then waited for her to answer. She couldn't because she didn't know what he meant. She liked sex; it was like putting down a weight she didn't know she carried. She worked better afterward, and she was grateful to him. She told him so once, and he'd laughed at her and explained very gently that gratitude for sex wasn't what he'd meant by love. Another man talked about love too; that was in Princeton and she couldn't remember his name right now. But she couldn't answer him, either. She loved her mother, and her sister. That feeling didn't confuse her.

The lights in the lodge went out, and there was nothing left on the snow but the dull gold of the light behind her in Faith's living room. The door slid open and John came out and put his arm around her. "She's finally going to feed us. Come inside."

Miles Carver watched them come in from the terrace. Ostrow kept his arm around Emily, and Carver thought he was a lovesick asshole. He saw nothing attractive about Emily Brand. She was a bone of a woman with pale skin and small features. She looked frail except for her hands, which were rough and strong-looking, almost like a man's. She *was* strong; he'd seen her lift things that were too heavy for him or Lipsky.

Ostrow led her to the dining room, where Faith Lawrence had finally put out her once-a-month "Science Bash" buffet. It was always the same. Meatballs that smelled like dogfood, frozen miniature franks still cold in the center, and potato salad from the deli on Main Street. The food made Carver sick but he ate because the liquor on an empty stomach would make him sicker.

Emily and Ostrow disappeared into the dining room, and Carver wanted to follow, but he controlled himself. She wasn't as spacy as she seemed, and she'd seen him watching her this afternoon. Besides, skulking after them like a character in a farce wouldn't tell him any more than he knew now, which was nothing . . . except that she'd gotten that same dreamy look on her face when she figured out how to pack the particle leak. But this time it wasn't a small solution because there weren't any more small problems left. He knew in his guts that this time she was on to something big, and he had to tell *them*. . . .

Next to him Bailey had started an argument with Lipsky. Bailey made snide cracks about the President, and Lipsky was losing his temper.

"He *is* honest, he *does* understand." Lipsky's voice was too loud. A few people nearby looked embarrassed, but Lipsky didn't notice. Then Bailey said something that Carver didn't hear, and Lipsky yelled, "Is that so?" The room quieted down. "His ass is on the line, just like mine and yours. He made a promise to us . . ." More smug mumbling from Bailey, and Lipsky shrieked, *"Us*, asswipe. The people. And he means to keep it. That's why he's seeing me *and* Mendel *and* Crowder *and* that fairy from Los Alamos."

Bailey grinned knowingly, and Carver thought he'd better stop it before Lipsky decked him. Lipsky had drunk enough, and he hadn't touched his food.

Bailey was in the vanguard of grad students and new Ph.D.'s that descended on the lab every May to clean out the vending machines, leave graffiti in the toilets, and try to learn something about plasma physics before they crawled back into their holes in September. Carver hated them and he half-hoped that Lipsky *would* lose it and smash the kid in the mouth. But Bailey's grin finally trembled and faded; he was getting scared of the famous physicist who was turning red with rage.

Emily came in from the dining room with a plate full of Faith Lawrence's slop while Lipsky was yelling about time running out for all the smug pigs in and out of government.

Everyone at this end of the room was silent. They looked at the walls, at the fireplace, anywhere but at Lipsky and Bailey. Only Emily watched the two men and ate her food. She probably liked the meatballs, Carver thought bitterly; she probably had the digestion of a python. She sat near Lipsky, eating and watching, always watching, Carver thought. Like a being from another planet collecting data on the lively earth folk.

He had to tell them about Emily soon, because Lipsky was right about time running out for the President. And if Orin Franklin, or any of the other jerk-offs in the White House, got even a smell that E. Brand had a chance of making that hunk of junk work, they'd be down on the lab like sleet on Whiteface, waving money or anything else that skinny bitch wanted.

He had to tell them—*him*, Carver corrected himself . . . he had to tell *him* now.

Carver looked up at the bark-and-twig mantel clock. It was ten-fifteen. He wouldn't be able to get Sheila out of here before twelve. He put his full plate down, made sure he had his address book with him, and walked out of the living room. No one noticed. No one ever noticed what he did.

He climbed the open oak stairs to the second floor and opened the first door he came to. It was a bedroom with coats covering the bed. No one would need a coat this early, and he shut the door and went to the phone on the bed table.

Mayhew had given him a number that was supposed to be manned day and night. The line was clear; he dialed the operator and made the call collect, because he didn't want that New York City number showing up on Faith Lawrence's phone bill. A woman with a voice like frozen metal answered on the second ring and asked the operator to wait. Carver knew she was checking a list. She came back quickly and accepted the call.

"Yes, Dr. Carver?"

"I need a meeting."

A pause; then she said, "You meet directly with Mr. Talbot . . ."

Carver didn't bother to answer, and she put him on hold. He heard footsteps in the hall outside the bedroom. His heart pounded and he wanted to slam the phone down and hide in a closet, but the steps passed the door, went on down the hall. His ear started to sweat against the dead air in the receiver; a toilet flushed, the footsteps passed again and went down the stairs. The woman came back on. "Monday at one-thirty, doctor."

"Tomorrow would be better," he said.

"Impossible." Her voice turned warmer. "Tomorrow is Mr. Talbot's grandson's fifth birthday and there is a big party . . ."

"Isn't that sweet."

The voice was bleak again. "Monday at one-thirty. There'll be a plane waiting for you at the Saranac Lake airfield at nine. Give your name at the charter counter."

He hung up and put his address book away.

Grandpa Talbot, he thought malevolently. Dear old Grandpa Talbot, who owned a billion dollars' worth of oil and the conglomerate that controlled half the utilities in

America. Sweet ol' Grandpa . . . one of the richest, most ruthless men in America. *The last prick on earth you ever want to cross*, Mayhew had said.

Carver wondered what Grandpa Talbot would do about Emily Brand.

CHAPTER

DAVID WAS LATE. He had to go to New York to settle the Vancouver Island permits mess, then home to dress, and the adult shift of his son's fifth birthday party had started without him.

He gave Raymond his coat and stopped in front of the mirror. He smiled at his reflection, let the smile freeze in place, and walked upstairs to the crowded drawing room. He had the feeling that they had all been watching for him. Marty Baron steamrolled through the crowd and grabbed David's hand.

"Congrats, Dave." Baron looked scared and jealous. They had been equals until yesterday, then Talbot made David his senior VP and deputy chairman of the board, and now every man in the room, except Talbot, answered to David. They should have expected it. He had married George Talbot's only child and fathered Talbot's only grandchild.

"Thanks, Marty," David said. Baron's palm was greasy with sweat, and David eased his hand free. Other men were moving toward him through the crowd for more sweaty hand-shakes and choked congratulations. David's head started to ache a little, and he grabbed a glass of champagne from a passing waiter.

An hour later, he'd gotten through the worst of it, and took refuge against the French doors at the far end of the room. The lights glanced off the crystal and the polished tabletops and into his eyes. The headache was getting worse.

The men toadied to him because they thought that he had the power now. They were wrong. It still belonged to his son, Anthony, and if Talbot left NARCON to his grandson, David would wind up working for the little boy who was upstairs sleeping in the soft glow of his pig-shaped nightlight and clutching his teddy bear. The prospect sent another throb of pain through David's head. He was jealous of his own son, and he hated Talbot for doing this to him. He wanted NARCON for himself. He wanted to see *his* name on the millions of stock certificates and over the Chairman of the Board title, and on the thick stationery.

He had thought it would happen yesterday. Talbot had given him the promotion, shaken his hand, and David waited for his father-in-law to tell him that he was his heir. That the gorgeous room they sat in, the huge building, the whole monster NARCON would belong to David when Talbot died or retired. But Talbot was quiet, watching David with a small smile, and David realized that his father-in-law was playing with him. He wanted David to ask, because asking would be a sign of weakness, and Talbot liked to see men falter, even David whom he loved.

David did not give him that satisfaction. He thanked Talbot in a steady voice, got out of there, and rode down to the executive floor trembling with anger and disappointment. . . .

David stayed out of circulation near the French doors, watching the other people, hoping they would forget about him if he stopped moving for a while. Joan Talbot was drunk already. The hem of her beaded gown was down, and she stopped to unhook her heel; then she weaved her way to the bar, smiling vacantly at her guests.

Talbot grinned at him from across the room; he was talking to Ralph Court. Court waved, and David waved back. Then his wife, Mary, came in leading another woman. As usual, the men turned to look at Mary. She was wearing gray chiffon, and the light glowed on her thick red hair. The woman with her was much older and dowdier, and she looked familiar to David. He tried to recall where he'd known her.

Mary spotted him and said something to the woman. She looked up and into David's eyes, and he remembered her. She was Rita Benson, his fourth-grade school teacher. He wanted to get away, but his stupid wife was towing Miss Benson through the crowd right at David. He was trapped, the way he had been trapped twenty-eight years ago in the classroom in Weston.

He thought he'd forgotten the game and Emily Brand, but as Miss Benson and his wife advanced on him through the crowd, it came back to him so clearly he could smell the chalkdust in the classroom, and the heavy must that came off of the green window shades next to his desk. He could see Rita Benson the way she'd been then, and worst of all, he could see little Emily Brand, her face pale, pinched, and ascetic in its subbornness. He could hear her clear little-girl's voice: *No, Miss Benson, I won't play that game . . . no, Miss Benson . . . no. . . .*

It was a miserable morning, just after Christmas, 1962. It had sleeted all night, the trees were coated with ice. Wind blew against the windows, the panes shuddered. The dry heat in the classroom fought drafts.

Miss Benson was wearing a tweed skirt and beige sweater and she looked pretty, and worried. She was telling them about a game they were supposed to play.

"The game," she said, "is called Masters; it takes two days . . ."

Masters. David liked the sound of it.

"Once we set up the rules," said Miss Benson, "everything will go on as usual." She didn't sound like she believed it, and suddenly David knew that something was wrong.

"Everybody will be a master for one day, and a servant for another. For one day, the servants must obey the masters. They must call the masters 'sir' or 'ma'am,' they must step aside for the masters in the hall. They must serve the masters' lunch in the cafeteria, and carry their books if they're told to. No servant can sit next to a master, no servant can talk to a master unless the master addresses him first. Are there any questions?"

Dorothy Scalzi raised her hand. "Who're the servants today?" she asked breathlessly. David held his breath too.

"Today the brown-eyed children will be masters; tomorrow the blue-eyed children will have their turn."

David exhaled and glanced around the room. This was Fairfield County, Connecticut; there were lots of Italians in

29

the towns, in this school. But the WASPs were still in force, and there were as many blue-eyed as brown-eyed children.

She went on, "The brown-eyed children will sit in the front for today, the blue-eyed children in the back. You can move to your new seats now."

David was supposed to move, to join the masters-for-a-day in the front. But he was smart and he knew something was wrong.

All the kids in this class were smart; they had to have IQ's over 140 just to be here. His was way over that, but it wasn't the highest. He'd heard Ellen Bernstein's was over 200, but she couldn't tie her own shoelaces. Emily Brand was supposed to be over 170, but all she did was draw intricate designs of machines that never existed. He wouldn't be surprised if she couldn't read. She'd probably wind up as an airplane mechanic for all her brains.

The children were moving. Pencils dropped, notebook pages fell and were picked up, a few kids brushed past David. He didn't know what to do because there was no way to win this game. Today's master could be tomorrow's if he gave the right orders; but that didn't make sense because then the blue eyes would never have a chance. Suddenly he knew it was a trap.

The children were settled. Miss Benson came down the aisle to his desk. "David," she said. She sounded intense. "David, you have brown eyes." Her eyes stared into his and he knew she wanted him to do something that she wasn't saying. The other kids turned in their seats to look at him. He was at a loss, and if he didn't figure out what to do in a second, he was going to lose this contest, whatever it was, and he'd never lost before.

He'd *almost* lost to Donny Broome. That was a year ago, before his father decided that the nuns were too stupid and rigid to teach his brilliant son. David was the best in his class. He always got the highest test scores, he was the class star in hockey, and he was only nine, but he could beat the thirteen-year-olds at chess. Only math didn't come easily. He had to study hard and get what help he could from his brother Joey to stay first in math. But Donny Broome was a natural at numbers. He barely studied and always came in just behind David in math. He was a short homely boy with spiky blond

30

hair and red-rimmed eyes behind thick round glasses, and David hated him.

Nights before the dreaded math tests, David studied until the numbers and signs blurred on the page and the lights in the house next door—in all the houses on his block—were out, and he was sure that he was the only person in the world still awake. The next day he would come to school pale and exhausted, and still, even after all the hours of lonely study, it would take him the whole period to finish the test. Donny Broome finished in twenty minutes, bounced up to the desk with his test paper, and spent the rest of the time poring over the field guide to birds he always had, or staring out the window.

David kept his edge until the fourth math test of the term. Then Sister Catherine announced proudly that Donny Broome was the first student she'd ever had to score a perfect hundred. The other boys looked quickly at Donny, who blushed to his hairline and ducked his head into his field guide. Then they looked at David, and he saw satisfaction and contempt in the boys' eyes, because he'd been beaten by little Donny Broome and they knew it would hurt him.

He didn't want his lunch that day, but he was sure the other boys watched him and forced himself to eat the bologna-and-cheese sandwich that his mother had packed. The brownie defeated him and he left it hidden in his lunchbox. He was closing the lunchbox when Donny Broome finished his lunch and squeezed past David's chair to leave the room. David imagined that he could feel the moist warmth of the other boy's pink skin, and rage overwhelmed him. He had to do something.

He waited for Donny after school. Father Jerome took some of the boys, Donny among them, bird-watching on the school grounds in the springtime, and David knew that Donny would be late. David didn't mind; he would wait hours if he had to.

At four-thirty Donny came through the gate. He walked along the path next to the stone wall toward the bus stop. He smiled shyly at David as he passed, and kept going. There was no one around; the wall hid them from the playing field on the other side. It was a nice afternoon; Donny walked lightly and swung the strap of his book bag. David waited another few seconds, then ran silently along the beaten dirt path until he was right behind Donny. Donny sensed his presence and turned. He looked questioning for a second, but something in David's expression must have warned him what was going to happen, and he whimpered.

David came up on his toes so he could feel the muscles pull in his legs. Words that he'd learned from his brother Joey came to him—*pig-fucker, motherfucker, dick-licker, cunt*—and he wanted to scream them into the red, scared face in front of him, but someone might hear him. His hand snaked out so fast, even he could barely see it. He grabbed Donny's jacket collar and rammed the boy back against the wall. Donny hiccuped and tried to catch his breath. David pulled him in from the wall, then shoved him back with all his might and let go. Donny's head thumped against the stone wall. He slid down and sat hard on the ground. His legs splayed open and he leaned over and threw up. David squatted down, careful to keep clear of the vomit. He grabbed Donny's blond hair and pulled the boy's head back. The sick dribbled down his chin; his eyes were glazed.

"If you tell anyone about this, Broome, I'll kill you. You know I will," David said.

Donny nodded and retched up more stuff.

David opened Donny's book bag and carefully emptied the books and papers into the pool of vomit. The field guide fell open. David left Donny Broome against the wall and walked quickly to the bus stop to catch the last bus.

Donny was out of school for two weeks. When he came back, he stayed away from David. He never told on him and he never scored a hundred again. David didn't have to think about Donny Broome again. He couldn't even remember what Donny looked like. For some reason, he did remember the field guide and the photograph of a small black-and-white bird spattered with vomit. . . .

The other kids were watching him.

"David," Miss Benson said again, "you have to move."

The trap was closing. He could refuse to play, but no one won a game he didn't play. Besides, all the other kids were playing, and if he didn't, he would be alone, cut off. Miss Benson couldn't expect that of him; she liked him, he was her favorite. She couldn't want to see him shut out like a freak. That would be too much to bear . . . she had no right to ask that of him. The other children waited for him to join them. Without them he would be like the stray dogs that the summer people left behind in autumn when they went back to the city. The dogs wandered the beaches, came up into the streets, and rooted through the garbage cans at night. Their fur was matted with filth, their eyes looked desperate and wild. They frightened children in the neighborhood and sometimes bit them. The dog catchers were busy in September and October rounding up the strays. Joey called them rogues and he said that they took them to the pound to wait for adoption or for their masters to claim them. Of course that never happened, Joey said. No one wanted a rogue dog, and after a week or so they put the dogs in a white-tiled room and filled the room with gas. Joey said that the dogs knew what was happening; they tried to hold their breath, to keep the poisoned air out of their lungs. But they were doomed, and in the end, when they couldn't hold out any longer, they gave one last horrible howl. Joey claimed that you could hear it on quiet fall nights, even out here near the beach, miles from the pound.

David would open his window some October nights to listen; and if the traffic on Route 1 was still, and the waves from the Sound were soft, he was sure he could hear it coming through the black, still autumn air. The wail of the rogue, full of loneliness and terror.

No one could expect him to risk such terrible aloneness. The other children didn't; they were waiting impatiently for him to join them. Only Miss Benson expected it, and he hated her for it.

Screw yourself, he thought, and he picked up his pencil box and notebook. Miss Benson looked at him sadly, and he knew he'd disappointed her. He hated her even more then, and he hurried to the front of the room and slid into the empty seat next to Dorothy Scalzi.

Maybe he had fallen into her trap, whatever it was, but so had all the other kids. Dorothy Scalzi smiled at him; so did the Jones twins, who sat on the other side of his new desk. Even Ellen Bernstein of the impossible IQ had remembered

33

that she had brown eyes and had come to the front with the others. They were all in it together, he consoled himself . . . playing the game that couldn't be won.

Then May Ruskin's tattletale whine rose from the back of the room. "Miss Benson . . . Miss Benson . . . Emily Brand's got brown eyes and she's back here with us. . . ."

"I know you don't remember me," Miss Benson was saying.

"But I remember you perfectly," David smiled. "Rita Benson, my fourth-grade teacher."

He filched a bottle of champagne, found two clean glasses and led Miss Benson, now Mrs. Reed, out of the drawing room and down the curving staircase to George Talbot's study. Mary watched from the landing with an indulgent smile on her beautiful face. He knew that she was thinking how sweet it was to see David and his old teacher find each other after all these years and have a lovely tête-à-tête, full of nostalgia and sentiment. That's how his wife's mind ran: no one ever died, no one was poor, and all evil was storybook, like the queen in *Snow White*.

He took Rita Benson Reed into Talbot's study, settled her next to the fire, then built it up, so the room glowed, and the corners were shadowed. The long windows looked out on the estate gardens, and they sat across from each other in a cozy circle of firelight.

He poured champagne and she took her glass and examined him with overt, kindly interest that reminded him of Madeline. He started to relax. She'd asked to hear about *him* so they would talk about him. There was no reason to mention the game or Emily Brand. He was in control; his headache was fading.

"You've done so well," she said.

"There's more," he said happily, and he told her about the promotion.

"And you've made a wonderful marriage."

"It wasn't like that," he said sharply.

She was surprised. "I never thought it was, David."

But he couldn't bear for her to think he'd married his success. He told her that he'd been at Yale and he worked her one summer cleaning the pool. He and Talbot started talking . . . he didn't even know who Talbot was then, or that he had a daughter. Anyway, Talbot liked him—very much, apparently, because he paid for his grad school—and when he got his MA, he went to work for NARCON. Still no Mary, he insisted. He was with NARCON five years, moving up in the ranks, before he even started seeing Mary. Then Mary . . .

David hesitated, and Rita said, "Mary fell in love with you."

He blushed, and nodded. Rita looked at his face in the firelight, and she knew why Mary Talbot had wanted this poor Italian boy from Bridgeport, whose father spoke with an accent and came to parents' nights wearing workclothes. David Lucci had been the most beautiful child Rita had ever seen, and he was the handsomest man. He was tall, but not huge. About six feet, she guessed. Under the tux, she could see that his body was lean and hard-muscled. His skin was the way she remembered it—smooth and dark, with a Mediterranean sheen—and his eyes were light brown against whites so clear they almost looked blue. She thought he had a saint's face—long, fine, Gothic; he belonged in a red robe, strolling through an ancient cloister in Constantinople. Of course Mary Talbot had wanted him, and now Mary had him, and she knew how he looked when he ate, slept, made love . . . she knew how he looked naked. Rita wouldn't mind knowing those things. She wanted to reach out and touch his thick black hair, to run her hand down his cheek. She blinked, and finished the wine in her glass.

He was talking about his work. He said it excited him, and it must have, because his eyes glowed. He poured more wine, and Rita knew she was getting drunk. His work was thrilling, he said, and the word lingered in her mind as she stared at him.

Thrilling.

NARCON ran the world's motor, he said. Stock markets in London and Tokyo fluctuated according to what they did at the top of the highest building in the world. But it wasn't all plush offices and stock boards. It was life on the rigs . . . eating fabulous food in a chamber ten feet wide and fifty long, with men from Spitsbergen and Baton Rouge, and everywhere in between . . . out on the North Sea, with a gale blowing, and the feeling that if the rig moved, it would crack

35

off its moorings and capsize. And not showing fear, no matter how the wind howled or how high the waves got. It was trips to Libya, Iran, Saudi Arabia . . . to fairy-tale cities that were old, decaying, incredibly beautiful . . . and feasts with the Arabs, who, in spite of politics and all the other crap, were the most gracious men on earth. . . .

He poured more wine. Rita watched his hands, imagined the play of muscles under the cloth of his jacket. The champagne was almost gone and they were both tight. He asked her about herself, and she was embarrassed that she didn't have much to tell him. She'd married Mayo Reed, the psychologist for the Weston schools. They had two children, both married . . . she went on teaching the accelerated classes —the geniuses of the ten towns of lower Fairfield County— and only stopped a few years ago. She worked part time in the library now; she volunteered for Meals on Wheels twice a week. She lived in the same town, in the same house where she was born. She was happy. . . .

She stopped talking and they were quiet. It was comfortable at first, then the atmosphere in the room changed. The fire had burned down, and she looked up at David. His eyes were in shadow and she couldn't see them. But she could feel tension that hadn't been there before, and his voice came out of the gloom of the dying fire.

"She won, didn't she?"

Rita didn't know what he was talking about.

"The game," he said impatiently. "Emily won."

He meant Mayo's game. But it wasn't Mayo's; it had been created by the American Society of Educational Psychologists. They said they were studying peer pressure and social domination in nine-year-olds, but Rita knew that was garbage. They really wanted to prove that everyone was born wanting to shove everyone else's face into the mud, and her kids weren't any better than the rest . . . for all their brains. So they forced teachers like her to play it in hundreds of schools in city ghettos, suburbs, fishing villages, and farm towns. Three thousand children, they said; and all of them lost . . . all of them went along with that cruel stupid game. Three thousand children, and not one refused to play. Until they got to Emily Brand.

"She did win, didn't she?" he asked. His voice was tight.

"No one won," Rita said thickly. "We never played."

They never did. Because of Emily.

Everyone plays, or no one plays, Mayo had told her when he explained the rules. She wasn't even going out with him then, but she knew that she liked him. *If one child refuses, tell them they'll ruin it for the others, and make sure that the other kids hear. That's the final threat, Rita. The real pressure. Not your disapproval or their parents'. It's the rejection of the other kids that finally gets them. No child can stand that.*

David was waiting for her to say something. Dance music was playing upstairs; it came through the walls faintly into the room. Over the music, and through the fog of too much wine, Rita could hear her own voice from twenty-eight years ago, threatening Emily . . .

"Emily Brand, if you don't move to the front of the class this second with the other children, I'm taking you to the principal's office. Do you want that?"

"No, Miss Benson."

"They'll call your mother. Do you want that?"

The little girl's dark eyes had been miserable behind her glasses. "No," she said softly. Rita thought Emily was going to cry, and Rita was ashamed of herself, but she had to go along.

"Then go to the front of the class," she commanded.

"No," Emily said.

"Why?" Rita demanded.

And Emily looked at her with calm, flat eyes and said, "It's not right."

"Would I tell you to do something that wasn't right?" Rita tried to sound indignant.

Emily answered without any arrogance, "You might not know. You can't know everything."

The children waited; it was time for Mayo's final threat, and Rita raised her voice so all the children could hear. "Emily Brand, if you don't play, no one can play; you'll ruin it for everyone."

Rita glanced around her; the other children were all staring at Emily, and the look in their eyes was frightful. Mayo was right: no nine-year-old could stand that pressure. Most adults couldn't. And sure enough, Emily started collecting her pencils, closing her notebooks, and Rita thought she'd capitulated. But then Emily said, "Will you take me to Mr. Ryder's, or should I have a note? . . ."

David leaned toward Rita. "Tell me," he whispered. "Say it. She won."

He was as drunk as she was. "We didn't play," she insisted.

"Because of her . . . and that was the point, wasn't it? I figured it out, but she figured it out first, and she won . . . she beat us all. You can say it, it's all right."

"Okay," Rita mumbled. "She won."

He leaned back as if hearing it out loud relieved him. The tension in the room eased a little.

"What happened to her?" he asked.

"She's a physicist."

"So you kept in touch." It was an accusation. Rita pleaded guilty. "A little. Once or twice a year we write. She got a Ph.D. from Princeton. She works in plasma physics, whatever that is."

"You liked her very much."

"No," Rita cried. Not guilty this time. "I liked you. I liked you better than any of the children I've ever had. Everyone liked you, David . . . you were special . . . the champion."

"But Emily was . . . What was Emily?"

Rita hesitated, then said, "Emily was alone. Her mother died that year, you know. And I went to the house after the funeral to see Emily. It was an awful place, huge, old, decaying. And I kept thinking of the little girl trapped in the rotting house with a dying woman. Her father was there to take her away, but she couldn't live with him. He had a new family, he didn't want her; I think just looking at her reminded him of things he longed to forget. That awful house, the sick woman he'd left . . . his guilt. So he was going to send her away, but Emily wasn't cowed. Not Emily. She stood on the porch to say good-bye to me with that house lowering over her, but she didn't cry. She shook my hand and let me kiss her. She was wearing a blue spring coat with hand-tatted lace collar. I've never seen such lace. And she had a little doll, a stuffed dinosaur . . . such a strange doll for a little girl, but she clutched it to her, defying grief and loneliness

38

and she was wearing white gloves. . . ." Tears came to Rita's eyes. "Poor little girl . . . I hugged her, and I told her that I'd help her if she ever needed it. I wrote down where I lived, and my phone number, and tucked it into her little pocketbook, and made her promise that she'd find me if she was in trouble. . . . I meant it, too."

"And did she ever need your help?" he asked.

"No. But I hope she will. Not that I ever in this world wish her trouble, but it would be a boon to help someone like Emily. You know what I mean?" David didn't answer; she finished her wine, and knew that she was going to have trouble getting back upstairs. The room turned slowly, inexorably around before her eyes, righted itself for a second, then started turning again. "A boon," she mumbled, "to help Emily . . . like Ben-Hur helped our Lord in his agony. . . ."

David couldn't stand any more, and he went to get Mary. Rita Benson Reed didn't seem to notice. He left it to Mary to get Rita to the bathroom to throw up, wash her face, whatever was needed; and he staggered out of the house and sat down in the snow on the front steps. The headache was very bad, and he knew it was only partly from the champagne. He took deep gulps of cold air, then got slowly to his feet, found his Jaguar in the jam of cars, eased out of the drive around a Rolls, and pulled out into the estate road that ran almost half a mile to the Round Hill Road. He drove fast, with all the windows open. The air rushing across his face helped a little, but by the time he got home to New Canaan, took a shower and a Tegretol, the pain was tearing, as if something inside his head was shearing off and running down his skull into his neck and back. Light was like daggers in his eyes, and he turned the lamps off and crawled into bed. He was scared that he'd keep replaying the scene in the study: little Emily, triumphant again, twenty-some years later. He was afraid he'd dream about her . . . see her wearing a lace collar . . . holding a dinosaur. But he didn't.

He woke up late. Mary was hanging solicitously over him, asking him something, but she was blocking his air, and he groaned at her to close the blinds, and he went back to sleep. The next time he opened his eyes, it was after four; there was a little gray light through the slit in the drapes, and he knew it was late afternoon. He heard Mary's light voice chattering into the phone in another room, dissecting the "wonderfully outrageous party." He staggered into the bathroom, took two more Tegretols, then went back to bed.

By Monday morning his eyes were swollen; so was one side of his face. He called Madeline and pleaded with her to see him in the afternoon, and she agreed. Then he called the office and told Sarah that he was too sick to come in. Talbot would worry and call, but Mary would take care of it. He went back to bed.

He was too sick to show up for his first day on the new job that he'd worked for and schemed for for fifteen years. All because of Emily Brand.

CHAPTER

3

TALBOT'S OFFICE was at least thirty by fifty; it was on the 115th floor, and the wall behind Talbot's desk was glass. Carver saw rivers, towns, counties, bridges, and the start of some distant mountain chain. The secretary, a tall classy-looking woman with gray hair and a good black suit, asked him if he would like a drink. He knew he shouldn't; acid already rolled in his stomach, but he thought the liquor might ease the burning. She brought him Scotch and water, then left him alone. The room was silent except for the whir of a quartz clock on the desk. He couldn't hear footsteps, typing, voices, anything. He was suspended on a column of granite and glass, cut off from the world. He wondered how Talbot could stand this place. But it was his office, designed for his taste and comfort, and no expense spared. The desk table was marble and chrome. The chairs around the room were gray suede, the walls were gray shading to lavender, the carpet was gray . . . everything was gray, except for streaks of black in the marble tables, the rainbow trapped in the crystal-based lamps, and slashes of color in the paintings.

There was nothing soft here, nothing on a human scale. It was designed to impress . . . to instill fear, and it worked, Carver thought ruefully.

Another door opened, and Talbot came in and crossed the yards of carpet gracefully.

"Good day, doctor; why don't we sit over here?"

Carver stood up. "Bring your drink," Talbot said, and Carver picked it up, balanced the coaster under the glass, and followed Talbot to an island of gray leather couches under a

41

Mondrian. Talbot remained standing until Carver was sitting with the drink in front of him on another marble-and-chrome table.

Talbot was very tall, six-three or more, and Carver had to crane to look up at him. He must have been handsome once, but now there were pouches of flesh under his eyes, his jowls sagged, the skin on his neck crinkled. His eyes were bright blue, still clear and kindly-looking, and he'd kept his figure, but Carver always thought of decay when he was in George Talbot's presence. There was an aura of rot held at bay by hairdressers, masseurs, and vitamin injections that clung to Talbot like a distinctive cologne.

Carver wished he were back with Mayhew. Mayhew had recruited him at Stanford seven years ago and their monthly sessions were almost pleasant. They talked over lunch or a good dinner, like old friends discussing Carver's work. Not like spy and spymaster. But since the last election, Carver reported to Talbot. So did the NARCON men at Stanford, Princeton, MIT, Mayhew had told him. Talbot didn't seem to like the man who'd become President, and Mayhew even speculated that the big boss was a little scared of Orin Franklin.

"Well, doctor, what's the emergency?" Talbot asked.

"No emergency, yet, but I have a feeling there will be soon."

"A feeling?" Talbot paused delicately.

Carver kept his voice tight and soft. "I'm not being coy, Mr. Talbot. I have a feeling something's going to happen at Placid. You can listen or not. It's your money."

Talbot smiled gently and leaned back in the couch. "Go on, doctor."

"There's a woman there . . . Emily Brand . . ." He told Talbot how good she was. A mechanic, he said, not one of those fey theoreticians who sit around with their thumbs up their asses, wondering if Newton would turn out right when all the votes were counted. She made things work. She'd packed a particle leak that Lipsky had been working on for months. He gave up and asked her to help him, and she'd walked around the machine with a dreamy look on her face, and Carver could have sworn that she was listening to the thing . . . like a doctor listens to a patient. She scribbled, thought, scribbled some more, then told them what to do, and it worked. Oh, she was good . . . a real mechanic. In another age, she'd have invented the wheel.

He finished his drink, Talbot replenished it and took plain soda for himself, and Carver went on.

Something had happened on Friday. They'd had their usual run, and everything was fine, which meant the reactor crapped out. "And then . . ." Carver said. "Something happened with her. She had a spell, like a walkabout. I would've sworn she'd fallen asleep, except that her eyes were open, like lights in her head, and she was staring down at that two-hundred-million-dollar hunk of junk and I knew she had something. Not all of it maybe, but something. She'll get the rest, Talbot. I've been watching her for four years. And when she gets it, Lipsky'll go along." He stopped.

Talbot waited, as if he expected to hear more. When he didn't, he said, "Is that all?"

"For now."

"I see. You flew down from Placid to tell me this."

"I think it's the most important report I've ever made."

Talbot nodded. "I respect your thoroughness and dedication, doctor. But it doesn't matter what Dr. Brand gets or doesn't get, because this afternoon"—he smiled—"even as we speak, the President and his committee are rejecting Marvin Lipsky's request for additional funding."

Carver wondered how Talbot knew that the President had turned Lipsky down. Then he figured it out . . . and next he wondered how much a Cabinet member—Secretary of Energy or of the Interior—cost NARCON. A fortune, he decided. Much more than Carver cost them.

"So that's the end of Brand and Placid," Talbot was saying.

"No it isn't," Carver said.

"I think it is," Talbot said smoothly.

Carver's gut turned. "Then you're a fool. Money doesn't buy ideas, being broke doesn't stop you from thinking. This is physics we're talking about—not market research . . . *physics*. Mind stuff. That skinny bitch is going to figure out how to sustain nuclear fusion. And when she does, Mr. Talbot, there'll be plenty of money. We'll be wiping our asses with twenties at Placid." He smacked his glass down on the table. It missed the coaster and cracked on the marble table. He didn't care; Talbot didn't seem to notice. "And then, Mr. Talbot, everybody in this country can light and heat their houses for about thirty bucks a year, and you and everybody else in this palace's going to have to drink the oil to get rid of it."

The room was quiet. Talbot had turned pale, but Carver knew he was scared, not angry. Talbot got up, stalked across the room, stopped at his desk but didn't sit down. He stared out through the wall of windows for a moment, then turned back to Carver. "You are very upset, Miles."

"You bet. When she does her trick, I'm going to be out sixty thousand dollars a year."

"What we pay you."

"Exactly."

Talbot wavered at the desk, fiddled with the pen set. Carver waited, and then Talbot seemed to come to a decision. He came back and sat down. His fingers twined, then untwined. "We need a wire . . ." he said softly.

"What?"

"Microphones in the lab, in their houses. Wires on the phones. We need to know what's going on."

"Not the lab. There're detectors for voltage spills. They'd pick up a mike in a second. Phones're okay."

"But you'll be in the lab, won't you, Miles?"

"Sure, George."

Talbot flinched but didn't say anything.

"And you'll keep tabs. . . ."

"All day every day."

"I appreciate this, doctor. You won't be sorry."

"I better not be," Carver said, and suddenly Talbot's expression changed. His eyes became blue pits in his face, his skin matched the gray chrome, the walls, the glass, except for spots of color on his cheeks, like rouge on a corpse. Carver had never seen a live man look dead before—dead and cold—and he remembered Mayhew's words: *the last prick on earth you ever want to cross.*

Carver jumped to his feet, took a step backward, and bumped the couch. "It's getting late," he said. "The pilot . . ."

"Of course," Talbot said softly. "Thank you for coming, Miles. I won't forget what you've said."

Carver almost ran out, left the door ajar, and Talbot watched him cross the silent marble-walled outer office to a steel-doored elevator. Miss Chrysler had to get up from her desk and shut Talbot's door.

Talbot went to the window and looked out at the game board of towns, hills, and rivers. As of now, President Franklin was helpless. He couldn't keep the price controls, but if Carver was right, they had real trouble. Talbot tried to imagine what that would mean. Think the worst, his grandfather used to say. Everything good should be a pleasant surprise. He tried to think the worst now. The woman would design—if "design" was the right word—a practical, economically viable fusion reactor. Then what? The country would have light and heat without oil. But NARCON would go on. NARCON wasn't just coal, oil, gas, and uranium. NARCON owned textile mills in Massachusetts and Alabama, banks from Iowa City to Hong Kong. They owned a movie studio, a publishing company, millions of acres of forests; they even had a big chunk of a pro football team. NARCON was lots of things. But the oil, coal, gas, and uranium were the bedrock. People *had* to have those; they would die without them. The rest was icing on the cake, and Talbot had no intention of finding out what it was like to deal in conveniences.

Once he'd asked his father why the company couldn't just buy fusion reactors, once they worked, of course, and still charge what they wanted for power. As usual, his father had sneered at him.

"You still don't get it, do you, George?"

Talbot's face had reddened as his father lectured him, and he felt his hands tighten into fists, but he had listened.

"By '88 we'll be getting two hundred dollars a month for every family in America," his father had said, "but it would take only five fusion reactors to light and heat America. Five! The people'll sit still for almost anything, but they won't swallow two hundred dollars a month if all we have to do is maintain five reactors fueled by a few glasses of water. No, George. Fusion's for the commies. Fusion'll kill us."

Talbot rang for his secretary. She came in and Talbot wrote

Emily Brand on his pad, tore off the slip, and handed it to the secretary.

"I want everything in the tapes on this woman," he said.

It was three, the outer office was empty, and David rang the receptionist's bell. Madeline called to him to come in, and he opened the door to her inner office.

He'd been seeing Madeline Warner for five years. Talbot's doctor told him he'd be better off seeing a psychiatrist for the headaches than swallowing so much crap for the pain. David didn't know if she was a psychiatrist or psychotherapist. He didn't care. She'd helped him, and he trusted her. She wasn't pretty. All her clothes were too tight; her black hair looked dyed, and her skin was coarse. She was direct and vulgar, and he relaxed with her and the headaches came only once or twice a year now. This was the worst one ever, and she looked shocked when she saw him.

"What happened?" she cried.

"Headache."

"Holy Jesus . . ." She made him sit down, and she went into the little lavatory off her sitting-room/office and brought back a wet washcloth. She put it gently across his forehead. "I'm going to give you a shot," she said. She filled a syringe and gave the shot quickly. "You want to talk yet?"

"That's what I'm here for," he snarled.

"Hey," she said softly. "Take it easy. Okay, what happened?"

"Saturday . . . it was Anthony's birthday, but she ruined it," he mumbled. "She ruined everything."

"Who?" Madeline asked.

"Emily Brand."

Madeline waited, and after a few minutes David started talking. . . .

The game ended because she wouldn't play. She'd controlled Miss Benson and the whole class. She controlled David, and worst of all, Miss Benson was paying as much attention to her as she did to him. He had to do something.

He and Joey caught wasps, and he picked the lock on her locker and left an open jar of angry wasps on the bottom shelf. They would sting her when she opened the locker—at

46

least they'd scare her. But during the day, the heat and air-lessness in the locker killed the wasps, and when she opened the locker door, they were lying on their backs or sides with their delicate legs and iridescent wings folded against their bodies. She didn't tell Miss Benson about the wasps, but he knew she wouldn't.

Then he stole her notebook during recess. Later he watched her search her desk, her book bag, and after school he stayed in the cloakroom and watched her search her locker. When she didn't find the notebook, she slumped down on the bench, and he thought she'd cry, but she didn't.

That night he looked in the notebook at the machines that she'd drawn. They were weird and horrible. Tubes ran in and out of them; they were cocooned in wires and girders. They were made to move, but he couldn't find out to what purpose or where their power source was. Some looked like the generators his father took out of cars, some looked like the motors of the cars themselves, except that they weren't. Some looked like rockets, some like pictures he'd seen of nuclear piles. She must have seen the same pictures; she was able to draw them from memory. He sat in his neat, tiny room with wallpaper covered in Ivy League pennants, and turned pages. He found a graph; along one arm she'd written "Binding energy per nucleon (MEV)." The other arm was labeled "Mass number." The graph was lines and small circles with numbers—4, 2, 56, 26, 10; and letters—He, Fe, Li, B. He stared at it. Nucleon, Mass, Energy. The skin at the back of his neck crawled. It was late, the house was dark, the heat was off, and suddenly he had an awful feeling that something dangerous had entered the room and was standing behind him, breathing icily on his neck. What were those numbers and letters? He didn't know. He would never have the patience to find out. The cold breath whispered up his neck into his scalp, and he slammed the notebook shut. It was just a cardboard-covered book. Her name, Emily Austen Brand, was printed on the cover, and her address, 490 Nod Hill Road, Wilton, Connecticut.

His mother and father were asleep by now, Joey's radio was turned way down, and he knew that Joey was lying in bed on his back, jerking off or just staring at the ceiling with that blank tired look that he had, even though he was only fourteen. Everybody and everything in this house was ugly, ordinary, stupid. If he went into the bathroom, he'd see his father's tube of hemorrhoid medicine, Joey's bottle of dimestore cologne, his mother's support stockings drying over the shower rod. No one in this house knew what a nucleon was, no one could help him, and he hated them. Most of all he hated Emily Brand. She haunted him. Donny Broome had learned his lesson and David never thought about him again. There were no stone walls around the Weston school, but the glacier had left a trillion rocks in Connecticut. One smack with a heavy piece of glacier detritus, and he would never have to think about Emily Brand again either.

At recess the next day he followed her into the woods surrounding the playing field. He moved as quietly as an Indian. A soft wind rustled the tree branches; sweat popped out on his upper lip and forehead. He looked for the perfect stone as he went, but they were all too small. Time was going, and he searched desperately. He found one that was big enough, but it was sunk deep in the ground. He tried to claw it free, but the bell rang in the distance, and to his right he saw her through the trees, heading back to the playground. He'd lost his chance for today, and he walked back to the playground. He was almost there when he found a long, heavy rock, jagged at one end. It looked like the head of an ax, and he pried it out of the leaves, carried it to the edge of the field, and left it for tomorrow, at the foot of the dying dogwood at the border of trees.

The next day, he was in class before anyone else. By eight they were all in their places except Emily. She was never late, and he knew she wasn't coming. He wasn't surprised; spring colds had decimated the class. But she didn't come to school on Friday or Monday. No cold lasted that long, and he started to worry. Then, on Tuesday, Miss Benson explained Emily's absence.

"Children," she said, "Emily Brand's mother died last Friday, and Emily won't be coming back to school this year."

At noon David slipped out of the cafeteria and got out the front door to the bike rack without being noticed. He pedaled madly down the drive, and out onto 53, heading for

Wilton. It was a hard ride, he had to wait a long time to get across Route 7, and it was almost one when he got to 490 Nod Hill Road. A sign pasted on the mailbox announced an "Estate Sale." He rode up a long rutted drive bordered by overgrown land, rounded a curve, and saw the house. It was huge, ten times bigger than his house. The front door was open and women crossed back and forth in front of it. The second-floor windows were blind mirrors in the sun, and he knew no one lived there anymore.

He put his bike on the kickstand and went up the steps to the front hall. Downstairs, the place was full of women. Tagged furniture was shoved into the downstairs rooms, and women were examining it. Dishes, draperies, linens, silver, knickknacks, covered long tables along the walls. He saw water marks on the walls, peeling paint and wallpaper, and he thought of his own spotless house where everything was replaced as soon it showed a sign of wear.

He went into a big room on one side of the hall. Most of the furniture was in here, but the room was so big it didn't look crowded. The ceilings were high, the floor was real wood, laid in a pattern he'd never seen before, but it was worn and buckling in places.

A woman wearing a tweed suit sat at a table near French doors. She looked like she was in charge, and he went up to her. "Can I help you?" she asked.

"What happened to the people who lived here?"

"It's a sad story. The mother died, and the little girl's gone to live with her father."

"Where does her father live?" David asked.

"Are you her friend?"

He nodded.

"I'm not sure," the woman told him. "Somewhere on Long Island. The real-estate agents would know, though. Your mother can call them."

David went back through to the hall and up the stairs. There weren't any women or furniture on the second floor. The water damage and disrepair were even worse up here, but the size of the rooms, the height of the ceilings, and the number of fireplaces amazed and tormented him. At one end of the hall he found a room with a tile fireplace and wallpaper covered with paintings of wild animals. He went in and shut the door after him. The room had its own white tile bathroom with a hideous tub on claw feet.

He used the toilet, then went back into the bedroom. The sun had passed this side of the house, and the animals on the walls looked mysterious and vibrant in the afternoon light. He knew this was her room. He thought he could feel an aura of her here. He searched the closets, cabinets, the corners of the room, the medicine chest in the bathroom, but everything was gone. The light was fading fast, the dust and the chips in the tile fireplace were hidden, and the room was beautiful. She'd slept in here, she'd used that bathroom, she'd opened her eyes in the morning and seen the animals on the walls. He noticed a loose corner on the wallpaper, down near the baseboard, and he pried at it until a corner came loose. He kept prying until he had enough to hold, and then he grabbed and ripped upward. It was a slaughter: a zebra was torn in half, a lion lost one eye, a giraffe was decapitated. In a frenzy, he pulled out his knife and pried up more seams and corners. He tore and ripped at the paper until nothing was left on the walls but ragged stripes of color, and the floor of her room was littered with torn, curling shreds of paper.

Madeline Warner watched him. He was breathing hard, his face was white. "It didn't help," he whispered.

"Tearing the wallpaper?"

He shook his head violently, then grabbed it because of the pain. "I knew . . ." He couldn't go on.

"What did you know?" she asked gently.

"I knew that if I never saw her again, if we never played again, then it would stay the way it was. She would be the winner, I would be the loser forever."

"But then you forgot her."

"No." He stared at her with swollen red eyes. "I kept the notebook. It's still in my mother's house in Fairfield or with my stuff in New Canaan. I still have it. I never forgot."

A pause, and then Madeline asked, even though she didn't want to know, "Did you mean to kill her with the rock?"

He didn't seem to hear, and for the first time in her career, Madeline didn't know what to say next; she'd been trained for this, but she wasn't ready for it. She saw lonely, unhappy housewives who drank too much and screwed the golf pro or the tennis pro then came to her to blow off some guilt. She'd seen menopausal men who hated their wives, their homes; sometimes their children. But not really. They were miserable and frightened . . . neurotic and alcoholic . . . disappointed and at a loss to understand what had happened to their lives, but they were still normal people.

She had never seen real hatred or sickness before, and she was lost. Old man Forrester had told them it would happen. *Call it soul sickness, if you like,* he'd said. *You won't see it often, maybe never. But if you do, have the sense to recognize that it's beyond your manipulation, and the humility to give up.*

She wanted to give up on David Lucci. He scared her with his hate and madness, and she wanted him out of her office. But then he pulled the wet cloth off his forehead and stared at her with eyes so full of pain, she had to look away from him. "Oh, my God," he said softly. "I *did* want to kill her." Tears filled his eyes and ran down his cheeks. "She was just a little girl, and I wanted to hit her with that rock until her head split open. . . . Oh, Jesus," he sobbed softly. "Help me. I want to be sorry, I want to love my wife, and my kid. Sweet Jesus, help me. Mad . . . help me." He slid out of the chair and knelt on the floor, holding his aching head in his hands.

Madeline was too shocked to move for a second. *The pain is horrible,* Forrester had told them. *Pity them, if they don't frighten you too much.*

Madeline came around her desk, knelt next to David and put her arms around him. He clung to her and buried his face against her shoulder.

She rocked him a little in her arms. She could smell his clean black hair, see the curve of his ear, the back of his smooth neck. She felt hard muscles in his chest and arms, and she fought desire. She'd imagined being in bed with him before; she knew most women would. And she knew that he'd make love to her if she wanted him to; she'd known that from the second he'd walked into her office five years ago. *Fuck her and leave her for dead,* she thought.

51

She forced her touch to stay firm and maternal, and after a few minutes his sobs subsided.

Emily watched the little plane bank in over the mountain, touch down and bounce across the ruts of the Mount Marcy airfield.

Lipsky trailed the other passengers into the Quonset hut they called the airport, and came toward Emily; his hair stood up from the wind and his coat and pants were wrinkled. He shook his head when he reached her.

"I know," she said. "We heard."

They drove out of Keene Valley toward Lake Placid without talking. They passed the slice of frozen lake without a name and the waterfalls hanging in fantastic shapes, ready to crack and come pouring down the rocks in a few weeks. They passed the concrete ski jump they'd built for the Olympics, rising sheer, gray, and eerie against the black mountains, and the first houses and motels.

"Stop here," Lipsky yelled. "I need a drink. Stop here."

They pulled into the parking lot of the Steak and Stinger and fought the wind across the parking lot to the door. It was early, the greenhouse-bar was empty; it was gray outside, threatening snow, but there was a fire in the wood stove and the hostess gave them the table closest to it. Emily took off her down jacket; Lipsky huddled inside his rumpled overcoat and put his battered briefcase on the empty chair next to him. It was too stuffed to close, and a manila folder stuck up out of the opening. On it he'd printed his name for the project: LIGHTSOURCE. Everyone else at the lab laughed at it behind his back and called it romantic crap, but Emily liked the sound of the word.

They brought him a double daiquiri and he was quiet until he'd drunk half. Then he said, "They gave us seven million. What the fuck are we supposed to do with seven million?"

"Keep going," Emily answered.

"Don't patronize me," he shouted. The waitress brought over a tub of cheese and some crackers, hoping, perhaps, that the food would calm him down.

"I'm not patronizing you," Emily said gently.

Lipsky dug into the cheese. "I know, I know . . . you never patronize anyone . . . you never humor anyone . . ."

He stuffed cheese and crackers into his mouth. "You never gossip or raise your voice . . . you're never venal or cruel or silly. You're a fucking bore, Dr. Brand."

Emily didn't say anything. Lipsky leaned across the table. "Goddammit, cry. You're a woman, I'm trying to hurt you. Cry!"

Emily waited and Lipsky sat back in his chair and downed the rest of the daiquiri. "You don't give a flying fuck what I think of you, do you?" he asked.

Emily didn't answer, and Lipsky leaned across the table, his voice soft and mean. "You don't. Not me, or your lover . . . or anybody. Did you even cry for your father, Emily?"

All at once Emily was tired. It was an old attack. Her stepmother had made it, and the girls at school and the man in Princeton. *Cold bitch. You feel nothing . . . you care about nothing.* Emily moved the knife in the cheese. She cared about the machine they'd built, she cared about Lipsky even if she didn't know how to show it.

"Did you?" Lipsky cried.

The waitress leaned against the bar, trying to ignore them.

"Did I what?" Emily asked.

"Cry for your father, goddammit."

"No," Emily answered. "I didn't know him very well."

Lipsky started to sob. The waitress rushed into the other room, the bartender ducked behind the bar, pretending to wash glasses, and Emily searched her purse for Kleenex. She found some and gave it to Lipsky. He cried into it. "I made such an ass of myself." His shoulders shook. "They knew they were going to turn me down before I got there, but they let me go through the whole show . . . and shit, I did. You know my number: we can light the city of New York with the energy in a glass of water . . ." He went on through his tears. The meeting was a total disaster. Three minutes into it Daniel Flynn, the Secretary of the Interior, was playing with his pencil. The President kept on listening and Lipsky tried to liven up the tired presentation. But as the worn phrases piled up, he saw the President's face turn cold, and then sad. His body sagged in his leather chair, and Lipsky had the feeling that he'd dashed a desperate hope.

But he'd gone on anyway. Oil was a dead issue, he'd told the President, who had stopped listening. In five years no one

53

would be able to afford it, in twenty years it would all be gone anyway. Coal was no answer, it polluted; its heat was trapped by the atmosphere. Coal would change the climate of the planet. Think, he'd said much too passionately, think if the ice caps melt and the oceans rise fifty feet . . . Then he tried the old joke, mainly to keep himself from bursting into tears then as he'd done now. *The good news about coal is that we have plenty of it . . . the bad news is that we might have to use it.*

No one smiled, and Lipsky had taken a deep, shuddering breath and asked the question they should have asked: *What about the dangers?* Minimal compared to fission, he told them. A runaway accident is impossible. When controlled fusion malfunctions, it stops. Simple. Yes, you get dangerous by-products of fusion, just as you do with fission . . . but we're talking about manageable half-lives with the proper shielding . . . which is possible with fusion and impossible with fission. No krypton, strontium, plutonium . . . no wondering how tight the canisters you bury today are going to be in ten thousand years. At this point, Flynn had smothered a yawn.

The waitress came back into the bar and Lipsky shouted for two brandies. The waitress brought them and Emily stared into her glass.

"You look as bored as they did," Lipsky said.

"I am," she said. "I've heard it all before too."

Then she smiled at him. She smiled so rarely, he forgot how pretty she could look.

"They'll listen next time you go," she said. "They'll carry you out of the Oval Office on their shoulders."

"What are you talking about?"

"What do you see when you look in a three-way mirror?" she asked.

He didn't think anything for a moment. Then suddenly he remembered the question Einstein had asked ninety-some years ago when he was a kid—the famous, simple, almost childish question that changed the world for all time: *How would the world look if I rode a beam of light?* A new view of the order of the universe came from that question and practical nuclear research. The reactor in Chicago, the bomb on Hiroshima, the trips to the moon and Mars and Jupiter, and the Adobe Head disaster were all responses to it. And if they ever lit the world with sustained nuclear fusion, it would be because Einstein had asked his innocent question.

Then he realized that *her* question wasn't like that after all; it wouldn't start a thousand years of speculation and experimentation or change mankind's vision of the universe. It was direct, like Emily; and it was designed to make something work. He was putting too much on it, as he tended to . . . as people tended to put too much onto Emily herself for some reason. *He* did. She awed him, and he was a fool. She wasn't a blind force of nature, a distant goddess watching from some ether over everyone else's head.

She was a genius, true. But he'd known other geniuses. He'd talked to Szillard when he was young, he'd had tea with Teller, and corresponded with Bronowski. But she was more than that, and less at the same time. She was a shy, handsome (at this moment beautiful) woman who'd never learned the games people played with each other, who'd never consented to the form contract for dominance that men made with women, parents with children, friends with each other. For some reason, this one little woman, out of all the people he'd ever known, simply did exactly what she was doing, without ego or artifice, and that was astonishing. That was more awesome than all the almost supernatural baggage he'd hung on his image of her.

"I'll bite, lady," he said softly. "What do you see when you look in a three-way mirror?"

Emily gave her perfectly magnificent smile and said, "If you angle it right, you see infinity."

The folder was labeled "Emily A. Brand, Ph.D. Sub ref/ LIGHTSOURCE," and David thought that he was hallucinating. But the headache was gone, he could still see the rain through the window; Esther was baking a cake and he smelled chocolate, and heard Talbot talking. The folder was real.

"We don't have much," Talbot was saying, "and I thought you'd go up there . . ." Talbot paused.

David had to say something. "Don't you trust Carver?" he asked.

"Yes. But he's a physicist, not a psychologist."

"I'm not a psychologist either," David said. He put his hand on the table, a few inches from the folder.

"I know," Talbot said, "but you see things other people don't. Carver believed what he said, but he was spooked. Spooked men imagine things."

David didn't say anything, and Talbot leaned forward. "I don't want chapter and verse, Dave. I know I can't have that. Just go up there. Meet her; meet Lipsky, sniff the air. Like you did in Karom."

Karom was a refinery town in Saudi Arabia. The profits were fine as far as anyone knew, and David had been sent there in '85 to trade compliments with the local sheikh and let the men from Galveston see a high-level company man out there in the sand with them. That's all he meant to do at Karom. But the first thing he noticed was that Samet, the little Arab who ran the refinery, was very nervous. He kept licking his fat liver-colored lips in David's presence and wiping the palms of his hands. The first night David was there, Samet threw a big, unnecessary feast in David's honor. David counted thirty different dishes, ten sweets, and four kinds of coffee. Samet even served whiskey and wine, and David knew that the little Arab would have put a roast pig on the table if David requested it. Samet had hired women for after dinner, whores from the north, where the women were thinner, lighter-skinned, more to Western tastes. He reserved the two youngest and prettiest for David. One was only twelve, a virgin, and tearing her open was the most sexually exciting thing David had ever done. But all night even as he jammed the young girl with barely formed breasts down on his erection and thrilled to her cries, which she tried to muffle, he couldn't forget the carafes of wine and bottles of whiskey on the Muslim's table.

He was supposed to leave in four days, but he stayed on in Karom, and at the end of three weeks he'd found the scam. There were two pipelines coming down from the fields in the north. One brought crude to the NARCON refinery, but the other split off fifteen miles north in the middle of the desert. At the end of it, in a narrow valley bordered by hills of red rock too hot to touch, was Samet's own refinery.

It was well done; the shippers and inspectors had been bought, the sheikh was in on it, so was one of the prince's ministers. Samet pleaded when David confronted him; he scratched his pitted cheeks with his nails, dribbled saliva, and sobbed piteously.

It would have been discovered in time without David. A revamped computer would have picked up the discrepancies. But the millions of gallons that Samet had already siphoned off were lost and he might have gotten away with millions more if David hadn't wondered why the Muslim served wine. The illegal refinery was dismantled, the inspectors were jailed for life, and the sheikh was allowed to exile himself. Samet was beheaded, and Talbot gave David a stock-and-cash bonus worth half a million dollars.

Karom was a victory, and David liked thinking about it. He moved his hand across the coffee table and touched Emily Brand's folder.

She the winner, and me the loser, he'd told Madeline. Unless they played again.

He picked up the folder and opened it.

There was a picture clipped inside the cover, the sort of portrait they use in annual reports. He studied it while Talbot finished his brandy. She wasn't plain, but she wasn't pretty, either. Not the sort of woman he'd turn to look at; nothing compared to Mary.

"You should have heard Carver on the subject of Dr. Brand," Talbot said. "You'd think she was a cross between Marie Curie and the god Shiva. He said she'd have been the one to invent the wheel if someone hadn't beaten her to it. . . ."

David turned to the dossier and read:

She was born in Danbury, Connecticut, on January 2, 1952. Her mother was Ruth Austen, her father was Isaac Brand, a Jew who manufactured women's clothes on Seventh Avenue under the name Judy Sherman. He'd started from nothing, and made a fortune . . . the computer picked up his progress, and David skipped. The mother's family had lived in northern Connecticut since the seventeenth century. They'd been rich once, but rotten financial management ate away the Austen fortune, and the Depression finished it off. He skipped again. Emily was sent to Trent School. David knew about Trent—it

57

was an institution for upper-class ladies-in-training. David thought of bunk beds, cold water, tennis sweaters, volleyball, and stables. They would try to teach her table setting, and ceramics, journalism, French, and interior decorating. Mary had gone to a school like that and loved it. But Emily was expelled from Trent after seven months. David wondered what she'd done, but the headmistress's report was vague.

After that, they sent her to school in Massachusetts; then Harvard, then Princeton. She was at Princeton until '86; then she went to Lake Placid. She'd had seven years of higher education, from freshman to Ph.D. in physics, and she'd gotten one incomplete. That was in an A-level sociology course which was required for freshmen back in the late sixties. Apparently they stopped trying to socialize Emily Brand, and from then on there was nothing but A's.

He read avidly now. She'd had a boyfriend at Princeton. A "sex con," the computer called it (for "sexual connection"), with a man named Richard Breemer. She had a sex con now at Placid with a John Ostrow, but she lived alone. She'd never married, she had no children and no abortions that had been paid for by the state. No evidence of promiscuity or homosexuality. The computer had picked up the provisions of her father's will. He'd divided his fortune equally among his wife and two daughters (the second daughter, with the second wife, was Susan Brand Cohen). The stepmother tried to contest the will and failed and Emily Brand inherited more than two million dollars.

So she had more money than he did. He closed the folder and rested it on his knees. The Brahms wound down, rain ran across the windows. He thought of the night in his room with her notebook, and remembered feeling that something treacherous was in there with him. Then he saw himself groveling on Madeline Warner's floor, crying for someone to love, and for a moment he seemed to see everything clearly, like a man riding the top of a train. He knew he should hand the folder back to Talbot and tell him to get another boy because he was getting out and taking his wife and kid with him. Maybe there was a spark of life in Mary after all and he'd find it if he got her away from her monster of a father, her catatonic drunk of a mother, and all the dead-asses of Greenwich and New Canaan. They'd go to Vancouver to run the new rigs together or up to Alaska or out to the New Mexico desert to start a trailer camp . . . The thought made him grin.

"What's so funny?" Talbot asked sharply.

The moment was passing. He tried to hold on to it. "What's so funny?"

The Brahms ended and the clarity faded like a light on shore that he was sailing away from. Then it was over.

Fate, coincidence, something was giving him another crack at Emily Brand. He put his hand in his jacket pocket just to be sure the Percodan was there; then he asked Talbot when he wanted him to go to Placid.

CHAPTER

"Something's going on," Carver told David. "She and Lipsky worked last night and the night before. No one' supposed to know. I wouldn't know if I didn't snoop."

They had turned off of the main road and driven up int the mountains. Melting ice cracked like rifle shots aroun them, the trees looked black in the bright sun, and water ra down the sides of the narrow road. David hated it here; h hated the pretty little town, the hotel that looked like desert fortress, the whole freezing place, but especially thos mountains. They looked like killers; worse than the Rockie or the Alps, even though they were half the size. It was th worn-down look that they had, the sense of having been ther forever. Unknowing, uncaring, indestructible, and dangerou Carver pointed out Whiteface, a malevolent white lump tha stuck up against the sky. Ice cracked again, David jumped and Carver laughed at him.

They passed a long modern building on a flat overlookin the town. It was glass and rough stone, with pruned spruc around it, and well-kept gravel walks.

"That's the tissue-culture lab," Carver told him. Her boy friend worked there. "Fuckbuddy," Carver called him. Hi name was John Ostrow, and the director thought he was th great white hope of genetic engineering, whatever that was.

They wound through a switchback, and at the end, behin a heavy cyclone fence with electric wire at the top and a incongruously open gate, was the Placid facility—TNF 121 —the backwater that nobody worried about.

It looked like a factory. The front stuck out into th

parking lot; the rest was buried in the mountain that rose up behind it. It was gray cinder block with aluminum-framed windows. The gravel path was dirty, and scraped almost bare; a few of the droopy junipers they usually planted around factories provided the only landscaping.

"Not much to look at, is it?" Carver said. David followed Carver up the path to the door. His heart was pounding; his hands sweated inside his gloves.

The front lobby was quiet. The floor was cracked asphalt tile, but it was clean and waxed. A semicircular counter was in the middle, with a guard behind it. The guard's uniform shirt was frayed at the cuffs, open at the neck.

He took David's NARCON ID, checked his list, then pinned a radiation badge on David's jacket. The man wore a gun; a closed-circuit TV screen hung behind his desk. Carver and David went down a short hall to double metal doors.

A speaker and a screen with digit pads were built into the wall next to the doors. Carver pushed a number; it flashed on the screen with the words: "Key if correct."

Carver pushed another pad, and a voice came out of the speaker: "Good morning, Dr. Carver."

"Good morning."

"Say again."

"I said good morning, you stupid bitch." Carver laughed. "You should hear what Lipsky calls it."

It. David realized that the doors were computerized for voice prints.

The voice came out of the speaker: "Thank you, Dr. Carver, have a nice day."

The doors were solid metal, six inches thick. They slid smoothly back into the walls and a long corridor rolled ahead of them. The walls and floor were gray composition that reflected the light fuzzily, so that the end of the hallway was lost in a shining haze. They stepped into the hall, and the door closed after them.

The shabbiness of the rest of the place was gone; the hall was silent, cold and new-looking; no cracked tile or peeling paint here. It got colder, and David realized that they were going into the mountain.

Carver talked. "This started as an industrial facility in the

61

fifties. Everybody wanted their own cyclotron and a lab dug into a mountain back then. Big time stuff in those days. The moguls sold it to the State in the sixties when they realized that their very expensive machine wasn't going to do anything but magnetize every piece of metal in sight. You couldn't go near one with a pen in your pocket. It wound up plastered to the nearest piece of metal, and if you didn't get it out of your pocket fast enough, you went with it."

They passed a door marked "Marvin Lipsky, Ph.D.," then another marked "Emily Brand, Ph.D." Sweat popped out on David's forehead in spite of the cold. His hands and armpits were clammy.

They came to the end of the corridor, and ahead he saw a door labeled "CONTROL."

He felt the first throb of a headache, and he stopped at a water fountain and swallowed a Percodan.

Last night, as he drove north, he had planned this day. Emily Brand was a woman; women always wanted something from David. Love, sex, pain, admiration. He'd figure out what *she* wanted and hold it out to her. He would start in the lab, with his first sight of her. He'd watch her with his special look compounded of surprise, admiration, and a little unwilling desire. She would notice, and maybe be embarrassed, but she'd be intrigued too, and flattered. He would follow her around the lab, admire the reactor (in his imagination, it was a fairly small, neat-looking contraption), and then ask her to have dinner with him. She couldn't refuse; he was a guest, and it would be rude. Besides, he was from NARCON, and NARCON might give them money, so she'd go. There had to be a decent restaurant even in Placid, someplace quiet and intimate, maybe with a fireplace. He'd ask her the right questions—nothing so crude as just coming out and asking about the reactor; he would ask her about herself. Women couldn't resist that, and once they started, the trick was to shut them up. So she'd talk, and he'd listen. The reactor was part of her life, the most important part, according to Carver.

He'd order good wine, their hands would brush across the table, all very subtle. He'd order brandy after dinner; then he'd take her home. They might talk more there, they might

make love. He'd never fucked a woman he hated before; it
was an exciting thought. She might not want to; some women
preferred fantasy. It didn't matter, though, because he knew
that by the time he left her, very late at night, and headed
down out of the mountains, he would know as much about
the future of fusion energy as she did. . . .

He knew which one she was the second he came through
the door. He only let himself glance at her, but he saw
everything about her. He saw a delicate blue vein trail out of
her hair, across her forehead to her eyebrows. Her features
were delicate, her face was pale; there were circles under her
eyes (Carver had said they were working late), and her
cheeks were hollow. Her glasses were old, out of style, and
didn't fit well anymore, and her hair was winter dry and
nondescript. He saw all this before he really looked at her.
Then he was facing her, and Carver introduced them.

He looked into the calm flat eyes behind the ugly glasses,
and he knew he'd been a fool. This woman didn't care how
he looked at her or what he thought. She wouldn't tell him
about herself or anything else, and she wanted nothing from
him. For all the interest in her eyes, he might have been
transparent. A ghost through which she could see the far wall.

They shook hands.

"We've met before," he said.

"Oh?"

"It was a long time ago. We were children."

"Oh," she said again. She wasn't interested and she started
to turn away, but he held onto her hand. The room was
quiet, with everyone wondering what was going on. He didn't
care, and for a second he let himself squeeze her hand so
hard he felt the bones rub. Then he let her go.

Lipsky started talking; Brand went back to the console and
didn't look at him again. She didn't know who he was, she
didn't care. He seethed; Carver leaned against the door and
watched with that shitty, spiteful little grin of his; Avery
stood as close to David as she dared, trying to get him to
look at her. The room was cold, the light came up off the
gray floor into his eyes, and the Percodan and the headache
fought it out.

"One hundred and fifty million dollars," Lipsky said
tiredly, "twenty-five feet of steel and molybdenum . . . internal

63

temperatures of seventy-five million degrees centigrade . . .
On and on he went, in the same tone. He tried for som
enthusiasm, but David thought it was an effort. Brand stayed
in her place, looking down at something in front of her
Lipsky pushed himself to go on.

"Laser-triggered . . . magnetic-shielded, magnetic . . ."

Finally Lipsky finished his spiel, and, with an overre
hearsed gesture, like a burlesque magician who was holding
the audience until the strippers came out, he waved his arm
at the glass wall that surrounded the control room and said
"And there it is. . . ."

David looked blankly at him. "The reactor," Lipsky said
"through the wall," and for the first time David looked down
through the glass wall and saw it.

It was enormous: a hundred times bigger than he had
thought it would be. The floor of the reactor room was two
stories deep, and the machine filled it. Metal tubes ran
around its body like vines; thick wires ran from even thicker
wires that were huge, zinc encased, and segmented like some
alien and fantastic worm. The top was an octagon or decagon
a heavy girder that seemed suspended from nothing ran across
it and ended. There were lines marked in tape on the black
floor, and big steel boxes sat next to the thing, with shining
hoses running out of them and into the reactor, like I.V. tubes
feeding a dying patient that couldn't eat on his own. It was
the ugliest thing David had ever seen.

"Would you like a closer look?" Lipsky said. "It's really
impressive close up."

A closer look was the last thing David wanted, but he said
"All right."

"Emily'll take you. It and Emily seem to understand each
other."

David followed her down pressed-metal stairs to the floor
of the room. The walls were metal; the floor was black tile
covered with the dirty tape. The room was enormous, silent
and smelled of metal. David felt the metal smell coating his
tongue, and the Percodan was losing the battle. Emily Brand
didn't look at him once, only at the reactor, and she ex
plained the controls as if she were describing a lover's face
He didn't listen to the words, only to the sound of her voice
Two months later, when he saw Emily Brand again, h

ealized he should have listened to every word. But then it
was too late.

David pulled up in front of the big Round Hill house. Raymond took his coat and led him to the study, where Talbot
and Joan were watching a tape of some old movie. David
smothered a grin; George Talbot, ruthless billionaire, owner
of half the world, watching old movies in his house shoes
with his alcoholic wife.

Joan Talbot was needlepointing, a glass of clear liquor on
the table next to her. David had never seen her actually do
anything but eat, drink, and needlepoint.

"Ah, David." Talbot stood up and turned off the machine.
The screen went blank and Joan Talbot picked up her drink,
her canvas, and crossed the room to the door.

He said hello to her, and she nodded without answering.
Gravy splotched her heavy silk blouse; her brassiere strap
had broken and one breast hung lower than the other. She
was a mess and he used to wonder why Talbot had married
her. Then Mary told him that her mother's father had been
a baronet and something very high up in North Sea Oil, which
almost explained it.

David had not known how to treat her at first. She never
spoke to him except for the amenities, but a few times he'd
caught her staring at him with unexpectedly clear eyes. He
would smile, and she would look away as if it hadn't
happened.

She did talk to him finally, on the day he married her
daughter. In the middle of toasts and uneasy congratulations,
David spotted his new mother-in-law weaving through the
crowd toward him, and he knew the time had come for a
boozy, teary heart-to-heart.

He was ready; he knew his lines. Sure enough, she'd taken
his arm and led him away from the crowd and out of
the room into the empty entrance hall. They stopped near the
coat room under the stairs, and he braced himself. But she
stepped back and looked at him for a few minutes. Her eyes
were red from drinking, her lipstick was smeared, but she
didn't look drunk or maudlin. She looked hard, sharp, and
suddenly very smart. Her smeared lips stretched back from

her still-perfect teeth in a snarling grin and she said softly "You're very pretty, Lucci. Pretty and sexy and smart, and my poor dumb little girl is quite besotted, isn't she? You've even seduced big bad George himself into a father-and son fantasy, and you deserve congratulations for that too I alone know you for the nasty piece of work that you are, Lucci. I have no power, I grant you that . . . but I still have a reflection of loyalty and remembered love in my husband's mind, and I shall use that to contain you, David dear. Somehow."

She reached out and patted his shoulder. He shrank away from her touch, and she laughed softly and said, "Fore warned is forearmed, pretty David." Then, deliberately, and still with that wolfish grin stretching her lips, she let her eyes glaze until she looked drunk again, and she turned and wove away from him back into the other room.

She had frightened him, and he avoided her after that But the years passed, she didn't "contain" him, and he almost stopped worrying about it.

"Well?" Talbot said.

Joan was just shutting the door. Talbot let her listen to anything, but David still remembered the warning she'd given him on his wedding day, and he waited until she was out of the room and the door was firmly closed behind her.

"Well?" Talbot said again.

"Carver's right," David said.

"How do you know?"

"I'm from NARCON, and Carver told them I might be worth grant money. So as far as they knew, I was a few billion dollars on the hoof. But they didn't give a shit. The woman wouldn't have anyway, but Lipsky's the money man He was polite and went through his number, but for all the enthusiasm he showed, I could have been the health in spector."

"So?" Talbot asked.

"Don't be thick, George. Lipsky didn't care about me or NARCON because he thought he could get his money else where."

"But Flynn said the President won't come across with major funding without a significant advance—"

"Exactly," David said patiently, "and Lipsky doesn't car

about *our* money, which means he thinks he can get money from Franklin, which means that he thinks he's got a significant advance."

Talbot stared at David. "This is very serious, David. Very, *very* serious." Then he whispered, his voice hissing eerily in the room, "David . . . you could be my heir. You know that. Not Mary or Anthony or Joan. *You*."

David kept quiet, and Talbot whispered again, "You want it, don't you?"

"More than anything else in the world."

"Good," Talbot said. He leaned forward until his strained face was close to David's. "But it's *this* NARCON you want, isn't it? Not a collection of textile mills and lumber companies with a few banks thrown in. *This* NARCON."

David said, "Yes."

David and Talbot were in a converted house in Georgetown, in a large parlor room with paneled walls, built-in bookcases, and antique furniture. The desk was bowed mahogany, the room was lit in pools from Chinese vases turned into lamps. It was a clubby room, a rich man's study, and David knew the man who got up from the desk and came toward them. David had seen him on TV occasionally and in news photos. He'd made the cover of *Time* a couple of years ago. He was Paul K. Stockton, the director of NCEC—the National Council of Energy Conservation. *Time* said that he was one of the few men in America who spoke the language of the environmentalists and of industry and could strike a balance that both sides could live with. He'd eased the way for congressional approval for the oil leases off Baja California (in spite of the furor over the gray whales) and on the Grand Banks (in spite of the fishery). David had never heard what he'd done for the environmentalists, but apparently he reassured them enough to keep them more or less quiet, and he had managed to keep the no-nukes nuts in line, even after the Adobe Head accident. He'd been a darling of the Reagan administration, but he kept his job after Orin Franklin was elected; some said that was because Franklin thought that Stockton had played fair, but others said Stockton had something on Franklin.

Stockton greeted Talbot like a friend, shook David's hand,

and told him how much he'd heard about him. Then he settled them in maroon leather wing chairs in front of the marble fireplace and mixed drinks.

He was better-looking than David thought he'd be. His cheeks had a healthy flush, his eyes were dark blue, and he had wavy gray hair. He brought their drinks, then settled himself across from them.

"Well met," he said cheerfully, and raised his glass and drank. Talbot leaned the snakeskin case he had carried from White Plains against the side of his chair and picked up his glass.

Stockton asked. "To what do I owe the honor?"

"I need help," Talbot said.

Stockton glanced quickly at the case, then away. Neither of them looked at it again.

Talbot said, "We may have trouble at Placid. That's TNF 1210."

"I don't know much about it."

"Marvin Lipsky runs it."

"I've heard of him," Stockton said. "Used to be at Stanford." Then Stockton's eyes narrowed. "You're talking fusion-type trouble, George?"

Talbot nodded.

"Flynn said they were cut off."

They were talking about Daniel Flynn, the Secretary of the Interior. David could hardly believe it.

Talbot said, "True, but money isn't everything in physics. So I was told, and so I believe. At least now. David was up there yesterday . . ."

They both looked at him. He was on.

David told Stockton what he'd told Talbot: Lipsky didn't want money from him, Brand barely knew he was there, Carver said they were working nights. But it sounded vague.

"Not much to pin a major effort on," Stockton said.

"I don't want a 'major' effort," Talbot said. "We'll do surveillance, but if something *does* happen, then one of your men should be there . . . in case . . ." He stopped dead.

In case of what? David wondered. What would Stockton's man do that the NARCON wireman couldn't? Talbot and Stockton were looking at him. Tension built in the room for a long time, then Talbot finished his sentence. "In case we've got another Klein on our hands." He stared hard at David; so did Stockton. Both men sending him the same message.

Talbot meant Howard Klein. David remembered him. He had been the director and general guru of a no-nukes bunch in Idaho eight years ago. Klein had energy and fanaticism. He wanted North Plains condemned before it was finished, and torn down. He lobbied, he raised money, and got himself on the local radio and TV stations. Of course the utility couldn't allow Klein to win. That would cost them several hundred million; so they fought back, and they had more money than Klein. But Klein had stirred the people up and gotten a referendum on the ballot. Local polls said he would win, and the utility spent more money and imported more PR men from the East. But three months before the election, Klein's lead was still growing. Then, late one night on a desolate road, Howard Klein's car smashed into a semi and exploded. The movement twitched like a fresh corpse that had lost its head, then subsided. The referendum was defeated, and the North Plains nuclear plant was built.

There'd been innuendos about the convenience of the accident, and questions about what a semi was doing on a road leading nowhere when it should have been plying the interstate. There was an investigation. But the truck driver swore that he got lost after stopping for dinner, there wasn't enough left of Klein's car to prove tampering, and the investigation folded up after three days.

Now David got the message the two men were sending him. They had killed Howard Klein. They wanted Stockton's men at Placid in case they had to kill Lipsky and Brand.

If David was going to stay in the game, he had two goals. One, figure it out. He'd done that. Two, stay where he was, in this chair, in this room, and handle his moral revulsion or whatever they imagined he would feel; then he could play with the big boys.

David made himself think about Howard Klein. He saw a long, empty road through flat fields. It was night. A car came on, going fast toward the distant mountain. Then, over a dip in the road, David heard the semi grinding, and then he saw it. It was going fast; its tires sloughed against the pavement. The little car hugged the right, but just as the vehicles came abreast of each other, the semi veered, and its huge featureless grille smashed into the little car. The car exploded, the windshield disintegrated, the doors popped off, and a black stick-shadow of the man inside raised its burning arms to its burning head.

David waited to feel something . . . but he didn't, and the vision of Howard Klein clutching his burning head in unimaginable agony was gone in a second.

Talbot and Stockton waited.

It was a clean decision for David. He could walk out now; no one had admitted anything and he was safe. He would keep his job, Talbot would still love him, but the love would be crippled, and when the time came, NARCON would go to trustees and then to Anthony.

Deliberately David leaned back in the chair, stretched out his legs, and crossed them at the ankles. Stockton smiled and asked if he could freshen David's drink.

CHAPTER

"Now it's up to the engineers," Lipsky said and took Emily's hands. She looked awful. She'd lost weight, and there were black circles under her eyes. He knew he looked lousy too. He hadn't been able to eat regularly the past two months, and he had trouble sleeping. He had a feeling that he was scared of something, but he didn't know what. He went on working every night anyway, and now they were finished.

"It'll work," he said.

"I think so," Emily answered.

"Tell me it'll work."

Emily smiled. "It'll work."

"You're sure?"

"No," she said. They both giggled.

The room was quiet, the building was cold.

"Emily?" he whispered.

She shook her head. He knew she'd stood all the emotion from him that she could.

"I'll make copies," she said gently. "One for you, one for me."

"One for the President. I'll bring it to him."

"Will he see you?"

"He'll see *us*."

She was quiet. She didn't want to see the President. The attention would make her miserable; she'd only cramp Lipsky's style. But she wasn't going to argue with him now. She gathered the careful set of drawings and the equations and stood up.

"Let me go," Lipsky said. "My ass is freezing, and I can't sit here another minute."

He took the papers to the Xerox room, and Emily went through the control-room door and down the stairs to the base of the reactor. The room was dark except for lights coming through the glass wall of the control room. The machine shone dully, the edges softened in the darkness around it. She reached out and touched one cold gleaming tube.

"You're done for," she whispered to it, "and I'm sorry. But you have an offspring, if it's any comfort. It'll carry on for you; it'll *work*." She laughed softly. "I *think* it will."

She hadn't closed the control-room door, and she didn't hear Lipsky come out onto the metal landing above the stairs.

"It'll look like you," she said softly, "but elongated . . . and at the apexes will be the mirrors." Not mirrors really, but obstacles of magnetic force. "Angled like . . . like mirrors," Emily said. "They will deflect the nuclei, send them crashing into each other, back into the mirrors, and into each other, and again into the mirrors, and into each other. Like the reflections in a three-way mirror, they will go on and on. I hope they will. Maybe not, though. But we'll learn. And the next one after that'll do it. I promise. But even that machine—that last machine—will be your offspring too."

"Meshugah!" Lipsky yelled from the balcony.

Emily held her hand against the machine tubing for another minute, then dropped it and turned around.

"Come up," Lipsky yelled. "Come up here, crazy lady."

She mounted the stairs, and he grabbed her shoulders and kissed her on the cheek, on the forehead, and on one eye. He was suddenly himself again. He handed her the copies.

"Keep these. One for you, one for me, one for the safe, crazy lady."

"You feel better."

He laughed wildly. "I went to the can and expunged a terrible fear."

"Were you afraid?"

"Yes," he said, suddenly serious.

"Of what?"

"Of failing. Of not failing. Who knows what scares a

sixty-year-old man who's trying to save the world? Come, we'll stash these, and then we're going to get drunk." He looked down over the railing at the machine. "Sorry, fella," he yelled. "You can't come with us."

They went to the Steak and Stinger. The place was jammed, but it was nine and diners were starting to leave. The hostess said it would take ten or fifteen minutes for a table. They went to the bar, ordered double vodkas, and ate cheese and crackers. At one point, something unidentifiable came over Emily, and halfway into her double vodka, without any warning, she reached out and put her arms around Lipsky's neck.

He froze in shock with his mouth full of cracker. "What's this?"

"I don't know," Emily said.

"Not sex. It must be affection. Affection from the ice bitch."

A few people looked at them. Lipsky glared back at them, and they looked away.

"You know what they think in here?" Lipsky said. "They think I'm a dirty old man and I just gave you sixty bucks to pretend that you like me."

Emily laughed and let him go.

"Let's call Marsha," she said.

"And John," Lipsky yelled. "A party."

They called, and fifteen minutes later they were sitting in the dining room with John Ostrow and Marsha Lipsky and two more double vodkas. They all ordered the big steaks, with onion rings, baked potatoes, and broiled mushrooms. They ordered a bottle of wine, and halfway into her second double vodka, Emily knew she had to eat or she'd be too drunk to.

John helped her to the salad bar; they each took two plates, so they could bring back food for Lipsky and Marsha. Emily concentrated on finding the right things to put on top of fresh lettuce and tomato, and she was sprinkling croutons on Marsha's full plate when she looked up and saw Miles Carver staring at her from the line of tables near the windows. She smiled drunkenly at him, but he didn't smile back. He glanced away as if he didn't know who she was, but not before she'd seen the look of startled fear on his face.

Suddenly she was almost sober. Carver leaned forward and talked to Sheila, pretending that he'd never noticed Emily in the first place. Emily finished filling the plates and brought them to the table. They went back to the same happy, excited talking, but some of the fun was gone for Emily.

Carver had been watching her for weeks now, sometimes gauging, sometimes looking blank or scared. She didn't understand. Maybe he just didn't like her. But she didn't think that was it. He didn't care about her one way or the other, except that she frightened him for some reason. That was stupid, she thought. She didn't have any power over him; she didn't want any.

She glanced back at the table where he and Sheila had been, but it was empty now, and the busboy was clearing for the next customers.

Carver stopped at the double metal doors. Even the lobby was cold this late at night. Kevin Starrett was on nights this week. He sat at the counter with a heavy sweater pulled over his shoulders and buttoned over his big belly, eating a huge grinder that dripped oil on the paper plate under it. Next to him on the counter, a nine-inch TV played, and actors' voices and romantic background music filled the lobby.

Carver punched his number and waited for the computer voice. It would record the time he'd entered, 11:32, and the time he left. But no one would check unless something was missing, and he could copy whatever he found and leave everything intact. He talked to the speaker, the doors opened and closed behind him, and he was alone, walking up the hall into the mountain. He went to Lipsky's office. If it was locked, he was screwed, but it was open and he went in and turned on the light. Lipsky's work table was a mess. He looked through the scattered papers quickly, then in the files, but he didn't find anything unusual. Then he opened Lipsky's closet and saw the safe. It had always been a joke, that safe, and most of the time Lipsky forgot to shut it. It was shut now.

He went back to Lipsky's desk and sat down. It was 11:45; Starrett said he didn't like leaving the alarm off for longer than ten minutes. Carver had to think fast. Lipsky was absentminded; he'd never remember the combination of a safe he rarely closed. He wouldn't leave the combination at home because he wouldn't want to call Marsha every time he did close the safe and had to open it again. He wouldn't carry it with him because he lost everything. He'd lost his American Express card so many times they took it away from him. The Lipskys never locked their back door because he kept losing the keys and had to wait outside in the cold or at Faith's until Marsha came home and let him in.

The combination wasn't at home, it wasn't on him. It had to be here.

Carver emptied the pencil box on the desk and looked in at the dusty bottom; then he went through the desk drawers and found more pencils, clips, and keys. He found a mezuzah that never got put up and a rock-hard doughnut with a few bites gone, but no combination. It was 11:55; Starrett might already be looking for him.

He pulled the middle drawer all the way out and felt under it, then the side drawers, and on the underside of the bottom-right-hand drawer he felt smooth tape and paper. He emptied the drawer, pulled it out and turned it over, and found the combination scrawled on a strip of paper.

"Assholes," he muttered as he copied the combination on one of Lipsky's memo pads.

He shoved everything back into the drawer, then slid it into place and went to the door. He turned out the light, opened the door slowly, and looked out into the hall. It rolled away, dim and empty. The metal doors were shut.

The phone rang in his office. He slammed Lipsky's door, and clutching the combination, he raced down the hall to his office, pulling the keys out of his pocket with his free hand. He got the door open and grabbed the phone on the fourth ring. It was Starrett.

"Sorry," Carver said. "I was in the can."

"Gonna have to arm the alarm, doctor."

"Give me a few more minutes."

Starrett sighed. "You're all nuts in this place. You should be home watching the tube. Okay, five minutes."

Carver shut his office and went back. He passed Emily's door and stopped for a second. She wasn't like Lipsky. She'd have it with her . . . whatever it was. Or she'd lock it up and she wouldn't lose the key. He went back into Lipsky's office, shut the door quietly, and went to the safe.

At one-thirty in the morning the phone rang in Talbot's mansion in North Greenwich, Connecticut. One of the house-men answered and tried to get Carver to call back in the morning.

"Listen," Carver said, "get massa on the phone now or you're gonna wind up shoveling shit for your supper." The houseman held the phone for a moment, then put Carver on hold, punched in the house phone, and dialed the master suite at the other end of the house.

Talbot waited until he heard the houseman hang up downstairs.

"I know you wouldn't call at this hour if it weren't important," he said.

"It's important," Carver told him. "They're finished."

"Finished?"

"You heard me," Carver said. "They were celebrating tonight, and I've got three pages of equations and a diagram—"

"Can you be more specific?" Talbot asked coolly.

Carver laughed into the phone and started reading equations.

"Okay," Talbot said. "What does it mean?"

"It means they can get their money."

"But if they get it and build the thing, will it work?"

The other end was quiet, and then Carver spoke, his voice soft and malicious. "I'd put *my* money on it, Talbot."

Talbot's insides lurched. He'd been waiting so long to hear this, it was almost relief. "Be here tomorrow, bring it with you," he said.

"Don't you believe me?"

"Yes. But I have to convince . . . other people. Tomorrow, as early as possible. I'll send the Falcon to Saranac."

Quiet again; then Carver laughed softly. "Sure, boss. Anything you say, boss."

Talbot hung up and turned around. Joan was awake, watching him. Her hair had come out of the rollers, cream smeared her face, and her eyes were red, but he could tell she was sober. He went back to his bed.

"Late for a call," she said.

"Trouble with Placid." He slipped back into bed and pulled the covers up but left the light on.

"Oh," she said. "Not serious, I hope."

"We'll see."

He'd never told his wife about Klein or Blair or his lovers, but he told her almost everything else. He never asked her advice, she never gave any, but he had to talk to someone, and she seemed to listen without hearing. She nodded in the right places, but her eyes were usually glazed, and he thought the nods corresponded to the rhythms, not the content, of his speech.

He heard her slide down under the covers and he looked over at her. Her eyes were closed and her greasy cheek rested on the pillow; in a few seconds her breathing changed.

She was still beautiful in spite of the sags and wrinkles and all the booze. She was fifty-six, seven years younger than he was, but she looked much younger, and he marveled at her, even though he knew that the liquor was finally making her sick; the tremor in her hands got worse every day. But he hoped she'd last a few more years anyway. He didn't love her anymore, he hadn't made love to her for years—since before Anthony was born—but she was a presence that he was used to and needed. The way a man needs a servant he's had for a long time, or a pet cat.

For sex, he had his pick of all the men and women who worked for NARCON. They could say no if they wanted; they wouldn't lose their jobs or chance of promotion, and he made sure that they knew that. But very few had turned him down through the years, and none recently, as if they understood that his advancing age would make him more sensitive to the slight. When he was younger, he had preferred men. They were harder to demean, and it was easier to hurt them physically without resorting to whips or thongs or any other nonsensical equipment. But lately, he wanted women; it was easier with them, and he felt a need for ease. He had one special girl now, a nineteen-year-old named Romy with thin hips and big tits who worked in the international section. She had a way of flattening herself to a bed that reminded him of a frog staked out for dissection, and she would let him do anything he wanted to her, without too much whimpering.

77

For love, there was David, the son he never had. Just as well, he thought as he listened to his wife's light, restless breathing. God knows what she would have produced. A boy as stupid and lifeless as her daughter. He pushed the thought away. He loved his daughter; he'd just hoped . . . He couldn't remember what he'd hoped.

He looked at the clock; it was almost two, and he knew he wouldn't sleep anymore. He could call Placid now; he'd wake them up, but they weren't being paid to sleep. He got out of bed, and then decided to use another phone. Not because he cared about what Joan heard, but because she was a light sleeper in spite of all she drank, and he didn't want to wake her.

The bedroom door closed, and Joan opened her eyes and sat up. She heard him pad down the hall, open the upstairs-sitting-room door, and close it. She slid out of bed and went out into the hall. Sure enough, there was a light under the sitting-room door.

She'd been eavesdropping on his conversations and going through his papers and files on the sly for years.

It was an interest in life besides this house, the endless yards of needlepoint, and her pretty empty-headed daughter, who seemed to want nothing more of life than planning tailgate picnics and bridge luncheons. The snooping made Joan feel part of things, and it gave her a feeling of power because she knew things that her husband didn't know she knew.

Eight years ago she had found the combination to his safe, and his tape file inside of it. On nights when he was out of town or at the club in New York, she would sit in his study with one lamp burning, and a cup of brandy-laced tea, and listen to Talbot and David, Talbot and Reynolds, Talbot and Court, Talbot and Paul Stockton. She knew who Stockton was, and she listened avidly to those tapes, which turned out to be a rotten idea, because on one old tape, a year after it had happened, she heard them plan the murder of Howard Klein.

She didn't do anything about it. She had reasons, she told herself. It was not up to her; Klein was only a name, and Talbot was her husband. She loved him, or remembered what it was like to love him. Besides, a wife couldn't testify against her husband, or some such rot. She drank more and lost weight.

A year passed, she started to feel better, and then two years, and she almost never thought about it. Then they killed Gerald Blair.

Blair had told the press that the specs on the Adobe Head nuclear plant were fudged, and he could prove it. If he did, the half-built facility would be dismantled and the NARCON dummy that owned it would lose two hundred million dollars. Blair and his wife came to this house, had dinner here, spent the night. Upstairs, Joan and Laura Blair drank (not so much then) and talked about men and love and children, like girls at school. Downstairs, George Talbot tried to buy Gerald Blair. Laura was pretty and fair, with pale hair and white eyelashes, and she blushed moist pink to her hairline when she told Joan that her husband was still the most exciting man she'd ever known.

They killed him a week later, in Ontario. The authorities said it was a hunting accident, but Joan knew better. Laura Blair waited to see him buried and to send her children to her mother's; then she ate mothballs and rat poison, and they found her body a few days after she'd died.

Joan Talbot didn't do anything about the Blairs either, except get drunk and stay that way for six years.

She still spied. It was a habit, and somewhere in the back of her mind, which she knew was getting dimmer all the time, she thought she might get something on David Lucci and make good yet on her old threat. She didn't spy because she had hope of finding some way to redeem herself.

She leaned the side of her head against the sitting-room door and heard Talbot dialing.

The phone rang in a run-down-looking fishing shack on the far side of Placid, about a quarter of a mile from Lipsky's house. It was one-thirty and the two men who stayed in the cabin, Patrick Bledsoe and Anthony Carmine, were asleep. Bledsoe snored, and Carmine pushed his head under his pillow. The phone kept ringing, and Carmine came out from under the pillow and opened his eyes. The remains of dinner—greasy dishes and an empty cardboard bucket of Kentucky Fried Chicken—were still on the counter. His mouth felt greasy like the plates. No one would call now, except for the piece at the Howard Johnson's who'd gotten a thing for Bledsoe. It rang again. Bledsoe didn't stir, and Carmine reached for it; as he did, he checked the other phones and the wall recorder out of habit. The lights were out; nothing was going on.

"Yeah."

"This is George Talbot."

Carmine sat up in bed. "Yes, Mr. Talbot."

"Anything from Lipsky?"

"Sure." Carmine went to the counter for the notebook, then came back and read to Talbot, "Lipsky called the Lake Placid cab company at eight this morning because he lost his car keys. Mrs. Lipsky called the locksmith at ten to get another set. Mrs. Lipsky called the Village Shell at ten-thirty. At eleven Mrs. Lipsky called her mother in a nursing home in New Rochelle. The electrician called at one. Then nothing until nine-fifteen, when Lipsky called to ask her to come to the Steak and Stinger to celebrate."

"Celebrate what?" Talbot asked.

"He didn't say."

Talbot was quiet.

"Mr. Talbot?"

Talbot said, "I have reason to think Lipsky's going to contact the President. You will call us immediately if he does."

Talbot hung up, and Carmine looked over at the lump Bledsoe's body made in the next bed. "The President," he whispered. "Is that enough action, you . . . you fed punk."

He hated Bledsoe almost as much as he hated Lake Placid. His last assignment had been a wire on the head of a no-nukes bunch in Rego Park, so Carmine could go home to Rosa every night. Lake Placid was his first long-term "away" assignment, and he was miserable. But he'd make six months' salary in one, so it was worth the cold and the lousy food and not seeing his wife and kids.

Bledsoe was different.

Once, when Bledsoe was out ice fishing, Carmine had searched his things and found his ID. He didn't work for the company like Carmine did; he worked for some government agency that Carmine had never heard of. He wasn't the first government man that Carmine had worked with. Carmine wasn't naive; North Atlantic Resources supported politicians, and one hand washes the other, Carmine thought. Fair enough. Still, the others had been regular enough guys, simple wiremen doing a job. Not like Bledsoe.

CHAPTER

DAVID STARED at the pages while Talbot, Carver, and Stockton watched him. He didn't understand one line or one number. It was like her old notebook; he even got a touch of the same chill he remembered. He thought of looking at the page upside down, and he grinned.

"Something funny?" Stockton asked. He sounded nasty and out of his depth. They all were, except Carver. No, David thought, Carver was too. He'd gone white when he'd walked in here, recognized Paul Stockton, and realized that he had gone too far and there was no turning back.

David shrugged and handed the pages to Talbot. Talbot examined them and looked helplessly at Carver.

"Will it work?" he asked.

"No one knows until they build it."

"But it's got a shot."

"A good one," Carver said.

They were quiet then.

Stockton cleared his throat. "What if we take action, and someone stumbles on the same thing next week?"

Carver laughed. It wasn't snide; he sounded honestly amused. He said, "Someone's as likely to 'stumble' on this as they are to 'stumble' on Mozart's *Requiem*. It's Emily Brand's work, gentlemen, like her fingerprints. That isn't a guarantee; there's always more than one answer, and someone might 'stumble' on it next week or next month. Take action, as you say, and you buy time. No one can guarantee how much. Maybe a year, maybe ten, maybe two hundred. I *do* guarantee a major government effort as soon as the President understands what's on those pages. Major, gentlemen, with all the money and engineers Brand and Lipsky need."

The intercom buzzed and Talbot answered it. He listened for a second, then put his hand on the mouthpiece. "Will you excuse us, Dr. Carver?"

He kept the phone covered until Carver had left the room and closed the door; then he said, "It's Bledsoe. Lipsky's calling the President."

Stockton straightened up in his chair, and Talbot uncovered the phone. He punched the intercom into a small speaker, so they could all hear.

Lipsky must have been on hold, because there was nothing for a moment; then a voice, not Lipsky's, came into the room. Stockton identified it for them. "William King . . . small-time aide."

King knew who Lipsky was; he explained that the President was not in Washington. Lipsky didn't rave or threaten; he didn't even tell King what he wanted or why. He told him it was extremely important that he talk with the President, and there was a simple confidence in the way he spoke that was terrible for the three men in Talbot's study to hear. King must have heard it too, because he told Lipsky that Orin Franklin was in New York, at the Waldorf Towers.

The phone disconnected, and they waited. Almost at once, Lipsky reconnected and started dialing. He talked his way through the Waldorf switchboard, the secretary who rode shotgun on the Towers phones, another secretary a little higher up, and finally Bruce Feinstein came on the line, and Lipsky said the magic words at last—*controlled nuclear fusion*.

Feinstein was quiet; so were the three men in Talbot's study. Then Feinstein said, "I'll tell him, Marvin, but he's got a rough schedule . . . he's very, very tired. Marvin, are you sure—?"

"I'm sure," Lipsky said firmly.

Another click and the silence of hold. One more click, and Orin Franklin's voice with its trace of Midwestern accent came through the speaker and into Talbot's study.

Orin Franklin held the phone against his chest while Feinstein punched up the calendar on the computer screen.

Feinstein said, "Maybe three weeks from Wednesday . . ."

Orin said into the phone, "Monday, Dr. Lipsky." Feinstein groaned. "Monday at three," Orin said, and hung up.

"Do you know who you're cutting out on Monday?" Feinstein asked.

"Don't tell me."

Feinstein crossed the enormous room and plopped down on a sofa across from the President. "Lipsky says he's got it?"

Orin nodded.

"And you believe him?"

"Why would he lie, Bruce?"

"Not lie. Exaggerate. He's excitable."

"We can get confirmation from Mendel at Princeton, and from Crowder," Orin said.

Feinstein shook his head. "They're not going to admit that Lipsky's beaten them until they have to."

"Maybe they have to," Orin said.

"If it's true."

"Let it be true," Orin said softly.

Feinstein felt terrible for his President. In seven weeks, oil-price controls would end unless Orin could convince Congress to keep them. But he had nothing to fight with, and if the controls stayed on, there would be the shortages again, and gas lines, and panic. It got worse every time. And this was an election year. Feinstein didn't have much faith in Lipsky, or in fusion itself. Flynn said it was at least twenty years down the road, and Crowder agreed. But Orin couldn't let go of it.

Orin was watching him. "You look worried, Bruce."

"I have a hard time buying it, that's all."

"But what if it works?" He looked distant. "What do we get if it works, Bruce?"

"I don't know. A lot of cheap energy . . ."

"No more old ladies freezing to death in shacks in the woods?"

He asked the question as if he really expected Feinstein to have an answer. Feinstein spoke gently. "Mr. President, old ladies will always freeze to death in little shacks or run-down apartments in the Bronx. It's in the nature of old ladies."

That night after the fund-raiser, Orin took off his tux and put on slacks and a sweater. Then he told Feinstein that he was going to take a walk, and went out into the foyer before Feinstein could argue. The six men in the foyer stood up. Orin went to the closet, put on his raincoat and a soft rain hat with a floppy brim that shadowed his face. Behind him, the men waited to get at the closet. He put on his dark glasses, then went down in the service elevator and out through the basement. The press was in the lobby or home in bed by now. It was just after eleven on a Saturday in New York. On Park and east of them the streets were quiet, but Orin walked west toward the porno houses and legit theaters in the Forties. Two of the men walked ahead, two on either side of him, two behind. Another ten or fifteen that he couldn't see were strung out behind and ahead of him. A nice quiet walk on a warm spring night. The men would be with him for the rest of his life, and he and Kathy could never walk alone again. Kathy had cried when she'd realized that, and she wasn't a crier.

There was a little mist now. The lights glowed softly. A perfect night; they didn't need much heat and it was too early for air conditioners. No brown-outs in New York tonight, or this month or next month. They would start in June and go on all summer . . . one a week if the weather was warm, more if it got really hot. Air conditioners all over the city would strain, sweat, falter; the lights would get dim here and on Eighth Avenue and downtown, everywhere. He would try to tough it out, but he knew he couldn't, and by the end of June the last of the price controls would come off. Then blessed cool air would rush out of millions of vents, the lights would brighten again . . . for a while. Then they'd burn it *all* up and the lights would go down for good. How long would it take? he wondered. Ten years? Twenty?

They passed a pizza parlor. The smell was luscious, and he stopped. It was open to the street, celebrating the mild night. The lights in here would go out, Orin thought; the bright steel ovens brought from Italy would cool down.

So what? Bunting of Tennessee had asked last month when they had discussed decontrol for the hundredth time. He was an old man with skin like paper and thin yellowish hair barely covering his skull. *So what?* he'd drawled. *The Lord's will be done.* (Webber of Iowa nodded as Bunting talked; so had a couple of the others—the good old boys for good old America.) *My grandpappy didn't have no air conditioner or electric lights. No one did a hundred years ago. They didn't die. . . .*

Liar, Orin had wanted to shout at him. *Of course they died. Old people gasped in the heat, couldn't find air, and died. Men and women died in factories, and on the streets, and in their beds on steaming nights, you old fart. . . .*

He went into the pizza parlor and ordered a slice with everything on it. Two of the men, Glover and Sanders, went with him and flanked him. The rest stayed outside.

. . . And in winter they froze, like Mrs. Marguery. . . .

His obsession with energy—with NARCON, George Talbot, Curran Mapes, and Mobil, and Exxon, and the whole mean, bloody-minded bunch—started with Mrs. Marguery.

Orin had met Talbot fifteen years ago, on Tom Gilligan's yacht, riding at anchor out on Superior, and they hated each other from the beginning. It was a hot, windless day. The boat rode a slow summer swell, and everyone was on the verge of being sick. Gilligan thought that had something to do with their dislike for each other, but Orin knew better. Their enmity was immediate and absolute, like cats and snakes, and nothing would ever mend it. Gilligan tried. Orin was running for the Senate and Gilligan wanted Talbot to fork out a couple of million to buy himself one more sympathetic senator. Gilligan didn't know yet what a rogue his Orin Franklin was. But *Talbot* knew a rogue when he saw one, and he closed up his checkbook and went home. Gilligan tried to reconcile them through the years, but it was no use. It worried Orin at first, because there should be an event or insult of some kind to justify their hatred. Then, in the middle of his third term in the Senate, Mrs. Marguery died and he had his reason. . . .

Orin and Kathy were home in Three Lakes for Christmas, 1986. He had snowshoed out on Cranberry Lake, enthralled with the silence and whiteness of the frozen lake. It was too cold to stay out, his fingers were numb, and he started back. He reached the lakeshore and heard Kathy calling, her voice sharp in the dead air. She sounded frightened, and he raced up the incline to the lodge, stumbling in the snowshoes.

Kathy was okay, but their housekeeper, Karen Brathen, had tried to call her mother and was told that the phone was disconnected. She called the little store in Crooked Lake, but they hadn't seen Mrs. Marguery since Sunday, and this was Wednesday. Karen huddled next to the phone, her sweater pulled tightly around her. Orin called the police; then he left the women and took the Jeep Cherokee for the long drive to Crooked Lake.

It was a tiny town on the edge of a vast wilderness preserve. Karen's mother lived two miles out of town on the border of the preserve itself. Her house stood alone in a spruce grove a hundred yards off the road; trackless snow reached the windowsills, the chimney was cold, and the windows were frosted. Orin strapped on his snowshoes and crossed the yard to the front door. The sky had turned white, and a few snowflakes hit his face. The window curtains were open, but there were no lights on in the house.

He cleared the front door and got it open. He called her name; there was no answer. The living room was spotless, freezing and empty, and the frost on the windows turned the thin light silver. He tramped through the living room, through the neat dining alcove with a few plants dying on the windowsills, to the kitchen.

Mrs. Marguery was lying on the floor, next to the table. Her face was white, her clothes stiff, and her body rested in a nest of blankets. He tried the phone; it was dead. He tried the lights, the stove, the heater. Nothing worked. The gauge on the oil tank read empty.

She'd died alone here in the freezing dark, wrapping her blankets around her for a last bit of warmth. He whirled around from the stove and looked at her. She'd been dead for days; there was no gleam in the half open eyes. Her legs stuck out of the blankets, and he looked at them before he could stop himself. They were thin brittle sticks with heavy stockings twisted around them, and the corpse wore old-lady sensible shoes that were too big now for the shrunken feet. She must have bought them in Eagle River or sent away to Rhinelander for them. Polish made them shine in the gray light. Orin's throat ached and tears filled his eyes. He touched the hand that still clutched the blanket. It was cold and empty, a dead beetle's carapace.

"How did this happen?" he whispered to the corpse. "Who did this?"

The front door slammed, and a man shouted, "Senator Franklin . . ."

Orin stood up and wiped his eyes. "In here, officer."

The cop saw the body and sagged against the kitchen door. "Oh, shit," he said sadly, "not again. . . . Shit . . ."

Later, while they waited for an ambulance to come for the body, the cop found a letter in Mrs. Marguery's desk and showed it to Orin. The letterhead read "Silver River Oil and Gas—NARCON: *Less Fuel to More People*." She owed them $754.00, they wrote, and deliveries would be reinstated when the balance was paid in full. "In full" was underlined.

The coroner made his report two days later; Mrs. Marguery's heart was fine, there were no clots or aneurysms or hidden tumors. She had frozen to death.

Orin and Kathy went to the funeral. He watched the coffin lowered into a cold black pit surrounded by snow and it hit him that he was attending the burial of a murder victim, and no one would ever be tried for the crime. A few days later he told Tom Gilligan that he wanted to try for the presidency.

There had been one point to his platform—end the energy crisis. It had been his constant and overriding promise to the delegates, then to the voters. He was obsessed, and they knew it and went for it, because they were obsessed too. At one point, a few weeks after the convention, he'd had the feeling that he could tell them he planned to bomb Moscow, cut off aid to Israel, and annex Mexico, and they'd have gone for it as long as he meant to keep that one promise. He didn't blame them; they were just coming out of the '88 gas riots and they were scared. He was scared too; and they must have sensed it and finally figured that shared fear would serve them better than arrogance. So a scared country elected a scared, obsessed President, and now they were in it together. Nixon would have sneered at the fear and Reagan would have decided that there was nothing to be frightened of, because God would provide in the end.

Old man Bunting would agree with Reagan. Orin knew what Bunting would say about Mrs. Marguery. He could hear the thin, mean voice with its long drawl: *She owed*

North Atlantic Resources seven hundred dollars but she had money for new shoes, didn't she, Mr. President? And the polish to shine them with. . . .

Orin looked up and saw the pizza man watching him. He straightened up, ready to get out of there, but the man rushed over to him. He was young, and looked Spanish.

"Excuse me," he said softly. "Are you—?"

Orin put his finger to his lips, and the man nodded, but then he couldn't help himself. "Are you?" Orin nodded, and the man looked totally confused. After a second he asked, "How's the pizza?"

"Terrific," Orin said. The man beamed, and Glover watched glumly.

"Then finish. No one'll bother you. I promise."

Orin finished the pizza, crust and all, while the man watched; then he wiped his mouth. Glover was waiting. Orin said, "It hit the spot," and he shook the man's hand over the counter.

"I voted for you," the man said softly.

"Thank you," Orin said.

He left the pizza parlor and went around the corner on Forty-ninth and into a construction walkway. His heels tapped the wood; he heard the men around him clumping together on the narrow walk. Glover had to shift back and walk behind him. He came to a jog in the walkway, and ahead of him on the ramshackle wooden wall he saw a handbill:

BE COUNTED.

COME TO WASHINGTON: PROTEST DECONTROL.

IT'S YOUR MONEY.

MONSTER DEMONSTRATION, MAY 2nd, ON THE MALL.

He paused for a second, then walked on with his head down. He prayed that the pizza man wouldn't regret the vote he'd cast. Then he prayed that Marvin Lipsky would not turn out to be full of shit.

CHAPTER

JOAN TALBOT listened at a chink in the French doors that led from Talbot's study to the greenhouse. The greenhouse was cold, her fingers were numb, and she wanted to go inside and warm up. She wanted a drink, but she couldn't leave until she'd heard everything . . . or as much as she could. The Carver person left, and then she listened to them listening to somebody named Lipsky. And then to the President and Lipsky making their appointment. That was over, and the real fun began because the three of them started arguing. She hoped it would turn into a real fight. Stockton would beat David to death with the good carved bronze lamp and Talbot would scream and burst a blood vessel in his head. She smiled and rocked in her chair as she imagined the mayhem. Now they were talking about a woman named Emily Brand. Joan liked what she heard about her. It seemed this Emily Brand had done something to put the wind up the vultures, and they wanted to buy her and Lipsky off.

David said it was impossible. Lipsky maybe; he didn't know Lipsky. But not Brand. He *did* know her, from a long time ago. Nothing could stop her. She was the stubbornest bitch that ever lived. David sounded intense, upset, and certain. She'd never heard him sound like that before and she believed him, but of course the vultures didn't.

"I tell you, it's no goddamn use," said David. "Don't believe me, ask Carver."

Stockton said they couldn't do that; then there was more back and forth while Joan wondered what the mysterious

90

Ms. Brand had done to upset pretty David so much. Good for her, whatever it was.

Then she heard Stockton ask in his smug, slimy way, "Then what do you suggest we do about Dr. Brand?"

The room was silent and then Stockton laughed and said that David was bloodthirsty. Suddenly Joan's fingers were freezing; she stuck the needle back into her embroidery and rubbed her hands together. *Poor Emily Brand.*

She went back to listening.

"Extreme," Stockton was saying, "precipitous, and possibly unnecessary. If we convince Dr. Lipsky not to go to Washington, Brand can't go either. If we buy Marvin Lipsky, we buy time to settle Dr. Brand's hash however we must. Doesn't that make sense?"

David didn't answer, but Joan could imagine his slow nod. She knew how pretty David's mind worked. He knew he was right, but he'd do what they wanted and let them hang themselves, so to speak. Actually they'd hang Emily Brand. It seemed settled then. David was going to Lake Placid in the morning to see Marvin Lipsky. Emily Brand wasn't mentioned again. The room was quiet for a moment, and Joan risked peeking around the back of her wicker chair and through the glass pane of the door. They were all still there. Stockton was handing David a slip of paper.

Stockton said, "That's a Lake Placid number. Call it when you've seen Lipsky, and talk to Mr. Bledsoe. Only to Mr. Bledsoe."

Joan smiled from her cold lookout. David Lucci was senior VP and deputy chairman of the board of North Atlantic Resources and Paul Stockton was giving him orders. How Lucci would hate that; it would eat at him, and he'd have trouble sleeping tonight. Maybe he'd get one of his famous headaches.

Stockton said, "If Lipsky says no, tell Bledsoe. Bledsoe knows what to do."

Lipsky was defrosting lox in the microwave when the doorbell rang. He took the plate out of the oven, picked up the skirt of his long robe, and went through the house to the door.

"The man from NARCON," he said when he saw David. He smiled and opened the door wide to let David in.

"I wanted to talk to you alone," David said.

"Oh, I'm alone. Marsha's still sleeping. That woman can sleep. So, what's so urgent?"

They were in the foyer, and David looked around. "Sorry . . . sorry," Lipsky said. "Come in. We'll have coffee, a lox sandwich. You like lox?"

He picked up the skirt of the plaid robe again, took David's arm, and led him through the house to the kitchen. The house was small, immaculate, and very pretty. The kitchen was warm and smelled of onion, lox, and fresh coffee. Lipsky settled David at the scrubbed wooden table and gave him a cup of coffee.

"The lox is frozen," he said, "but what can you expect from Lake Placid, New York? I'll make you a sandwich, I got bagels—frozen too, I'm afraid. It's better in summer. . . ."

"Just coffee's fine," David said.

"You don't mind if I do?" David shook his head, and Lipsky brought David coffee, then sliced a bagel while David looked around. Sun filled the room; he saw the lake through the window. The kitchen was spotless, like the rest of the house; gingham curtains hung at the windows. The table was big and old with carved legs, and they probably carted it with them wherever they went, along with the comfortable old wood chairs. The house was a haven, warm and safe on a beautiful lake in the mountains. It would be hard to leave it.

Lipsky spread cream cheese on the bagel and piled on the lox and onion. "So," he said as he worked, "what can I do for you, man from NARCON?"

"I'm here on behalf of George Talbot," David said. Lipsky smiled tolerantly, brought the sandwich to the table, and took a huge bite. "And who's George Talbot?" he asked with his mouth full.

"Chairman of the board of North Atlantic Resources, doctor."

"Ah," Lipsky said, "a *macher*; and what does he want with me?"

"He wants you to work with us."

Lipsky stopped chewing and put the sandwich slowly back on his plate. "Doing what?"

"We plan to start supporting fusion research to the tune of two or three hundred million dollars."

92

Lipsky wiped his mouth and waited.

David said, "All fusion research is not created equal."

"No," Lipsky said, "it's not."

"We need to know which is more equal."

"And you want me to run around and tell you who should have the millions, and who should have zilch."

"Yes. We buy research . . . you know how that works?"

"Vaguely."

"For instance, we supported the research on shale oil extraction, and when they finally made it work, we owned the process."

"Did you, now?" Lipsky said softly. His bright eyes had narrowed. "And now you want to buy fusion futures, is that it, Mr. Lucci? Come waltzing in here one Sunday morning with your checkbook and buy the little Jew before he can even swallow his frozen lox, and waltz out again with fusion futures in your pocket."

"Please, doctor," David said gently, "it's an important job, and the salary would reflect that."

"And what would this important salary be?" Lipsky asked.

"A quarter of a million a year," David said.

The amount shocked Lipsky, and he was silent a moment. Then he said, "A lot of money."

David smiled. The smile was seductive and seemed to hint that a quarter of a million was only the beginning. He said, "Fusion's the future, and NARCON wants in. Nothing crummy about that. And the job itself . . . Christ you'd have a ball, doctor. There'd be Novembers in Minneapolis, sure. But there'd be Januarys in Honolulu, too." He smiled, felt his eyes light up, and knew he was cooking. "Your wife would love it."

"She would," Lipsky murmured. "January in Honolulu . . ." He giggled softly and wiped his mouth again. "A quarter of a million dollars a year, and January in Honolulu." Suddenly he looked sharply at David. "You're not jerking me off here?"

They smiled at each other; David felt his own smile reach his eyes, and he knew his face looked warm and kind. But Lipsky's smile faded slowly, like a man going from a nice dream into a bad one.

Neither of them said anything; David heard ice melting off the roof, running through the gutters.

Then Lipsky said, softly, "Not kosher."

"I beg your pardon?"

"I said 'not kosher,' boychik. You heard me."

"Don't decide this second."

"But I have decided, Mr. Lucci. Thank you for coming here, and all that. You can take a bagel with you for the trip home if you like."

"Look, the plane's waiting at Saranac. Come back with me, talk to Mr. Talbot yourself. I'm sure he can settle any fears—"

"Oh, boychik," Lipsky said in a gentle half-moaning tone, "what are we playing here? Look, I'm not so young, and I forget my own kids' names sometimes, but I'm not a fool. I got my Ph.D. when I was twenty, at the University of Chicago under the aura of the ghost of Enrico Fermi. Not a fool at all, Mr. Lucci. So let's get it all out now. Ass on the table."

"I told you."

"I know what you told me, and we both know it's bullshit. Oh, I don't want to lose my temper and ruin my breakfast. And I love the sound of that figure—a quarter of a million dollars sounds so pretty—but you're insulting my intelligence, Mr. Lucci. This is Sunday, and even quarter-of-a-million-dollar job offers can wait until Monday. We've been sucking mud here for ten years, and as far as you're *supposed* to know, we're still sucking it. But you know something you're not supposed to, don't you? You're not here to buy 'future' anything. You're here to buy fusion, and you think I've got it to sell."

David gave Lipsky his "young-man-getting-caught" smile and nodded.

Lipsky said, "And you want to keep it for yourselves, nu? You and *macher* Talbot."

"That's right," David said easily, "and we'll pay a fortune for it."

"Don't tell me how much. I might be tempted, and I would have to live with the shame of that temptation. I see you finished your coffee; I think you can leave now, Mr. Lucci."

David made his face smooth and expressionless, and he looked into the little man's eyes. At first Lipsky looked back almost gaily; then he must have seen the menace that David meant him to see, and he looked away.

"It's not that simple," David said.

Lipsky faced him firmly. "No?" he said. "You make me an offer with all your heart and goodwill, and I refuse with all my heart and goodwill. What's not simple?"

Lipsky heard the front door close after David, and suddenly he didn't feel well. He threw the rest of his sandwich away, then covered the food and put it in the refrigerator for Marsha. He sat at the table for a few minutes, then left the kitchen and went upstairs. Marsha was asleep; he got dressed, left a note on her dresser: "Dearest Marsh, Went to the lab, home for lunch."

He left the house and drove to the lab.

Ellis was on this afternoon. His wife had packed some of their Sunday dinner into a foil pan for him, and he was eating pork chops, stuffing, gravy, and potatoes when Lipsky came in. The smell filled the rotunda, and Lipsky started to feel definitely sick. He stood back from the counter so he wouldn't have to look at the food. He wiped his face as Ellis looked up.

"Hey, doc, you're pale. You okay?"

"Fine," Lipsky said.

"Want something to eat?"

"No, thanks. Has anybody been in here?"

"Not today or yesterday. Place is a tomb."

"What about nights?"

"Starrett's on nights this weekend, but he's up in Blue Ridge duck hunting. You can ask Katie."

Katie was the computer. Sally said the voice tape sounded like Katharine Hepburn, which it sort of did, and now everyone called the computer Katie. Lipsky couldn't ask Katie because the retrieval terminals were shut down and he didn't know how to activate them. He nodded to Ellis and went in through the double doors and down the hall to his office. He opened the closet door; the safe was shut and everything looked like he'd left it on Friday.

He slid the drawer out of the desk, held it over his head to read the combination, then put it back, and repeating the combination to himself, he went back to the closet and opened the safe. The papers were there, maybe in the same place he'd put them. He closed the safe and went down the hall to the Xerox room.

He opened the side of the copier and knelt down to read the white numbers. 1507. He went back down the hall to Sally's office. She was a neat woman; her office was clean, dark, and freezing. He turned on the light and went to her desk. She kept a record of the last number on the Xerox every night so no one could use it for unauthorized copies.

Her desk calendar was open to Friday, April 19, and under the reminders to buy panty hose and cat food he saw the number 1492, and his stomach heaved.

He had copied three pages four times on Friday night. That made 1504. But the copier said 1507. He went back to the Xerox room to be sure. But he had remembered right. It was 1507.

So someone had come in here and copied three more pages. Not in daylight, because Ellis hadn't seen anyone. A faceless man or woman had come here in the dead of night, opened his safe, copied those three precious pages, and took them to Lucci and big man Talbot.

Lipsky knew at once that Carver was the spy. Carver had a big house with five bedrooms right on Placid. He drove a Mercedes, his wife had a Porsche. One son was at Harvard, the other at Deerfield, and no one could manage all that on what the state university system paid physicists.

So it was Carver. Then sometime yesterday Carver went to Lucci and Chairman Talbot with those three pages and told them that they'd done it at last, and now they would get their money and build the magic machine. So Talbot sent Lucci with the gold to buy Lipsky, because after all, how much would their very own first-off-the-line fusion reactor be worth to NARCON? And out of nowhere came the answer: *Nothing. Worse than nothing.*

Lipsky stood up painfully.

They owned the coal, oil, gas, uranium. If poor America ever had to go back to wood on some dismal day in the future, they'd find that NARCON, Exxon, Mobil, and the rest owned the forests. But they couldn't buy the Mississippi, the Ohio, the Great Lakes; they sure as shit couldn't buy the oceans. So the gold was a bribe *not* to build the thing, *not* to remember that it could be built. But what did they think they were going to do about Emily? They could have bribed him, maybe. He'd have a hell of a time turning down a couple of million bucks *not* to do something. He didn't like that Lucci, but another man, not so handsome, who didn't have chilling yellow flecks in his eyes and who'd been up front about what he wanted, might indeed have walked out with Lipsky's honor in his pocket. But that was Lipsky, not Emily. He laughed out loud, and felt a great pride in Emily Brand. They could promise her the gross from the Saudi oil fields for the next twenty years, and she would still build her reactor. They could hold him, and Ostrow, and even that pretty little sister of hers hostage at the edge of a pit of cobras, and she would build her reactor.

Tomorrow at three o'clock he would put the whole thing on Orin Franklin's desk and let him worry about Talbot and Lucci and the jerks who ran the oil companies. Then he and Emily would go out on the town. He'd take her to L'Enfant Plaza. He started humming to himself. Emily was a genius, but she was the most parochial woman in the western hemisphere. She'd probably never been in a first-class restaurant. She spent money on her car, and nothing else. The woman was nuts about cars. He hummed louder; tomorrow would be a triumph, and a relief. He couldn't wait. They'd eat châteaubriand, get drunk on champagne, and then he'd come back here and fire Carver. He could do it now, but there would be pleas of need and protestations of innocence, and Lipsky was suddenly feeling so good, he might pity the little shmuck and let him stay, or at least let him leave without prejudice. The only way to make sure that Miles Carver got what he deserved was to fire him on Tuesday morning, when Lipsky was sure to have a hangover.

He called the airfield at Mount Marcy. The phone rang for a long time, and finally a very bored-sounding woman answered. Lipsky had called the reservations in yesterday, and after five minutes the woman admitted to him that she had a record of them. Then she said, "But you better pick up the tickets today. We can't hold them past eight tonight, there's a waiting list for the flight."

The "flight" was a little six-passenger toonerville that snorted and rattled its way from Marcy to Albany. She made it sound like an SST plying the Arctic route from New York to Tokyo. Normally he'd have picked a fight with her, but he felt forgiving and told her he'd be right by to get the tickets for himself and Dr. Brand.

Carmine trudged along the shore. He was cold and miserable, and his pants cuffs were caked with mud. It was only three, and Bledsoe had told him to stay out until four. But Carmine decided defiantly that he'd go back now, get warm, change his clothes . . . only he knew he wouldn't because Bledsoe scared him.

He climbed up the bank from the lake, through the tiny park to the street; the wind whipped the bare twigs. Dying begonias drooped in the window boxes. The sun was gone, and the street was empty and desolate. He went into the only open bar.

An old man with a torn felt hat sat at the end, nursing a beer and whiskey; the bartender was watching TV chapel or some such shit. The preacher had a face as soft and bland as white bread and he was exhorting his flock to send money and to love Christ, in that order. Carmine had two beers, ate stale nuts, and waited. The TV picture changed and a beaker of stomach acid replaced the preacher. The bartender watched in a daze of boredom; the old man stared at his reflection on the finger-marked bartop. Carmine paid and left, then walked slowly . . . slowly around the lake and back to the cabin.

It was five to four. He sat on the bench next to the shore, freezing his ass. The lights were on in the cabin, and smoke came out of the chimney. At four he went to the door and knocked hard.

Something flat and heavy slid across the floor; then Bledsoe shouted, "Okay, fucko, come in." But the door was bolted and Bledsoe had to open it.

Bledsoe flopped in the only comfortable chair, and Carmine sat on the bed. There were thin scrape marks on the floor at his feet. Bledsoe must have pulled Carmine's toolbox out from under Carmine's bed, then shoved it back. Carmine looked a the recorders. The lights were out; everything was quiet.

He waited until Bledsoe was asleep; then he slipped out of his bed and knelt on the floor. He didn't dare pull the case out—it would scrape and wake Bledsoe. But he knew the contents by heart, and he unlatched the case under the bed and felt around blind. His tools were out of place, and his roll of wire was smaller. He relatched the case, then went to the recorders to see if Bledsoe had done something to the wires. He hadn't.

Carmine opened the tape drawer. There was one marked with today's date, and he fitted it into the recorder, plugged in the headphones, and played the tape.

Marsha Lipsky talked to her mother in a nursing home, John Ostrow called Emily Brand and asked her to come for the night; then there was a dial tone, the beeps of dialing, then silence. Carmine rewound and played it again. It was louder than the other dial beeps and it sounded close to the mike. He looked over at the phone, next to the mike. Bledsoe had made a call from this phone, and not talked, or he had talked and then erased the conversation, but he had forgotten the beeps, or maybe he didn't think they were important.

Carmine rewound again, punched in the counter, and got the number Bledsoe had called. Only seven digits, so it was local. He looked in the number-to-name directory for Keene, Placid, Saranac, and Wilmington and found that Bledsoe had called Mountain Air, at the Mount Marcy Airfield.

That almost made sense. Lipsky and Brand were flying out of here tomorrow, and Bledsoe wanted to know for sure what time they were leaving and when they'd get to Washington. But why? NARCON wasn't going to be at Friendship with a red carpet. And why would he get such neutral information and then erase the tape?

Carmine took off the headphones and looked around the room. Bledsoe was on his back, snoring lightly; the room was warm, and Carmine went out onto the tiny back porch for some air. It was pitch black. He turned on the dim yellow porch light and saw a black case he'd never seen before, half-hidden by the fishing rods and tackle box.

Cautiously Carmine moved the tackle box and looked at the name tag. The case belonged to Warren Beecham of Wilmington, New York. Carmine had never heard of Warren Beecham. The case was zippered shut, with a luggage padlock, and he couldn't open it without cutting the plastic or breaking the lock. Either way, Bledsoe would know.

Carmine stared at it. A wind came off the lake and through the jalousies that enclosed the porch. Carmine shivered, and suddenly he didn't want to know what was in Mr. Beecham's mysterious case or why Bledsoe had called the airfield and then erased the tape. The shivering got worse. He turned off the light, eased his way back into the room, and shut the door gently.

Talbot prowled his house in the dark. It was twelve-thirty. T minus ten and a half hours, he thought.

His muscles were knotted and he ached for action. He went into the greenhouse and looked up through the glass at the sky. The moon was bright, but they said it would rain by morning. No sign of it yet. If the weather was too bad, the flight would be canceled and they'd have to start all over. But Lipsky and Brand would be delayed getting to Washington, so they'd have time.

He stalked out of the greenhouse and through the sitting room. He heard the TV playing upstairs, and he knew Joan was up, watching a late movie.

He hated waiting like this. If only he could do it himself . . . but that wasn't the way the world worked anymore. He didn't even have an active part in running the drilling or mining anymore. David did that; now Talbot had endless dinners with greasy, ugly sheikhs, reckless heads of one state or another, and covered the company's ass.

He turned on the light in the study and looked up at his father's portrait. The painted face was as stern and cold as it had been when he was alive. Talbot went closer and looked up into the painted gray eyes. His father hadn't done his own killing either, but his grandfather had. When his grandfather was old and sick and knew he would die soon, he'd bragged about it to his grandson. Talbot had been enthralled and made the old man tell him about it over and over. The first killing was an accident. A brawl in a bar in Shreveport. The second had been murder, done with a hammer, and a fire afterward to explain the body. That time it had been his partner, another wildcatter from Texarcana who thought that he and Dean Shepard Talbot would control the infant NARCON together. Poor bastard, Talbot thought. He should've looked into his grandfather's soft blue eyes, just like Talbot's eyes, and taken his money and run. But he'd be dead now anyway, Talbot thought, and what difference did those years make? Better to die fast like that than like the old man had—alone after months in a strange white room that smelled of alcohol and excrement; yellow-skinned, drooling, and not even knowing his own name. Even so, his grandfather had done the right thing; if he hadn't, there would have been a horde of squabbling heirs selling off shares, and by now NARCON would be controlled by a bunch of thin-blooded, alcohol-pickled preppies.

Talbot was doing the right thing too; if Lipsky and Brand got to that prick in the White House, the bureaucrats and old ladies would devour NARCON, like termites eating a dying sequoia. And the first up the trunk—the queen termite, the empress of all the insects—would be Orin Franklin.

David knew something would happen between now and three o'clock tomorrow afternoon, but he didn't know what, or when. Talbot spared him, and he was sorry in a way, because he knew he could take it. But he was glad, too, because if he did know, he would be waiting helplessly, like the other two must be waiting now. As it was, he was calm. He read quietly in front of the fire while Mary entertained the New Canaan Bridge Club in the family room.

The women left, and they got ready for bed. David wondered if he would have trouble getting to sleep, but the session with Lipsky and the flight back must have exhausted him, because he fell asleep at once.

Lipsky was still in his bathrobe when Emily came into the kitchen at eight o'clock on Monday morning.

"You're going like that?" Lipsky asked.

She was wearing slacks and her down jacket.

"I told you, Marvin, I'm not going."

"I got the tickets," Lipsky wailed. He picked them up off the table and waved them at her. "Look . . . all paid. My treat. I'll even buy you dinner."

"Please, Marvin," Emily said.

Marsha brought coffee to the table. "She doesn't want to, she doesn't want to," she told Lipsky. "Leave her alone."

"How can she not want to?" He glared at Emily. "Dinner

101

at L'Enfant Plaza," he yelled. "It's a palace, you'll love it. They're going to kiss your ass . . . for Christ's sake. Go home and change your clothes."

"No."

"Why?" he cried.

"Because I won't know what to say to them, and you'll worry about me sitting in the corner, and I'd hate it."

"It's your day, you did this."

"It doesn't matter. It only matters that we get the money. You'll do better without me. You've been getting money from them for years for nothing—"

He jumped up. "Goddammit, we got an hour and a half, go home and change your clothes."

"No." Emily said it quietly, but her eyes got that flat look that Marvin had seen a few times before, and he knew he could rant and scream and tear his hair out of his head, but she wouldn't budge. When Emily looked like that, *no* was *no*. He sank back into his chair. He was truly sorry. Today was a triumph, and he would have loved to share it with her. But maybe she'd have her day after all. When the thing was built and running and she stood close to it listening to the power inside of it that no one else could hear, maybe then she'd feel joy he couldn't imagine. He hoped so.

"Okay, *maidl*," he said. "You win. I'll come home tonight. We'll celebrate tonight. Get drunk again . . . all of us. Screw L'Enfant Plaza." He looked at the clock. "You'll take me to the airport . . ."

"That's why I'm here," Emily said.

He went upstairs to get dressed, and Marsha made Emily some toast.

Lipsky yelled from the top of the stairs, "I can't find my blue cufflinks!"

"He probably sent them to the laundry with the shirt," Marsha said; then she shouted, "Wear the gold ones, you're going to see the President of the United States."

He appeared at the kitchen door fifteen minutes later. There was a piece of bloody toilet paper stuck to his jaw, and the points of his shirt collar stuck out.

"You forgot the stays," Marsha said, and she raced upstairs to get them.

"Nothing's ever right," he grumbled, "nothing." She came

back with the stays, and he had to take off his jacket and tie while she fixed the shirt and peeled the paper off his face. Then he was ready again.

"Nu?" he asked.

"You look wonderful," Emily said.

"So what do I do with this ticket?" he asked her.

"They'll give you your money back. That flight is always full," she said.

He was quiet during the first part of the ride, thinking about NARCON and their Mr. Lucci. He couldn't forget the chill the man inspired, but maybe all short men his age were threatened by men who looked like David Lucci. Or maybe Lucci had meant well enough but was just a klutz. There were people like that. His own son, for one; the kid couldn't give away quarters in Calcutta.

He looked over at Emily and wondered if he should tell her about NARCON; then he decided not to. If they had wanted to bribe her, they'd have tried it, and good luck to them. He would tell her about Carver when he got back, and about the extra copies that were probably on the big man Talbot's desk right now. That *was* his business, and hers. And the President's, if he cared. But he wouldn't tell Emily today . . . today should be unmarred. Besides, there was nothing the NARCON *machers* could do now. He was on his way, and nothing could stop him.

He hummed a little under his breath, then said, "You excited?"

"Yes," Emily answered. She was surprised to find that she was. "You'll call me?" she asked.

"Of course . . . dummy, you should've gone." He looked through the windshield. It had been raining since early morning, but now fog came down out of the mountains and turned the air white.

He turned back to her. "Fog!" he cried. "What if that miserable little plane won't take off? What if they cancel?"

She glanced at him. His eyes were wide and he was chewing his bottom lip. "I'll wait. If they cancel or bring you back, I'll drive you to Albany."

"That's two hours," he cried. "I'll miss the connection."

"You'll take the next plane."

"The next plane's too late! I'll be late to see the President

103

of the United States. Shit . . ." He hit the dashboard with his fist. "I should've gone last night."

"There was no flight last night."

He ignored her. "Oh, my God, look at that fog."

But it must not have been as bad as it looked, and according to the flight board the Albany flight was delayed only ten minutes. Lipsky wouldn't calm down. "Sure, they'll get half-way up the mountain, and turn back. You'll wait . . . promise you'll wait till we're gone."

"I'll wait," Emily said. He returned the extra ticket, then came back and sat next to her. He was quiet for a moment; then he said in horror, "What if they have to land at Glens Falls? You won't know it . . . I'll never get to Albany . . ."

They called the flight. "It could be worse south of here," he moaned. "I won't get there until—"

Suddenly Emily grabbed his arm and pulled him to his feet. She was strong, she almost hurt him, and he was startled. She said, "You've got the fire, Marvin. They'll see you when-ever you get there."

He was quiet after that. She went with him to the rolling door that passed for the gate. He gave the attendant his ticket and suitcase, and when the five passengers were together, the attendant slid open the door to the field and a chilly wet wind blew in. Lipsky turned to her. "Don't leave until we're over the mountain."

"I won't."

Then he smiled at her. " 'The fire,' " he said. "That's good. That's really good." They looked at each other for a moment, then shook hands. He joined the ragged line of passengers as they crossed the windblown field to the little jet, and Emily moved to the window next to the ticket counter. She saw his brown coat go up the stairs into the plane and a few minutes later they shut the door, rolled away the staircase, and the plane taxied up the runway. Emily stood to the side to see better. The plane reached the end of the runway, turned, and started back toward them. She could hear the whine of the motor as the plane picked up speed. It ran like a streak over the winter-rutted runway, then gathered itself, lifted, banked, and started to climb over the mountains. Emily could barely see it through the rain as it climbed toward the peak of Mount Marcy. It reached the top, leveled out, and she heard a crack, then a huge thump echoed across the valley, and the little plane exploded in flames.

The fireball hung there, and dark shapes—suitcases, boxes, people—fell through the flames to the ground. A woman screamed behind her, other people screamed, and finally the burning mass fell to the ground and the fire went out.

CHAPTER

"I'M SORRY, Mr. Beecham," said the man on the phone. "Sorrier than I can say." He had just told Ed Beecham that his father was dead.

"It was over in an instant," he said. "They didn't know anything ..."

Tears filled Beecham's eyes, spilled down his face through the smudges of the machine oil.

"Mr. Beecham?" Beecham didn't answer.

"Mr. Beecham, we want to help you any way we can. A Mr. Gregory—"

"What happened?" Beecham cried.

"The plane exploded. We don't know why yet. We'll know more this afternoon. As I was saying, Mr. Gregory from the Mountain Air underwriters will be there in an hour to see what you need—"

Beecham hung up without letting the man finish. He wiped the tears off his face with his bandanna, then crossed the garage to the Audi. He let the lift down, waiting for the car to settle, then started putting his tools away. Tears blinded him, but he forced himself to put them all in their proper slots; then he closed and locked his toolbox and walked unsteadily out of his garage—Ed's Service: Foreign and Domestic Auto Repair—into the cool, foggy air. The phone rang; he knew it was the same man calling to tell him more about Mr. Gregory, but he shoved the doors shut and locked them. He couldn't stand talking to lawyers now. They would come and sniff around, with phony sad eyes and oily voices, then try to put a price on his father's life. He pulled himself up into the tow and drove out Route 86, heading home.

It was two when he stopped at the bottom of the dirt track that led up to his house for the mail, then drove up to the old farmhouse. He'd been born here, his mother and his poor frail wife of three years had died here, and there'd been no one left but him and his father. Now his father was gone.

He stopped the truck and got out. The house was freshly painted, his father had planted yew around the stone foundation, but now the place looked desolate and abandoned. Chickens ran across the yard squawking. The old man was supposed to feed them before he left this morning, but it was his first time out of these mountains since World War II, and he must have been too excited to remember his chickens. He was going to Schenectady to visit his sister, who'd been sick. They were old, he'd told Beecham, and he wanted to see her one more time, so he'd bought his ticket to Albany, and a new white shirt.

Beecham got feed out of the shed, scattered it, then went up the worn wooden steps into the kitchen. He dropped the mail, got a beer out of the refrigerator, then came back to the old scrubbed wood table. There were bills, a flier from the Grand Union, and a thick envelope from the Rockland Insurance Company, Burlington, Vermont, addressed to him in his father's writing. He tore open the envelope and pulled out a sheaf of paper. He skimmed the first page, then the second, then read more slowly, sinking down in his chair, his beer forgotten. He got to the last page, read it, then spread the whole thing out on the table. The room was silent, even the chickens were quiet, and the old regulator clock on the wall had stopped. He couldn't believe what was in front of him, but it was printed and official, and on the bottom of the last page was the signature, Warren Thomas Beecham.

It was an in-flight insurance policy for one hundred and fifty thousand dollars, bought this morning at the Mount Marcy Airfield by one Warren Beecham, to the benefit of his son, Edward, and it was the most official piece of paper that had lain on this table since the notice of his brother's VA insurance for ten thousand dollars.

Beecham was shocked; his father must have been terrified to fork out money for this, and he'd never said a word. He'd gone off this morning in his one dark suit that was green with age, humming to himself, generally pleased with the world.

But the old man had been scared after all, and suddenly Beecham thought of the spring fog this morning, rising up out of the streams and cataracts all through the mountains, and the little plane climbing gallantly into it, cresting Marcy, then blowing itself and all the people in it to fragments. He threw himself forward across the table and sobbed out loud. He prayed that it had been like that; that his daddy was dead or unconscious and never saw the flames coming for him, or the mountain-peak rocks rushing up to tear him apart.

A car pulled into the yard. The chickens screeched, and Beecham ran to the sink, splashed his face with cold water, and dried it on the clean dish towel his father had put out this morning. His people didn't prize shows of emotion, and he wouldn't shame his father's ghost by letting anyone see his son crying at the age of thirty-six.

He went to the door and looked out. It was his best friend, Karl Banyan, in a state cruiser. Banyan was in uniform. He got out of the car, nudged the chickens out of the way with his foot, and came up the steps. Beecham opened the door, and Banyan stopped on the second step and looked up at his old friend. He had a peculiar expression on his face, but Beecham put it down to shock at the news about the old man.

Banyan said, "Need to see my badge?"

Beecham didn't know what he was talking about. They stood without moving, until Beecham said, "Come in, if you're coming." Banyan walked past Beecham into the kitchen.

"Sorry about the old man," he said. He sounded as weird as he looked.

Beecham nodded. "I'll get you a beer."

Banyan went to the table and saw the papers. "What's this?" he asked.

Beecham was at the refrigerator. "The old man bought insurance at the airport. One hundred and fifty thousand dollars' worth. I still can't believe it . . ." He swallowed hard and went on, "Had to have been mailed this morning, and here it is. I didn't even think the old man knew what insurance was."

He turned with the beer intended for Banyon in one hand, his other hand still on the refrigerator door, and he froze where he stood.

His old friend Karl Banyan, who'd gone to grade school

and high school with him, who went fishing with him in the spring, deer hunting in the fall, and whoring over to Burlington or Plattsburg every couple of weeks—his best friend and the only person left in the world who gave a shit if he lived or died . . . was staring at Ed Beecham as if he hated him.

"Listen to the news at noon," Talbot had told David on the interoffice phone. David did, and heard about the crash. He listened for her name, but there were still rescue teams at the top of the mountain; no names were given.

At three the newscaster reported that Marvin Lipsky was dead, and then he said, "The names of the other victims are being withheld, pending notification of relatives."

He missed the news at six; at six-thirty he parked the Jaguar in the garage on Sixty-eighth and Lex, and he walked into the club lobby at six-forty-five. He found a copy of the *Post* in the coat room, and saw a minor headline announcing the plane crash on page three. He would read it after dinner, taking as long as possible, making himself wait to see her name until he got to it in the column.

He tucked the paper under his arm, went to the elevator, and rode up to the dining room. Talbot and Stockton were at the prize table in the corner overlooking Park. They saw David and stood up. When he was settled, the sommelier came over and poured the wine.

Talbot tasted, then nodded, and the glasses were filled.

No one mentioned the plane crash or Lipsky or Brand. David's heart pounded, but he raised his glass like they did, smelled the wine, sipped.

"Wonderful," Stockton said, "truly wonderful."

The wine tasted sharp and brittle, like dead leaves.

"Ah," Stockton enthused, "I see they have shad and roe. The first of the season. This will be a feast."

They all ordered the shad, and David thought that now they would talk about it, but Talbot was telling Stockton about fishing on Jasper Lake in Alberta. The waiter brought their dinners. Stockton bent over his plate and sniffed appreciatively, and they started to eat without agonizing over what they had done or wondering how they were going to cover their asses for murdering seven people. It was amazing, and David admired them.

The tender fish melted in his mouth, butter slid down his

throat. The food was delicious, and he was starving. He attacked the shad ravenously. She was dead . . . she would never beat him again, there would be no more challenges. Stupid clichés jumped through his mind—the luck of the game, the luck of the toss . . . staying the course . . . he who laughs last . . .

At last Stockton got around to it. "Bledsoe's remarkable," he said. "All he knew was that old man Beechman lived with his son and that he was on his way to see his sister in Schenectady. And this afternoon, Edward, son of Warren, received an insurance policy in the mail, signed—a not totally convincing forgery—by old man Warren." Stockton sliced neatly into his pod of roe.

"What would the son—?" Talbot started to ask, but Stockton shook his head and swallowed.

"We're very thorough, George. Fifteen years ago, son Edward worked on the Northway construction. And what do you suppose comprised the major part of that work?"

Talbot smiled. "Blasting," he said.

"Bledsoe'll get a bonus?" Stockton looked up at Talbot, holding his fork in midair.

"It's been taken care of," Talbot said.

Stockton went back to his fish, and David marveled at the two men. They weren't old yet—Talbot was sixty-three, Stockton looked about the same age. They'd had a man and woman killed this morning, along with five other people they didn't know, and now they were enjoying their shad and roe and wine, without guilt or fear. They were like forest animals who come out on the plains to raid the herds of gazelles or wildebeests. It was a good image and David dwelt on it as he drank wine. The kills were clean, done to a plan that none of them had made, and it was as hard for David to hate these men as it would be for him to hate a cheetah or lion, or even a pack of hyenas. Now he could feel sorry for Emily Brand because she had challenged them. She had been one of those pretty, delicate herd animals—a gazelle, he thought, remembering how slight she'd looked as she led him around the base of the reactor. Slight and shy. Poor gazelle, he thought. Then he remembered her calm, expressionless eyes behind the big heavy glasses, and all at once he was uneasy. Slowly he put his fork down next to his plate, took the newspaper off the

110

empty chair, and opened it to page three. The other two men stopped talking and looked at him. He skimmed the story and found the paragraph of names, addresses, and occupations.

Her name wasn't there.

There were six names, but the paper said that the plane carried six passengers and a pilot.

"David?" Talbot said. "Is something wrong, David?"

David put his napkin on the table. "I have to make a call." He walked carefully across the dining room and out into the hall. The phone booths were on the main floor, and he took the elevator down and went into the phone room. Each phone had its own tiny wood-paneled room with a door and a lamp.

He got the number from information and called Mountain Air in Albany. A woman answered after seven rings.

"I need some information about the plane crash this morning in Keene—"

"I'm sorry," she said. "If you're from the press, we have a number—"

"No. I need to know if there was an Emily Brand on that plane. She was supposed to be, but I didn't see her name . . ."

"Are you a relative?" the woman asked.

"I'm her husband. I've been out of town. She was supposed to be on that plane, and I just heard . . ." He sounded desperate. "Please," he said.

"One moment."

He waited. The little box was stifling, the fan was weak, and he shoved open the door.

The woman came back on the line. "Mr. Brand?" She sounded happy. "I have good news for you. Mrs. Brand was not on that plane."

"But there were six passengers," he said. "Only five were listed in the paper."

"One of the tickets was turned in, and the weather was so bad there weren't any standbys—thank God." The woman sounded ready to cry. "I'm so happy for you; it must've been a terrible—"

David hung up and left the phone booth.

He didn't remember getting upstairs, and the next thing he knew, he was in the wide paneled hall that led to the dining room. Ahead he could hear the voices of the men having their dinners, talking about the day on the street, or the week in Houston, or the weekend in Palm Beach or some other neighborhood of money and power. The entrance to the club library opened off the hall; it was dark, and looked empty, and he ducked in there.

She was alive. She would ruin them—*this* NARCON, Talbot had said, and that was what David wanted. For himself and for Anthony, and finally just for the idea of the company. It had an existence, it had a soul; it was all the people who worked for it, build it, fed it, coddled it. The men out on the rigs, the drillers in Arabia and Alaska were NARCON too. But the company was even more than all of them. It was a collective. People playing along . . . all in it together. Even the consumers who talked about getting screwed were accomplices in a game they all played and understood. NARCON was a pyramid of covenants—of people standing on each other's shoulders. And she could bring the whole thing down with three pages of chicken scratches that had come out of her head. No one should have that much power, and he was going to stop her.

He left the dark library and went back to his seat in the dining room.

"Why, Mr. Lucci . . ." Stockton said in his oily voice.

"Shut up, you old fart." David snarled, "She's alive. She wasn't on that plane. She's alive."

Watching them was almost funny. Stockton turned dark red, and David wondered if the man was going to have a stroke. Talbot sat stone still as if someone had just bashed in the back of his head and he was getting ready to crumple across the top of the table.

They started whispering, "It can't be . . . how do you know . . . Bledsoe said . . ."

"Shut up," David said. They were quiet.

David looked at Stockton. "Call that fool Bledsoe. Tell him to stay where he is." Then he turned on Talbot. "Get Carver, too. I'll need him."

"Carver's in Washington," Talbot said.

"Why?"

"Franklin had Feinstein call him when they heard about Lipsky."

"It's no good going to Placid without Carver. If she gets

into that lab, no one can go in after her." David was quiet; the other men waited. Then he said, "We have to wait. She won't suspect anything yet . . . she's not going anywhere. And the paper said there's a service for Lipsky tomorrow. She won't miss that." He looked at Talbot. "Is Red bringing Carver back from Washington?"

Talbot nodded, and David said, "Tell him to pick me up on his way. I'll be at Westchester from ten o'clock in the morning until he gets there. Tell him to plan to land at Saranac, it's closer." Now he looked at Stockton. "We need another man. I've never used a gun, and Carver would probably shoot his dick off. One more man, someone good. No more fuck-ups, Mr. Stockton."

Talbot said, "Gelb."

Stockton shook his head.

"Who's Gelb?" David asked.

They didn't answer. David had the feeling that Mr. Gelb frightened them. He asked again, "Who's Gelb?"

Stockton said, "Mr. Gelb is valuable, and highly specialized. Not to be overused. I prefer to save him for extreme situations."

"And this isn't extreme?" David demanded.

Stockton looked amused. "Hardly, Mr. Lucci. We're talking about one woman with no allies or organization."

Carmine never officially knew that Emily Brand was supposed to be dead, so no one told him that she was alive. But he'd known all day. She'd been the one who'd called Lipsky's son and daughter. He was surprised when he heard her voice because he thought she was on her way to Washington with her boss. And then he heard her tell Evelyn Lipsky that the plane her father was on blew up, and Carmine remembered Mr. Beecham's black bag. He still didn't know who Beecham was, but now he knew what was in the bag, and he was furious at Bledsoe for leaving it out where he could see it. Bledsoe was stupid. Big, brutal, and stupid, with an almost handsome pudding face and mean little eyes—like raisins, Carmine thought.

Now he knew that they'd killed Lipsky and meant to kill Brand. But she had escaped. They told Carmine to dismantle everything and go home, but Bledsoe was staying. So they were going to try again, and Bledsoe was their hit man. If Carmine hadn't seen that bag, he wouldn't know all this. He would have gone home in the morning and forgotten that he'd ever heard of Lake Placid. But Bledsoe was the *cheminude* of all time, and now Carmine knew, and he was scared that he had to do something about it. He longed to talk to Father Danilo. Father Danilo never cared about the taps. "The church ain't big on privacy," the old priest had told Carmine. But Carmine knew what he'd say about this: "Murder's something else, Anthony . . . murder'll damn you."

Carmine lay on his bed in the dark end of the room; Bledsoe ate pizza. Marsha Lipsky was home with her children and her grief, Emily Brand was God knows where, the lab was closed and the machines were silent. He had to warn Brand, but he had to be careful. They'd disconnected the Lipsky wire this afternoon; no point in tapping a dead man's phone. But the wire was still on Brand and still on the lab. He couldn't call Brand . . . but he could call Marsha Lipsky and *she* would warn Brand. Good. But how to call her . . . where to call her from? Bledsoe hadn't left the cabin, and since the call he'd gotten at eight—from his boss, Carmine suspected, whoever that was—Bledsoe had been silent and absorbed. He'd sent out for the pizza, they'd bought coffee and milk yesterday, and Bledsoe didn't smoke. He wouldn't leave the cabin, and he might try to stop Carmine from leaving.

Bledsoe solved the problem himself. He finished the pizza, shoved the greasy carton away, and then went into the can. Carmine heard the door lock.

He put on his jacket and waited to be sure Bledsoe was settled on the pot; then he called through the door, "Going out for some ice cream. Want anything?"

"What about the wire?" Bledsoe yelled.

"The recorder's running," Carmine said. "No problem." And he slipped out the door before Bledsoe could answer.

The Howard Johnson's was open; they had a phone, and ice cream to make his story good, so he went there. It was after ten; the place was empty except for a couple of men who looked like truckers. Carmine passed the cleaned-out salad bar and went to the semienclosed phone near the rest rooms. He would've liked a booth better, but there was no one nearby; he wouldn't be heard.

He picked up the receiver, dropped in money, then hesitated. He would give his warning and then hang up; he wouldn't answer questions or explain. He wouldn't even tell Mrs. Lipsky where the danger was coming from. He was a good Catholic, and he had a responsibility. But within limits, he told himself as he dialed. Certainly God didn't expect him to get himself killed. The phone rang, and he turned to watch the front of the restaurant. Marsha Lipsky answered.

"You don't know me," Carmine said, "but I have an urgent message for Dr. Brand. Tell Dr. Brand—"

Bledsoe opened the door from the parking lot and came into the restaurant. He saw Carmine at once, and Carmine hung up without saying any more.

The rabbi prayed, but Emily didn't listen. Sally watched her from across the aisle with tears streaming down her face. Emily glanced over at her, and Sally looked away, but Emily saw disapproval in her eyes. Emily wasn't crying, and Sally thought she should. The rabbi rocked and intoned in the soft, beautiful language that Emily had heard at her nephew's *rit*. Marvin's son and a few other men in the tiny Lake Placid congregation rocked with him. John was a Jew; he would have prayed and rocked like the others, but he was some sick. Very sick, she thought, or he'd be here.

Finally it was over. Emily stood up, Sally walked away from her, her head down, her handkerchief to her face. Marsha Lipsky came up the aisle and stopped in front of Emily. Her children hesitated, but she waved them to go on. Marsha's skin was dry and red, her pretty hair had shrunk against her scalp, and she looked like an old woman.

She said, "I'm taking him back to Illinois." Emily's throat worked, but nothing came out of her mouth. She couldn't cry, and now she couldn't seem to talk.

"The house is for sale," Marsha said with a weird calm in her voice, "and once it's gone, there'll be nothing. As if we never lived anywhere, as if we never lived at all."

"The children . . ." Emily croaked.

"Of course . . . the children." Suddenly Marsha stepped up very close to Emily and put her arms around her and held her close; her voice lowered to a whisper. "Em, he cared about you. And he cared desperately about what you were

115

working on. I don't know what it was . . . But you'll take care of it, whatever it was, won't you?"

Emily nodded, and then Marsha kissed her on the cheek, and with tears running down her face, gently brushed back a strand of Emily's hair that had fallen over her eyes. "I don't think I'll ever see you again, Em. Marry John, he loves you. Love's all that matters." She went past Emily, and got half-way up the aisle; then she stopped and came back. "I almost forgot. A man called last night. He didn't leave his name, but he said he had a message for you. Then he hung up before he told me what it was. I wouldn't've bothered to tell you but he said it was urgent, and what with the business with the President and all . . . He sent a telegram, by the way. I'll save it for the grandchildren. I got the feeling the man was interrupted, not disconnected . . . and I know this sounds crazy, but I think he was frightened."

Clouds piled up. Emily sat in the kitchen without taking off her coat or turning on the lights. She wanted to call John but she might wake him; he needed to sleep, so she sat at the table. The ache in her throat was terrible. It would be better if she could cry, but she hadn't cried since her mother died. . .

Her father's limousine had pulled away from the old house and she knew that she would never see her mother or the house again. Her father and Miss Benson had come back from the cemetery. Miss Benson hugged her and wrote down her address, and now her father was in a hurry. Emily wanted to go back for a last look at her mother's room and the animals that had been poised on the walls of her room for as long as she could remember. But her father said there wasn't time, and he hustled her into the back of the huge black car. They turned the curve of the drive and she lost sight of Miss Benson standing on the front steps and the sun on the panes of the old greenhouse and even the tops of the stone chimneys through the trees, and she cried. Her nose ran; she didn't have a handkerchief, and she sniveled. Her father glared at her, and she had wiped her nose on the sleeve of her good coat and forced the tears back down her throat into her chest. But they left an ache that stayed there for days—like the ache she had in her throat now.

"You'll take care of it," Marsha had said.

She would. She didn't know how, but she'd figure it out.

She couldn't call the switchboard of the White House and ask for Orin Franklin. Marvin had to have a contact, but she didn't know his name. Marsha probably didn't know it either. It would be in the coffee-stained Rolodex on Lipsky's desk, indexed under "money" or "White House" or some other mnemonic. She'd find it—unless it had been in his briefcase on that plane. . . . She saw the fireball again before she could stop herself, and the black objects falling helplessly through it to the ground. One of them was the briefcase . . . one of them was Marvin. . . . The doorbell rang, and Emily thought it might be John, miraculously cured, coming to help her. She ran through her house to the vestibule and opened the door.

A short, swarthy man with dark frightened eyes stood on the doorstep. He put his finger to his lips to signal silence, and then he opened his coat like a man exposing himself and held a yellow pad with block printing on it in front of her face. It read: THE PHONE IS TAPPED. THE HOUSE IS BUGGED. COME OUTSIDE. IT'S ABOUT MARVIN LIPSKY.

His eyes pleaded, he looked *urgent*, and she knew that this was the man who'd called Marsha Lipsky last night with the message he never gave. She nodded to him, stepped through the door, and closed it after her.

You're crazy, Susie would say. *How can you go outside with a wild-looking man you've never seen before?* But Emily wasn't frightened. *Nothing frightens you*, Susie had said once. *That's not healthy. Fear is a survival mechanism.*

Emily led the man around the side of the house to the backyard; then he walked away from her, putting distance between himself and the house, until he was at the lakeshore. Emily followed, and then he stopped and faced her and started talking in a hoarse, scared voice.

"My name is Anthony Carmine, I work for NARCON . . . I tap phones for them, so maybe they won't want to tell you that I'm on their payroll, if you ask. But, lady, you can't ask. Swear to me you won't tell anyone you know me."

"Yes," Emily said.

"Swear," Mr. Carmine insisted.

"I swear."

Then he said, "They killed Marvin Lipsky . . . they put a bomb on that plane."

Suddenly Emily was freezing. She pulled her coat around

her, and had to clench her teeth to keep them from clicking
against each other.

"Don't say nothing," Carmine said, "and don't faint on me
I got two minutes, so just listen, okay?"

Emily nodded.

"They killed him; guy named Bledsoe put the bomb on th
plane sometime last night or this morning. I can't prove any
thing. But I know he did it. He's some kind of government
man, hooked up with NARCON. I don't know what you and
Lipsky were working on, I'm an electrician, I don't know
about physics. But they didn't want the President or anybody
else to see whatever it is. So they did . . . this." He took
breath and raced on.

"I worked for them for seventeen years, and I've been
loyal all that time. There's nothing wrong with the taps, to
my mind—information gathering, that's all it is. All th
other biggies do it, even if it isn't all legal, so why shouldn'
NARCON? Right?"

Emily nodded again.

"But they *murdered* Lipsky, and . . . lady, you were sup
posed to be on that plane with him. I don't want to know
why you weren't. I don't want to know another thing about
you. But it stands to reason that Bledsoe'll try again."

Emily's voice grated in her aching throat. "What does Mr
Bledsoe look like?"

He looked surprised that she had the wit to ask that ques
tion. "He's tall and mean-looking, with dishwater hair, dark
eyes, and a face like a pudding. Remember . . . your phone
the lab, your boyfriend's phone." Then Carmine nodded to
her and walked away, around the house to the front. She
stood in the yard for a second, then ran up the back stair
and in through the kitchen door. She went right to the wall
phone over the kitchen counter, picked up the receiver, and
brought it quickly to her ear. There was no click, no obvious
sound, but there was something—a vague noise that came
over the wires that ran up across the mountains and around
the lake. If they were listening, she had to make a call. She
dialed John's number, and she thought the dialing itself set
up the hint of an echo. He answered on the second ring; he
sounded terrible, but he said his fever was down. He asked
her about the service. She didn't know what to say, and she

118

was silent. Then he said very gently, "Don't sit there alone toughing it out, Emily. Come here. Come to me. Maybe it'll help."

Over his raspy voice that was painful to listen to, she heard Carmine. *You were supposed to be on that plane.*

She said she'd be there in half an hour and hung up. She went upstairs, took off the blue dress from Razook's, and hung it way to the side of the closet, so she wouldn't see it and think of Marvin every time she opened the closet door. Then she took off her slip and stockings and went into the bathroom. She meant to wash at the sink, but suddenly she remembered the other NARCON man—Lucy or Lucia—who'd said they'd known each other from a long time ago. Sally had talked about him for days afterward; she thought he was the most beautiful man she'd ever seen, especially his eyes. But Emily didn't think those eyes were beautiful. He had looked at her with fear and fascination, the way a child looks at a snake, and he'd grabbed her hand and held on to it as if he wanted to break it. She didn't know why; she had no idea who he was or where she'd known him from. But NARCON had sent him, and Carmine said NARCON and some government agency had killed Marvin and meant to kill her.

She turned off the water in the sink, stripped, and got into the shower.

Maybe the storm on Monday had caused the noise in the phone, and maybe Carmine was crazy, but *something* had happened to that plane.

It was all over town that Ed Beecham sabotaged the plane for his father's insurance, and the police had fragments of the suitcase he'd used and a copy of the forged insurance policy Beecham bought. But Emily knew he didn't do it. They were friends of a sort. He worked on her car, and let her watch him because she'd told him that she liked motors. He hummed while he worked, he handled the parts and tools gently, as if they had a life of their own, and he'd glowed with pride when she'd told him that the Volvo custom turbo that he'd told her to buy was the best car she'd ever had. He liked cars, he loved his work; he wouldn't kill his father or anybody else for money, and that was another reason to believe Anthony Carmine.

She got out of the shower and went into the bedroom. She put on heavy slacks, a work shirt, a heavy sweater, and thick socks. She was shoving her feet into her boots when she realized that she was rigging herself up for a long cold trip although she had no idea where she was going or why. She thought of taking her mother's clock and the dinosaur, but that was crazy. She was going to John's across the lake; she would be home tonight. But she shoved her feet into her boots anyway, then sat on the bed in the bulky clothes and tried to think.

Lipsky kept everything secret, and if Carmine was right all she had to do was tell Sally, Carver, or Bailey and give them a copy of the three pages in her desk, and she'd be safe. They couldn't kill everyone in the lab.

She barely knew Bailey; Carver was a better physicist than Sally, but she trusted Sally more, so she called her. She let it ring ten times, then hung up and fished in her purse for her address book and picked up the phone again. She heard the noise, and her heart pounded. Susie would approve, she thought as she dialed Carver's number. She'd go there and wait for him to come home.

"Hello," Sheila Carver answered, and suddenly Emily realized that if Bledsoe was listening, he'd be waiting for her at Carver's.

"Miles had to go to Washington," Sheila said. "He was sick about missing the service."

Emily's mouth was dry; she tried to raise some spit.

"Emily . . . ?"

"I'm here, Sheila. Will he be back tomorrow?"

"Oh, he'll be back this afternoon," Sheila said, "about four. Do you want him to call you?"

"No, I'll see him in the lab tomorrow." She hung up and wanted to grab the phone again to see if the noise was still there. But she made herself sit still, and just when the beating of her heart slowed, she heard a soft scraping noise downstairs. It was the fabric bottom of the weather stripping on the kitchen door. She held her breath, and heard it again. Someone had opened the back door, which she never locked, come into the house, and closed it after him.

CHAPTER

THE PRESIDENT closed the file folder on his desk. Carver saw the word "Lightsource" written across the front in a Flair pen.

The President said, "He said he had something new. He was very excited about it. He also said that it was someone else's idea. He was very clear about that."

"It wasn't mine," Carver said.

"But you knew about the 'breakthrough'?"

"Dr. Lipsky had become very secretive about his work."

"But you knew. You had to know."

"I'm sorry, sir." Carver tried to keep the contempt out of his voice. This poor confused-looking sap was, after all, the President of the United States. But Carver wasn't impressed. Orin Franklin looked like he'd just been kicked in the balls, and the room—whatever they called it—was small-time and fussy. Nothing compared to George Talbot's office. *There* was the look of power, Carver thought. If this man wanted to impress people, he should send his decorator to George Talbot's shining glass-and-chrome-steel retreat at the top of the highest building in the world.

"I went to Lipsky's last night," he told Franklin, "after I talked to Mr. Feinstein." He nodded at Bruce Feinstein, who sat near the fireplace.

The Jew in the corner, Carver thought.

"And I got his wife's permission to look through his desk and the files he kept there, but there was nothing. I even asked his wife if she knew anything. She was very broken up of course . . ." Too broken even to cry. She had stood in the doorway watching Carver go through her husband's papers. Carver found Lipsky's will, dated 1980; two insurance policies; and a bunch of letters. One was from Leo Szillard and another from Jacob Bronowski. The good old boy network that Carver would never belong to because even though his mind was good—very good, he told himself—his work was mediocre. He was over fifty now; it would never be anything else. He'd shoved the letters back into the desk without reading them. Fuck them, he'd thought. In the end, they were nobodies too. Szillard had begged Truman not to drop the bomb—fat lot of good that did him. Maybe there was another George Talbot behind the scenes in 1945, too. Probably, he'd told himself. And in the end, the Szillards and Oppenheimers had been as impotent as Carver.

"I asked her, as upset as she was—because Mr. Feinstein told me how important it was—and she told me he'd never said a word to her about any new development, and he told her everything. They'd been married thirty years."

Then Orin Franklin took his glasses off and polished them with a handkerchief. Without the glasses, Franklin looked hard and cold, and suddenly very competent. Carver grew uneasy. He wanted to say his piece and get out of there.

Don't say too much, Lucci had told him on the phone this morning. *Volunteer nothing*. Carver knew it was good advice. Silence was a weapon. But it was hard to keep quiet with those eyes on him.

"You see," Carver said quickly, "Marvin was upset by his last meeting with you, and he wanted to get back. Not *at* you"—Carver felt himself talking faster, but he couldn't stop—"nothing like that, Mr. President. I mean back into your good graces. And he'd been working very hard the last few months, and he wasn't a young man. Maybe he . . . you know."

"I don't know," Orin said.

"Maybe he just didn't have as much as he thought he did."

"Do you think he made it up?" Orin asked. Carver heard Feinstein shift in his seat.

"Not exactly."

"Then what, exactly?"

After a minute Carver said helplessly, "Yes, I think he made it up."

"And the colleague. Did he make him up too, like a child imagines a playmate?"

Carver didn't answer.

"Did he imagine the colleague, Dr. Carver?"

"He didn't mention her name, did he?"

The room was suddenly so quiet Carver wondered if they'd all turned to stone. A clock chimed, and Carver jumped.

The President said quietly, *"Her?"*

"The others are women," Carver said.

Orin put his glasses back on and examined the pages on his desk.

"There're seven physicists at the facility," Orin said. "Only two of them have women's names."

"But we four—me, Lipsky, and the two women—we're the . . . the . . . the . . ."

"Executive staff?" Feinstein suggested from behind him.

"Exactly," Carver said, giggling softly. "Executive staff."

"Then, assuming that Dr. Lipsky didn't imagine his colleague, you think it was one of the two women." Again Orin consulted his desk. "Dr. Avery or Dr. Brand." He looked up at Carver. "Perhaps you could guess which one."

"I can't do that," Carver cried. Franklin took the glasses off again, and Carver thought that this man didn't need chrome steel and glass. He didn't need portraits of Lincoln or Feinstein crouching in the shadows.

"Can't?" the President asked.

"I mean I don't know. Besides . . . you're right. There're seven of us . . . I mean six now. It might be one of the others."

"But you do think it was one of the women, don't you, doctor?"

"I don't think it was anybody," Carver said desperately.

The President stood up, and Carver struggled to his feet. He waited to see if Franklin would shake hands, but he didn't.

The door closed behind Carver and Orin picked up the phone.

"Don't call Placid," Feinstein said urgently.

"Why?"

Marilyn was on the line waiting for instruction, and Feinstein had to think fast. He didn't like Carver; he felt lousy

123

about what had happened to Lipsky. He was uneasy and he didn't want to leave. But Ruthie had been planning their trip for months, and he couldn't cancel for a vague feeling he barely had words for. He didn't think that Carver had lied; Carver just didn't know. But Lipsky hadn't lied either. He might exaggerate a "breakthrough," but he didn't imagine the woman. All at once, as he thought that, she had a substance of sorts. *The woman.*

Feinstein spoke haltingly. "Lipsky's on his way here . . . his plane blows up. Planes . . . don't just blow up. . . ."

Orin told Marilyn he didn't need her after all, and put the phone down. "Who?" he asked.

"I could make a list half a mile long, so could you. And whoever stopped Lipsky—if someone did—is going to try to stop her. If she exists and they know it."

If this, maybe that. . . . But Orin listened intently.

Feinstein rubbed the skin on his forehead. His words were choppy: "They knew Lipsky was coming here. If you contact her, they'll know who she is, and that she matters, and they . . ." He stopped; then he said slowly, "I think you should send someone to bring her in."

"Who?"

"Me."

"Ruthie'd kill both of us."

"Yeah," Feinstein said. The old friends were quiet; then Feinstein said, "Someone small-time and discreet. Dan Flynn's an agency watcher and you trust him. . . . He'll know who to send."

"Why small-time?"

"A big agency would leak it to the press, and we'll wind up looking like the paranoid assholes we probably are."

Carver gulped a milk shake, trying to ease the burning in his stomach. He was at Friendship, talking to Talbot on the phone. He was going to be sick, and he hated Talbot and the waiting room and the sweet malt taste of what he was drinking. He hated Feinstein and Orin Franklin. He hated himself.

"He knows," Carver told Talbot.

A beat of silence, and Talbot said, "Knows what?"

"That it was Avery or Brand. If it was anyone. All he has to do is ask, and when he does . . ."

"That's not your problem, doctor."

"Maybe you didn't hear me. All he has to do is talk to her—"

"Dr. Brand isn't going to talk to anybody, Dr. Carver."

"I see," Carver said.

"I'm sure you do, Miles. Is Red there?" Red was the pilot. Carver motioned him over and gave him the phone, then took the remains of his milk shake to a molded plastic chair next to the gate.

Dr. Brand isn't going to talk to anybody.

Carver sat in the chair and looked out at what he could see of the field. It was cold and cloudy. There were lights on inside, he could see his reflection in the glass, and through it, the gray field and the Lears and Falcons waiting for the big-time men doing big-time business. He hated all of them too; he even hated the sleek little planes.

Dr. Brand isn't going to talk to anybody.

Did Talbot think he could buy her? If he did, Carver thought, he was even a bigger asshole than Orin Franklin. He watched one plane taxi by, heading for the runway, and all at once he knew why Brand wasn't going to talk to anybody, and what had happened to Marvin Lipsky. She was supposed to be on the plane too—Lipsky had told them that he and Emily would be gone for the day. He didn't say why, or where they were going—in keeping with his new secrecy. But she hadn't gone. Carver could have told them that she wouldn't. Emily Brand didn't need credit or adulation. She didn't need anything except an occasional fuck from that asshole Ostrow.

Carver hated her too; suddenly he hated her more than anyone else, and that was a good thing, he thought, because he was going to have to go along with whatever happened to her. Even if it bothered him, even if Marvin Lipsky, who'd never hurt anyone that Carver knew about—who'd never hurt Carver, certainly—had gotten blown to pieces in the rain at the top of that miserable mountain . . . even if that bothered him just a little, even if the pain in his gut was rolling like a lake of acid . . . even then, he was going to have to go along. He'd spied for NARCON for seven years. They would certainly keep records against just such an occasion. If it ever got out—and he knew that George Talbot would make sure it did—then Carver would never work in another physics lab. He'd be lucky to wind up slicing salami in a meat-packing plant in fucking Siberia. Then he realized how naive he was. Professional espionage didn't matter, his career didn't matter, because if Talbot ever thought that Carver would talk, Carver wouldn't wind up anywhere at all.

As soon as they were in the air, he put his head back and tried to sleep. He prayed that he'd get lucky for once, and that whatever they were going to do to Emily Brand would be done before he got into Placid. He managed to doze, and woke up startled because the plane had touched down. He looked at his watch; it was too early to be at Placid; then he looked out of the window, and didn't see anything familiar. The cockpit door opened, and Red came out.

"Where are we?" Carved asked.

"White Plains," Red answered.

Red went to the door, unbarred it, and shoved it open. Cold damp air came into the plane, and Carver's head cleared a little.

"Why are we stopped here?"

Red didn't answer. A limousine drove out onto the field next to the waiting plane, and Red unfolded the stairs. Carver peered through the afternoon gloom. The chauffeur went around the car and opened the trunk. Then the back door opened, and David Lucci and a man with blond hair got out and walked toward the stairs.

Carver staggered back to his seat and sank down in it. He never had any luck, he thought bitterly.

Whoever it was crossed the kitchen. Emily untied her boots and took them off, then ran silently to the guest room and looked out of the front window. A strange car was parked behind hers, blocking it into the driveway. She went back to the bedroom, got her purse and the boots, and carried them to the head of the stairs. He came out of the kitchen, and she heard him go down the back hall to her study. She heard the door open, and she bent down and shoved her feet back into the boots. They'd clump, but she could move faster in them.

It was quiet, and she imagined him standing behind her

desk with his head raised, listening. She got the boots tied, settled her purse strap on her shoulder, and clutched the car keys.

"Dr. Brand?" he called.

His voice was loud; he must be at the study door. She wouldn't have time to get her jacket. She should take a map, but there wasn't time to find one. Besides, why did she need a map? Why was she running? The man in the study would appear any second, and he'd be wearing blue coveralls with his name and "North New York Electric" embroidered on the pocket in red.

But once, a long time ago, Susie had told her, "If you think you see a fire, yell 'Fire.' If you're wrong, they'll call you *pisher*. So what?"

Emily braced herself and ran, taking the stairs two at a time; her boots clumped, but they grabbed the treads, and she leaped the last four stairs and landed hard on the foyer floor. She heard him run up the back hall.

"Dr. Brand . . ."

She ran across the foyer and got the door open. Take the time to shut it, she told herself; he'll have to stop to open it. She slammed the door and ran across the lawn to her Volvo 780. The car that blocked her in was a Chevy Burro. The TV ads claimed it was made for today's needs, which meant it had a fiberglass body, four cylinders, and all the horsepower, according to Ed Beecham, of a lawnmower.

She started the Volvo, put it in reverse, and backed hard into the Chevy. She heard the parking-gear pin break, and the car slid back, squealing. She kept her foot to the floor, and the Chevy squealed out into the middle of the road. The road was empty in both directions. She put the Volvo in first and pulled back up almost to the house to give herself a running start. The man opened the door. He was wearing fishermen's clothes, not the blue uniform; he was very tall, with dishwater hair and brown eyes. Mr. Carmine's Mr. Bledsoe. He had a gun in one hand. He raised his arm straight out, elbow locked, and she looked into the muzzle, pointing at her through the windshield. She jammed the car in reverse, and hit the accelerator. The Volvo slammed down the driveway full throttle and hit the Chevy again. This time it sent it up over the shoulder and over the rock border of Mr. Spriggen's lawn. If flew down the incline and stopped in the middle of the grass, halfway to Mr. Spriggen's house.

Bledsoe ran down the path at the road. The back wheels of the Volvo were in the shoulder; Emily shifted, hit the accelerator again and shoved the wheel hard over. The Volvo screeched up over the shoulder and onto the road and made the turn. *The tightest turning ratio of any stock car*, Ed Beecham had told her. He was right. The Volvo screamed around and raced past the end of the walkway to her house just as Bledsoe got there. It passed Bledsoe and tore up the road toward town.

Emily looked in the mirror. Bledsoe was in the middle of the road. He'd dropped to one knee, and he was aiming at the back of the car, gun in both hands. He looked very professional; he would hit one of the tires, or the gas tank, or blow out the rear window and the back of her head. She chivied the wheel violently. The car careened from one side of the road to the other, but held the pavement. Someday she'd write to the Volvo people and tell them that they made a good getaway car. They could put it in their ads along with the EPA. She laughed out loud, then realized that she'd heard two shots. She kept the car careening, but in control. She didn't hear the bullets hit metal, or glass breaking. The gas tank didn't rupture and engulf her in flames. She glanced in the mirror again. Bledsoe was dwindling away behind her. She righted the car and drove flat out toward town. He wouldn't be coming after her for a while; it would take a tow to get the Chevy off Mr. Spriggen's lawn.

Round one to me, she thought when she got to the stop sign that marked the main road. She was shaking, and she wanted to keep running, straight east on 73. But she made herself come to a full stop at the sign and think. Seventy-three led out of town . . . and all she seemed to want to do was put distance between herself and the man with the gun. But where would she go? She didn't know. The name of Marvin's contact in Washington and her copy of the three pages were in the lab. Besides, once she was behind the double metal doors, no one except lab staff could reach her without blasting out half of the mountain.

She turned right and headed west. She passed the Howard

Johnson's and realized that she hadn't eaten anything, but Bledsoe would get the tow fast—she had to keep going.

She turned up the road to the lab. She passed the cell-culture lab, and thought of John waiting for her at his house. She'd call him from the lab.

The lab parking lot was empty except for Starrett's ancient Datsun pickup. The tattered flag hung at half-mast for Marvin. She pulled around the back and parked in the shadow of the building so her car was hidden from the road, and she crossed the lot to the front door.

Starrett was asleep in his chair, his head resting on the desktop. The nine-inch TV was playing and a quiz-show contestant struggled to decide whether to take the money while the women in the audience shrieked advice. Starrett's mouth was open, his lips pushed aside by the desktop. His gun holster was at the back of his belt, and Emily went around the end of the counter and stood over him, looking down at the gun. It was snapped in place; she couldn't get it out without waking him. His belly stuck out over his belt; his arms filled his shirt sleeves. If she had to wrestle him for the gun, she'd lose. She disarmed the alarm, then went back around the end of the desk and down the hall to the doors and entered her code.

"Good afternoon, Dr. Brand," the computer voice said in its genteel tone.

"Good afternoon, Katie," Emily answered. "It's a lovely day—cold, but clear. The wind has died."

The doors slid open.

"Have a nice day," the computer told her, and the doors closed behind her.

She went to the vending machines and bought a cup of chicken broth and a Baby Ruth bar and took them to Marvin Lipsky's office. The broth was scalding and tasteless, the candy was stale, but she was hungry and she ate and drank as she searched Lipsky's Rolodex. She found the name under W for White House. Bruce Feinstein, with his number and an address in Chevy Chase. She lifted the phone and heard the same distant, vaguely audible snap. She slammed the phone back on the hook and waited. If she called, they'd know where she was. But they'd figure that out soon enough anyway.

She picked up the phone again and dialed the number on the card.

The woman who answered had a Southern accent. "Feinstein residence."

"Mr. Feinstein, please." Emily tried to sound official. "Long distance calling."

"I'm sorry, Mr. Feinstein is out."

"Where can I reach him? It's important."

She couldn't bring herself to say things like "emergency" or "life and death" yet.

"Just a moment," the woman said.

Another woman came on. "This is Ruth Feinstein. Who is this, please?" She didn't have an accent.

"Dr. Emily Brand," Emily said. "I work with Marvin Lipsky."

Ruth Feinstein was in the rose-colored chintz-and-velvet master bedroom. On the luggage rack across the room, new leather suitcases waited half-packed.

Emily said, "Mr. Feinstein doesn't know me, but he knows Dr. Lipsky."

Ruth said coolly, "I remember Marvin Lipsky." She'd met him three or four times and thought he was ugly, loud, and vulgar. Only last month Lipsky'd had called at eleven, wakened them, and kept Bruce on the phone for an hour. Her poor husband couldn't go back to sleep. Of course she was sorry that the man was dead, but she'd thought that at least there would be no more late-night phone calls from Marvin Lipsky. Now this soft-voiced woman was calling in his name, which could only mean trouble and maybe delay. Delay was intolerable because they were leaving today at five for Nassau and their first vacation together in over two years.

"Please," Emily said, "it's urgent that I talk to him . . . it's about the work that Dr. Lipsky and I were doing. Mr. Feinstein knows—"

Ruth Feinstein made her decision. "He won't be home until three, Dr. . . ."

"Brand," Emily said. "Tell him Dr. Emily Brand from the Lake Placid facility."

"Dr. Brand. I'll tell him as soon as he comes home. Does he have your number?"

Emily gave her the number, then said, "It is urgent, Mrs. Feinstein. Is there anywhere I can reach him now?"

Ruth looked at her bedside clock. "Really, Dr. Brand, it's almost two; he'll be here in a little over an hour—"

"An emergency," Emily said.

God, the woman's persistent, Ruth thought. Like Lipsky. She hesitated, then gave Emily the White House switchboard number. That way the message would go to the bottom of a pile of the hundred or more "urgent" messages her husband got every day. Maybe he'd get it before he left for the day, maybe he wouldn't. She wasn't *preventing* anything. She— Ruth Roth Feinstein of Long Beach—was not standing in the way of fate. If Dr. Brand was lucky, he'd see the message today right before he left, and he'd call back, of course, because the President had some cockamamie idea that plasma physics was going to save the world. And if Ruth was the lucky one, then he'd come home, finish packing, and by this time tomorrow they'd be eating conch chowder and blinking against white sun on the green ocean. The world had waited a thousand million years to get saved, she told herself. Two more weeks weren't going to matter.

Ruth hung up. She'd written, "Emily Brand . . . Lake Placid" and the phone number on the pad next to the phone. She tore off the page and slid it under the other messages so that the top one read, "Your mother called to wish us bon voyage."

Emily checked the doors. The computer panel was dark; no one had tried to get in, no one was punching numbers on the other side. She went back to the phone, and she tried not to hear the noise, but she did. She dialed and waited, and then a very cultured voice said, "Good afternoon. This is the White House."

Bitch, Emily thought. She gave me the switchboard.

"Bruce Feinstein," she said, "long distance calling."

"One moment, please." The same woman came back on. "I'm sorry. Mr. Feinstein's secretary is out. But if you care to leave—"

"I want to talk to Mr. Feinstein. Not his secretary. It's urgent."

The voice went on inexorably. "If you care to leave a message . . ."

"Is there any chance . . . ? Can I talk to the President?"

A long pause this time, and the voice came back sounding kinder. It was humoring her. "We will see that the President knows how you feel about any of the questions—"

"I don't feel anything about anything," Emily said. "It's urgent that I talk to the President or Bruce Feinstein. It's a matter of life or death."

"We will be glad to take any message—"

"Shit," Emily said.

The voice hesitated, then went on lugubriously, "There's no need for—"

"I'm sorry," Emily said. "Tell Mr. Feinstein that Dr. Emily Brand called. Tell him I'm calling for Marvin Lipsky; tell him that I can build a fusion reactor that works. Tell him that it'll light and heat the city of New York for six months with the energy in a bucket of water. Tell him I can do that. . . ."

"We will see that Mr. Feinstein—"

"Is this a recording?" Emily asked.

The voice ignored her. "—gets your message. Thank you for calling." The connection was broken.

She should call the police. The man had tried to shoot her. But Carmine had said that Bledsoe was government; the police might be on his side. If they were, they would lead her out of the lab, out of Starrett's sight, and then hand her and the three pages over to Mr. Bledsoe.

She went back out into the hall. It was quiet. She went down to her office, unlocked her desk, took the three pages. She rolled them up and put them in her purse, then went back to Marvin's office to wait. Feinstein hadn't called by three-thirty. The lab got chilly; she put Marvin's old janitor-type cardigan over her sweater and tried to read the latest copy of *Nature*.

Feinstein hadn't called by four, or four-fifteen, or four-thirty, and she called Chevy Chase again.

The woman with the Southern accent answered. "I'm sorry," she drawled, "the Feinsteins left about fifteen minutes ago. . . . No, they won't be back tonight. They'll be in the Bahamas until May 1. But if you leave your name—"

"Which Bahama?" Emily cried, but the woman wouldn't say.

Emily slammed the phone down. It was getting cold, and she shoved her hands into the pockets of the cardigan. That left Sally and Carver. She tried Sally. Still no answer. Then she called Carver.

Sheila answered. "He got back about twenty minutes ago," she said.

"Can I talk to him?"

Sheila said, "They just left. He'll be home for dinner."

After a second Emily said, "*They?*"

"Miles and that David Lucci. You met him last month. Very mannerly man, tall and handsome. You remember."

Emily remembered.

"He said he'd come for poor Marvin's funeral, and he was very upset that he missed it. He thought it was tomorrow. But Jewish people get those things over with so quickly, don't they? Anyway, he and Miles are on their way—"

Emily put the phone down, grabbed her purse, and went to the door. She had the pages, her car keys, and about a hundred dollars in cash. It wasn't enough to get to Washington, but she'd hole up somewhere tonight and go to the bank in the morning. They might be ruthless, but they couldn't watch the lab, her house, and the banks too. She didn't think they could. Hole up, she thought. Eat something first, because she felt empty, then sleep, because she was exhausted.

She went out into the hall and saw the computer panel light up on her side of the door. It had to be Carver; he was punching his code into Katie, and in a second he would have voice contact and the doors would slide open. She ran back to Lipsky's office and pulled the center desk drawer open.

"Let them be there," she prayed. "Let them be there."

She scrabbled in the papers. No keys. She shut the drawer and opened the one on the right; her pulse thumped hard and fast and she made herself breathe steadily as she searched under the papers and bits of junk in the drawer. She felt metal, shoved papers away, and pulled the keys out of the drawer. She ran back to the hall and looked again at the doors. The panel was lit; he'd finished keying his number.

She turned and ran for the control room. The floor was slippery, but her boot soles gripped. She got to the glass wall with the steel-rimmed glass-topped door and made herself look at the lock. It was an Emery. She found the key that had "Emery Lock, Omaha" stamped on it.

"Carefully," she whispered, and slid the key in slowly. It fit and turned, and she opened the door, stepped through, and shut it and locked it. She was alone in the control room, the only way into the reactor. She glanced through the glass panels on the other side. The machine looked abandoned. The room was empty; steel walls caught dull light. She knelt between the control benches and stretched up to look over the top. The doors at the end of the hall slid open, and four men came through them: Carver, Lucci, Mr. Bledsoe, and another man she'd never seen before. They had to search five offices, the rest rooms, and the lounge before they got to the control room. If they divided up, they'd reach her in a few minutes and she wouldn't have time.

She reached up over the top of the bench and slid her hand along the controls. Her fingers remembered for her; the shield control was the fourth pad in. She touched it, then made her hand go back to the first and do it again to be sure. Again her fingers found the fourth indentation, and this time she pressed her finger against it and activated the reactor's magnetic shield. She looked back to the hall. Lucci and Carver were at Lipsky's door, and the other two were heading for her office.

Fools, she thought. They couldn't bear to search alone, and in twos they were lost. She turned on her knees to the next panel. There was only one lever, and she released the safety, then found the thin magnetic key on Lipsky's ring. Her fingers found the slot, and she inserted the key and turned it.

She had three minutes to go, and she sat flat on the floor between the benches and looked down at herself. The lace eyelets on her boots were metal; the shank inside probably was, too. She unlaced them and pulled them off. She opened her purse and found the pack of Dentyne she'd bought last summer when she and Sally had had pizza for lunch and were afraid their breath would be stupefying in the closed control room. The sticks were stiff as wood, but she raised as much spit as she could and put three of them in her mouth. All her fillings were in her bottom teeth, and as soon as the gum softened, she took the wad out of her mouth, divided it, and wedged half over her bottom teeth on one side and half over the other. She pulled her mother's gold ring off and put it in her purse; then she took off her metal-framed glasses and looked down at herself.

The zipper on her pants was metal; so was the fly button. She opened the fly and pulled the pants down, raising her butt off the floor to get them off. Then she took another inventory. The buttons on the cardigan were bone . . . she wasn't wearing earrings. At the last minute she remembered her watch, and she took it off and put it into her purse with the ring. She thought again; she was clean.

She raised her head up over the bench: Carver was at Sally's office door; Lucci must be inside. The door to the women's room opened, and Bledsoe and the other man came out and shook their heads. Carver said something to them. He was probably telling them that she had to be here. Her code was still on the computer, so she'd gone in and not come out. She glanced up at the green digits on the panel. Shielding had less than three seconds to go. She reached up, found the unlocked lever, pulled it down, and sent twenty billion volts through the doughnut run searching for the nuclei of deuterium and tritium atoms. But they weren't there. Nothing was there but four force fields contained by the shields, building to catch the missing nuclei. She tried to calculate the magnetic power under the shielding, but she couldn't. It would be enough, she thought—more than enough.

She peered up over the bench. They were at the control-room door. Carver tried the door, then looked back at them. Bledsoe moved in front of him, and Carver grabbed his arm and shook his head violently. Bledsoe yanked his arm away, reached inside his jacket, pulled out the gun. Carver grabbed Bledsoe's arm again; his mouth moved furiously. Bledsoe shoved him, and Carver stumbled back. Then Emily stood up. The hall light fell on her, and they saw her at once. Bledsoe banged on the door. Carver looked down, then turned and moved a few feet down the hall. Lucci smiled at her through the glass, and she smiled back at him. Then Bledsoe fired at the door. The glass in the door was shatterproof; it splintered into a web of cracks, but it didn't break. Bledsoe stepped closer, fired again, and then shoved the door open.

Emily stepped backward to the reactor-room door and grabbed the handle behind her.

Three of them came into the control room; Carver stayed outside with his back turned resolutely. Emily pulled the handle down and felt the door open a few inches.

"Dr. Brand," Lucci said, "this isn't really necessary. I don't know what you've been told—"

"That you killed Marvin Lipsky," Emily said. Her words were muffled because of the gum covering her teeth.

Lucci's eyes had an elated look, and the corners of his mouth twitched. Sally was right: he was beautiful . . . and she couldn't take her eyes off him. "I'm sorry about the melodrama," he said, "but this is very important to us . . . to our company." His voice was gentle. None of them seemed to wonder why she wasn't wearing pants.

Bledsoe was closing in on one side of her, the other man on the other side. She kept her eyes on Lucci and pushed the door open a little wider.

All he had to do was signal, and Bledsoe and the other man would shoot. She thought of bullets tearing through Marvin's sweater, and her own, then through her skin into her flesh, and her hand on the door lever was slippery with sweat. But he didn't make the gesture, and she had a feeling he had more to say. Good, she thought. Talk, Mr. Lucci, keep talking. . . .

"You do remember me?" he asked.

She pushed the door open a little wider. "Yes," she said. She was amazed at how calm she sounded. "You were here last month—"

"Not last month. Before."

His eyes never left hers, and she supposed the other two were concentrating on her too. Carver stayed in the hall with his back turned. She knew he wouldn't look around until she was dead. If she slammed the door hard enough to latch, she'd have a few seconds to get down the stairs and around the reactor to the control panel on the far side. The wall and door here were high-impact plastic. Lipsky had told her it would stop anything smaller than a rocket.

The men still didn't seem to wonder why she wasn't wearing her slacks, why she was opening the door, or why the control lights were on, threading across the panels in blips. Lucci looked young and excited, and suddenly she had the feeling that she *did* know him from a long time ago. She gave herself a second to try to remember, but it was hopeless. She couldn't remember the name of her first lover; she'd admitted that once to Susie, and Susie had been horrified, then amused.

"Emily," Lucci said softly, "look at me . . . think . . . it was twenty-eight years ago. . . ."

The shield was on, and she opened her mouth as if she were going to say something. Then she slid back through the partly open door onto the landing of the stairs to the reactor room and slammed the door. She ran down the stairs; her stocking feet skidded on the stairs, so she had to go slower, but they were already at the door. She jumped the last few steps and felt her feet slide out from under her. She fell to the side and tried to roll, but she hit hard, and her left arm took the shock and went numb. She scrambled to her feet and half-ran, half-slid across the floor and around the reactor. They opened the door, and Lucci and Bledsoe came out onto the landing. The other man stood in the doorway.

She crouched behind the reactor and watched them. She wasn't wearing her glasses; the men were blurred, but she could tell them apart. Bledsoe came down the stairs first, gun ready. Lucci was behind him, and the other man was in the open door.

She scuttled backward toward the ground-floor control panel. It was there, just in case, Lipsky had told her. In case of what? she'd asked him. That was years ago. Lipsky had laughed. *In case of nothing*, he'd said. *It's here because granting committees are a bunch of jerks who know as much about fusion as my ass does.*

The last man shut the door and trailed the others down the stairs to the floor of the room. He was balding; the light from the control room showed scalp through his thin hair, and suddenly it hit her that the three men on the stairs would bleed and feel pain. They had wives and children, and they didn't look like killers. *Horsefeathers*, her mother would have told her. *Who looks like a killer? Jack the Ripper probably wore a stiff collar and a watch chain and trimmed his beard.*

But the sudden doubt wouldn't let her alone. She bent her numb left arm across her body and cradled it with her right one, ready to step out of the shadow of the reactor. She stopped. Bledsoe had tried to kill her on the road three hours ago. No, she thought—stop her, not kill her. He'd fired at the car, not at her. She moved out of the shadow of the reactor.

Lucci saw her first. "Emily," he cried joyfully, which she didn't understand at all, and then Bledsoe saw her and the gun came up. She whirled, caught one of the tubes that ran down the side of the machine, and pulled herself back behind it. She slipped, went down on one knee, and grabbed for the side of the control panel as Bledsoe fired. The blast echoed off the steel walls, reverberated around them, picking up volume as the echoes piled up. Emily pulled herself up to the panel, yelled at Bledsoe to drop the gun, and yanked the shield lever all the way down. She thought she could feel the reactor lurch (although of course it didn't), and the shielding shut down.

Nothing happened for a split second; then the men screamed and Bledsoe's gun went off again.

"Drop the gun," Emily shouted again. But it was too late and she heard metal clang against metal, and a softer smack of bone against steel.

She waited; then she heard someone moan, and she came out from behind the reactor.

Lucci and Bledsoe were plastered against the same wall. Lucci's feet barely touched the ground; Bledsoe's feet were clear of the floor, and he hung on the steel wall like a mad decoration. The third man was on his side on the floor, his back wedged in the corner where the floor met the reactor tubing. He must have carried his gun at the back of his belt, like Starrett, and the unshielded force from the reactor magnetized the metal and slammed him against itself in this position. He was closest to her, and she walked over to him. He'd banged his head, and a line of blood ran out of his hair and down his cheek. He was dazed but conscious. It would take him a while to figure out that he had to take off his belt to get free. Even then, the metal in his shoes or watch, or the change in his pocket, would keep him immobilized. She looked him over quickly; he wasn't badly hurt.

Lucci and Bledsoe were on the other side of the room. She started toward them and then saw a sheet of blood streaming down the steel wall under Bledsoe's body. She went closer. Bledsoe didn't move; the blood collected in the cuffs of his trousers and darkened his shoes. It poured down his back, soaked his shirt, the seat of his pants, and pooled on the floor. Something pinkish-white and blurred stuck out through the plaid flannel cloth that covered his back. She went closer, the white thing came into focus, and her stomach heaved. Bledsoe hadn't dropped the gun. The magnetized gun, the hand holding it, and his arm had hit the wall so hard that the bones of his arm and shoulder had smashed back through skin, muscle, and flesh, and the scapula had stabbed all the way out of his back and through the shirt. The gun was wedged between the wall and his body, and he was held in place by his belt buckle, pocket change, shoes. She stepped around the pool of blood spreading on the floor and looked up at Bledsoe in his magnetic crucifixion against the wall.

His head was wrenched sideways, his eyes open and blank.

Lucci groaned, and she whirled around. His head was turned too, held sideways against the wall by the fillings in his teeth. The one eye she could see rolled to look at her.

"He's dead," she said.

The beautiful light brown eye stared down at her, and she stared back for a minute. Then she said, "You won't get me."

"On't ah," Lucci groaned.

"No," she said, "you won't."

She turned away from the mess. "Ooh a ed oma," Lucci cried. She looked back up at him; the eye she could see wept tears of pain and rage. "Ooh a ed oma," he screeched at her, but she couldn't understand him. She ran up the stairs to the control room. She opened the door just enough to slip through; even so, her purse, boots, and pants started to slide across the floor. She shut the door in time, put her trousers, ring, and glasses back on, slung her purse over her shoulder, and picked up the boots. She looked through the shattered glass door; the hall was empty. She opened the control-room door and went out into the hall.

The door to Carver's office was closed, and she knew he was cowering in there, waiting for it all to be over. He hadn't heard anything, except maybe the sound of the shots. They must have frightened him, because he hadn't come out to see what was going on.

She knocked on the door, then put her purse on the floor, grasped the tops of her steel-shanked boots in one hand. She knocked again, then slid along the side of the wall next to the door. She heard him cross the office, saw the doorknob turn, and he opened the door. She mashed herself against the wall, and he stepped out into the hall, his head turned toward the control room and away from her. She stepped out from the wall.

"Miles," she said.

He turned and went white when he saw her. She swung the boots as hard as she could, and smashed them against the side of his head. He fell against the wall, lurched out toward her, and she hit him again. His head smacked back against the wall, and then he slid down to the floor, half-sitting, half-lying, and didn't move.

She pulled her boots on, grabbed her purse, and punched herself out through the double doors. The lobby was silent; Starrett's head still rested on the desk. He looked peaceful, but she saw blood running down the back of his neck, and a welt showed under his hair.

"Mr. Starrett?"

He didn't respond. His back and shoulders raised, his breath was slow and steady. Emily pried the gum out of her teeth and went back to the doors. She keyed in numbers at random, and the panel lit up. "Sorry, Katie," she said, and pressed the gum against the numbers. The gum would hold the heat long enough to keep the digits engaged and jam the computer; it would be a while before anyone got in or out of the lab.

She went back to the desk, unsnapped the holster on Starrett's belt, and pulled out the gun. It was a revolver; she'd seen them opened in movies. She found the catch, pressed it, and the circular chamber popped out. The slots were loaded, and she pushed the chamber back in and opened the drawer in Starrett's desk. There was a full box of shells, and she stuck them into her purse, closed the drawer, and hefted the gun in her hand. It was heavy, but it fit her palm easily and she knew she could hold it steady enough to fire it. She thought she could calculate and imagine the kick from the size, even though she didn't know the caliber. She thought she could handle that all right, too. She was strong, and fast; she could get the gun out in time for anything. The problem was aiming it. Her eyes were bad, and she'd never tried to hit anything before in her life, not even a dart board. She would have to aim slowly, and at things that were big and close to her . . . if she had to aim at all.

She stuck the gun in her purse and felt the strap pull against her shoulder. She crossed the empty, gloomy lobby and went out into the parking lot.

It was almost dark; the arc lights had come on, and the red and blue on the ragged flag looked black in the green light. The mountains were purple against the dark gray sky, and to the north a couple of early stars shone over Whiteface. She stopped and looked back at the lab door. The reactor would shut itself down if anything went wrong. That was basic. Besides, Carver would wake up soon and shut it down anyway. He wouldn't be able to get out, and Starrett wouldn't be able to get them out without the computer man from Tupper Lake. She might have made a real mess of the thing, and then they'd have to wait for someone to come from Plattsburg. She had hours.

Two cars were in the front lot: Starrett's pickup and Carver's Mercedes. She pulled back the safety on Starrett's revolver with both thumbs and felt it click into place. She went to the Mercedes and aimed at the right-front tire. Then slowly and steadily she pulled the trigger. The report died against the mountains. It was duck-hunting season, or almost; hunters always started early, and no one would wonder about the shots. She went to the next tire, and the next. By the time she had blown out the tires on both cars, her ears had a high singing ring in them that she thought she could live with if she had to. Her right hand and arm felt like someone

141

had stabbed a million tiny pins into them, and her left arm was getting stiff. She was hungry, and muscles in her back and thighs jumped with exhaustion and strain.

She was getting into her car when she remembered the sheet of blood streaming down the steel from Bledsoe's body and the blood-smeared bone rammed out through his shirt, with strings of muscle fiber clinging to it, and she ran to the edge of the lot and threw up over the ground pine until her throat was raw.

"Mother," she whispered, "I killed someone."

She could see her mother very clearly. She was lying on a white pillow, her skin slick and yellow like stained glass. It was just before she died, and she'd stretched out her skinny yellow hand with its ridged chipped nails to her daughter. The hand was hideous, but Emily had taken it and held it against her cheek.

Then her mother had said softly, "Be a brave girl, Emily. A fine brave girl." Those weren't her last words. She had lived two days after that, and she had said things like, "Can I have some water . . . I think I need the bedpan . . . please close the door . . ."

But "Be a brave girl, Emily," were the words Emily was meant to remember, because Ruth Austen Brand had prized bravery above all things.

Emily raised her head and looked into the woods that sloped up the side of the mountain. She heard water running through the trees, and she left the edge of the parking lot and walked toward it. A spring had broken out of the frozen ground under a boulder and rushed in rivulets around the rock and through the ground pine and wintergreen. Emily knelt down next to it, washed her face, and swilled the fresh cold water around in her mouth, then raised it in her hands and drank in gulps. Then she stood up and went back to the car. This time she got in, started it, and drove quickly to the front lot and down the ramp out of the installation. Behind her the building looked deserted, the flag moved dispiritedly in a cold breeze, and the cars already looked like junk.

Ooh a ed oma, Lucci had cried at her.

She knew now that he'd said, "You're a dead woman."

She downshifted and took the curves down the mountain as fast as she could.

PART
II

CHAPTER
10

STOCKTON WAS CALM. It was six, Feinstein's flight to Nassau was taxiing for takeoff, and Stockton knew that no matter what Orin Franklin suspected about Lipsky and the plane, and perhaps the woman, he didn't *know* anything. And Stockton did. Still, he'd been a touch nervous when he came in here and settled himself in the ugly damask chair across from the President. But he had examined Orin Franklin covertly and quickly and hadn't found him a very imposing presence. On the order of Jimmy Carter, he thought. Obsessive but ineffective.

An incompetent fanatic, Stockton thought.

"What do you know about the fusion installation at Lake Placid?" Orin asked.

"Nothing."

"And Marvin Lipsky?"

"No . . ."

"He was the director."

"*Was*?" Stockton said.

"He was killed in a plane crash on Monday."

Stockton didn't say anything, and Orin watched him for a moment. He didn't like or not like Paul Stockton. He didn't know him. Flynn said he was a well-entrenched bureaucrat . . . twelve years of collecting dossiers and scratching the right backs. But Flynn swore that Stockton could be trusted.

Orin went on. "Before he was killed, he told me that he and a colleague had designed what he called the next and maybe final generation of fusion reactors."

"Oh?" Stockton didn't sound impressed.

"A fusion reactor that works," Orin said.

"Oh," Stockton said again.

"Do you know what that could mean, Mr. Stockton?"

"Not exactly."

"It means that we could light and heat every home and factory in America with a few gallons of water."

"I see."

"The idea doesn't seem to excite you."

Stockton hesitated, then asked, "What would you like me to do about this, Mr. President?"

"Get excited," Orin said coldly.

Stockton smiled. "Ah, Mr. President, I've heard so many solutions to our energy problems." His voice was velvety, but clear. "In eighty-four it was a formula for synthetic oil. Not the synfuels, Mr. President, but real, go-to-hell oil. It came from nutshells or cactus . . . I can't remember exactly." He laughed softly. "I don't have to tell you the furor, do I? The Arabs wanted it because if it worked, they'd be out several trillion dollars and have to stop buying up Fifth Avenue. The Israelis wanted it to stick it to the Arabs. And the Russians wanted it to keep us on our backsides, because they figured that nothing compromises Americans as much as gas lines. They were right, too." Then he asked conversationally, "Do you know how many people were killed in the gas shortage of eighty-eight?"

"Twenty-eight," Orin said.

"Why, yes. The Russians are right, Mr. President. We are as serious about gas lines as Argentinians abont soccer games. So naturally, synthetic oil was a very hot item. Maybe the Chinese wanted it too, and the Albanians . . . I don't know. But we got it, and it worked. It made honest-to-God oil. Only thing," Stockton said softly, "it was expensive. A tankful for your average Chevy would have cost about six hundred dollars." He laughed and went on in the same soft, almost hypnotic voice, "Then there was synthetic coal. Nonpolluting—almost nonpolluting—and cheap, so it would save billions on all those scrubbers. Only it wouldn't burn. An acetylene torch wasn't hot enough to ignite it. Foolish . . . foolish," he intoned. "You'd think they'd have noticed before they spent all that money developing it, wouldn't you?

"I don't have to tell you what's happened to solar energy—ich people build it into their homes and save money . . . and I suppose that a few farms out on the prairie are still powered by the wind. I don't know how much we've invested in fusion, but I suspect it's enough to buy Libya itself, never mind its oil."

"And you advise me to forget the whole thing," Orin said.

"Why, no," Stockton smiled kindly. "Just don't expect me to get excited. Not that I blame you, Mr. President. The other presidents got excited too—about fision or fusion or synoil or syncoal; they were like medieval kings investing in their pet alchemists. The presidents tended to get very excited. Not the oil men, though. They're the real bellwether." He looked up at Orin, then past him through the window at the dusk starting to cover the lawn, the shrubs, the fence in the distance. He couldn't see the tops of the buildings. "I've stayed where I am because I believe in bellwethers, Mr. President. The oil are the big frost. They've been with us in one form or another for all of history. They sold us coal or wood or corn seed or cattle or flints. They don't move fast or easy because they deal in the basics. I'll get excited when they get excited. But then you know what'll happen, don't you?"

Stockton was a good talker, if a little theatrical, and Orin waited to hear the rest. Stockton said, "They'll buy your reactors, or the water to run them. If this is the breakthrough you think it is, in a few years, somehow or other, it'll belong to them, and the few people in this country who have the guts will form committees and task forces and clubs to find out why electricity from water—*water*—costs more than oil ever did. The rest will watch the frost gather."

"You don't seem to have much faith in the future, Mr. Stockton."

"Oh, but I do. I have infinite faith that it will be just like the past."

Suddenly Orin had the awful, inexpressibly draining feeling that Stockton was right. That he should tear up the thin file marked "Lightsource" and leave Talbot and the rest of them alone, like they'd always said he should, like they'd said Reagan should, and Carter and Ford. If Stockton was right, fusion wouldn't save America; nothing would. The feeling dragged at Orin until he wanted to let his head fall on his

147

desk and sleep. He had to stifle a yawn; his eyes watered. The controls would come off, the people would pay the freight, and when they couldn't, then the companies would have to come down on their own, and when the oil finally gave out . . . when the oil gave out . . . Orin couldn't see that far. Something would turn up. *God would provide.* So said Reagan and Orin's mother-in-law, and senators, secretaries, old ladies, and preachers would agree.

Orin couldn't suppress this yawn; it pulled his mouth half open, and he had to wipe his eyes. From the shadows Stockton smiled, and Orin wondered madly if the man had put a spell on him. *God would provide.* Except for Mrs. Marguery. For her there'd been the black pit in the frozen ground, and that last night alone in the dark, trying to stay awake, to keep warm, because if she died so stupidly, what would happen to her little house, to the plants in the dining room? Orin wondered what had happened to them, and then he wondered if freezing to death was as gentle as it was cracked up to be. Or did Mrs. Marguery struggle against the torpor; did she bang her old poor head against the clean kitchen table to stay awake? Did she pinch herself, rub her hands and legs; and at the end, when her eyelids were lead and she'd lost her meager battle against the silent cold, did she know it? Did she mourn her own death in the last seconds before she couldn't keep her head up any longer, as she felt herself sliding out of the chair to the floor?

Orin said, "Maybe you're right, Mr. Stockton. Maybe God stacked the deck, and nothing can ever change. But what if there is no God, or what if he leaves us alone, and the future is exactly what we make it into?"

"If you say so, Mr. President."

"I say so," Orin said, and he opened the Lightsource file and handed Stockton a sheet of paper.

"There're two women at TNF 1210," he said. Stockton took the paper. "One of them may have been working with Marvin Lipsky. Find out which one as discreetly as possible because she might be in danger, and see that she gets to me or to Bruce Feinstein."

Stockton glanced at the list, and the name jumped out at him—Emily Austen Brand, Ph.D.—and for the first time since he'd walked in here, he was scared. He shouldn't be. She was dead by now, and he had expected to see that name, but as one of seven or eight others, not stuck out on a page with only Brenda Salome Avery for company. Stockton felt sweat collect at his hairline.

Lipsky hadn't said "she" when he called the President. But now Franklin knew it was a woman, so Carver had screwed up. Everything else was okay, he told himself. Wonderful, in fact, because Orin Franklin was asking him to find Emily Brand.

Stockton's limousine was stuck in the evening traffic, and he snapped on the radio. The newscaster talked about the demonstration against decontrol. It was scheduled for eight days from now. It was growing; a hundred thousand had been expected, but now it looked like twice that would show. Stockton turned off the radio and allowed himself a second of pity for the man he'd just left. If Franklin kept the controls, he faced the wrath of the oil companies and the shortages and gas lines. If he let the controls come off, he faced the people.

Stockton opened the bar at the back and poured himself a small portion of Pimm's and added soda.

It was six-thirty, and she'd been dead for hours. Stockton sipped his drink and planned. Her disappearance would have been a local matter. When she didn't show up, the boyfriend would call the sister and then the cops. The cops would look for a while, then figure she was dead or off on her own because she was shocked by the death of her boss, sick of the boyfriend, and didn't give a shit for the sister. They'd stop looking in a month at most. Then the boyfriend and the sister would hire a PI, and he'd look for another month or two. But that would run into money, and one day the boyfriend would look at his check register and figure she was gone for good. The sister might hang on longer . . . blood ties and all that. Besides, the sister was rich. But she was only a half-sister, and soon the kids would stop asking about Aunt Emily, and the holidays would be coming; there would be shopping to do, decorating and baking . . . and then the sister would give up too, and that would be the end of Emily Brand.

But now tne President was involved, and there had to be a real search.

Stockton sweetened his drink; his mind moved smoothly. A real search meant a real trail. That was easy. A check on Emily Brand's account would be cashed in Syracuse and a gas-station attendant in Scranton would remember a woman who looked like Emily Brand. *The lady was moving west.* She would stop in a motel near Pittsburgh, and another near Iowa City, and there, just east of Iowa City and south of Clinton, the trail would end. She could have gone south to New Orleans or Texas, and from there into Mexico. Or she could have gone north to Fargo and Thunder Bay.

A woman who looked like her had been seen in Puerto Vallarta or Vancouver. He could stretch it out with false clues. A year's manhunt could run into a few million, and sooner or later Franklin would start feeling foolish. He'd have to accept that Emily Brand had disappeared because she had been bribed or doubted the validity of the work or its safety. Stockton would think of more reasons when he had time.

By then there would be nothing left of the body at the bottom of Union Falls pond but crumbling bones and long filmy shreds of flesh too insubstantial for anything but minnows to feed on.

Talbot was finishing his favorite spring supper, cold leg of lamb and artichoke vinaigrette. He would hear from Placid soon, or Stockton would. Stockton had seen the President and everything had gone smoothly. Talbot had known it would; Stockton had a cynicism about him that people confused with honesty, and Franklin had made that mistake.

He looked down at the table. Joan was cutting her meat raggedly and describing a wall hanging that she was going to embroider for Anthony's room. He wished she could find something to do besides drink and needlepoint. Maybe they'd take a trip now that Placid was settled. Joan loved Rome—she had cousins there. He'd leave her with them and go on to Tunis. The Tunisian whores were wonderful, especially for a man his age. Lately there were times when he didn't want to see Romy because he knew he couldn't perform. A week in Tunis would fix that. Joan was talking about the pattern for

Mr. Toad in *Wind in the Willows,* and Raymond came into the room.

"Call, sir. Dr. Carver from Lake Placid."

Talbot put his napkin down next to his plate.

"Lake Placid . . ." Joan said.

He smiled at her. "I won't be long. There's some champagne cooling."

He left the table and went down the hall to his study. Now he was excited, and he knew that if Romy were here this minute, he'd show her a good time. Maybe he'd call her tonight. Then he decided he wouldn't. He'd rest tonight; the excitement would last. The details he was about to hear would feed it, keep it alive until tomorrow. He walked lightly, he felt young and vigorous, and he was smiling as he went into the study and closed the door.

He crossed the room to the phone, engaged the scrambler, started to raise the receiver, then stopped.

Why was Carver calling instead of David?

He tried to think of what could go wrong. Nothing. Bledsoe and Kelsey were pros. David was there; David could handle anything. Emily Brand was dead. Her body was at the bottom of the bottomless pond between Placid and Dannemora, tiny fish already feasting on her flesh. He closed his eyes and imagined the freezing darkness that they'd dropped the body into, and felt a stab of pity for the corpse that he knew he would never have felt for the live woman. She was dead, the plans were destroyed, everything was normal again . . .

But Carver was on the phone, not David.

Talbot left the desk, went to the bar and poured a slug of brandy. He glanced up at his father's portrait.

"It's okay," he said softly. He took the brandy back to the desk and picked up the phone.

"Carver?"

"Listen to me, Talbot. We're locked in the lab." Carver's voice shook. "She jammed the computer and we can't get out. Bledsoe's dead, I think Lucci's jaw's broken. Someone's coming from Plattsburg to fix this mother, but it'll take hours. I think Lucci's in shock, I think I have a concussion, and I don't know how long I was out. The clocks are frozen so I don't know what time . . . Oh, Christ, what time is it?" Carver cried.

"Seven," Talbot said mechanically.

"I think it was about six when she beaned me, so she's been gone an hour."

"Gone where?"

"How the fuck should I know? Gone . . . that's all. Gone Tell Stockton she made hash out of his big bad hit man. She made hash out of all of us."

"What about the other man . . . Kelsey?"

"He's okay. Banged up, but nothing serious."

Bledsoe dead, David in shock, Kelsey banged up . . Talbot remembered the description of her in the file: five four, one hundred fifteen pounds. He felt a hysterical giggle rise in his throat. He forced it down. "What did she do?" he asked.

"She magnetized all the metal on us with the reactor. I did it. It's on her side, like I told you. Now she's loose . . she's got the plans. . . ."

Joan waited at the table. She thought of Lake Placid and the Emily Brand woman. Talbot had looked young and happy when he left the table, so Emily Brand was disposed of. Joan raised her vodka to drink, then put it down untasted.

Talbot had said that David was in Placid; David, the master troubleshooter, sent to neutralize poor Emily Brand. But David reported his own successes; he wouldn't leave it to that Carver, and it was *Carver* who'd called from Placid.

Joan rang for Raymond and asked him to bring the champagne ice bucket and two glasses on a tray. He came back and she took the tray from him with almost steady hands. The tray was heavy, but she got it down the hall to the study. She put it on the hall table and knocked on the study door. "It's me," she called.

Talbot told her to come in. She opened the door, then picked up the tray and brought it to the cocktail table.

"The champagne was ready," she said. He didn't answer.

He was dialing. His face was gray, and the scrambler was on. "David's hurt," he said.

"Oh? An accident?" she asked.

"No."

Then he said into the phone, "Paul, it didn't work."

Joan spilled a bit of champagne on the table. She mopped it up, and finished pouring. She brought the glass to Talbot, then went back to the fireplace and sat down.

David was hurt, and it was not an accident. George had just told Paul Stockton that *it* didn't work. Emily Brand must still be alive. She poured champagne for herself, stared straight ahead, and listened.

"We need to cover the sister," Talbot said. "Brand ran, she may need money. I can get a wire on the sister in half an hour. The boyfriend's covered."

They were going to tap the sister's phone, Joan thought, and when Brand called her for money, or food, or someplace to sleep, they'd hear, and they'd be waiting for her.

Then Talbot said, "An hour, but she won't hang around Placid. She'll head for Washington. I don't think she could have called anyone yet."

Joan knew Placid, she used to take Mary skiing there years ago. There was nothing around the town but more little mountain towns that closed down in March and didn't open up again until July, when the black flies were gone. Saranac was big, and stayed alive, but it was miles west of Placid, and Emily Brand wouldn't go there. She'd head southeast, for the Northway, and there was nothing in that direction until she got to Schroon Lake. But Schroon Lake was over an hour from Placid, so by the time she found a phone, the sister's phone would be tapped.

Joan looked up at the clock. It was seven-ten. Her eyes went to the portrait of the old man over the mantel. His funeral had marked one of the happiest days of her life. She stood up and approached the mantel. Talbot was still talking to Stockton—something about a man named Carmine and another named Simmons. Those names meant nothing to her, but then Talbot said "Gelb." She remembered that the man named Gelb had taken care of Gerald Blair. Her heart broke for Emily.

She looked into the painted gray eyes.

She's a woman all alone, running for her life, she told the portrait silently. *Let her go.*

But the eyes stared past her at the far wall. They were pitiless.

Talbot dialed another number, and she heard: ". . . Albany

153

tolls . . . the airport." But that was all right. If Emily Brand was smart enough to take out David Lucci, she wouldn't come barreling straight down the Northway to the tolls, or go to the Albany airport. She'd stick to side roads, she'd lie low.

She heard Talbot say, "Great Neck." Then, "Cohen . . . Steven and Susan." He gave an address and phone number, but she knew she couldn't remember them, and she couldn't write them down. She sipped the wine and looked at Talbot. He looked scared and ugly. She thought of him naked, his slack belly drooping over his crotch, the sparse hair on his body, the flaccid skin on his arms and legs. She hated him as much as she had hated his father, and she thought that this . . . this cruel, ugly, incredibly willful creature . . . this monster, had given an order, and now Emily Brand was going to die. Rage made her weak. He finished his call and reached for the champagne. She looked at the clock again. It was seven-twenty.

"How is it?" he asked.

"Excellent," she answered; then she said, "Oh, I have to go to Ann Devore's."

"What for?"

"She's having trouble with a seat cushion. I promised I'd help."

"At this hour?" He wanted her to stay with him until Emily Brand was found and killed, or whatever they were going to do to her.

"Ben's out of town, and I was supposed to go this afternoon, but I forgot." She stood up. "I'll be home by nine." She looked at him, making sure that her eyes were vacant. "I'm sorry about David . . . not too bad, I hope?"

"I don't think so."

"Well, don't tell Mary until you know definitely." She went to the door, remembering to stagger slightly. She smiled dully at him and left the room.

The Devores lived next door, which was almost half a mile away. She didn't dare wait for a car, and she grabbed her needlepoint bag and ran down the drive to the road. The air was cold, but it was clear, the moon lighted everything, and running was exhilarating for a few minutes. Then her side started aching, the bag banged against her leg, and stones clipped up from the road and into her shoes. She had to stop and catch her breath. She thought her shaky legs and burning lungs would stop her. But after a minute of breathing slowly, she went on, and a few yards along, she started to run again.

The outside lights were on the Devore house; their drive was as long as hers, and by the time she got to it, she was limping and holding her side. But she didn't stop until she reached the front door.

The butler showed her into the library. Ann was there, in her bathrobe, although it was only seven-thirty. Her bare feet were up on a pillow, and she was drinking tea and watching a tape of *War of the Worlds*. On the screen, glittering space ships hovered over half ruined buildings, and the earth people screamed and ran for their lives. Joan giggled, still gasping for breath.

Ann rayed off the machine. "What on earth . . . ?"

"I have to make a call, and I can't do it from home. Now, Ann. Please." She was afraid she'd burst into tears.

Ann beamed. "Oh, Joanie, you've got a boyfriend after all these years."

"Yes," Joan cried, "a boyfriend. Please . . . I don't have much time."

"You'll tell me—"

"Everything. I swear."

"You don't look very romantic."

"Oh, God, Ann. Please!"

"Yes . . . the sitting room. Turn right; it's just down the hall. The door should be open."

Joan dropped the bag and ran out of the room.

"There's brandy in the cabinet," Ann called.

Joan found the room. The phone was on a tiny table next to a spindly chair, and Joan called 516 information. There were two Steven Cohens in Great Neck, and Joan took both numbers. She'd forgotten her watch; she didn't see a clock in the room, and she didn't know what time it was. Maybe Emily Brand had just reached Schroon Lake, found an open gas station, and was lifting the phone in the booth. Joan started dialing the first number, and suddenly it occurred to her that the wire might be on by now. They would hear her warn Susan Cohen, and they'd tell Talbot. That scared her so much that her throat seemed to dwindle in her neck. But she was in the grip of something now, and she couldn't have stopped if she'd wanted to.

The phone rang twice, and a woman answered.

"Mrs. Cohen?" Joan tried to sound calm.

"This is Mrs. Cohen."

"You have a sister named Emily Brand."

Joan heard the woman catch her breath. "Has something happened to Emily?"

It was the right Mrs. Steven Cohen, and she cared about her sister. Joan said, "Not yet."

"Who is this?"

"It doesn't matter. You don't know me. But your sister is in danger. I don't know why but NAR is after her . . . to capture her . . . hurt her." She couldn't say kill; it would sound absurd. "They think she'll call you for help, and they're tapping your phone. Someone could be listening this minute. Do you understand?"

The woman did not answer and Joan was afraid she had hung up. Then she heard breathing. She said, "If Emily Brand calls you, they'll be listening. Don't let her come to you, and don't let her tell you where she is."

"This is crazy," the sister cried.

"If it's crazy, there's no harm done. If it's not, then we'll . . ." Joan was amazed to find that there were tears in her eyes and that she was smiling stupidly into the phone. "We'll help to save Emily Brand," she said softly. And then she put the phone down.

Talbot was in bed when she got home, propped up on pillows, reading. He looked strained but not as if he'd just heard that his wife of thirty-two years had betrayed him.

"How's Ann?" he asked.

"Learning," she said.

He looked sharply at her. "You're looking nervy," he said.

"You'd look nervy too if you'd just spent an hour trying to teach Ann Devore how to use her hands."

Susie Cohen held the phone for a second after the woman hung up, then put it down and looked at Steven.

"What was that?" he asked.

"I don't know."

"What do you mean you don't know?"

"Steve, what's NAR?"

"You buy their gas for the car."

"NARCON," Susie said.

"Yeah. They probably supply the oil for the house too. They're the biggest in the northeast, maybe in the country since they bought Texoil in eighty-four during the glut."

"What glut?"

"The eighty-two oil glut. You remember, they took the controls off, the prices zoomed, and everybody stopped buying. The companies had stockpiled all this oil to cash in. But they couldn't sell the stuff because everybody was running out of money." He laughed, his bulk shook, and Susie looked away. The current diet wasn't working either.

He said, "That was probably the first and only time in history that greed was self-defeating."

"But they put the controls back . . ."

"Sure. The recession ended, people got more money, bought bigger cars and filled 'em with gas, and bigger houses with bigger furnaces, and the prices went up again." Then he asked, "What does NARCON have to do with that nuts conversation you had?"

"Steve, what would NARCON want with my sister Emily?"

"I don't know what anybody would want with that crazy bitch."

"Don't call her that," Susie said. "She's my sister."

"She's your half-sister."

Susie stood up to leave the room and Steven raised his hand in a peace gesture. "Okay, I'm sorry. But she *is* crazy." He had never forgiven Emily for inheriting a third of Isaac Brand's estate.

He said, "I don't know what NARCON would want with Emily. What did they say?"

"Not they, she," and Susie told her husband what Joan Talbot had said.

"No name?"

Susie shook her head.

"No reason?"

"She said she didn't know. Only that they were after Emily. That Emily is in danger."

"So just like that, someone from North Atlantic Resources taps our phone and goes after Emily."

"The woman on the phone meant what she said," Susie said.

"Then she's crazier than your sister. Emily's not in business. She's got as much sense for any of that stuff as Pudgy." Pudgy was their dog, a mutt who seemed to have a glandular problem, because she got fatter and fatter, no matter how little they fed her or how many miles a day Susie and the kids walked her. The dog reminded Steven of himself, and he loved her.

"Maybe they want to kidnap her—" Susie said.

"Why the fuck would anybody kidnap a thirty-seven-year-old spinster physicist . . . ?" He stopped talking suddenly.

Emily was crazy, and he'd never liked her, but no one could call her dumb. Had she found something . . . invented something that they wanted, that they had to have, and she wouldn't give it to them or sell it to them, because she was crazy and stubborn and she was running away with it, whatever it was?

"Steven!"

He looked up.

"What should I do?"

"Call Emily," he said. He turned back to the TV, a fifteenth-time rerun of *MASH*, and pretended to watch it while Susie called Placid.

After a while she put the phone down. "She's not there." Her voice had an edge of panic.

"Maybe she's at John's." He went back to the TV. In the background he heard Susie talking to John Ostrow, another nut case. The conversation was short.

"She isn't there," she told Steven. "She called him this morning, and she was supposed to come to him after poor Marvin's funeral. He's got spring flu . . ."

Spring flu, Steven thought disgustedly. A fine way for a microbiologist to talk.

"But she never showed up. . . . Steve, I'm scared."

She looked terrified, and he damned Emily. "There's nothing you can do, sweetheart. If she's in trouble, she'll call."

"But they'll be listening . . ."

He gentled her down as best he could; made her a cup of tea and brought it to her, along with a plate of cookies that

158

he wanted to eat himself. He took only one, and made himself leave the rest for her. He got her upstairs and undressed and into bed okay; then he looked in on the kids. His son was a slim, hard-bodied little boy, wiry like his mother. He slept on his stomach with his head burrowed into the pillow. He was four and still carried his Teddy wherever he went. It was in bed with him, his arm draped over it. Pudgy was at the foot of his bed, lying on her hefty side, her fat body spreading on the floor. Steven Cohen stroked the dog's ears and turned to his daughter. She was six and ran to fat like he and Pudgy did. She slept on her back, her puffy little cheeks pink even in the dim light that came through the window. It was bad for a boy to be fat, it was a disaster for a little girl, and he felt so sorry for her as he watched her chubby little chest move with her breathing that he wanted to cry.

The phone call bothered him more than he let on to Susie. He thought it was nuts, but even if there was a little bit of truth in it . . . He went to the door of the room and looked back at his sleeping children. He'd kill for them. He'd die for them too, and for Susie. He was a fat middle-aged man with thinning hair, a fair-to-good lawyer who'd never make a quarter of the money his wife had inherited, and he knew he didn't have much to pat himself on the back about, but he loved his family; they were his life.

He went back downstairs into the den, turned off the TV, avoided the cookies Susie hadn't eaten, picked up the phone and heard the distant echo of something. It frightened him so badly he couldn't do anything but stand stupidly holding the receiver. After a second he dialed his mother's number.

"Steven?"

"Yeah, Ma. What're you doing?"

"I'm sleeping." Then she asked, "What's wrong?"

"Nothing. I just forgot to call you today."

"You forget to call me every day. You sure you're okay?"

"Everyone's fine."

"So go to sleep."

He stared at the phone for a few minutes, then picked it up again. He heard it right before the dial tone came in, a distant sound like a twig breaking underfoot across the road or an ice cube cracking in a glass in another room. He dialed the weather, listened to the whole forecast, then went upstairs to Susie. The lights were on; she was sitting up staring at nothing.

"The phone's tapped," he said stupidly.

"I know that."

He sat on the edge of the bed and turned on the light. His face was damp and flushed; he grabbed her hand. "Emily will call."

"I hope so," Susie said.

"When she does, you say nothing. Do nothing. Tell her you're sick, tell her you can't talk . . ." Steven pleaded.

"I won't do that, Steven."

He sagged, and she reached out and touched his damp fat cheek. "She's my sister," she said softly.

He hadn't expected any other answer from her. "Not even for me and the kids?" he tried.

"It has nothing to do with you and the kids, Steven. That's not fair."

He nodded. "Okay, then we've got to be ready. You've got to know what to say to her so you won't give anything away."

"I'll—"

"No you won't Suse. You'll panic. That won't help Emily, it won't help us. Figure out someplace to meet her that only the two of you know about . . . that you don't have to tell her about in detail. Like someplace you went when you were kids."

"I know one," Susie said excitedly.

He nodded again and wiped his face. "Mostly we mustn't panic. So they tapped the phone. It goes on all the time. We're talking about industrial espionage, not murder, for Christ's sake."

Carmine was home at last. He filled the bathtub with hot water, he even used some of Rosa's bubble bath, and he soaked for an hour, and came downstairs for dinner smelling of lavender. The hot water got some of the kinks out of his neck and shoulder muscles, but he was still edgy. Rosa had made his favorites for dinner, osso bucco and a side dish of escarole. The kids were glad to have him back and they were on their best behavior. They sat at the round table in the spotless kitchen and tried to have a good family dinner

160

But Carmine's nervousness must have communicated itself, because there were long stiff silences and even the kids were uncomfortable. The food smelled wonderful, and he tried to enjoy it, but the fragrant veal was like sawdust in his mouth, and it was an effort to swallow. Rosa kept asking him if there was anything wrong, and he kept telling her that there wasn't. By dessert—homemade buddino—Vinnie and little Rosa were squabbling and Rosa made them leave the table. She cleared the table and left him with a cup of coffee and a glass of his uncle's homemade cordial.

He was scared and he could barely admit it even to himself, much less to Rosa. When Bledsoe had seen him on the phone in the Howard Johnson's in that cold miserable little town, he'd kept cool. He was calling his Rosa, he'd told Bledsoe. He was going home tomorrow and it just hit him and he had to call. Bledsoe seemed to buy it. They bought the ice cream and drove back to the cabin in separate cars, Carmine in his van and Bledsoe in his little Chevy. They watched a tape of *The Longest Day* (Bledsoe wouldn't sit still for anything but war movies) and in the middle of it Carmine caught Bledsoe staring at him. Bledsoe looked away, but Carmine imagined he could still feel the man's small mean eyes on him, and he kept waking up during his last night in the cabin, half-expecting to find Bledsoe's huge black form standing over his bed in the dark. But Bledsoe slept, and in the morning Carmine felt a little better. He said good-bye to Bledsoe, who nodded without looking at him. He didn't even offer to shake hands, after a month of living in the same cabin, and Carmine decided that Bledsoe was truly an animal, a beast, and he'd shuddered for Emily Brand.

In spite of that, he'd meant to hit 73 and keep going, even though he hadn't been able to warn her about Bledsoe. But as he drove abreast of the turnoff to her house, he thought of Bledsoe's eyes. The meanest eyes in the world, eyes to leave blisters on your skin where they looked at you, and he knew he couldn't leave her to that *faccine* without at least a warning. She was a woman, after all. She had a gentle voice and she worked hard. Father Danilo would have a hard time forgiving Carmine for not at least warning her. He would have a hard time forgiving himself. He pulled up and printed the note, then drove to her house. He reasoned that he was safe. He reasoned that murder was night work and that Bledsoe would wait until dark to do his business. But when he'd left Emily Brand and was driving back toward 73, he happened to look in the rearview mirror and he was sure he'd seen Bledsoe's car pull into the other end of her street. It *was* Bledsoe's car. The only question was whether or not Bledsoe had seen him. Maybe not—Bledsoe had come from the other direction, along the back road that wound around Mirror Lake from the other end of town—but it was possible. That was his only question, and he'd waited all evening since he'd gotten home for the answer. He ate what he could of his dinner; he listened to the early news, and there was no mention of a woman physicist dying in Lake Placid. He watched a puppet show on cable with the kids, who'd calmed down, and then he listened to the late news, and there was still nothing. No one called except his mother to say that they were having dinner at her house tomorrow and then his brother with a tip on the sixth at Aqueduct. He started to relax. Rosa had bought a bottle of white Chianti and they drank some of the wine and watched a night-owl movie on cable which was so hot that he and Rosa made love on the couch. Then she went upstairs to get ready for bed and he sat alone on the couch in the dark.

Thoughts came to him. He would go to NARCON in the morning and resign. But that would make them suspicious. He'd worked out his time; he would take his money and his next assignment and try to forget about Emily Brand. He wouldn't look at the paper tomorrow, he wouldn't listen to the news.

He could have called the cops, but he'd never called the cops in his life . . . it wasn't his way. Besides, he had a feeling that somehow—between NARCON and whatever bunch of Nazis Bledsoe worked for—the cops wouldn't do anything anyway. No, he thought, he'd done what he could for her. He'd done all that was right to do. After all, he had a wife and kids, and his life mattered too.

He heard the toilet flush; then water ran and was shut off. He waited until he thought Rosa was in bed and asleep because he wasn't ready to talk about anything yet, and then he went upstairs, got undressed, and slipped at last between the clean sheets on his own bed. Rosa slept, and the warmth of her body in the bed with him was more relaxing than anything, and he fell asleep.

Something woke him. Something in the house. He sat up and listened. Everything was quiet, but he had a feeling that something was wrong. He looked over at Rosa; she was usually the one to have such feelings, but she was still sleeping. He got out of bed and went to the window. The sky had cleared, the moon was up, and it shone on the gas barbecue he'd bought last summer. If it was warm enough, he would use it on Sunday. He stayed at the window for a moment listening. He didn't hear anything and he was ready to go back to bed when he heard a car start up near the house and drive toward the stop sign at the end of Twenty-third Avenue. He could see the stop sign from the window, and the lights of the car paused, then turned the corner and stopped. The lights went out and he glanced at the clock. It was three, pretty late for anyone from around here to be coming home, and all his fear came back. The street was empty and silent again. He went to the bedroom door and looked out into the hall. The stairs were dark, the first floor stretched at the foot of them in blackness. He listened. Nothing. He turned on the light from the top of the stairs; the foyer was empty, the front door was still double-locked and chained the way he'd left it. He'd been looking out at the garden, so no one could have come in or gone out the back door, and he knew he'd double-locked and chained it too. He was too worked up, he told himself, and he made himself turn to go back to his warm bed, when he thought he smelled something. He took a deep breath. Definitely something. Faint, but there. A whiff of gas.

He raced down the stairs to the first floor, and through the dark, silent house to the kitchen. It was much stronger in here, and he ran to the stove. But the gas was off here; the pilot lights glowed in the dark. He blew them out, just in case; then he noticed that the window over the sink was open. A fresh breeze came through and dispelled the smell for a second. Stupid, he thought. Stupid to start a gas leak in his house and leave the window open with a fresh wind filling the kitchen. But the smell fought the fresh air, overcame it, and Carmine unlocked the back door and went out to the grill. He walked along the line, sniffing, all the way to the grill itself. But there was no smell. He ran back into the house, remembering to lock the door after him, and he raced to the phone. It could be something to do with the Bledsoe bunch, but this whole neighborhood was honeycombed with gas lines, and leaks were common. Well, he'd report another, he thought. Just a gas leak, he told himself. Happens all the time; but sweat collected under his arms and ran down his ribs. He'd call and then he'd get Rosa and the kids out of the house. Although they'd probably get it fixed in no time. They usually did. But better to miss a couple of hours of sleep than take any chances. He was ready to shout up the stairs when a man answered at 911. Carmine told him what was wrong, and it only took a second for the next connection. This man had a strong West Indian accent.

"We be dere in a flash," he said. "Whea de furnace?"

"In the basement . . . where the fuck do you think it is?"

"Calmly, my mon. Some folks got no basement. Now, you turn your thermostat all de way down, den you hop down to dat lovely basement and blow out dat pilot light. You hear me? Move!"

Carmine slammed down the phone and ran for the thermostat. He had a nightmare vision of the ring of blue flame flickering on in the gas-filled basement. He got to the thermostat and jammed the control all the way down, then ran for the basement. He recrossed the living room, the dining area, and thought the smell was much, much stronger. He started to choke, the fumes burned his eyes, and tears streamed out of them. He tore open the basement doors, ready to leap half the stairs, and, too late, he remembered the open window and the draft. He watched helplessly as the fresh air passed him and the little blue flame on the furnace gas ring danced high for a second. Then the air around him gave a giant whumf, and a fireball filled the basement and rolled up at him. It seemed slow, almost lazy. He thought he could outrun it, and he tried, screaming his wife's name as he ran.

"Rosa . . . Rosa . . ." he shrieked. The flame ball caught him in the middle of the kitchen, but he kept going. His hair burned; the flames devoured his pajamas and licked at his eyelids. The air burned, he was breathing in flames, but he kept going. He almost made it to the foot of the stairs before he collapsed.

Kurt Gelb waited around the corner in the car until he heard the muted sound of a gas explosion. He got out of the van and walked quickly to the corner with the stop sign. Lights came on in the houses around him. Across the street a man ran out onto his concrete stoop in his underwear, shrugging on a robe. A woman with a scarf around her head came out of another house. He heard cries and gasps, but he knew it was from the bystanders. Not from anyone inside the house. He waited patiently. Flames leaped at the windows, he heard glass break, and sirens screamed a few blocks away. He waited until he saw the flames at the upper windows and the whole second floor was suffused in a glow. No one came out the front door. He walked back down the block. More people had come out on the street. Some were yelling in terror and sympathy; some watched quietly. All their attention was on the burning house; no one looked at him. He walked back almost to the van, then stepped up to a Cyclone fence at the edge of the sidewalk.

The second yard in from the street belonged to the Carmine house. The sun-room back porch of the house had blown out. The yard glittered with broken glass, and the air on what had been the porch glowed red-orange. As he watched, the barbecue puffed and started to burn quietly. The yard was empty. No one had gotten out of the house at the back either.

He got into the car and drove away as the sound of the sirens closed in on the block. He had to stay in New York tonight because he had an appointment with Emily Brand's banker first thing in the morning.

CHAPTER

11

IT WAS DARK when Emily woke up, and it took her a second to remember where she was. This was Bessie's Tourist Court on old Route 9 in North Hudson. She'd escaped, and Bledsoe was dead. She looked at her watch. It was six-thirty. The room was cold and she was naked because she didn't have a nightgown. She jumped out of bed, turned on the oil heater, and raced across the cold linoleum to the bathroom. The underwear she'd washed last night hung stiff and freezing over the shower rod. She pulled it down and turned on the shower. The shower stall was freshly painted, there was plenty of hot water, and by the time she was done, the bathroom and the tiny bedroom next to it were warm and full of steam. She pulled her clothes on and looked in her wallet. She'd bought gas last night, and when she paid for the room she'd have about twenty dollars left. Not enough. She had to get more money. She hadn't eaten last night, and her stomach was sour with hunger. Maybe Mr. Bessie served breakfast. She'd seen scrubbed wooden tables with napkin holders on them in the office last night.

She went to the window. The road was empty; a dirt-and-gravel drive led to the office. The lights were on, and smoke drifted up out of the chimney. She put on Marvin's sweater, checked her purse for the rolled papers, even though she knew that they were there. She pushed the gun down under them and under the wallet and card case, and she left the cabin and crossed the driveway to the office.

Mr. Bessie was behind the counter. She smelled ham frying and fresh coffee.

" 'Morning, young lady."

She nodded. "Can I get breakfast?"

"Been serving breakfast here some thirty years. No one throws biscuits like Mrs. Bessie. Sit down."

Emily went to one of the tables, and Mr. Bessie tied on a clean white apron around his middle and came out from behind the counter.

"We got ham'n eggs, bacon'n eggs, and fresh sausage. We got hash-browns, and them biscuits, and we got hotcakes. But I should warn you, they're real Adirondack flannel cakes." He grinned at her. "Stay with you the whole day, maybe longer."

She smiled back. "Ham and eggs," she said, "and could I have three eggs . . . and the biscuits?"

Mr. Bessie left her to put in the order. It was light now; across the deserted road, she saw an old frame house with the paint blistered off the siding. It leaned out crazily in the middle, as if it had been caught in a wind. Route 9 used to be the main road from New York to Montreal, and then Rockefeller built the Northway in the sixties, and now this was almost a side road. People had to get off the highway to come here. She wondered how Mr. Bessie sold enough gas and breakfasts to stay alive. But he must have managed. The place was spotless and in good repair. Nothing defeated about Mr. Bessie or his tourist court. She heard a car crunch across the gravel and stop. Her heart jumped and she reached deep into her purse and grasped the handle of the gun.

The door opened and two men came in. They were wearing plaid wool hats and flannel jackets. Their faces were creased and their eyes had a squint, as if they spent a lot of time in the glare of the sun. They nodded to her and went to another table, and she relaxed and pulled her hand out of her purse.

They wouldn't look for her here, she thought. They'd look at Frontier Town, right off the Northway. She'd stopped there for lunch once when she drove back from New York. It was crowded and bright; there was a huge parking lot and a wild-west show for the kids. But then she heard a truck zoom by on the Northway less than half a mile away, and she knew that they'd think of Route 9 sooner or later. She couldn't get to Orin Franklin until Feinstein got back; maybe she could find Feinstein in the Bahamas . . . wherever they

167

were. Somewhere in the Caribbean, probably. If they were big with Hiltons and gambling casinos, she didn't have a chance. But they might be small and out-of-the-way. One of those places she'd seen advertised in magazines where a tanned, almost nude couple played in water that looked hot, green, and thick like paint. She'd never been to the Caribbean, she'd never even been to Florida. She'd never seen a palm tree that wasn't potted, and if they caught her, she never would. She'd spent her life in Ivy League schools and gray-painted installations from New Jersey north, and she vowed that if she got out of this she'd go to Florida or Venezuela or the Costa del Sol. If she lived.

Mr. Bessie brought out covered foil pans for the two men, and her plate of food. The men paid and left, and Emily fell to. Mr. Bessie went back around the counter and watched her eat.

"Hey, young lady, savor a little. No one's going to take it away from you."

But she couldn't slow down; she wiped egg off her plate with the biscuits, washed it all down with coffee, and heard another truck pass on the Northway. It was eight, traffic was building.

She paid, and sure enough, she had twenty dollars left. She'd have to stop at a bank somewhere. She had an ID and they could call Placid or New York to verify her account if they had to. She was rich, moderately rich; surely she could get a few thousand dollars.

And then what?

"Do you have a map?" Emily asked Mr. Bessie.

"Don't need no map," he said. "Tell me where you're going, I'll tell you how to get there."

"I don't know," she said. "I'm just touring."

He looked closely at her. "Oh?"

"Yes, I'm a schoolteacher on vacation. Thought I'd see upstate New York."

She never lied, and she must be making a mess of it, because his eyes narrowed. "I see," he said.

"So if you have any maps . . ." She trailed off.

They were quiet for a minute; then Mr. Bessie said, "None of my business, mind you, but that's a dumb story, and I wouldn't tell it around if I was you. Point one, it's too late for Easter recess and too early for summer vacation. Point two, you look as much like a schoolteacher in that outfit as Bill Purcell does—Bill Purcell drives for United Van Lines. Point three, there's been about 200 million schoolteachers on these roads in the past twenty years—schoolteachers love the mountains—but I ain't never seen one of them without another. I don't think they even take a dunk alone. Excuse the rudeness. Point four, you ain't got a scrap of luggage with you. Not even one of them little overnight duffel things that they seem to give schoolteachers along with their certificates. Point five, that car of yours is a Volvo custom turbo. Sells for around sixty thousand. No schoolteacher spends sixty thousand dollars on a car."

Mr. Bessie leaned across the counter at her. His eyes were bright in the morning light. "Now, don't get me wrong, young lady. I don't care who you are or what you do for a living. You could be a hooker for all of me. In fact the great Adirondack park could use a couple of loose ladies who'd give a man a nice piece for a K spot." Emily had no idea how much a K spot was. "But you go telling folks that story, and someone's gonna figure that maybe the trunk of that fancy car of yours is full of whatever white powder people are pumping into their arms or sniffing up their noses these days." He shook his head sadly. "That story stinks. Find another." He reached under the counter and came up with a dusty map. "Got these in eighty five," he said, "but nothing's changed much." He handed it to her. "Good luck, young lady. Don't worry, I won't tell no one I saw you, and thank you for stopping at Bessie's."

Schroon Lake was the next town south. But it was right off the highway, and she decided to go east. It was less than twenty miles to Port Grace, the next black dot on the map, but the road was so rutted and winding that it took her almost an hour to get there. Somewhere along the way she passed a place that the map said was Moriah. She expected a little town as lovely as the name, but all she saw were a few trailers and two houses. One was extremely neat, with a patch of lawn reclaimed from the woods. The other had a torn screen porch covering the front, and an abandoned car rusting in the front yard. She could smell Port Grace before she got there; industrial fumes that smelled like sulfur filled

169

the air and hung over the big lake that separated New York and Vermont. It must have been a pretty town once. From a distance, it still was. But on the town streets the smell reigned, paint peeled on the houses, porches sagged, and the downtown stucco buildings were patched with rot. The people on the street looked dispirited, the one movie house was "temporarily" closed for repairs. But the marquee sagged, the ticket window was broken, the frame around it rusted.

The Union Bank and Trust Building had patches of stain on the front that made the stone look diseased. The uniformed guard seemed snappy in spite of the decay around him, and he unlocked the door ceremoniously at the stroke of nine and opened it with a flourish. Emily told him what she wanted and he directed her to a group of desks at the end of the room. Emily picked a woman with gray curls piled on top of her head, held by a silver-colored hair net. The woman's nameplate read "Mrs. H. Porter." The woman eyed Emily uncertainly. Emily was still wearing Marvin's old sweater, and her work pants were wrinkled and too heavy for the sunny day.

"May I help you?" the woman asked.

"I have to cash a large out-of-town check," Emily said. She opened her purse, saw Starrett's gun, and held the flap of the purse over the opening so Mrs. Porter couldn't see the gleam of metal. "It's on American Trust." Emily found the right card and gave it to Mrs. Porter. Mrs. Porter took it gingerly. "The man's name is Simmons," Emily said, "and he'll verify my accounts there."

Mrs. Porter stared at the card, then back at Emily. She'd been in banking for fifteen years, and even though Port Grace was a backwater, she prided herself on not being a hick. The card was gray plastic—not gold or silver, but plain gray—and was signed by one of the American Trust senior officers. Mrs. Porter examined Emily and what she saw wasn't reassuring; her nails were unpolished, her hands were rough, she wore no makeup, her hair looked like she cut it herself, and her work pants—*work pants*—were too heavy for the warm day. She had on one of those Polack sweaters, and surely no one had worn glasses like those in fifteen years. Mrs. Porter's own glasses were huge with pale pink frames and a tiny diamond embedded in the lower corner of the right lens. She knew rich people didn't necesarily wear good clothes and stylish glasses with diamonds in them. But they didn't look like this, either. Mrs. Porter examined the card. Emily A. Brand, Ph.D. The degree reassured Mrs. Porter somewhat, because she believed that too much education made women eccentric.

"Does Mr. Simmons know you personally?" she asked.

Emily nodded.

"How large a check do you wish to cash?"

Emily thought a moment. She didn't know when she'd get to another bank. She never thought much about money, and she had no idea how much she'd need.

"Twenty thousand," Emily said.

The woman inhaled sharply. "That is a great deal of money."

"Yes," Emily said. "I see that."

The woman wasn't eccentric, Mrs. Porter decided, she was insane. But it was her money . . . maybe.

"I'll have to call Mr. Simmons. He will be able to describe you?"

"Yes. But I have a license with my picture. And my ID from the lab. I *am* Emily Brand."

"Then the only question is whether or not you have twenty thousand dollars," Mrs. Porter said coolly.

Emily smiled, and Mrs. Porter had to stop herself from smiling back. The woman had a pretty smile; it almost made *her* pretty, Mrs. Porter thought.

"Oh, I do," Emily said. "I have a great deal more."

The happiness was infectious. For a second Mrs. Porter almost felt as if it were her money too, and in spite of herself, she reached out and patted the rough veiny hand clutching the pocketbook.

"Well, sit right here, dear. We'll see what we can do."

Mrs. Porter was buzzed through a steel gate in the back, and Emily waited.

At nine-twenty, N. Barton Simmons' secretary buzzed him to tell him that there was a customer call from the Union Bank in Port Grace, New York.

"What's the customer's name?" he asked softly.

"Emily Brand."

Simmons was quiet.

"Mr. Simmons?"

He said, "I'll call back."

"But the customer's waiting."

"I said I'll call back."

He put the phone down, crossed his arms on his desk, and rested his head against them. He hated what he had to do but they would ruin his life if he didn't do it.

Kurt Gelb had come to see him at nine this morning. Only twenty minutes ago. The appointment had been made late last night by Paul Stockton, director of the NCEC. Simmons said he would give Mr. Gelb a few minutes of his time and Stockton had been smoothly grateful.

Gelb was tall and rugged-looking with an actorish face. His features were regular, he had good skin and all his hair and he should have been handsome, but wasn't. He carried a manila envelope without a case and he showed Simmons his ID, which was government but vague. He didn't tell Mr. Simmons that he was glad to meet him, he didn't comment on the fine spring weather. Without preamble he had said, "You have a substantial trust account in the name of Emily A. Brand."

Simmons felt himself flush. "We don't discuss our customers, Mr. Gelb."

"We don't want to discuss her, we want to know if she tries to get money."

"Then we don't have anything else to say to each other, Mr. Gelb. Please leave my office."

Gelb didn't answer. He pried open the envelope.

"Mr. Gelb, if you're not out of my office in three minutes, I'm going to call a guard."

Gelb drew out several eight-by-ten photographic prints.

Simmons went on, his voice tight and angry. "I don't know who you people think you are, but you can tell Mr. Stockton . . ." He stopped with a catch, like a machine shorting out, because Geld had laid the photographs on his desk facing him.

Simmons stared silently at the top one. It was a photograph of him, taken two years ago. In it Simmons was naked on his back on a bed. His head was straining back, his lips were pulled over his teeth in an expression of ecstasy. His

172

face looked shockingly young, almost beautiful. A young man was kneeling over him. His name was Bobby Millet, and Simmons had picked him up one dead-freezing and despairing night at the Trinity in the West Village. He'd seen him on and off for almost a year; then Bobby drifted away.

Gelb moved the top photograph so Simmons could see the one under it. It was the same bed, the same man. Now Simmons was crouching behind Bobby, his arms wrapped around his body.

Simmons put his hands flat on the top of his desk; he felt the blotter soak up sweat from his palms. He knew how Paul Stockton and this ice-faced man had gotten the pictures. Bobby Millet was a hooker who'd do anything for a hundred bucks. But why Paul Stockton and the NCEC should have wanted to blackmail Simmons two years ago was harder to figure. Simmons wasn't a political man. He was a Republican, but that was by birth, not conviction, and he'd never given any campaign more than a hundred dollars. The only cause that ever moved him involved a toxic-waste dump in New Jersey about five years ago. The people's wells had been poisoned, their livestock was sick, the vegetables and flowers that they tried to grow died. Their children's teeth rotted, they had asthma. He'd seen them on TV; the cameras caught them as they left their homes for the last time because the houses and land were condemned. Some looked angry, some cried; but most of them couldn't find words for the reporters, even to complain. They looked unutterably lost and bewildered, and in a rare flash of fellow feeling Simmons realized that he was lost and bewildered too, and had been most of his life.

He sent money to the relief fund. He started supporting groups that fought for toxic-waste control. He was a rich man, and by the end of three years he'd contributed over half a million dollars to the cause of toxic-waste control. Maybe that had worried Stockton and the NCEC and made them want leverage against him. He stared down at his middle-aged, almost flabby body in the photograph. They had it now. He grinned sourly; the board of directors of American Trust would never understand. His wife, Kaye, might forgive him because she loved him. But she might not; he might lose her, and he realized as he looked at the grainy,

173

shiny black-and-white of himself riding Bobby Millet that he loved her too, and couldn't imagine his life without her.

He looked up at Gelb. The man's eyes were clear, disinterested, without malice. Gelb wasn't bluffing; he would show the pictures to Kaye and to old man Gamadge. He would send copies of them to Simmons' son at Williams and to his daughter and her husband. Mr. Gelb didn't care one way or the other.

Simmons wasn't frightened any longer. He did not sweat or tremble; he was terribly, exhaustingly sad. "What do you want to me to?" he asked Gelb.

Gelb had told him, and now he was going to do it. He was going to betray a customer because he was a scared faggot, and then he was going to lunch at the Downtown Association and pretend to his friends, his colleagues, and the men he'd gone to school with, that he was still an honorable man.

He went to the window of his office and looked down. Even if Kaye and his children forgave him, he could never make it right because he could never give up the Trinity or the Bobby Millets.

He looked down at the street. Traffic was thick, and the street was so narrow he couldn't see the sidewalk. He wondered how it would be to climb out, hang on to the stone gargoyles that framed the windows, then let go. He imagined the freedom of sailing silently out into space wrapped in his own momentum until he hit the top of the blue car stuck in traffic. His body would shatter and spill. He would spatter the cars and pedestrians with blood . . .

He jerked himself back from the window and went to the phone. Emily Brand waited in Port Grace; Gelb, or someone like him, waited at the 518 number, wherever that was. He picked up the phone and dialed the number Gelb had given him.

"I can't imagine what's keeping him," Mrs. Porter told Emily. "Maybe the computer won't come on line. It happens. . . ."

It was ten; Emily had been waiting an hour. She knew something was wrong. Simmons knew her and Susie, he'd known her father. He knew she had money. She had only twenty dollars, but it would have to do. She stood up.

174

Mrs. Porter looked worried. "Dr. Brand—"

"I have to go to the ladies' room," Emily said, and just then two men came through the front door into the bank. One wore a blazer, the other a raincoat. They weren't dressed like local people. They stood at the door and looked around.

The one in the raincoat saw Emily; his eyes stopped on her for an instant, then moved on, but she knew that he had recognized her. He said something to the one in the blazer. Both men walked over to the armed guard who'd opened the door for Emily. They took out card cases and showed them to the guard. Emily strained to see. The guard's eyes widened.

Emily shoved her hand into her purse and gripped Starrett's gun. She stepped back away from Mrs. Porter's desk. Her butt bumped the iron gate that Mrs. Porter had gone through to make her call.

The guard looked at her, and all three of them started toward her across the stone floor. Emily smiled at the guard as dazzlingly as she could.

Some smile, John once said. *Smile at the reactor, Emily, and it'll light the world for you.*

The guard smiled back before he could stop himself, and hesitated. The other two kept coming, and Emily turned her back on them and faced the area behind the waist-high metal fence. Another armed guard stood next to an open vault door. He was looking out the side window, probably wishing that he were out of here on such a nice day, fishing or swimming at the lake. Emily shuddered. The fish were gone; no one could swim in the acid-filled water anymore. She slid the gun out of her purse, keeping it low, hoping the folds of Marvin's sweater would cover it. The gate lock was large, and she was close. She didn't have to aim to hit it. She pulled back the safety and then the guard behind the gate had to take off his hat and wipe his forehead. Everything slowed down. The guard moved as if he were trapped in taffy. His handkerchief came up to his head a micron at a time and he wiped the sweat in slow motion. She heard the men's footsteps behind her, and the guard finally put his hat back on. His hands were free, and Emily fired at the lock on the gate.

The shot roared through the stone chamber, crashed against the gate, echoed off the walls and floor, and the alarm went off. A siren screamed, sank, screamed again and Emily whirled around to face the two men. They were reaching inside their coats.

Move, Emily wanted to yell. *Faster!*

The guns came out and cleared their clothes, and Emily glanced back. The guard's gun was out too, his arm stretched to aim, as soon as he could figure out what to aim at, and Emily dropped to the floor, leaving the armed men facing the armed guard.

The men froze. They were supposed to get Emily Brand, not some hick bank guard in a dying town. But the guard saw the guns, and he fired. He hit the man in the raincoat midbody. The man spun around, careened into Mrs. Porter's desk, and fell. The man in the blazer knew what to do now, and he aimed dead at the guard, but he'd forgotten the door guard; his gun was out too, and he must have been unwilling to let anyone shoot his partner, no matter what kind of ID they had, because he aimed to kill. His first shot hit the man in the blazer in the back of the neck. His throat exploded out over his collar, and blood spewed through the air, splashed the gate and Emily's leg. The guard fired again, and the man crashed forward across the gate and hung there.

Emily stayed flat and pulled herself across the floor by her arms, like a commando in an old war movie. The floor was slick, and she slid easily along the wall behind the desks. Men and women screamed, the siren crashed around them. She kept pulling herself until she was a few feet from the door. She shoved the gun back into her purse and stood up, back to the wall.

Everyone in the bank—tellers, customers, and the guard —ran toward the back where the two men lay. No one looked at Emily. She stepped clear of the wall and walked sedately out of the bank into the sunny sulfur-stinking air.

People were running out of the few stores up the street toward the bank. Cars screeched to a stop and people climbed out to see what was going on. More sirens wailed in the distance.

Emily crossed the street to the Volvo. A man was leaning against the fender, watching the bank door.

"What happened?" he asked. His voice was laconic, but his eyes were full of excitement.

176

She didn't have time; the door guard would remember her in a second. Look for her. The man glanced down at Emily's leg.

"That blood?" he asked.

"Yes," she said. "Two men are shot in there."

"Holy shit," the man said. He leaped away from the car and ran across the street to the crowd collecting at the bank entrance. Emily got into the car and started it just as three squad cars raced into the block, lights and sirens going. They pulled over and stopped. Men poured out of the cars and ran into the bank, pulling at their holsters. The center of the street was clear, and Emily pulled away from the curb and drove slowly down the main street toward Lake Champlain. She kept the windows closed against the smell. She didn't want to use up extra gas for the air conditioner, and sweat ran down her face and neck and wet the collar of her shirt. A mile south of town the grass looked brighter, the houses cleaner. She opened the window; the sulfur came in faint streams through the air. Then it was gone and the air was fresh and cool. She saw the turnoff for the bridge to Vermont and decided to take it.

CHAPTER

DAVID OPENED HIS eyes and saw his wife's face hanging over him like a mask suspended from the ceiling. He closed his eyes and let himself lose consciousness again.

He dreamed that *she* was standing in a pool of blood looking up at him. She was bare-legged except for heavy socks that were soaked with blood. Her eyes were clear and calm.

You won't get me, she said. It wasn't a cry or a threat, but a statement of fact.

He tried to move, but he was pinned to a metal wall. She walked away, and he bellowed at her and fought the wall, but it held him, and then it started to absorb him. He felt the metal soften; his fingers melted into the steel and were gone. She was on the stairs, almost to the door. She'd won again, she was free. The wall sucked in his hand and the toe of his shoe . . .

Close by, he heard his father's voice, "Don't cry, Davy, it's all right. Davy . . . wake up," and he opened his eyes.

His father stood next to the bed. The ceiling was pale green, the light was too bright. Something stuck to his face, and he pulled his hand free and raised it to his face, half-expecting to feel molten steel sliding across his cheek. He felt dry gauze and tape. His face was bandaged. He looked at his father.

"It's not broken," his father said. "Only a gash, inside your mouth. They stitched it. You had a concussion . . . but not so bad . . . and you lost a tooth. You'll be fine in a couple of days."

David worked his tongue around in his mouth, looking for the empty space, but he couldn't find it. He looked past his father. His mother was sitting in a chair, her knitting in her lap.

"Abo," David groaned. His father looked at her helplessly. She came to the bed.

"Abo," David said again.

She took a pad and pencil out of her knitting bag and handed it to him. The white light hit the paper and jabbed into his eyes.

"Ite."

"The light off?" she asked. He nodded and she turned off the bed lamp and the overhead light. The room turned dim, the pain eased, and he wrote, "Talbot."

She nodded. "He's been here all morning. I'll get him."

David closed his eyes. When he opened them again, Talbot was next to the bed and his mother and father hovered in the background. Talbot smiled at David and drew a pair of mirrored sunglasses out of a plastic case.

"Your mother said the light bothered you," Talbot said gently. "I got these downstairs in the gift shop."

David put them on, fitting the earpiece over the bandage. The glasses turned the room green; Talbot and his parents were gray and ghostly.

David wrote on the pad, "Where is she?"

Talbot spoke to the Luccis. "Please excuse us for a few minutes."

David's mother left the room, but his father came to the bed, leaned over, and kissed David on his unbandaged cheek. Then his father said sternly to Talbot, "Not too long, he needs rest," and he left them alone.

David tapped the pad in Talbot's hand. Talbot pulled up one of the chairs and sat down. "We found her in a bank on Lake Champlain. Stockton got two of the men who were watching the Northway over there . . ." He stopped. David groaned at him to go on, and Talbot took a deep breath and said, "One of them was shot in the gut. He's in a hospital in Burlington. The other got it in the neck. He's dead. She . . . she's gone."

David made a strangled sound and Talbot looked scared

179

and reached for the call button. Then he saw that David was laughing. The enormity of the fuck-up hit him too, and he giggled softly, then laughed until the two of them were howling.

Outside in the hall, David's mother and father heard them and looked at each other. A nurse passed the door, heard the noise, and rushed into the room.

"Mr. Lucci," she cried.

Talbot jumped up and barred her way. "Get out."

She looked at David. He goggled at her through the mirrored sunglasses, half of his face twisted in a snarling grin. She backed away.

"Out . . ." David moaned at her. "Out."

She fled, and Talbot stood over the bed.

"We'll get Brand," he said. "She'll pay for what she did to you. She went to the bank for money she didn't get. She wouldn't have done that unless she needed it, so she's broke. Or almost broke. Stockton's alerted every major computer in the Northeast, so she can't use plastic. She's probably running out of gas . . . Stockton's got the White House covered. She can't get to Franklin. Feinstein's out of the country. The boyfriend's wired, so is the sister. They've covered the people at Princeton . . ."

David grabbed the pad and wrote, "Too much to cover."

Talbot shook his head. "Only three at Princeton." He smiled. "She wasn't exactly sociable."

See, Emily, David thought, *you need other people. Other people are everything. If you had five friends in the whole fucking world, you might make it. But now you're dead.*

His cheek and jaw hurt and he needed Demerol. But it would make him groggy and he had to think. After a minute he wrote, "Police."

Talbot answered, "She hadn't gone to them. Stockton and Gelb—Gelb's with us now, by the way—don't think she will."

David shook his head and wrote, "Use police. Beecham thing stupid."

Talbot didn't know what David meant at first. Then he figured it out, and he smiled slowly at his son-in-law. "Yes," he said. "Of course."

"Now," David wrote.

"Immediately," Talbot said.

"You had access to explosives," Denny Robinson accused Ed Beecham. Karl Banyan stared out of the window, and Beecham wanted to shake him and yell: *Look at me, Karl. It's Eddie. The one who pushed your nose back straight that time that Johnny Boston broke it in the school yard. Eddie, who took Rags home when your mother wouldn't let you keep her . . . Eddie, who pulled you out of Tupper when the ice broke that time in November. It's Eddie Beecham, Karl. I couldn't kill my daddy, I couldn't kill anybody.*

Robinson said, "You could have hidden them—"

"Sure," Beecham sneered, "for fifteen years, just in case I take a notion to blow my father to hell one day. And if I did, Denny, then where were they? Why couldn't you and your big-time dogs get a smell of them?"

Robinson didn't answer because Beecham had him there. This morning ten men and three dogs had pulled Ed Beecham's house apart. They pulled boxes off the closet shelves, searched the attic, and found the desiccated remains of the moose head his father had tried to stuff himself. They found his mother's wedding dress and his poor dead Elaine's poetry books from high school, but no explosives. They tore up the shed floors and half-demolished the chicken coop, and found nothing. The dogs gave up, lay down and refused to move, but the men wouldn't stop. They ripped up the garden, destroying the early peas that his father had planted; then they went down to the riverbank, dug in a likely spot, and found the skeleton of Rags where he and his brother Will had buried her almost thirty years ago. The little mutt had been hit by a car one dead black summer night, and dragged herself all the way from Route 86 to the front porch before she died. Will had been killed in El Salvador in '85. He stepped on a land mine and the army said that there wasn't enough left to send home. So Will didn't even have as much grave as poor old Rags.

Ed Beecham's throat burned. He stared down at the table-top and swallowed hard. The noon whistle blew and Sheriff Steuben came in with a tray of sandwiches and coffee. Robinson grabbed one and started to eat.

Steuben said, "Two more feds just arrived. They want to talk to us. One of you stay with the prisoner." Banyan rushed out of the room without looking back and Beecham and Robinson were alone.

Robinson finished his sandwich, then looked at Beecham's. It was fresh tuna salad, on Mrs. Steuben's homemade bread, but just the smell turned Beecham's stomach.

"Want that?" Robinson said.

Beecham shook his head, and Robinson slid the paper plate in front of him and started eating.

"Who're the feds?" Beecham asked.

Robinson shrugged. "Snotty bunch who think we fill our pants because we don't work for something with initials and its own building in Maryland."

Robinson washed down the last of Beecham's sandwich with the coffee. They heard voices in the hall, Banyan laughed loudly, and the door banged open. Banyan stood on the threshold; he was red-faced and beaming, and for the first time since the nightmare had started, he looked right into Ed Beecham's eyes.

"Get your skinny ass outta here," Banyan said. Then he gave a high wild laugh and shrieked, "Go home, shitbreath. It's over. You're innocent . . . of murder anyway."

That night they bought a quart of Old Crow and tried to drink the whole thing in Ed Beecham's kitchen. The feds brought new evidence with them, Banyan told Beecham; the old man had bought the policy after all. "Must have been scared that his jerk-off, ass-faced son would lose the farm without him."

Beecham drank and let Banyan ramble on for a few minutes, then he said, "Someone blew up that plane, Karl. Who?"

Banyan stared into his Dixie cup of bourbon. "Can't say."

"Yes you can. I got a right to know."

After a minute Banyan said solemnly, "That's the truth. But you gotta keep your hole shut."

Beecham nodded, and Banyan said, "It was one of the women up at the physics lab. Name of Brand."

Beecham turned white and whispered, "*No*," but Banyan kept talking.

"Seems she had a crazy fight with her boss up there. Something about a new design that she wanted the credit for. Wasn't that important, it turns out, but she's not all there—"

"No!" Beecham yelled.

Banyan was startled. "Whadaya mean, no? What do you know about her?"

"She's a no bullshit woman, keeps her tongue attached to her brain. She wouldn't kill—"

"Well, maybe you don't know as much as you think you do," Banyan yelled back. "Babe's way over thirty, lives alone, works in that hole in the hill, in this ass-end-of-nowhere town. They got a psych sheet on her longer than Tom Crandall's dork. God knows the last time the poor bitch got laid, if ever."

Banyan stopped because Beecham wasn't listening to him. He was staring past Banyan as if he saw something, and maybe he did. They were drunk enough, Banyan thought. Maybe, while he was palavering about that crazy bitch, old nan Beecham's ghost had slipped into the kitchen and projected itself on the refrigerator door.

"Eddie?" Banyan said uncertainly.

"How'd you know about the policy?" Beecham asked, still staring past his friend.

"What?"

"The policy got to me at three, you were here at three-fifteen. How'd you know about it?"

"A tip."

"Who from?" Beecham asked.

"Anonymous." Banyan was uneasy. He wanted to bury the whole thing, because he thought it had been too close . . . closer than Eddie would ever know. The federals weren't just law-enforcement men; they smelled of murder, and looking back now, he'd have bet his pension that Ed Beecham would never have made it to Elizabethtown alive, much less to trial.

Beecham pulled his eyes away from whatever specter he saw, and looked at Banyan. "Karl, how much did that policy cost?"

"Look, Eddie, let's drop it."

"How much?"

"Fifty bucks."

Beecham said thickly, "But my daddy only had thirty on him, Karl. And he didn't have no checking account or credit cards. So how'd he buy it?"

Banyan didn't answer.

"He didn't," Beecham said. "*They* did. But to do that they had to know it was going to happen. Karl . . . they killed my daddy."

"Blow it out your ass," Banyan cried.

Beecham ignored him. "They killed the old man and framed me, and now they're framing her. We gotta stop 'em Karl. You gotta help me. . . ."

Beecham's eyes were glazing fast; he was very drunk, and Banyan didn't want to hear another word of this madness. He poured a stiff slug for Beecham, and Beecham threw it down. "Stinks, officer," he moaned. "The whole thing stinks. They killed my daddy . . . we gotta get 'em . . ." Beecham's head sank to the tabletop and rested on one arm. The other arm dangled at his side.

"Eddie?" Banyan said. There was no answer. Banyan capped the bottle and put it in the cupboard for another night. Now there would *be* another night, thank God. He staggered out of the kitchen to the back bedroom, found an afghan folded at the foot of the bed, and brought it back to the kitchen without falling over anything. He draped it across Beecham's shoulders, tucking it around the front so it would stay on, and he went to the kitchen door. Halfway across the dooryard he stumbled and almost went flat on his ass in the mud. He was too drunk to drive home or anywhere else. He turned and made it back up the steps and through the kitchen to the living room. He collapsed on the couch, and blackness closed around him. He started to fade into it; then he came to with a start. He had a sudden sickening feeling that Ed Beecham was right. The evidence stank, the feds stank. They killed the old man and all those other poor slobs. That meant that Brand would never make it back to Elizabethtown, any more than Eddie would have. Eddie wanted him to do something about it, but that was out of the question. They were big boys, and he was a small-time pigshit state cop from the hills. No way he could let his ass get into this one. Not even for Eddie. Against his will, he thought about Emily Brand. No one knew where she was. On the run, he thought, as his mind—at long last, and thank God—finally started to go blank. On the run with half of the Western world on her tail.

Red shimmered behind her closed eyelids. Her back ached, and the red glowed and ran like the blood on the reactor-room wall. Two men were dead, and Emily hated death. Just before her mother had died, Harriet found mouse turds in the kitchen of the house and called the exterminator. He was an old man with eyes so light they almost blended into the whites. He smelled of old sweat and DDT. He came with packets of poisoned pellets, and he put them all through the house, grumbling that houses this old always had mice, and if people had any sense, they'd buy cats and stop trying to poison the whole world.

After a few days, the pellets had disappeared and Emily heard scrabbling in the walls. She knew it was the mice running to escape the poison burning in their guts. In a week the scrabbling stopped and certain rooms started to smell. Emily knew that the mice were rotting in the wall; the magical mechanism that had sparked their tiny brains, pumped blood through thread-thin veins, was destroyed and putrefying. It made Emily sick. She stayed outside in the afternoons until it was time to see her mother, and she had trouble sleeping at night. Harriet had killed the mice, and Emily was angry at her. She'd never been angry before or since that she could remember, but she still hated death.

The red light brightened and she shaded her face with her hand and opened her eyes. It was the sun coming through the stained-glass window of the church she'd slept in last night. She sat up. Brilliant red fragments slid across her hands and clothes.

Two men—billions of atoms arranged in a pattern that could never be repeated—were dead because of a roll of paper in her purse. She would call NARCON and tell them they could have the plans and she would swear to disappear. NARCON could build the reactor themselves or burn the plans, and no one else would die.

The door next to the altar opened and an old man wearing a sweater like the one she had on came out carrying a dust mop and an aerosol can. He saw Emily and stopped. " 'Morning," he said.

"Good morning. Is there a bathroom here?"

He squinted at her. "D'ja sleep here last night?"

"Yes, I'm sorry."

"Don't be. Church is meant to be a sanctuary, ain't it? Toilet's down the stairs from the vestibule. Let the water run in the sink, it'll get hot by and by."

The little lavatory was tiled and freezing. She used the toilet, then ran the water until it was hot and filled the basin. She took off her clothes and washed. The hot water felt good for a second; then she started shivering. She dried her skin with brown paper towels and put her clothes back on. She started to comb her hair, and was arrested by her face in the mirror. She took off her glasses and leaned close to the mirror to see herself. Her face was pale, there were circles under her eyes, and her cheekbones stood out like rocks.

Lucci and NARCON didn't want her plans or vows of secrecy, they wanted her dead. She knew it was true the instant she thought it.

They'd come out killing. First Marvin and the people on the plane. Then they had tried to kill her, and they'd keep trying. That was wise of them, she thought in a detached way that felt more normal for her, because she wasn't going to send them the papers in her purse or disappear and stop causing trouble.

"Stubborn bitch," Marvin used to call her when he got mad.

He was right. She was going to build the thing, unless they killed her.

Poor broad, Luther thought.

The woman in front of the counter looked exhausted; her clothes were wrinkled as if she'd slept in them. He weighed the three envelopes she gave him, then looked at the addresses. One was to the President of the United States, one to a Bruce Feinstein, also at the White House, and the last was to the New York *Times*.

Poor, crazy broad, he thought sadly. "That'll be seven dollars," he said.

She opened her wallet and he saw that it was almost empty. She gave him a ten, probably her last, and he made change.

"Thank you," she said. Her voice was low and cultured.

"Thank *you*," Luther said politely. She walked away, and Luther noticed a stain on one leg of her trousers. It was a long, ugly rust-colored streak, and it looked like blood. She opened the door of the Marbleton, Vermont, post office and walked out.

He kept seeing that stain. It startled him, like a bug running out of a cabinet. She'd bled on herself, then let the blood soak in and dry and didn't change her clothes. It was sickening; it didn't go with the image he'd had of an eccentric young woman who sent rambling letters to the President and the *Times* protesting vivisection or the fate of some little bird that no one gave a shit for. Then he thought it might not be her blood, and that frightened him.

He examined the envelopes. They were cheap and handwritten. There was no return address, only a name, E. A. Brand, Ph.D. They seemed tainted, like the woman, and he picked them up gingerly to put them in the mail bin. They were stuffed and heavy, and suddenly he remembered that the French consul had been blown out of the window of his apartment by a letter bomb last month, and a few weeks before that a secretary at the Israeli embassy had her face blown off. He put the envelopes carefully on the ledge under the counter and went in back to call the sheriff.

Emily was on Vermont 303 heading south out of Marbleton when she saw flashing lights in the mirror. She slowed to let the cruiser pass, but it stayed on her tail. She was doing forty in a fifty zone, her taillights were all right, and she hadn't braked for miles anyway. The road was empty; she was the one they wanted, and she didn't know why.

The bank guard back in New York hadn't seen her car and didn't know her license number. The other men might know, but they didn't look like they could tell anyone.

She pulled over on the shoulder, making sure that the tires on the left side stayed on the pavement. The cruiser pulled all the way into the gravel and stopped. Emily left the motor running and the clutch engaged. The cruiser left its motor running too, and both men got out and came up on the Volvo. They moved cautiously, their feet crunching in the gravel as they came up around the car. She watched them in the side-view mirrors. They held their hands out from their sides; the straps on their holsters were unsnapped and flapped as they walked. They were ready to draw and shoot and she didn't know why. Then she remembered that the bank guard had been impressed with the men's ID; a NARCON employee card wouldn't do that, so they weren't NARCON men, they were government, like Bledsoe. NARCON and whatever government agency they owned could tell the police anything. The police would believe them. Why shouldn't they? What did they know about Emily Brand and the roll of papers in her purse?

Emily eased the car into first. The men were at the back door, their hands taut and ready for anything.

She waited another second, then she floored the accelerator and popped the clutch. The car leaped ahead on the shoulder. The left wheels gripped pavement, the right rear skidded slightly on gravel, and the car raced up the shoulder. She shifted up, turned the wheel, and the Volvo came roaring up out of the gravel and onto the road. She heard shouts and looked in the mirror. They were racing back to the cruiser.

The Volvo speedometer went to 110, but Ed Beecham had said the car would do 130 or more, and he'd patted the hood like he would a dog. She shifted up, then floored it again and felt the turbo slide in.

The police car charged forward, trying to get onto the road; the wheels spun, gravel and white dust blew up from the shoulder. They hit the siren and it screamed after her. The turbo whined like an excited animal; the needle froze at 110. The siren receded, the Volvo lay to the road, and the wind crashed around her. Trees, rocks, brooks, and little houses flashed past her; the siren was gone, and now she had no idea how fast she was going. The turbo was quiet; she was cruising. The wind tore around her, but inside the car it was quiet, as if she were outrunning noise. She was drunk with the speed and she knew that she should slow down, but she kept her foot to the floor and the car ran as if it were glued to the road. Mr. Beecham was right. It was a wonderful car.

A sign flashed past—Route 30 West. She remembered the map; the road led back into New York, and she decided to take it. There were more roads in New York, it was harder to patrol. By instinct, she knew to brake with gentle, steady pressure; the car slowed evenly, slowed more, and she raced around the turn into Route 30 at seventy.

The road was bumpy, and windier than the one she'd come off. She slowed more, and the scenery caught up with her. The road was empty and quiet; the siren and cruiser were back on 303, struggling south toward Poultney.

Route 30 changed to 22A, and she was in New York. Little towns slipped by: Raceville, North Granville, West Granville, and a place called Rock Corners which was nothing more than a sign with an empty farm truck parked next to it. She saw a few other cars, but none of them tried to follow her. She turned onto Route 4, and just south of Glens Falls she pulled into a McDonald's, parked next to another Volvo, and bought a Big Mac and a thick shake. She brought the food back to the car and ate in the parking lot while she looked at the map and tried to plan.

They'd set the police on her; they knew her car and her license plate. She had to get another car. Glens Falls was small, but there'd be a used-car dealer somewhere. He'd trade even for the Volvo—it was worth a fortune. But used-car dealers kept records, the transaction would go into a computer, and NARCON would know about the new car. She could steal a car, but she'd have to leave the Volvo behind, and they would find it, so it would come to the same thing. She could try to make a private trade with someone, but it was too risky. There might be a reward out for her—they did a lot of that lately. Or the person might get scared afterward and go to the police: "I'm sorry, officer; it seemed like a good deal, that's all. I didn't know Emily Brand was a wanted woman. I can keep the Volvo? Great. She's in a gray Mazda, license number . . ."

It wouldn't work. She could just abandon the car and try to hitch a ride south, but that was madness. They'd found her on tiny 303, they were certainly watching all the state routes south. She could try to get to a plane, but there were only a few airports between here and Albany, and they'd be able to watch all of them. Even the little private ones. Besides, she didn't have money for a plane ticket or bus ticket. The Volvo had already saved her twice; it might save her again. She didn't want to give it up.

The custom Volvo looked like the other big Volvos. Only

189

the weight and the motor set it apart—and the color. It was the only black sedan that Volvo shipped to the U.S. and she'd had to wait months for it to get here.

She finished her hamburger and shake. She had six dollars, and a quarter of a tank of gas left. She would have to risk using a card soon.

She pulled out of the parking lot and drove into Glens Falls. The sun was high, but the town looked gray and tired; a huge smelter of some kind stood out against the sky and dominated the horizon over the town. She came to a small variety store off at the edge of the main drag. The parking lot next to it was empty except for a big truck with green paint peeling off its sides. She pulled around the truck and parked, and when she looked back from the road, the Volvo was hidden. Inside, the store was plain, with thin-slate wood floors and painted bins of merchandise. It was dim and cool, there was a musty, homey smell, and she leaned against the cash-register counter in a daze of tiredness. An old man came out of the back. His skin was thin and pale; tiny black veins crossed his cheeks and the sides of his nose.

"Can I use your phone book?" she asked.

He groaned as he bent down behind the counter and lifted the thin book onto the top next to the register. Then he leaned on his crossed arms and watched her open it. She stepped back, holding the book up so he couldn't see the "Auto Paint" heading in the Yellow Pages.

"From around here?" he asked.

"No," she answered. She found an ad for "Smitty's Paint Shop, *collision specialists*" in Glens Falls.

"Where from?"

She almost said Lake Placid, then caught herself. She wasn't really from there anyway. She wasn't from anywhere. She might as well have sprung full grown from the ground pine at the base of an old spruce, walked out of the forest and seen the world for the first time five minutes ago. She didn't seem to have as much substance as this old man with black veins in his nose. He had this store and a wife, probably, and children. John loved her, and would help her if he could, but Carmine said they'd tapped his phone. If they killed her and hid her body, he would look for her for a while. A long time, to give him credit. But Susie was like Emily. Susie was

190

stubborn and she would look for Emily for the next thirty years, and Steven would help her because he couldn't touch Emily's money until he could prove that she was dead. Poor sweet, fat Steven, she thought. If she lived, she would make a new will and leave everything to him alone. Thinking about John and Susie and Steven and all the plans she was making if she got out of this alive made her smile.

"Something funny?" the old man snapped at her.

"No . . . nothing . . ." She handed the phone book back.

"Well," he asked, "where're you from?"

"Wilton, Connecticut," she said. That seemed to satisfy him, and he put the phone book back under the counter. She asked him if he knew where Don's Market was, because the ad for Smitty's had said it was right across the street.

Smitty's Paint Shop was just a cut-out place in the road with a neatly paved drive and turn-around. The mountains were black pyramids in the distance. She had six dollars and the credit cards she was afraid to use. She would have to give Smitty a Lake Placid check.

The entrance to the paint shop looked like a car wash. It was empty, the sprayers silent, and she went into the office. A man about thirty with a beard like golden thread sat behind a desk made from crates and a slab of granite. A radio on the desk next to him played Handel's Largo, and the stately, incredibly beautiful music went out the open door, across the dusty yard. Emily imagined the fading chords spreading into the mountains and across the lakes to the north, and for a second she was almost homesick.

"I wanted to get my car painted," she said.

He swung his feet off the desk and looked at the clock. "It's after two. Might not finish before dark. Can you leave—?"

Emily shook her head violently.

He stared at her. Then he said, "Okay, miss, let's see what we've got."

He stopped dead in the doorway when he saw the Volvo. "Is it scraped?" he asked.

"I don't know."

He walked around the car. Inside, the music changed to a medieval chant with a slow insistent minor beat. "Gregorian chants," Smitty said. "I love them. You have the registration?"

"It's in the glove compartment," she said, but he didn' ask to see it.

"It'll cost one-twenty-five," he said.

"All right."

He went through the entrance of the paint tunnel, she heard blowers start up. He came out with a bucket of soapy water, unhooked a hose from the side of the building, and washed the car. After that, he taped plastic-coated paper over the windows and chrome. He worked carefully.

"Been real slow," he said.

"I'm sorry," Emily said.

"Doesn't matter. Spring's always slow. People concentrate on their houses. Save the cars for summer. Gives me a chance to read and do some writing. I'm a writer. Had some stories published in one of those reviews no one's ever heard of, and I'm writing a novel. Winters're good too. Me and my girl go up into the mountains on the weekends, to Blue Lake. There's a museum there with a small window in a kind of chamber overlooking the lake. The chamber's dark, the lake's light, so it's like a lantern show. But not like anything any man ever made." Then in the same gentle conversational tone he said, "I know who you are."

Emily couldn't answer.

"They showed around a picture up at the diner this morning."

"Who?" Emily's voice was amazingly steady.

"State cops," Smitty said easily, "from up near Saranac. What color do you want the car?" he asked.

Emily couldn't think.

"Most Volvos are green," he said. "Didn't you ever notice that? Dark green. Now, you can have metallic or flat. I recommend the metallic. It'll cost another twenty-five, but it covers a multitude of sins."

"Metallic green," Emily said automatically. He nodded and went to a control panel and punched in the numbers for the color. He talked as he worked.

"One of the cops fishes at Blue Lake; nice guy, named Banyan. He wasn't happy about this business."

He drove the car to the track, hooked it in, and came back to Emily. The car inched its way into the tunnel entrance. "Nope," Smitty said, "he wasn't happy at all. The

192

other cop loved it all. Made him feel real important. You know how some people get. Seems the government's in on it too. The charge is felony homicide, by which I guess they mean murder."

"Who am I supposed to have murdered?" she asked. Her legs were trembling.

"Six people on an airplane," Smitty told her.

Emily said, "I have to sit down," and she made it across the yard to the steps of the office and sank down on them. The Gregorian chant throbbed in the warm spring air, and Smitty watched her, then walked across the yard and stood over her.

"At first the other cop did all the talking—Banyan didn't look at anyone. Then the other cop said that you were armed and dangerous, and Banyan got mad. He said that anyone who took potshots at you because you were supposed to be dangerous would be in big trouble. Then some old codger—the kind who itches to shoot anything that moves—says that after all you killed six people, and Banyan started yelling that the evidence against you was *brought* up here by some lousy Feds. No one *found* it. The other cop tried to shush him up, but Banyan wouldn't keep quiet. He said that he didn't like that evidence, if anyone asked him, which they weren't likely to. It was 'closing' evidence, he said."

"What's that?" Emily asked.

"I didn't know either," Smitty said, "and I followed them out to their car to ask. The other guy wouldn't talk to me. I guess he was angry at Banyan trying to ruin his big show with the locals, but Banyan told me; Banyan wanted to talk. He said it was the kind of evidence you use to close a case, not try one."

Emily looked blank, and Smitty said, "The kind of evidence you use when you can't try the accused because he's dead or in a straitjacket."

He squatted down next to Emily so his face was level with hers. "A lot of the men in that diner loved hearing that 'armed-and-dangerous' shit, especially about a woman, and they're home now oiling their guns. You need help . . . I'll help you."

"Why?"

Smitty was quiet for a second; then he said, "Because of

an old bear." He smiled. "When I was a kid, my grandpa told me about this rogue bear that'd mauled a man in the woods up around the falls; scraped half of the guy's scalp away before he could get free. They got up a posse, went to the lodge at eight o'clock in the morning, fortified themselves with big talk and lots of liquor, then took their guns and flasks and went out to get themselves that bear. My grandpa was a good tracker and he picked up a trail at one end of Bass Lake. In those days it was pure wilderness, not even a track around that lake, and it was hard going. But Grandpa followed that trail all day, coming around the lake, clinging to a sheer cliff with almost no footholds. Even his dog gave up and went home, but Grandpa was stubborn and kept going. Then, as it was getting dark, he heard thrashing and saw a break in the trees ahead. He crouched down and crept through the trees. He got to the clearing, and sure enough, there was the bear. It had sprung a trap and it was stuck at the end of the chain. The trap was old, the teeth were rusty, and the chain squeaked when the bear moved, but it wasn't hurt too bad, just held fast. The bear saw my grandpa and it stopped moving. Grandpa came into the clearing, stopped, and raised the gun. The bear just looked at him. It didn't move, it didn't make a sound. Grandpa had doubts. There were lots of bears in the Adirondack woods then, and this might not be the rogue. But he was puffed up with all the talk from the morning, and tired and mad at the bear for leading him such a hard chase, and a little drunk, so he took aim. The bear still didn't move, still didn't do anything but look at him, and then my grandfather shot it. It was a bad shot . . . caught the bear in the shoulder, and the bear howled and thrashed around. But when my grandpa brought his gun down, that old bear stopped moving and snarling, and he looked at Grandpa again, right into his eyes. Blood poured out of its shoulder, its fur was all matted with it. Grandpa aimed again, only now he couldn't see anything but those eyes staring at him. The second shot was good, and the bear hunkered down and died. But he seemed to go down very slowly, and all the time, even as he was dying, his eyes looked into my grandpa's. The bear's eyes looking into the man's." Smitty's

194

voice was very soft; the sun was setting and it was turning cold. "Grandpa said he never forgot those eyes. At first he saw them every night as he was falling off to sleep—soft, calm animal eyes, impersonal and without hate. Sometimes he dreamed about them. And all the rest of his life, once or twice a week, without wanting to, he'd see that bear again, looking at him as it died."

Smitty stopped talking, and Emily asked, "Was it the rogue?"

"Don't know. There were no more attacks, so it could've been. But the rogue could just have moved on and that could've been any old bear who'd been dumb enough to get himself trapped. My grandpa said he consoled himself that the bear would've starved to death in that old trap if he hadn't come along and killed it quick. But he knew that wasn't why he killed the bear. It was vanity and booze that made him do it, and he told me that he never felt as good about himself after that. He said that the final memory of all of his life would be of that bear's eyes."

He watched Emily's face in the light that came through the office door. "If I called them, and they got you . . . if I didn't help you and they got you, I have an awful feeling I would see your eyes looking at me every night for a long time." He smiled. "My grandpa was one hell of a storyteller, Dr. Brand; he left me with no taste for killing or trapping anything."

Emily opened her purse and pulled out the three pages. "You should know—" she said, but he shook his head.

"Don't want to. It's big trouble, whatever it is, isn't it?"

"It seems to be."

"Put it away. I'll help you, and in return, you won't get me in any deeper than I am now. Fair enough?"

He gave her a sleeping bag and clean clothes that belonged to his girlfriend—slacks and a heavy woman's sweater. "It won't stick out like that janitor job you're wearing," he said. He gave her a clean blue T-shirt, with "U.S. Open 1987" emblazoned in yellow across it. He let her use the toilet and shower, gave her a clean towel, eight gallons of gas that he siphoned out of his car, a Connecticut license plate he'd taken off a wreck last month, and twenty dollars, which was all the money he had. He bought her a bag of doughnuts from Don's Market across the way. "For the road," he said.

It was dark when she and Smitty solemnly shook hands and she drove the metallic green Volvo out of the clearing. She looked back. The office was lit and friendly-looking in the dark. The market was closing, the road was empty.

She kept to back roads until about nine. She passed a town called Bacon Hill, and crossed the Hudson, which was just a wide stream up here. Then, on the west side of Greenwich, New York, she stopped in a closed gas station that had an outside phone booth and called Susie collect.

CHAPTER

13

We don't know any Emily Brand, Steven wanted to say. But Susie was listening. He covered the mouthpiece. "It's her."

Susie grabbed the phone out of his hand. "Emily—"

"I have a collect call from Emily Brand," the operator intoned. "Will you—?"

"Yes . . . yes. Emily, don't tell me where you are. They tapped the phone."

It was quiet. Susie was terrified that Emily had hung up. "Emily . . ."

"I'm here," Emily said calmly. Emily's voice neutralized Steven's jitters and soothed the panic that had been building in the house since the anonymous phone call.

"Oh, Emily, honey . . ."

"Susie, I didn't think they'd get to you. I should have known. I'm going to hang up now. They're dangerous, Susie, they . . ." She stopped.

"They what? Tell me."

"I have to go now."

"Nooo . . ." Susie shrieked. Steven grabbed her arm, but she yanked free and said into the phone. "I'll be at the place where Daddy took us for ice cream and I cried. The time you tried to kill that girl. I'll be there tomorrow at five, no matter what you say."

"They'll follow you," Emily said gently. "You'll lead them right to me."

Susie gasped, then said, "I didn't think of that. But I'll lose them, Em. If I can't, I won't show up. I'll bring money, anything you need. Oh, Em, what do you need?"

After a second Emily said, "Money." Then she hung up and Susie put the phone down. Steven collapsed in his chair. From the next room where the kids were watching TV, Susie heard gunshots and chase music, and she giggled softly to herself.

Emily found an abandoned lumber track and drove to the end of it. The car heaved over ruts and exposed rocks, and she drove very slowly, not to break an axle. The tracks ended in a wall of deep woods three miles in from the road. Disturbed birds screeched overhead, then were quiet. The moon was hidden, the woods were black except for the headlights.

She was shaking; sweat dripped off her jaw, ran down her cheeks. She had almost told Susie that they killed Marvin . . . almost said those words into a tapped phone. If she had, they would have had to get rid of Susie, and maybe Steven and the kids, just to be sure. But she hadn't done it and a miss was as good as a mile.

She got out of the car and unrolled Smitty's sleeping bag across the backseat. It was too early for black flies; the forest was quiet except for the wind whining in the treetops. Smitty had told her to take off everything but her underwear before she got into the bag. She did what he said, crawled into the back and locked the doors, then slid into the nest of down and nylon. It was chilly at first; then it warmed up and she closed her eyes. It was cramped, but better than the hard church pews. She was exhausted and still a little shaky, but she didn't fall asleep.

Susie would show up tomorrow looking pretty and stylish, with a purse full of all the money she could get her hands on. Emily couldn't wait to see her. It would be safe. Susie was no fool. She'd know if she were followed, she'd lose them, or she'd go somewhere else. If she couldn't make the rendezvous, they'd figure out another. Maybe in the city. They had a hundred secret restaurants and galleries that they'd gone to when they were kids. Emily would find a way to get to New York.

She smiled in the dark. Susie still thought that she'd tried to kill her roommate at Trent. Emily told her it wasn't true, but Mrs. Brand repeated the story in horrified whispers for years to anyone who would listen. Maybe Susie had heard it too many times not to believe it. Or maybe she thought there was something romantic about her big sister risking murder to defend her honor. But honor had had nothing to do with it; saving the stuffed dinosaur was all Emily had in mind. . . .

It was almost the end of her first year at Trent. April or May, Emily wasn't sure which. She had just read Zeno's paradoxes, and she didn't understand them. She usually understood everything she read without thinking about it, but not this time. Zeno was deep. He said a runner couldn't get to the finish line. He couldn't get halfway up the track . . . he couldn't even leave the starting post. If he was right, Emily couldn't get from the end of the hall to her room. But she was doing it; she passed the window, the shower room, the fire door, Thea and Beth's room, and her own door was in sight. Zeno was wrong, but she knew that he wasn't. He was about motion—discontinuous (like the frames of an animated movie) versus continuous motion. She didn't understand, and she was annoyed and frustrated and felt like a baby. She'd get back to it in the morning. She'd cut French and go right to the library.

She reached out for the handle of the door to her room and heard a giggle that wasn't Maggie's. It was a sly, nasty sound, and she stopped with her hand on the knob. She heard it again; then someone else whispered and Emily opened the door. Maggie, Beth Simmons, and Brett Fairley gasped when they saw her, their faces turned red, and Maggie whimpered. Maggie had the plush dinosaur in one hand and an Xacto knife from craft class in the other. The dinosaur's underside was slit open, and clouds of bunting hung down like pale guts. The neck was empty; the small head hung from a strip of limp plush.

Brett Fairley recovered and grinned defiantly at Emily. "Go on, finish it," she said to Maggie. "Finish it."

Emily looked at Maggie. Her roommate trembled, the hand holding the knife drooped, and Emily leaped across the room and smashed full force into Maggie's body. Maggie yelped and dropped the knife; Emily grabbed it before it hit the floor and raised its point up toward Maggie's face. The other girls jumped in place and squealed, but they couldn't think fast enough to do anything. Emily held the knife so it caught the light; Maggie stared at the point, hypnotized, and Emily moved in on her, keeping the girls to the side, where she could see if they moved. She backed Maggie against the wall, pressed her own body against the other girl's, and put the tip of the knife to Maggie's throat.

"Put it down," Emily said gently. "Put it on the bed."

Maggie's neck was smooth and pink, the color of some rare and wonderful marble, and Emily could never do anything to mar that surface. But they didn't know that. Maggie leaned over, staring at the knife point, and put the dinosaur on the bed.

Emily glanced at the others. "Get out," she said.

They ran out of the room, slamming the door after them.

Emily picked up what was left of the dinosaur. The hump had collapsed, the tail was almost empty. Her mother had made it for her, and when she gave it to Emily she'd said, "This isn't just a toy, Emily. It's a representation of a creature that walked this earth for millions of years and then somehow, catastrophically, disappeared. We don't know what happened to them, or why. But one of them—the brontosaurus—looked like this." She'd held the dinosaur out to Emily. She was sick by then; the veins on the backs of her hands were dark blue and looked like swollen rivers running under her skin. "He's a wonderful-looking creature, isn't he?" her mother had said. "Take good care of him. . . ."

Emily turned to Maggie. "Why?" she asked. They'd never been enemies.

"They made me," Maggie sobbed. "Brett and Beth and Mary Joe. Brett hates you."

Emily was startled. Brett was older than Emily, and very pretty. She had black curly hair and blue eyes and she was popular. Emily barely knew her. Algebra was the only class they had together. The course was too easy for Emily, and she spent most of the time looking out the window or drawing in her notebook. She couldn't understand why Brett Fairley would think enough about her to hate her. Emily never thought about Brett.

"How did they make you do it?" Emily asked.

"All of them got together . . . you know."

Emily didn't know and she was going to ask again, but the door crashed open and Miss Jones, the art teacher, stood on the threshold.

By late afternoon Emily was in Miss Iselin's office.

"I never meant to hurt her," Emily explained, "only to make her leave my dinosaur alone." She kept her tone reasonable, as she had through the first two tellings, first to Miss Jones, then to Miss Arnhault, and now to the headmistress. Miss Iselin stared at Emily's file open on her desk, then raised her head. Her eyes were bright blue and piercing, the lashes pale and thick. Emily was holding the cut-up dinosaur, and Miss Iselin's beautiful eyes went to it, then back to Emily.

"What if the knife had slipped, what if Margaret had panicked and moved the wrong way? What then, Emily?" she asked.

"That couldn't happen," Emily said.

"You can't be sure."

Emily didn't argue, but she *was* sure.

"It was a terrible risk to take, Emily," Miss Iselin said, "and whatever that little doll means to you, it's only a toy."

"No!" Emily said.

"Oh? What is it, then?"

Emily explained what the dinosaur represented.

"Where did you hear all that?" Miss Iselin asked.

"From my mother."

Miss Iselin's eyes turned luminous with sympathy. But Emily didn't want sympathy. She wanted Miss Iselin to understand what had happened, not to feel sorry for her because her mother was dead. She tried another tack.

"Suppose I'd hit Maggie. The girls hit each other all the time—it's not so terrible."

"Well, not all the time . . . but you're right, it's not so terrible."

"Okay, say I hit her."

Miss Iselin leaned forward. A crease appeared between her eyebrows and she seemed to be listening at last instead of seeing blood that had not been spilled.

Emily said, "I might have hurt her. I'm stronger than she is, and faster. The other girls would have grabbed me and

201

held me down, and Maggie would have had to go on cutting up the dinosaur. She said she was forced in some way, and I believe her. Why would she lie?"

Miss Iselin nodded, and Emily went on, "Don't you see? Maggie would have a black eye or bloody nose. I might have hurt one of the other girls too, or they might have hurt me, and the dinosaur would have been destroyed. This way, no one got hurt, and the dinosaur . . ." She looked at it. The head hung from the empty neck, and she stopped talking.

Greta Iselin was at a loss. Emily was ten and it was hard to believe that she'd figured out how to save the dinosaur without hurting anyone between the time she opened the door and leaped at Margaret Pleasance. *It was only a second*, the Fairley girl had said. *She moved so fast she was a blur.*

But even if Emily Brand was the brightest child in the world, and had the fastest reaction time, and never meant to hurt anybody, they couldn't keep one little girl who'd threatened another little girl with a knife.

"I'm sorry, Emily," Miss Iselin said. She closed the folder. "I'm afraid you don't belong here."

Emily clutched the ruined dinosaur. She didn't belong in Great Neck, in the long, low glass house that looked like a motel. She didn't belong in Wilton—her father had told her that the house was sold now; the stream belonged to somebody else . . . so did the dam and the swamp cabbage she used to walk through in the spring. She looked up at Miss Iselin, who was still watching her with her wonderful eyes. Miss Iselin was probably right, Emily thought. She didn't belong here, either.

Late that night Emily's door opened and the light from the hall woke her. They'd moved Margaret in with Barbara for the night, and Emily was alone.

"Emily?" It was Miss Iselin.

"Is my father here already?" she asked.

Miss Iselin turned on the light. She was wearing a heavy flannel robe and fur house shoes.

"No, he won't be here until morning," she said. She took Emily's robe off the end of the bed. "The heat's way down," she told Emily. "Put your slippers on."

"Where're we going?"

"To my room," Miss Iselin told her. "Bring the dinosaur."

Miss Iselin had cocoa ready and a plate of cookies; and while Emily ate and drank, staring dreamily into the fire, Miss Iselin took out her sewing box, chose a thin needle and matching thread, and started to mend the dinosaur. As she sewed, she talked quietly to Emily.

"You'll be better off," she said. "We don't have the staff for someone like you."

Emily looked up sharply. "You mean guards or psychologists?" she asked.

Miss Iselin laughed. "No, that's not what I mean. I don't have a mind like yours, but I can imagine things. I was always very good at that. And I can imagine what it's like to catch on before anybody else and to know that if you *do* need help, no one around you will be smart enough to give it to you. I can imagine more," she said, taking small neat stitches and replacing the batting so that the dinosaur started to look like itself again. "I can imagine what it's like when the people who can't keep up make you feel like a freak and like a conscienceless monster because you won't stay back with them. To a lot of people in the world," Miss Iselin said, almost to herself, "intelligence is the mark of the beast. . . ." She finished another seam, bit the thread.

"I've told your father about a school in Massachusetts and he's agreed to send you there. There'll be a lot more math and science, a lot less French and handicrafts. The children's talents will be closer to yours."

"What kind of science?" Emily asked.

Miss Iselin began a soothing litany as her fingers replaced the bunting and took tiny stitches in the plush. Now, lying in the back of the car in Smitty's sleeping bag, Emily could remember Miss Iselin's exact words and the order in which she'd said them: "Zoology, biology, chemistry, mathematics, astronomy, physics. . . ."

Steven was too nervous to go to the office. He prowled the house all morning, and Susie found him in the kitchen at the refrigerator.

"Hungry?" she asked.

"Starving." It was almost noon; she said she was leaving at

twelve-thirty. He watched her fill a plate for him with low-fat cottage cheese, sliced tomato, and melba toast. Her eyes glistened with excitement and her hand trembled as she scooped the cottage cheese out of the container. He sat at the table, and when she put the plate in front of him, he grabbed her hand.

"Susie, you can't go."

She didn't answer.

"You're not going," he said sternly. "I forbid it."

She looked into his eyes and Steven saw the brutal, powerful Isaac Brand looking down at him. "I'm not leaving my sister waiting there and not knowing, Steven. Don't ask again."

He let go of her hand and looked down at the unappetizing approved food. "You'll lead them to her," he wailed.

"I'll lose them."

"How?"

"I think I have a way."

"Tell me," he cried.

She leaned over, kissed his cheek, and crossed the kitchen. He left the food and followed her.

Pudgy heaved herself up off the floor and followed him. Susie went to the basement door.

"Where're you going?" he asked.

"The safe." She opened the door and went down the carpeted stairs to the basement. He hesitated, grabbed a couple of cherries out of the bowl on the counter, and went after her.

Susie slid a redwood panel back and started to work the combination.

"Where're you meeting her?"

"You don't have to know, Steve."

He wanted to cry. "Do you think I'd tell—?"

He stopped because he knew he'd give Emily to NARCON to protect Susie from even a hint of danger. He also knew that if anything happened to Emily, Susie would never get over it and he'd have to live with her sorrow and his guilt. This way was better. He didn't know, so he couldn't tell. Susie was wise.

She opened the safe and took out all the money they had

in the house. She didn't leave anything in case *they* had an emergency. Everything for Emily, he thought with loathing. She carried the money through the house and up the front stairs to the bedroom. He and Pudgy followed helplessly. He knew there was almost fifteen thousand dollars there, and the wad was so thick she had to force the purse closed. Then she changed into jeans, which she almost never wore, and rolled them up.

"They'll think I'm wearing a skirt," she said.

She went back downstairs to the hall closet and Steven and the dog traipsed after her. "You can warm up the big can of Chef Boyardee ravioli for the kids' dinner. They love it."

"What about me?" He was ashamed at the whine in his voice, but he couldn't help it.

"There's leftover roast. You can slice it." She took her old khaki raincoat out of the closet. It was years out of style and very long. "Maybe you can go out later and buy some coleslaw." She tied a scarf around her head, covering her lovely soft blond hair. He wanted to rip it off, but he stood frozen next to the closet watching her. The long coat covered the rolled-up jeans, he noticed. She did look like she had a skirt on and he was surprised at her cleverness. Then she put on sunglasses.

"They can't miss you in that getup."

"That's the idea," she said. She kissed him again. "I'll be home for the late show," she said, and she went out the door and across the lawn to the driveway. He watched through the sidelights as she pulled the Continental out of the driveway and into their little road. She hated that car; she said it looked like a land ark. It did, but he thought it was the shiniest, most glamorous car in the world. They'd have no trouble following her in the Continental. But maybe that was part of the point too.

He watched her drive to the end of the road and turn right toward the expressway. The street was empty, and for a second he thought that nothing would happen. Then a big dark blue Chevy that needed washing pulled out of the tiny side street that ran down to the beach, drove to the corner, and turned right too.

The Chevy followed Susie to the expressway. She stayed in the far-right lane and kept her speed at thirty-five—twenty miles an hour slower than the stream of traffic. The Chevy stayed behind her. She hung back until she passed the turnoff for Grand Central and the airports, then speeded up and pulled into the center lane. The Chevy followed.

The traffic built up and they were crawling by the time they reached the Midtown Tunnel. The Chevy stayed three cars behind through the tunnel and up the streets to Third Avenue, where she turned uptown. She kept a steady speed, slid across lanes smoothly. She was sure the Continental impressed the other drivers. Even the taxis seemed less aggressive than when she drove her little Mercedes.

The traffic stalled at Fifty-third and she and the blue Chevy crawled through the lunch-hour rush and the bridge traffic. It opened again at Fifty-eighth, and she zoomed around a truck, half-ran the light at Fifty-ninth, cut around the construction and raced the last four blocks. She swung left at Sixty-third and pulled down the ramp of the garage she used in this neighborhood.

She got her parking ticket and walked up the ramp to the street. She didn't see the Chevy, but she knew it was there somewhere. Up near Lexington, probably, or hovering in the driveway of the garage on the other side of the street. She didn't look for it, but walked back to Third, then down the avenue to Bloomingdale's.

The store was mobbed. It was early for air conditioning and the customers and salespeople sweated. Susie knew every inch of the store. She swept across the floor of men's furnishings to the up escalator, and halfway to the second floor she looked back. Women jammed the steps, and a few men in sport jackets. They all looked like they belonged in the lunch-hour throng. Then she saw a man in a business suit ease his way through the crowd and step onto the escalator. His suit was wrinkled and he looked like he needed a shave. He didn't look up, but stared at the backs of the people in front of him. He carried a wrinkled raincoat and a newspaper. There was nothing odd about that, but he didn't look like the other people on the escalator; maybe the polyester suit set him apart, or the cheap raincoat.

Susie got off on three and went into the designer-sportswear section. The man in the business suit browsed outside among the ladies' better blouses. She went to the sales racks and chose two heavy tweed blazers, a couple of blouses, and a pair of slacks. She carried everything to the sales desk next to the fitting rooms; the man couldn't see her from here; he wouldn't know what she was trying on.

A woman with pencils stuck in her hair took the hangers from Susie and led her back to one of the cubicles. "Let me know if you need any help," the woman said, and hung the clothes on the back of the door and left Susie alone.

Susie picked a heavy gray tweed jacket that looked like most of the other jackets she'd seen that spring. The woman came back after a few minutes.

"I'll take this one," Susie said. "And would you wrap it back here? It's for my mother. She's waiting outside, and I don't want her to see it."

The woman took Susie's charge card and came back with the sales slip, tissue, and a shopping bag. Susie asked her to cut the tags off, because she always forgot, and the woman smiled at her, took off the tags, wrapped the jacket in tissue, and slid it into the bag. Susie took the bag and left the designer boutique.

The man was behind a rack of Ralph Lauren skirts. She went right to the escalator and rode up to four. She didn't look back as she went through the maternity shop and the section of clothes for fat women and into the ladies' room.

The ladies' room was full, but all of the women looked too short or tall. Susie went into one of the cubicles, took off the raincoat, changed to smaller sunglasses, and put on the jacket she'd bought. She rolled down her jeans, untied the scarf, and shook her hair loose. Then she came out. A woman about her age was leaning toward the mirror, putting on eyeliner. She was a little taller than Susie, but she was about the same build and she was blond. Susie stood next to her at the mirror.

"Will you help me?" she asked softly.

The woman looked startled, then frightened. Around them toilets flushed, the other women washed their hands, combed their hair, and applied makeup. No one noticed them.

"Please," Susie said, "it's very important." She took the

207

woman's arm. "It's a divorce thing. His lawyer's got some-one following me with a subpoena, and he's got me trapped in here. I'll pay you . . ."

The woman looked at Susie's expensive new jacket, the designer jeans, and the perfectly bleached hair. Susie smiled bravely. "It's been going on for weeks. He wants the chil-dren . . ."

The woman still hesitated. "I can't even go into Blooming-dale's," Susie whined. She thought she could cry if she had to.

The woman's face changed; she frowned with sympathy. "What do you want me to do?" she asked.

"Just wear this coat and the scarf and glasses and carry the shopping bag. Go anywhere you like, but keep them on for an hour. After that you can just throw them away."

The woman still looked uncertain.

"I'll give you a hundred dollars," Susie said.

"What if he gives *me* the subpoena?" the woman asked.

"He'll ask you if you're me first. And you're not me. So it can't hurt," Susie answered. The woman's face cleared. She nodded, and they went back to the cubicles to change.

They left the ladies' room with a bunch of other women, and Susie stopped in the shoe department. The woman in the raincoat got on the escalator, and the man in the rumpled suit followed her. Susie gave them time to get almost to the next floor, then made her way through the crowds to the front escalator and rode down to the first floor. She didn't want to go out on Lexington—it went the wrong way, and it could take half an hour to get around the block this time of day. She walked steadily through the cosmetics department, into the men's section, crossed it without looking around, and left the store by the Third Avenue exit. The traffic was bad, and she was frightened that she wouldn't get a taxi. She shoved her way through the slowly moving crowd to the curb and waved at the taxis crawling up the avenue. But they were full. Then one stopped right in front of her and a woman paid and got out while Susie held on to the door handle.

Luck is with me, she thought.

"Where to?" the cabbie asked.

"Olins Rent-a-Car on Seventy-sixth and Broadway," she

said. She looked back as the cab pulled into the traffic. There was no sign of the man with the raincoat over his arm. She looked left at Sixty-third but there was no sign of the blue Chevy, either.

She'd lost them.

CHAPTER
14

SUSIE COHEN'S breathy voice came through the speaker: ". . . Daddy took us for ice cream, I cried . . . you tried to kill that girl . . ."

David stopped the tape.

"I'll call the computer," Stockton said. David shook his head. He didn't need the computer. He read her file every day until her life was part of his mind: where she was born, where she'd gone to school, whom she'd been to bed with. There were two summer camps. Both in Maine. They had lost Susie Cohen in Bloomingdale's on Fifty-ninth Street at one-fifty. She couldn't get to northern Maine by five. So it was a school. There were two schools. She'd spent seven years in Evington in Massachusetts, and seven months at Trent in Washington Depot, Connecticut. Now he knew why she was expelled from Trent; twenty-eight years ago, in the northern reaches of Connecticut horse country, little Emily Brand's arrogant indifference broke and she cared enough about something to try to kill for it. He wondered what.

He turned the tape on again. *"They'll follow . . ."*

He switched the recorder off and raised his hand to his aching jaw. He had checked himself out of the hospital this morning; his eyes were tender to light, so he kept the sunglasses on.

Talbot and Stockton watched him anxiously. He ran through it one more time in his head, just to be sure, even though he already was. Twenty-eight years ago she was expelled from Trent. Her father had gone to get her, and he'd brought little Susan along for the ride. Then he took the girls for ice cream, and sister Susan had cried because her brilliant half-sister was coming home and poor little sister Susan would have to share father's love and attention.

The father wouldn't plan the excursion for ice cream. He must have seen the place on the way to the school or on the way back . . . a spur-of-the-moment treat to cheer Emily up and stop Susan from crying. School towns always had sweet shops or ice-cream parlors.

He shut off the machine and looked at Stockton. "I want to be there," he said.

"Kelsey thinks it might have gone the other way in Placid if you hadn't been there."

"Kelsey's wrong."

Stockton shook his head. David jumped out of his chair, leaned on the desktop, and shoved his face close to Stockton's. His mirrored sunglasses zoomed in, and Stockton flinched away.

David said softly, "She's taken out two of your finest. How?"

Stockton didn't answer.

"She thought faster than they did, Stockton, and this time it'll be worse. Her sister's there, and I think she cares about the sister—didn't you think so, just listening to her talk to her? Emily Brand cares . . . and that'll make her even more dangerous."

"And I suppose you can handle her," Stockton sneered.

"That's right."

From the sidelines Talbot said nervously, "We need Gelb. Where's Gelb? . . ."

David drew back. They didn't have time to get sidetracked about Gelb. The thought flashed through his mind that he was as good as this Gelb, anyway. Then he thought that maybe he wasn't, and he was intrigued, but it didn't matter. Gelb was somewhere else.

"Gelb's not here," David said. "I'm all you've got, Stockton. Because if you send two more dead-brained pigeons after her, they'll wind up at the bottom of some gravel pit or hanging from a pine tree, not knowing how the fuck they got there, and she'll be gone . . . one more time."

"He's right," Talbot said. "Besides, he knows where she is."

"He figured it out, we can too," Stockton said.

David looked at his watch.

"Can you get there by five?" Talbot asked.

"If we leave now," David said.

Stockton gave up. "Okay. Where is she?"

"I'm going?"

Stockton nodded.

"She'll be in an ice-cream parlor on the main street of Washington Depot, Connecticut."

"Christ," Talbot cried nervously. "You can't shoot down an unarmed woman in an ice-cream parlor or on the main street of some dink town."

Stockton grinned. "It seems Mr. Lucci hasn't thought of everything after all."

David grinned back, but the movement twisted his face, and pain shot up his cheek and into his eye. He kept the smile in place. "She had a gun in the bank in Champlain. She still has it, so she's not unarmed. And she's not just a woman . . . she's a fugitive, remember? She's wanted for murdering six people."

Talbot laughed softly, and Stockton deflated and picked up the phone. David had seen two men outside lounging against the car, so he wasn't calling to his stable of killers. He was calling to verify the existence of Washington Depot and to find out if there was an ice cream parlor on the main street. Talbot listened, but David didn't need confirmation. He was thinking about Mr. Gelb. The two old farts were intimidated by him, and David was curious. Maybe he'd meet him someday . . . when this was over. He hoped he would not need his help. He wasn't as sure as he sounded; she'd outsmarted him in Placid, she might do it again.

Stockton put the phone down. "It's there," he said.

David didn't know what he was talking about for a second.

"Washington Depot exists," Stockton said, "and there's an ice-cream parlor on the main street, just like you said there'd be."

It was called Scoops, and Susie didn't think it had changed since their father had taken them there twenty-seven years ago. The front glass reflected the street and trees wavily; the entrance was white, with stained-glass sidelights.

She opened the door and a bell tinkled in the back. The

counter was marble and the old-fashioned long-necked soda spigots stuck over the top like swans' necks. There were the same round tables and wire chairs, and the white booths against the wall with latticework on the top of the wooden seat backs.

Susie remembered perfectly. It had been a Sunday and she thought Emily was coming home with them for good. Emily's only toy was a stuffed green animal with a strange hump on its back. She didn't have any proper dolls, and after thinking about it all the way from Great Neck to Washington Depot, Susie decided that she would give Emily Barbie Ann, her favorite doll. Susie would have visitation rights, of course, and sometimes she would ask Emily if she could sleep with Barbie Ann, just for the one night. But the doll would belong to Emily.

They got to Washington Depot about two, Susie remembered. Her father stopped on the curving drive in front of the school, left Susie in the car, and went in to get Emily. The trees were budding out then too, and Susie had been weak with joy and excitement. It was spring and her sister was coming home.

She and Emily sat on the jump seats, their father stowed Emily's books and suitcase in the trunk, and they drove into town. Susie was too excited to talk. She grabbed Emily's hand once, but was too shy to kiss her. She'd thought that Emily was the most wonderful person in the world. She'd tried to kill someone and they'd expelled her. If it'd been Susie, she would've died of shame, but Emily was calm; she held Susie's hand gently.

Then they were in the ice-cream parlor . . . in this booth . . . and Susie ate her hot-fudge sundae and rattled on about how she and Emily were going to go to the beach together and play badminton in the backyard and swim in the pool in the morning. She noticed how grim and quiet their father was, and she ran down.

"Emily's going to another school," he said.

Susie stuck her spoon straight up in the ice cream. "School's almost over," she proclaimed.

"Almost, but not quite," her father said. "She's leaving next Wednesday. Aren't you, Emily?"

Emily had stared straight ahead and said nothing.

"But school'll be over," Susie said.

"Then Emily's going to camp. She'll learn to ride there, and take care of a horse. You'll love that, won't you, Emily?"

Emily still didn't say anything, and Susie realized that they were never going to let Emily come home. Emily would never get to have Barbie Ann and Susie would sleep alone in her room for the rest of her life. Susie started to cry.

"Hush," her father whispered sharply.

The other tables were full of students from Trent and their families on Sunday outings at the ice-cream parlor, and they were turning in their spindly chairs to stare at the Brands. Susie sobbed with her mouth open; ice cream and spit dribbled out of her mouth and down her chin.

"Stop that," her father said.

Emily grabbed a paper napkin out of the holder on the table and started wiping Susie's mouth; then she sort of sagged, balled the napkin up, put it on the table, and took Susie in her arms. Even now, all these years later, Susie could still remember how strong and warm her sister's arms were; she could almost feel her sister's dry soft hair against her cheek.

Susie smiled to herself as she remembered. Anybody but Emily would have cried too, she thought. The waitress cleared up after a teenage couple, then came over to see what Susie wanted.

"A double martini," Susie said.

The waitress smiled grimly. "Me too."

"I'll have a hot-fudge sundae. Chocolate ice cream, nuts instead of sprinkles." The waitress left her alone and Susie looked up at the clock. It was three minutes to five; her heart beat faster and she pulled the stuffed purse into her lap. The waitress brought her sundae. Through the wavy glass front she saw a black Mercedes go slowly up the street past the shop. Then the street was empty. It was five. She wanted to wait for Emily to eat, but the hot fudge was already congealing and she clamped her purse in her lap against the table edge and picked up her spoon.

She heard a shot out in the street, and the waitress said, "Someone's driving a clunker."

Emily had come into town at the residential end of the main street and pulled into a driveway. The house next to the drive was dark, the blinds were drawn, and no one opened a window or door and yelled at her to get away. The people were still at work, or in the city for the week.

She walked up the drive and looked in the garage. It was empty. She went back to the street. The drive was lined with yews, so no one could see the Volvo until they were abreast of it.

It was almost time; Susie was always early, and she would be there by now. Emily shoved her hand into her shoulder bag, grasped the gun butt, and started walking toward the shopping center.

The street was empty and tree-lined. All the houses were white, with dates like 1783 and 1801 painted over the doors. Emily imagined that the people behind the doors had been born here, like their fathers and grandfathers. They would live here all of their lives; so would their children. They belonged here.

She passed a Ford with a New York license plate with a Z in it. A cabbie had once told her that the Z meant the car was rented. She looked in and saw a blazer with a Bloomingdale's label lying on the front seat, and she knew Susie was only half a block away. If Scoops was gone, Susie would be waiting in the shop that had replaced it. Then she saw that the ice-cream parlor was still there, and she wanted to run.

A Mercedes with a Maryland license plate pulled into the street and came slowly up the block. She saw three men inside, two in the front, one in the back, and she ducked into a doorway.

The Mercedes screeched to a stop, and the doors flung open. Two of the men jumped out and came sliding up the street toward the doorway; the third leaned against the fender of the car.

"Good evening, Dr. Brand," the third man called. He was wearing sunglasses with mirrored lenses.

The other two men kept moving; their figures were distorted by the angled glass of the shop. She pulled the gun out of her purse. They must have seen her do it, and one of them shot at her. He was good; the bullet went through angled layers of wavy glass and hit her in the side. Her body flew sideways, her head cracked against the door, and her glasses flew off and hit the pavement. She didn't feel any pain, but her legs buckled, and she went down hard on her knees.

The men were almost directly across the street. She couldn't shoot them—she could barely see them. She could see the plate-glass window of the shop behind them.

She felt blood soak her T-shirt and trousers; it was running down inside her clothes, and she wanted to press her hand against her side, but she made herself hold the gun with both hands. She fired at the bottom of the window, and kept firing. The bottom of the glass shattered and blew back into the shop. The top slid down, hit the sill, and crashed out on top of the men. They fell flat and threw their arms over their heads. The glass shattered across their backs, splinters of glass glittered in midair. The sound of crashing glass filled the street, then died with the echo of the shots, and the street was quiet.

She crawled through the blood around her to her glasses and put them on. One lens was gone, but she could see a little better. The third man was coming at her. She braced her back against the wall of the entryway and slid to her feet. The third man stopped in the middle of the street and tore the mirrored glasses off. It was Lucci. He didn't have a gun, or he would have shot her by now. She raised the gun at him and he leaped behind the Mercedes.

She clamped her palm flat against her side and limped out of the doorway onto the street. She had to run, but she wound up staggering along the street. He would get a gun from one of the men, and he'd come after her. He'd shoot her or grab her by the hair or the back of her bloodstained shirt any second. But she was moving faster than she had thought, and she was passing the stately houses again. They were still dark and quiet; the people were gone or deaf.

Blood squished in her shoes, and she staggered another few feet, then leaned against a tree and threw up in the grass. Strings of bile ran out of her mouth and nose and collected in a disgusting pool on the ground next to the tree.

How awful, she thought, as if she were watching herself from the end of the block. *How perfectly awful.*

216

She didn't think she could move again, but then she heard Susie's voice: "Run, Emily . . ."

She pushed herself away from the tree and hobbled on a few more feet. She heard car doors slam; then she heard the crunch of metal ramming metal, and she looked back.

Lucci had decided to come after her in the car. It made sense; he would shoot her and pull her body into the car instead of having to drag it back down the block. But he'd forgotten about Susie. Susie had run out of Scoops and gotten to the Ford before they knew what she was doing. She had driven it crosswise to the street and blocked the Mercedes. Lucci was trying to get past her. He'd crashed into her once, and now he drove up on the sidewalk to get around her. But Susie did the same and he smashed the Mercedes into the side of the Ford. The Ford held its ground and Emily pushed the pain and blood out of her mind and ran. Behind her, she heard Lucci scream, "Move the bitch or we'll lose her. Christ, we'll lose her. . . ."

She was getting dizzy, but she didn't have far to go. She heard a car door slam again. Lucci was coming after her on foot and Susie couldn't stop him. Then she saw the nose of the Volvo. She got the door open and thought she'd faint across the front seat. But she got in and started the car. If she drove straight out on the street, he'd shoot her through the car windows. She looked behind her. The driveway ended in the garage, but there was a footpath around the garage. The house was almost at the end of the street; there might be another road perpendicular to it, and she could reach it by driving across the lot next door.

She raced backward to the garage, turned the car hard over, and drove across lawn, over a bed of daffodils and through a hedge of evergreen shrubs. She came out on the lawn of the corner lot. The wheels sank in the wet grass, but the car plowed across the lawn to the drive, then down the drive to the other road. She turned left without thinking. The road was gravel; the back wheels skidded, then held, and she drove west into the sun. She was heading right back into New York. There was no help there, but there wasn't any help anywhere, and she couldn't think anymore or do anything but drive.

David got to the intersection and looked up the dirt road. She was gone, but he saw dust settling. She had the car, but he hadn't seen it. He ran back and saw a driveway with rutted gravel. He went up it, and found a torn up flowerbed, crushed evergreens, and tire tracks across the next-door lawn leading to another drive.

She'd gone up here, then taken the dirt road. An unpaved road would slow her down. They could still get her, if they could move.

He ran back to the street, down to the shops where the Ford blocked the Mercedes. Kelsey was dazed; he'd wiped his face and neck, but blood still seeped out of the cuts.

David grabbed Kelsey's gun. He'd never fired a handgun, but the gun's weight and size felt good in his hand. He ran to the Ford.

Susie Cohen stared at him through the dusty closed window. Her face was slick with sweat, her eyes red and fierce with stubbornness. He yelled at her to open the door. She didn't move. He pounded on the window with his fist, but all she did was look at him. Then he brought the gun up to the window and aimed the muzzle point-blank in the middle of her face. He knew he could do it. She was nothing now but an obstruction. Another round had gone to Emily Brand because of this stubborn bitch, and he knew he could blow that sweaty face to pulp. He pried off the safety; Susie threw herself sideways on the seat.

Stu Levenson grabbed his arm.

David looked at Levenson's bloodied face, then past him at the street. People had come out of the shops and stood silently watching him. A woman in a waitress uniform was standing in front of the ice-cream parlor, staring at him wide-eyed, and sirens screamed down the street toward them.

It was one thing to shoot a murder suspect, something else to kill an unarmed suburban matron who was trying to help her sister.

Three cop cars pulled into the street, and uniformed men poured out. David disengaged the safety.

"You got a carrying permit?" Levenson whispered.

David shook his head, and Levenson took the gun out of his hand. "The locals probably hate feds enough to throw you in the can," he said, and he slipped it into his jacket pocket.

The cops swarmed around the Mercedes and the Ford. Susie Cohen sat up and stared wildly at them but she wouldn't unlock the car or open the window, and the road stayed blocked.

A huge cop whose belly strained against his gray uniform shirt lumbered over to them.

"It's the Brand woman," David cried. "We're going to lose her."

"Which way'd she go?" the cop asked.

"West," David said. "Move that car—"

"We got a tow coming."

"That'll take too long," David cried.

The cop looked at him calmly. "What would you suggest?"

"Get that woman out of the car."

"Don't quite see how we can do that, do you?"

"We'll lose her . . ."

The cop looked up at the sky as if he were trying to gauge the wind, and David wanted to hit him. "Well . . ." the cop said, very slow, very country, "if she's headin' west, and pushing it, which I imagine she is—don't you?—then she'll be at the New York border in ten or fifteen minutes. Don't think we'll catch her by then."

"Call somebody," David yelled. "Get a roadblock . . ."

The cop lowered his head slowly and looked at David. David knew the man was having a good time. "Oh, we'll radio into New York," the cop said. "But there's about twenty roads heading across the line, some paved, some dirt. Lumber tracks, farm roads, quarry trails. Which roads would you like us to block, Mr. . . . ?" The man paused, waiting for David to supply his name, and David whirled away from him. Susie Cohen grinned at him through the car window and rage made him light-headed. He stalked across the street to the doorway where Emily'd been. There was a lot of blood on the sidewalk, drying into the concrete. A track of it went up the walk, and he followed it for a few yards. The splotches turned to footprints. Blood had run down her leg and covered her shoes. He turned back. Susie Cohen had finally gotten out of the car, and two of the numbskulls held guns on her. David wanted

219

to laugh. A tow truck clanked up to the shambles in the middle of the main street and stopped, and David turned back to the trail. The sidewalk ended under the trees, and he stepped off the concrete onto grass. He saw blood here too; it colored the grass and soaked into the dirt.

Then he saw the pool of vomit and thought of Donny Broome.

CHAPTER
15

THE NEWS CONFERENCE was a disaster. The questions came fast, and Orin was ready with answers at first. Yes, there were going to be farm supports if he had anything to say about it, and a profit freeze on foodstuffs. And finally, maybe, they'd be able to squeeze the middleman instead of the farmers and consumers. Yes, the U.S.–Soviet space treaty was ready to go to Congress, and, yes, they had a protocol agreement for a new round of inspections for the nuclear-arms freeze. He had good news: unemployment was down to 12 percent last month, and the bankruptcy rate was the lowest it had been since '86. He knew the deficit was horrendous . . . but not as bad as it was last year, and it would get better, he pledged (although he didn't know how he was going to do it). He had three minutes left and he thought he might make it, and then Claire Ryan asked, "Are you going to ask Congress to extend oil-price controls?"

And for a second, Orin couldn't talk. Years ago, during his first run for the Senate, Tom Gilligan had told him: *The price of honesty is not having an answer for every question. But politicians gotta have answers. Don't let honesty cut your balls off.*

It was good advice, and Orin had prepared the necessary equivocations, but this minute he couldn't remember what they were. Even if he did—even if he tried to tell this bunch of hawkish-looking men and women that he might if this . . . and might not if that—he had an awful feeling that he would start laughing hysterically and not be able to stop. The silence was almost worse than laughing would have been. It seemed to go on for a long time; then Orin cleared his throat and said simply, "I don't know yet."

They were shocked, and it took a few seconds for them to recover and go after him.

Claire again: "Isn't it true that decontrolled gas prices could go to seven dollars a gallon?"

"Yes," Orin said, and he recognized Herman DiSalva of the *Times*:

"But extended controls will mean a repeat of the eighty-eight mess. Isn't that right, Mr. President?"

Again Orin said, "Yes." He couldn't seem to think of any other word, and in front of him there was a pandemonium of waving hands, but DiSalva stayed on his feet.

"There was a committee to study rationing . . ." DiSalva said, and Orin said his "Yes" and nothing else. He saw a number of the reporters glance at each other.

DiSalva still had the floor. "What were their findings?"

"It's difficult . . ." Orin said, and finally he managed to collect himself. "It's difficult to balance the problems of rationing, which would be considerable, against the hardship of higher prices." *No shit, Sherlock*, he thought. And he hated himself because he sounded like the last three mealy-mouthed men who'd stood here before him trying to evade the same questions. Control vs. rationing vs. staggering prices in a weakened economy. "But we are studying the options very carefully," Orin went on, "with a view of finding more than a temporary Band-Aid solution. . . ."

He owed Mrs. Marguery more than this. He owed Herman DiSalva more, and his old friend and patron Tom Gilligan, and everybody who was listening to him tonight, and everybody who wasn't. But all he could do was go on telling them one more time what they all knew: it was difficult.

DiSalva was asking him something else, and he had to concentrate to hear.

"I asked if you will speak at the demonstration next week."

He hadn't decided that yet. Glover was against it, so was Feinstein, but Orin saw a chance to redeem the gutlessness of his performance this evening, and he said, "Yes, I'll be there."

Rockland of UP stood, and Orin recognized him. He was tall and thin, with sallow skin and deep lines running down his face.

"And what'll you say to the people, Mr. President?" He sounded mean.

"I'll explain to them . . ." Orin stopped and looked past the lights at the reporter's cadaverous face. Orin smiled, then said, with that odd gentle honesty that the voters seemed to love, ". . . as soon as I understand myself."

There were a few laughs, then it was over, and King came to the mike. "Thank you, ladies and gentlemen," and then Orin was walking up the aisle past them with the spate of applause—faint praise—following him out of the room into the hall.

He got around the corner and stopped. The entourage stopped with him, and he took out his handkerchief and wiped his face.

"They're waiting . . ." King paused, and Orin nodded and went on to the office. The group around him broke up, and he was alone with King and Glover by the time he reached the office. He touched the door handle, and hesitated. Talbot was in there, along with Flynn and Mapes. The first discussion of what would happen in six weeks.

If only Lipsky had made it with . . . whatever. But three days ago, a few hours after the crash, they'd sifted through the ash and debris of the little plane and they'd found charred scraps of his briefcase and nothing else. It was gone, if it ever existed, and maybe it was all a dream anyway. Orin still wasn't ready to believe that, but he was going to have to jump one way or the other soon.

He went into the office; the three men stood, then sat in a row facing his desk. Talbot's face looked smooth and confident. Orin closed the door, leaving Glover and King outside.

Orin knew it would be between him and Talbot; the other two men were window dressing. They had no niceties to exchange, and Talbot got right to the point. "We're going to have to hear your decision on this, Mr. President."

Orin threw his folder of notes on the desk. He didn't waste words either. "Okay. How the hell much more will it cost the people if the controls come off?"

223

Talbot shrugged lightly, and Mapes leaned into the light.
"We realize the burden is heavy on the people—"

"Then lighten it," Orin said.

Mapes looked helplessly at Talbot.

"We can't do that, Mr. President."

Orin turned to his Secretary of Energy. Daniel Flynn was
staring intently at the backs of his hands. A year ago Daniel
Flynn had been a ball of fire, he'd known everything.

"We're up to our asses in options," Flynn had said then.
"Synfuels, shale oil, solar . . ."

Flynn knew everything sixteen months ago. Now he studied his hands, folded schoolgirl fashion in his lap.

"I guess we're not up to our asses in options after all, are
we, Mr. Secretary?"

Flynn looked up miserably for a second; then his eyes went
back to his hands. Orin had known Flynn for years and
thought he was honest and smart. Now he knew the man
was a fool. They were all fools, himself included.

What the fuck have we been doing all these years? he wondered. Reagan knew what was going to happen, so did Carter
and . . . Suddenly he couldn't remember who'd been President before Carter. Mapes was talking, but he didn't listen;
he had to remember. Ford, Jerry Ford, and before him Nixon.
Who was the first one to know? Did it go back to Eisenhower
or even Truman? Did some little secretary of whatever the
department was in those days sit in this office and plead with
Harry Truman: *Mr. President . . . about our energy problems*. Orin tried to imagine Truman's answer: *Shit, man, the
communists have China, we're at war in Korea, our State
Department is up to its balls in reds, and I used the most
destructive weapon in history on a hundred thousand men,
women, and children who weren't even carrying guns. Stick
your energy problems up your ass, boy. I've got real things
to think about. We'll worry about that pansy stuff later. We'll
worry about it in thirty years. Yeah . . . ask me about energy
in 1980."*

Mapes was still talking. Orin interrupted him. "That's all
bullshit, isn't it, Curran?"

Mapes shut his mouth with a snap. Nobody smiled or
spoke. The mantel clock that had belonged to John Kennedy

chimed sweetly. It was ten, the city was hunkering down for the night.

"How much do you have left at the old price?" Orin asked.

The oil men didn't answer.

"Flynn?" Orin asked.

Flynn finally looked up from his lap. "Enough for three months. Two months if people panic and start hoarding."

"But they will panic, won't they?" Talbot asked.

"Yes, George," Orin answered. "You can scare them; you can dictate how far they can go to their jobs and how much money they'll have left by the end of August; you can tell them how fast they can drive and make them sweat on hot still nights and freeze on cold ones . . ." Orin's voice was tight with fury. Mapes and Flynn looked embarrassed, and Orin took a deep breath to get control of himself. He wasn't sure he'd ever been so angry; in a way, it felt good. He said, "It seems I have a week or two, anyway."

Talbot said, "The controls come off June 15—unless you try to extend them, Mr. President. I heartily advise you not to, but if you do, the summer of ninety will make the summer of eighty-eight look like a church picnic."

"That's a threat," Orin said. His voice shook, but he couldn't help it.

"Of course it's a threat," Talbot said easily.

It was between them now; the other two men were forgotten.

"Threat-counterthreat," Orin said.

"What do you have in mind?" Talbot asked.

"Rationing, George, and if that doesn't work, I'll nationalize the companies . . . and NARCON, Exxon, Mobil, will become part of the National Trust. Like Yosemite and Yellowstone. And I'll back that up with the National Guard."

Mapes gasped and Talbot's face went white and Flynn seemed to be turning to stone. Any minute, Orin thought, he'll crack, and chunks of him will hit the floor with a thud. He decided that he would ask for Daniel Flynn's resignation on Monday.

"You wouldn't dare!" Talbot yelled.

He wouldn't. The companies could tie him up in the courts for years, and all that time the same people who stamped driver's licenses and administered welfare claims would be doling out the oil and gas. At the end of a year the country would be on its knees. Talbot was right: he wouldn't dare. But Talbot didn't know that, and Orin didn't want him to.

Talbot spoke to Mapes and Flynn, keeping his eyes on Orin. "I'd like to talk to the President alone. If you don't mind, Orin?" He managed to sound humble.

"I don't mind," Orin said.

Flynn and Mapes filed out. Talbot and Orin didn't say anything for a moment after they left. The silence was almost pleasant; it was late, and they were both tired. Then Orin stood up. "Would you like a drink, George?"

Talbot nodded.

"Cognac, right?"

"Yes. If it's good."

Orin laughed. "I'm sure they only buy me the best." He opened the cabinet next to the fireplace and took out the bottle. "Delamain Reserve," he read from the label. "Nineteen-thirty."

Talbot whistled silently and they were quiet again until Orin had poured the drinks and they'd sipped at them. The brandy was beautiful, Orin thought. Smoky and smooth, it slid down his throat and set up a glow.

Talbot smiled. "God, that's nice." Then in the same tone he asked, "Why're you doing this, Orin?"

"Why're you?"

"It's my oil. I have a right to get what I can for it."

"Ah, free enterprise."

"My enterprise. My company, and my daddy's before me, and his daddy's. Not got easy, I can tell you. Nothing 'free' about it."

"Okay," Orin said, "your oil. What do you want for it?"

Talbot shrugged. "Whatever I can get, Orin. Whatever the people can pay. That's the point. And you know as well as I do that Gilligan would've said I was right."

Would he? Orin wondered. Maybe. Gilligan had loved simple arguments, and God knows this was simple. It's mine, you want it, you pay what I charge or you don't get it. Nothing simpler. But when Orin had told Gilligan about old Mrs. Marguery in her little freezing cabin, he'd seen tears in Gilligan's eyes. True feeling, Orin wondered, or ersatz Irish sentimentality? Orin didn't know, and now he couldn't ask, because Gilligan had died three years ago in his beloved Eagle River.

"Gilligan didn't believe in stealing," Talbot said.

"Who's stealing?" Orin asked as calmly as he could.

"You are. You want to tell me who I can sell my property to and for how much. And if I don't go along, you'll take it away from me. What would you call it, Orin? What would Gilligan call it? I have as much right to what I own as some little son of a bitch in Yonkers has to his house and his half-acre. And Gilligan would say I was right."

"Gilligan loved this country, and you're wrecking it."

"You sanctimonious fart," Talbot said. "How am I wrecking it? What kind of shit do they feed you . . . what kind of shit do you feed yourself? That the people will freeze or die if we raise our prices? Humbug."

The word was so unexpected, Orin grinned, but Talbot was deadly serious. He bolted out of his chair and stood over Orin's desk. "What do you think you see from the window behind you . . ." Talbot gestured out behind Orin at the big many-paned window that opened out to the Rose Garden. "Or from your helicopter or your yacht or Camp David? What do you think you see in the woods of Three Lakes, or Wausau. The tired, the hungry, the poor? Humbug!" Talbot cried. "Those poor wretches that you think are starving and freezing and frying to death because they can't pay for gas for their cars or oil for their houses are spending twenty billion dollars a year on cosmetics, liquor, cigarettes, and movies. Another few billion on video games and VCR's and home computers. They're taking the oil my granddaddy sold his soul to get and they're fueling their dishwashers and toaster ovens and food processors and electric can openers. Electric can openers! Watch the consumer lists like we do. And when they stop spending their dough and my oil on all that crap, then we can talk about who can afford what. Until then, it's *my* oil and Mapes's and Gordon's and our stockholders'—I suppose you still consider them citizens too. Or maybe you don't. It doesn't matter, it belongs to us and we'll sell it for what we can get for it, and if you try to stop us, I'll take this government to every court between Presque Isle and Galveston. And if you try any shit with the National

227

Guard, our men'll be there to meet them, armed, if it comes to that. And let's just see what happens in this country the first time one of your soldiers kills an American citizen for protecting private property. Let's just see." Talbot whirled away from the desk, grabbed his brandy glass, and drained it. He sat down again, took his handkerchief out of his pocket, and wiped his face.

The room was quiet. Orin looked at Talbot for a while, then spoke mildly. "You're right," he said.

"What?"

"I said you're right."

Orin got up and went back to the liquor cabinet. He picked up Talbot's glass on the way. He moved calmly, but he was frightened because in six days he was going to have to face a mob of some two hundred thousand people and tell them that they were going to have to spend the money they'd put aside for the kids' school or their vacation or their once-a-week beef roast, to heat their houses and buy gas for their cars.

"A shorty for the road?" he asked. Talbot stared at him without answering.

"Don't look like that," Orin said. "It's your oil, just like you said."

He poured the brandy and brought it back to Talbot. Talbot reached for it slowly, like a man in a daze.

"We've all been on a big party for a long time. Since . . . since when, George?"

No answer from Talbot.

"Since fifty, I'd say. And it's over. I guess it's been over for years. But we're still here waiting for the band to strike up again." He swished the brandy around in the glass. "It finally ended about seventy-three, wouldn't you say? The embargo ended it, but here it is 1990 and we're still waiting. The ballroom floor is thick with dust, spiders have spun webs over empty chafing dishes and silver trays, and we still don't go home." He laughed softly. Talbot didn't move. "It's time. You're right."

"You'll let the controls come off?"

Orin nodded.

"No rationing?" Talbot asked. "No National Guard, no last-ditch fights in Congress?"

"No, none of it."

"What'll you do?" Talbot asked wonderingly.

"Try to find a way to beat you fair and square."

Talbot turned slowly to look at Orin. His eyes were almost childlike. "What way, Mr. President?"

Orin shrugged and went back to the liquor cabinet to sweeten his drink. Talbot watched.

Orin stood at the cabinet with his back to Talbot. "What do you think about fusion, George?"

He knew the question would scare Talbot, and he'd think that Orin had something going after all. He didn't. Stockton had not reported yet; there must be nothing to report. The playmate was probably imaginary after all, and the whole thing was Lipsky's delusion. But Talbot deserved a couple of bad minutes; he was going to give the country a lot of bad years. The silence went on for a long time, and Orin turned around to see the effect of his jab. Talbot's cheeks were chalky, his eyes seemed to have sunk in his head.

"I think it's a dream," Talbot said. "Like monkey glands for impotence and royal jelly for wrinkles. I think it's a tale people tell each other on cold nights." He looked sharply at Orin. "Have you been telling yourself tales, Mr. President?"

"Maybe. It'd do it, though, wouldn't it?"

"Do what?"

"Beat you fair and square."

Emily pulled herself up in the seat. Her clothes and the car seat were covered with blood. Blood dried on the floor, on the accelerator and clutch pedal.

She held on to the steering wheel and leaned over. Smitty's doughnuts were still in the glove compartment. She opened it and got them out. They were hard, the sugar crusted on them, but she ate two of them and licked her fingers. They made her sick at first. She was afraid she was going to throw up again, and opened the car door to lean out. But the feeling passed.

It was daylight. Somehow, last night, she'd managed to pull the car off the road and into the patch of wintergreen and ground pine. The smell of crushed wintergreen was sharp, her head cleared, and she heard rustling in the underbrush.

Her fingers scrabbled madly across the floor of the car until she found her one-lensed glasses. The rustling got louder; then a figure came out of the trees and brush and froze at the edge of the clearing where the car was parked. Her heart pounded; she threw one arm across her chest in a futile gesture of protection and jammed her glasses onto her face. The figure came into focus.

It was a little boy, about seven. He was holding a plastic soccer ball and staring at her.

She tried to say something to him, but her throat was dry and her voice came out as a croak; then she tried to smile, and that must have been even worse, because the boy gave a thin wail and ran away into the woods clutching the ball.

She had to move. He'd run home and tell his mother he saw a blood-covered woman in the woods where he played. The mother might believe him—he looked scared enough—and she would call the police.

Emily eased around behind the wheel and saw her face in the rearview mirror. Her skin was light green, her eyes were black rimmed. She looked dead already, and she didn't blame the boy for running away. She had to find water somewhere; her gas was getting low. She'd lost too much blood, but the bleeding had stopped and she didn't *think* that she was dying. She had to call Susie and find out if she was all right. She had to get more food. The list of chores was growing, and she laughed out loud, making a strange sound that worried her.

She started the car, and looked in the mirror again to back out. She remembered Lucci's face half-covered by the mirrored glasses, and then his eyes without the glasses staring at her with pain and hatred. Suddenly she almost remembered the eyes. They reminded her of a jar of dead wasps.

They had been in her locker at some school, she couldn't remember which one. She didn't know how the jar had gotten there or why someone had put dead wasps in her locker. She'd shaken the jar, hoping that one might still be alive and she could open the window and let it go. But the bodies had rattled dryly against the glass and the beautiful iridescent wings had lost their shine and started to crumble. Eyes like Lucci's had watched her. Maybe it *was* Lucci. She tried to remember more, but she couldn't, and she backed the car out into the track and headed back for the road.

Karl Banyan called Eric Greeley as soon as he saw the report on the wire. It was after three, State Trooper Greeley was in off the road, and he came to the phone.

Banyan told him who he was; then he said, "You signed this. . . . You talked to the kid who saw her?"

Greeley said that he had.

"How bad was it?"

Greeley was quiet for a second; then he said, "Hard to tell. The kid thought she was a zombie. Really a zombie. His older sister made him watch one of those ratty horror movies last week, so seeing the woman and all the blood spooked him half-crazy. He'll get over it. His mother was baking him a cherry pie when I left, and I guess they'll spoil him rotten for a couple of days. I told him he'd be a real hero if we do get her. I don't think that mattered to him so much, though. I think once he realized she wasn't one of the walking dead, he started to feel a little sorry for her. He's a nice little boy . . . name of Jimmy Burrows. But I guess that's in the report."

Banyan cleared his throat, and Greeley said, "Sorry to ramble, but we're not used to shit like this around here. Got us all a little spooked. I'm sorry, officer, what was it you wanted to know?"

"How bad the Brand woman was hurt."

"Bad," Greeley said. "Kid said the blood was everywhere. We drove out there. Car was gone by then, but we found tire tracks, and some blood on the ground. It looked like she'd bled all over her shoes, then put her feet outside the car. Like she was trying to stand up. . . ."

Banyan looked out the window next to the desk he shared with Robinson. It would be cold when the sun went down— damp, bone-eating spring cold. He thought of her trapped in her car, awash in her own blood in a dark, freezing patch of woods. He shivered and said, "Thanks, officer. Friend of mine knows her, and I told him I'd let him know."

"Sure," Greeley said. Banyan was ready to hang up, but Greeley kept talking in a soft sad voice. "Hate to think of a woman doing all this . . . killing those people, getting shot

herself. Young, nice-looking woman, too, from the picture."
Banyan didn't answer, and after a minute Greeley said, "Feds
shot her, you know. But it didn't go all that smooth for them.
She blasted out a window behind them, and two of them
came in here bleeding like pigs in the slaughter trough." He
chuckled. Banyan joined him weakly, and they said their
good-byes.

Banyan knew he should tell Ed. But he wasn't going to.
All Beecham talked about now was how she'd been framed
and they had to help her. But Banyan had resolved that he
wasn't going to sling his ass out over the pit for some half-
crazed woman he'd never seen. No matter what. Maybe he'd
have tried if it weren't for the feds. But these boys scared
him, especially a big bastard named Gelb with eyes like
bleached bones who'd come smelling around Placid this
morning.

This thing was driving a wedge between him and Eddie,
and Banyan hated it. He'd have hated her if he didn't feel
so sorry for her. In spite of himself, he looked at the map.
She'd been on the run since Tuesday. Millbridge was west of
Washington Depot, so she was heading into New York. The
poor dumb bitch hadn't made two hundred miles in three
days. Now she was shot, maybe dying, maybe dead already.
He almost hoped she was. Then he and Eddie could go back
to being friends.

Beecham called him later to see if he wanted to meet at
the Hungry Trout and get a light buzz on. Banyan said he
had a headache, and he hung up on Beecham, hating himself
for sounding like a frigid wife. He took home a box of fried
chicken and a six-pack. He finished the beer, all right, but he
couldn't eat the food. He kept thinking about the poor bitch
bleeding to death in the cold night, lost and alone on some
abandoned lumber track, and he couldn't sleep either. Finally
he gave up and took one of the Valiums his wife had left
behind when she took off last year.

The next day he looked in all the local papers, figuring
that he'd hear from Beecham as soon as Beecham read about
it. But there was no mention of a murder suspect being shot
and wounded in Washington Depot or anywhere else. He
went down to the newsstand and bought the Albany *Courier*
and the Hartford *Courant*. There was nothing about Emily

Brand in either paper, and there should have been. He thought he'd be relieved, but he was more troubled than ever.

It was an old mill. The wheel was rotted, some of the spokes caught in the rocks of the dam, and ice-cold water ran over them into the pool.

Emily cupped her hands under the small cataract and drank; then she sat back on the bank and looked down at her side. The T-shirt and the waistband of the slacks were stuck to her skin with dried blood, and she was afraid that pulling the cloth would tear her skin and start the wound bleeding again. She took off her shoes and socks and put her feet into the water. It was so cold it made her ankles ache, but cold slowed liquid; it might keep blood from running. Besides, she couldn't stand the crusted clothes stuck to her anymore.

She waded toward the center of the pool, where a soft eddy came off the dam. A bird watched from the other side, chattered at her, then flew away. She stood still until her body was numb and the blood softened and washed away in small patches of pink foam. Then she held her breath and ducked all the way under. The cold tore at her scalp and her cheeks, but she came up slowly, afraid that a sudden move would open the wound.

She waded back and crawled up on the bank. Most of the blood was gone, and she eased the T-shirt over her head, took off her slacks and underwear, and looked at the wound.

It was deep, but the bullet had gone all the way through, tearing her flesh. The edges were whitish and weeping and the scar would be hideous if she lived long enough for it to heal. She wondered in a distant way how long it would take for the worms to find her revolting wound and make a home in it.

She spread her clothes out in the afternoon sun, then crawled back into the car, unrolled Smitty's bedroll, unzipped it, and wrapped it around her. She was warm and dry, and she fell asleep again. When she woke up, the sun was still up, but it was after five. The clothes were dry and she put them back on, only she put on her old shirt and Marvin's sweater instead of the T-shirt, which still had some stain on it. She was in New York—it didn't seem to matter exactly where. Her forehead was hot, and she was light-headed. She had to find a phone. The stain on her pants was very light now, and the sweater was clean. She looked in the mirror again. She was still terribly pale, and spots of color had come out high on her cheeks, but she wouldn't look that bad from a distance. At least she wasn't covered with blood. It hurt to raise her arm, but she managed to comb her hair, and she drove back out onto the road.

Most of the paving on the road was cracked, there were wide potholes, and every bump hurt. It was almost an hour before she found a gas station with an outside phone; her gas was getting low, but she had only three dollars and change. She parked near the phone and got slowly out of the car. Another car pulled up next to the pumps, and the driver, a man wearing a windbreaker and cloth cap, was talking to the gas jockey. They both looked over at her, and she smiled and nodded. They were about fifty feet away, and they went back to their conversation. They didn't act like they'd seen a ghastly-looking woman on the edge of death who was wanted for murder.

It was cold, but there was sweat on her forehead. She clutched Marvin's sweater around her, found a quarter, and called Susie collect. The phone rang four times. "Please, Susie, be okay. Please, please," she whispered. One of the men at the gas pump laughed raucously, and then Steven answered the phone. He hesitated, and she was terrified that he'd refuse to accept a collect call from Emily Brand, but he did.

"Steven . . . Steven, it's Emily," she said stupidly. "Is Susie there?"

"She's here. She finally fell asleep an hour ago after sitting up all night and all day trying to figure out how to help you. Do you know what you've done to your sister?" His voice was hoarse with anger. "You don't care enough to ask, but I'm going to tell you, Emily. They arrested her. They booked her—obstructing justice—and I had to drive to some godforsaken bullshit-colonial town in Connecticut last night and bail my wife out of jail. Do you hear me, Emily? Do you?"

"Yes, Steven, I hear you."

"She had fifteen thousand dollars on her. For you. So they set the bail at twenty, the pricks. The miserable pricks. They won't get away with this, Emily. I swear they won't.

Let them bring her to trial—but they won't. They won't even get an indictment, the pricks. And then they gave us some shit about you blowing up a plane and killing six people. I think you're crazy, Emily, but I know fucking A—"

There was a click, and Susie's voice came on the line. "Emily . . . Emily is that you? Oh, I tried to lose them. I *did* lose them . . ."

Susie was crying, but she was all right; no one had hurt her. Lucky thing for them, Emily thought feverishly. " 'S okay Susie." Her voice sounded too weak and she hung up without saying any more and went back to the car.

She could call John, but his phone was tapped. Of course, she could do what Susie did. She could hear the conversation, and she giggled at her dream voice saying: *Do you remember the place where you fished last spring, and you caught the seven-pound trout, and I couldn't watch you cut its head off?*

She couldn't do it. John would come to her, and they'd follow him. Susie couldn't lose them, John wouldn't either. Emily had no strength left, and this time Lucci would kill her. John would be a witness and an accessory. Lucci would kill him too. She searched her purse and pulled out her old ragged address book, then put it back without opening it. NARCON had money and computers. They knew everyone she knew. She couldn't ask Herb or Ann Mendel or Sally or Marsha Lipsky to risk their lives or her.

The President would never see her letter. It was in some obscure file or the waste can by now. But Feinstein would be home next week—at least she *thought* it was next week. The *Times* would find out that she was wanted for murder, but she was a respected physicist, too. The murder charge would only make them pay more attention, make them check the three pages that she'd sent them.

She just had to buy a few more days.

Time for the Times.

She would have laughed if she didn't feel so sick and light-headed. But she was aware enough to be glad of the fever and touches of delirium, because they kept the pain at bay.

She pulled out Starrett's gun.

The lights came on over the gas pumps and made a safe, secret-looking pool of light around the two men talking. She couldn't point the gun at them; there were two of them, she told herself. Besides, she wasn't ready yet. She needed a little time to work herself up to pointing the gun at people who'd never done her any harm and taking their money.

Money is time, her father had said. She nodded her aching head firmly. He was right, and it was the first time in her life that she'd ever remembered or agreed with a word that man had said. She was going to steal some innocent person's time—all the time and work it had taken him to get the money she had to take. She would make it as little as possible. She tried to calculate how much she'd need for another three days.

Better make it five days, she thought. But suddenly she couldn't add gallons of gas at so much a gallon, and a couple of meals here and there. She couldn't add anything. She decided on two hundred dollars. It was an arbitrary figure, and might be too much or too little, but she couldn't help that now; besides she had a consolation gift for her victim. A wonderful gift—energy from nanograms of the components of a glass of water, using the secrets of the sun. Surely that would be worth the sorrow and fear she'd cause, and the loss of the precious hours it had taken him to get that money.

She opened the gun. There was one shot left, and she pulled the ammunition box out of the glove compartment and started to reload the gun. The half-lensed glasses made it harder to see the holes in the chamber, and she took them off. She'd gotten four shells loaded when she remembered the reactor-room wall—not just remembered it in a normal way, but actually saw it again: the wall, the blood, the body with its poor shard of bone exposed through flesh and a flannel shirt. She saw the scene in Washington Depot, her blood staining a street that hadn't seen violence since the Revolution.

Whoever she pointed the gun at might need the money so badly he would fight for it. He might have his own gun. Her control wasn't good just now, and she might pull the trigger, and there'd be more blood: her unwilling benefactor's blood, or more of her own.

She left the gun open, then turned it up and shook it so that the bullets fell out onto the front seat and rolled back. Then she closed the gun, put it in her purse with the roll of papers that were still miraculously clean, though ragging at the edges, and her useless address book, and she pulled out of the station and back onto the road.

The gas-station lights disappeared, it was almost dark, the road was empty.

She'd have to risk a bigger road if she didn't come to something soon. Then she passed a sign for the Taconic Parkway, and another for a town called Grant Union. The signs were old and faded and peppered with buckshot. She pulled over and looked at Mr. Bessie's map.

Grant Union was right before the parkway. There might be a liquor store or gas station or a little grocery store open late. She headed for Grant Union. But a mile on, roaring started up in her ears and her legs trembled so badly she could barely drive.

She pulled into the turn-around of a shut-up fruit stand and let her head fall back against the seat. She meant to rest only, but she fell into a deep, dreamless void that, later, when she woke up with a start, seemed more like dying than sleeping. She wondered if she *was* dying. Her skin was hot and tender, her head hurt. But the roaring sound was gone, and she seemed to have better control of her legs.

She started again. It was dark; the moon hadn't risen yet.

Grant Union wasn't much of a town. She passed some run-down-looking houses, a town hall, and a handsome well-kept building that was the Taconic Valley Water and Power Authority. All the stores were shut, and she thought she would have to cross the highway and go on to the next town. Then, just ahead, she saw a lighted island of gas pumps.

The station had an "Open" sign on the door, and a small deli that sold cold cuts and canned goods was attached to it. Their sign announced that they had hot coffee and sand-wiches to go.

Emily pulled into the station, out of the light, and walked back toward the deli entrance.

She had to stop and lean against a pump.

The sounds around her—the night birds calling, the frogs, odd cars passing on the parkway—were muted, as if she had cotton in her ears. She took the gun out of her purse, held it down at her side, then walked into the light. Someone had put a vase of daffodils in the window along with rows of canned tuna fish and olives and coffee. Emily opened the door. The floor was spotless; glass cases of potato salad, coleslaw, and prepared meats shone. All around her, can labels blazed with color, and the steel shelves reflected the light. A short, fat woman in a blue housedress stood behind the counter. Her cheeks were pink and glossy; she had light brown and gray hair and round blue eyes.

"Can I help you?" she asked Emily.

Emily raised the gun above the counter so the woman could see it.

The woman gasped, and Emily tried to tell her to give her two hundred dollars. She knew she was saying it, she could feel her mouth moving, but she couldn't hear her own voice. All the normal noises around her disappeared, and the roaring came back in waves. The colors and shapes in the shop spread, faded, vanished, and suddenly she was on her back looking up at the white ceiling. That started to fade too. She was going to black out, and she realized with a terrible ache of regret that this was the end of her.

CHAPTER

16

SHE HAD WHIPPED him again, and the men in Stockton's office knew it, even Gelb. Gelb sat in the corner, in the shadow of the bookcases, listening without talking.

David wanted to get Mr. Gelb alone. To tell him that they were not dealing with an ordinary woman, but with a demon. He couldn't use those words, he'd sound insane; but he could make Gelb understand how serious it was. The old farts didn't seem to know. Stockton was talking about some letters. Then David realized that they were *her* letters, and he made himself concentrate.

"We had to let them go," Stockton said.

Talbot used his Mafia Don whisper, "I hope you had a good reason for that, Paul."

"We did," Stockton said quickly. "The Marbleton sheriff had fluoroscoped them and knew they were harmless. He wouldn't waylay them without a warrant. They don't like government men up there, and it was risky to try bribing him. We could have gotten a warrant, but then the judge would have seen the letters, and maybe the sheriff, and God knows who else. We could have forced the issue, but we didn't want another incident"—he looked pityingly at David—"so we let them go. The two to the White House were intercepted there and destroyed. But the *Times* mail is sorted and distributed by computer. She isn't famous. The computer may not even send the letter on. But if it does, and the science editor sees it, we're covered. Not the editor himself. He's a Paul Garner, and he has an M.A. in biology. He doesn't know much about physics, so he has a consultant."

Stockton paused and smiled. "The consultant is Charles Owens."

Talbot chuckled, and David knew that they owned Charles Owens, the way they owned Carver and Flynn. The old farts had one more flunky in place, and they were pleased with themselves and thought they were safe, while all the time she was out there, free and making her plans. His fists clenched, sweat rolled down his ribs, and he had to fight to control himself. Then Stockton said something so stupid that David literally wanted to kill him:

"Of course, we may be out of the woods anyway. There's a good chance—seventy-thirty, according to the computer—that the wound was mortal and she bled to death somewhere between Washington Depot and the New York border."

"No," David whispered.

Stockton ignored him. "The men in Washington Depot said the wound was bad. A little boy saw her yesterday morning and thought she was dead until she moved. She called the sister last evening. She didn't talk long enough for a trace, but we listened to the tape, didn't we, Kurt?"

Gelb didn't answer.

"And we thought she stopped talking because she was too weak to go on. Isn't that right, Kurt?"

Gelb didn't even nod.

"We put all this together," Stockton said, "and decided—"

"No," David cried out.

It was quiet for a second; then Stockton snapped, "Then where is she, Lucci?"

"Holed up somewhere."

"Without food, money, or medical treatment for two days . . ."

"Someone's helping her."

"Ridiculous. I can't imagine anyone helping a total stranger who's wanted for murdering six—"

"You incompetent coward," David yelled. "You've got fifty trained killers and half the cops in the Northeast running down one woman who has nothing but a car and a bullet in her side, and you can't kill her. So you decide that she's dead, so you can save your stupid face . . ."

Stockton turned red and started to tremble, but David couldn't stop.

"She's alive; she's holed up and healing somewhere, and she'll come out and keep going until she scores, Stockton. And when she does, you're going to spend the rest of your limp little life in the slammer giving blow-jobs—"

"Get out!" Stockton screamed. "Out!"

David slammed out of the office into the hall and stood against the wall to catch his breath. The outburst eased the tension and he felt better. Talbot would soothe Stockton. Talbot wouldn't mind because he enjoyed watching David lose his temper and he loved seeing men at each other's throats.

The door opened, and Gelb came out into the hall. "Come with me," he said, and walked down the hall.

David followed him without asking questions. Gelb led him downstairs, through a modern room with women typing, computer terminals on the desks, and into another room at the back of the house. It was fixed up like a parlor, and looked out on a neat, beautifully arranged garden. It was a comfortable room, with chintzy furniture and homespun-type drapes. Gelb sat on a settee; David sat across from him in a wing chair.

It was late afternoon; the room was dim and full of shadows. Gelb leaned over and snapped on a lamp next to him, and David saw his face clearly for the first time. One look and he understood why Stockton was scared of him and Talbot treated him like a member of the board. Bledsoe had been beefy and stupid-looking, like a worker in a meat-packing plant. Kelsey was pale and watery-eyed and looked like a tenth-rate accountant. But Gelb had the face of a killer. He was handsome except for his eyes. They were the color of tarnished metal, and they looked dead. David wondered if they'd frighten him too; he knew they should, but he didn't feel anything, and he waited calmly to see what Gelb wanted.

Gelb said, "You don't think she's dead."

"No."

"Why?"

"I'd know if she were dead. Don't ask me any more. She's alive."

Gelb nodded. "Stockton wants to believe it for obvious reasons. Saving face, as you said, and because he's in much deeper than he'd planned. Two of his men are dead, the target's still on the loose, and he'd planned a quick neat operation. He wants desperately to believe that she's dead. He's scared; so is your father-in-law. Fascinating."

"What's fascinating about it?"

"As you said, she's alone, broke, and wounded. A woman without training or allies, and she got rid of Bledsoe—nasty customer, by the way—and she's made dogshit out of the whole agency. Fascinating. Of course, most of it's luck. But it's something else, too."

David nodded.

"What?" Gelb asked.

"She's smart."

"I have heard that you are too. Very neat, the way you figured out she'd be in Washington Depot. You should have killed her then. Why didn't you?"

"I didn't have a gun."

"Stupid," Gelb said blandly.

"Not really. I've never fired one."

"We'll have to take care of that."

"Why?" David asked.

"Stockton told me you've been there for two of the . . . confrontations. That you insisted on it. I have the feeling that you'll insist again, and I don't want a man with me who doesn't know how to use a gun."

David felt a warning chill. It reminded him of looking in her notebook and knowing that something dangerous was in the room with him. He pushed the feeling down and nodded.

Gelb stood up. "There's a practice range upstairs. I have to go to New York in a couple of hours, but we can start tomorrow. That is, if no one finds Emily Brand's body rotting in a patch of woods by then."

"Why New York?"

"In case the *Times* editor gets that letter after all."

At the door of the room, Gelb touched David's arm; David had to stop himself from pulling away. Gelb said, "The others are worried about their business, their money, what they think of as their power. It's something else with you, isn't it?"

David didn't answer.

"Do you know her?" Gelb asked.

"I knew her a long time ago."

"Some kind of love thing?"

David laughed, and Gelb watched with his calm empty yes. He didn't even smile. When David stopped laughing, ;elb said, "I have a couple of hours before the plane leaves. Vould you like to go somewhere for a drink?"

"Yes," David said. He was flattered.

Paul Garner had been science editor for two years. He ead his own mail except for ads and charity pleas. He got nly five or six letters a day (not like the health editor, who /as inundated), and it seemed arrogant and unnecessary to :t the computer dispose of any of them. Sometimes it was /orthwhile—a lay reader would have an intelligent comment r insight he could use. Most of the time, the letters were 'orthless.

"Junk," Garner muttered as he looked through this 1orning's mail. A woman in Minnesota wrote that she had ured her advanced breast cancer with grape juice—three uarts a day. She didn't say if she drank it, bathed in it, or sed it in an enema. A man in California was doing genetic ngineering in his garage, and he was sure that he'd created bacterium that converted grain alcohol to gasoline. An- ther man wrote that he'd identified a tenth moon orbiting upiter.

The letters annoyed Garner and made him sad. He didn't ke to think of people as fools, and as he shoved the letters 2gether in a sloppy pile, he hoped that the people who'd /ritten them weren't as mentally lazy and ignorant and ungry for attention as they seemed. They were just lonely, e told himself, and a little desperate for contact.

The last of the bunch was three Xerox pages of equations hat he didn't understand. There was a short note attached:

> Plans for a fusion reactor capable of
> sustained neutron discharge and capture.
> Please investigate and disseminate as soon
> as you can. My situation is difficult.

he note was signed E. A. Brand, Ph.D. There was no title r affiliation with the signature, and the note was handwritten. It wasn't like the rest of the junk, and Garner went to his bookcase, pulled out Volume I of *American Men and Women of Science*, and was surprised to find an entry for Emily A(usten) Brand, and a respectable CV.

He dialed the computer, and found a file on her. He sent Celia down to get it. There were three articles, all from the *Times*. The last one was three days old. A plane had blown up over Mount Marcy seven days ago, the FAA investigator had evidence of sabotage, and Emily Brand was wanted for questioning. She had disappeared; the state and local police were on the alert for her. The *Times* didn't use the word "suspect," but Garner knew that the other papers would come right out with it. *Woman physicist blows up boss and five innocents*. But the stories were terse, even for the *Times*, and there was nothing for the past two days.

He picked up the pages of equations. Nothing there to help the police. Then he looked at her note again.

My situation is difficult.

"Well," he said softly, "I guess it is, lady. You're wanted for murder."

He put the letter and pages of chicken scratches in the out-file box and ordered his lunch—egg salad and bacon on rye—and went back to his series on the crisis in education in the basic sciences. His sandwich arrived, and he stopped working to eat it. He looked again at the small pile of paper. The note was short and reserved, and he liked that. Celia came to collect file material, and on impulse, he took the Brand stuff off the top and laid it on his desk. He finished his sandwich, lit a cigarette, and stared at the indecipherable marks trailing across the page. She could have put anything on those pages and he wouldn't have known the difference. He read the note again. The words meant something to him, and he made himself remember some recent articles they'd published. He looked from the words to the equations, and back to the words, and all at once he got a sense of something, and the skin at the back of his neck crept. Neutron discharge . . . neutron capture . . . *fusion*.

He picked up his phone, got an outside line, and called Charles Owens.

Dr. Owens was the executive editor of the *Journal of the American Society of Nuclear Physicists*. He had an office on

105th Street in a fine old graystone just east of Fifth. There was a vanity about him that always put Garner off a little. He was a short, very thin man with thick gray hair and a pointed well-groomed beard. His clothes looked tailor-made, and the midnight-blue jacket of today's suit hung perfectly from his thin shoulders. Owens was on the board of the AAAS and an adviser, to the White House during two administrations. Most of all, he could convert physics into English, and the *Times* and a number of journals paid him a lot of money to do it.

Owens was going over the three pages while Garner sat across the desk and waited. On the wall behind his desk, Owens had hung pictures of himself with Leo Szillard, Robert Oppenheimer, Edward Teller. There was one of him shaking hands with Ronald Reagan. Owens shuffled the papers together and looked up.

"You'll have to leave these with me," he said.

"Okay," Garner said. "I got a copy made. I thought I'd show it to Ira Benson too."

There was a tic of something—Garner couldn't tell what—on Owens' face. His skinny fingers roved over E. Brand's pages.

"Do you think that's necessary? I could give you a 'reading' now, but I thought I'd give the lady a bit more of my time."

"Fine, but I just thought Ira'd be interested too."

Owens' face was cold. "Ira Benson hasn't done physics for thirty years," he said.

Neither have you, Garner thought.

"Besides, this stuff"—Owens flicked at the paper with the back of his hand—"is hardly new. It's good enough work, but it was done—by which I mean built and tried—four years ago at Livermore."

"Oh?"

"Yes. It failed . . . that is, it didn't do what was hoped."

"Which was?" Garner asked.

"Sustain nuclear fusion for practical use, Mr. Garner. Of course, it wasn't a failure in the sense that the work deepened our understanding of the problem. Always worthwhile."

Owens sounded like he'd done the work himself. He was

oilier than ever today, and he was something else that Garner couldn't figure out.

Garner said, "Why don't you hang on to it, anyway. Look again, just in case . . ."

"In case of what?" Owens asked sharply.

"I don't know. In case you missed something."

"That's hardly likely," Owens said. Then he asked tightly, "You're not still taking this to Benson?"

"Sure. Why not?"

Garner stood up, and Owens snapped, "I told you that isn't necessary." Garner was surprised. He looked back at the other man.

Owens didn't meet his eyes. "Benson can't tell you any more. He can't tell you as much." Owens did look at Garner then, and Garner thought he saw pleading in his eyes.

The whole thing was getting very strange, and Garner tried to lighten the air a little. "Of course I'm going to show it to Ira," he said. "Maybe he'll call you, and you can both knock it around a little."

Owens still wore that pleading look. "I can't dissuade you, Mr. Garner?" he asked softly.

"Why on earth would you want to?"

Owens didn't answer, and Garner said good-bye and left the office. Owens barely waited until the door was closed, and he reshuffled the pages and looked at them again. Very closely this time. He pulled a pad over and made a few equations of his own, then went to his files and pulled out a sheaf of articles and brought them back to his desk. Half an hour later, he sat back in his chair, took off his glasses, and rubbed his eyes. Then he lifted the papers almost reverently in his hands. It was magical work, and for a few seconds he let himself feel privileged to have been one of the first people on earth to see it. He didn't want to call NARCON. At this moment, everything in him wanted to call his staff and start these three pages into print for everyone to see and marvel at. But he couldn't. Eight years ago, George Talbot had hired him as casually as he would have hired a typist. Owens had been insulted by everything about the deal, except the money. He'd taken that, and kept taking it. NARCON had records, and last night on the phone George Talbot had said, "You've been very valuable to us, Dr. Owens," and then the gentle phone voice had turned cold and Owens had found himself holding the phone so tightly his hand cramped. "You're one of the most respected men in American science, doctor. Your reputation has always been enviable. . . ."

Owens closed his eyes and sat still, holding the precious pages for as long as he dared, but Garner had been gone almost an hour, too long already, and Owens grasped the edges of the pages and tore them in half. Then he picked up the phone.

CHAPTER
17

EMILY HAD TO swallow, choke, or spit up. She didn't know
which she did. Her body and hair were drenched in sweat.
The left side of her body was raw; she couldn't move. Some
one tugged at her clothes; she tried to pull away and cry out
but she couldn't, and she passed out again.

Later she saw a watercolor of a casement window with
starched white eyelet curtains and sunlight coming through
it. It was from a children's book she'd had in the old house
in Wilton. There were trees outside, and she knew that if
she could sit up, she would see hollyhocks growing under the
window. A breeze came, moved the curtains, and touched
her burning skin. She thought she groaned, and started to
tremble. Someone murmured—she couldn't make out the
words; she closed her eyes, and when she peeked again, the
window was closed, the curtains hung still, and reflections on
the glass hid the trees. The watercolor faded and turned to
paint washing off in a heavy rain. She thought she'd see gray
walls behind the running colors. Not the reactor room, but
a cell. She waited for Lucci to come into view. He would be
there; he would not miss the kill. Sure enough, his head rose
up along the side of whatever she lay on like the head of a
snake. He had a gun; he was grinning in anticipation as he
raised it and put the muzzle gently against her lips. Cold
metal touched her teeth. He pulled the safety back, put his
hand behind her head, and gently raised it. She saw his finger
squeezing at the trigger. Her grief was unbearable. She would
never see Susie or John again, the machine was done for . . .
no one would build it, the old one was already in ruins, like

the house in Wilton, but much worse; the sides were dented, the dents filled with rust, the girder had fallen across the top, and the wires were disconnected and trailed across the floor, corroded and useless. There was nothing to take its place because he was going to kill her in an instant. She had to stop him. She raised her hand, contorted her fingers so her hand was a claw; the hand was yellow, slick, with swollen black veins. It was her mother's hand; it reached out for his smiling beautiful face. He flinched back, but it was too late. Her mother's chipped, cracked nails snatched into his eye. The gun sagged, cracked against Emily's teeth. He fought, thrashed, the gun waved in the air. It was no use; her mother's fingers scooped out the socket, and blood poured down his smooth cheek. He opened his mouth to scream. Emily could see his tongue, back teeth, the uvula fluttering. . . .

"Can you sit up?"

She was expecting shrieks of pain and terror.

"Can you sit up?" He sounded like a woman, and she opened her eyes.

It was the woman from behind the counter in the deli. The watercolor window was there, but it was real. It was closed, and Emily could see the room in it, and half of herself. She seemed to be lying on a bed.

"Try," the woman said.

Emily tried to raise her head. Something inside of her pulled at her side, and she thought she would split open. The woman held her head, and Emily relaxed. The pain eased. The woman slid another pillow under her head. Emily smelled clean linen; her head lay against the cool sheet. Her skin was dry; her eyes didn't ache.

"Could you eat something?" the woman asked.

Emily tried to use her voice and made a hoarse, rusty sound. She tried again. Her mouth and tongue were dry, her lips were rough. "I don't know," she whispered.

"Would you like to try?" Emily managed to nod. The woman left the bed, crossed the room, and went through the door.

Emily looked around. The room was out of focus, but she could see the walls were white and covered with paintings of flowers in delicate colors. There was a bright rag rug on the dark, polished floor. She was covered with a blue wool blanket, and an ivory candlewick spread was folded at the end of the bed. She pulled back the cover. She was wearing a short nightgown with blue flowers on it. A white enameled chair sat next to the bed with a clean bedpan on it. The chrome of the bedpan caught the light, gleamed into her eyes, and she looked away and wondered where her glasses were. The nightgown was clean, like everything else in the room. There were no bloodstains. She pulled at it; it was short and loose, and she managed to uncover the front of her body.

Her skin looked like paper; her pelvic bones made sharp humps. Her side was black and yellow and looked like someone had taken a saw to it. But the wound wasn't weeping; it was dry, scabs had formed.

The door opened, and the woman came in carrying a tray. "Oh, no," she said gently. She put the tray down and came to the bed. "You'll get chilled, dear."

Emily couldn't get herself covered in time, and she was embarrassed at being nude in front of a stranger. The woman pulled the nightgown back down, raised the covers, smoothed them into place, and went back for the tray.

"I wanted to give you some chicken, but Jesse said nothing but liquid at first. See how it goes down. She's right, I'm sure. She used to be a nurse . . . only an LPN, but Jesse's always been the bright one. I was sure she could have been a doctor if our folks had had the money and it had been more usual for a woman to go to medical school back then."

She put the bed tray across the bed. "Try to eat," she said gently.

Emily croaked, "Thank you, Miss . . ."

"Perth," the woman said. "Mrs. Roy Perth. But Roy's been dead nine years. Call me Jenny."

Steam came out of the bowl on the tray. Emily smelled beef, and her mouth filled with water. It was brown broth, and a bowl of Jell-O sat next to it. Emily picked up the spoon and dipped it into the soup.

"Hold on a second," Jenny said. She took a napkin off the tray and draped it over Emily's chest and neck.

Emily sipped the soup; it mixed with the water in her mouth and slid down her throat like silk. She took another spoonful, then picked up the bowl and brought it to her mouth.

"Not too fast," Jenny cried. "You'll sick up. Use the spoon, dear, use the spoon."

Reluctantly Emily put the bowl down and went back to the spoon.

Jenny took the bedpan off the chair and sat down next to the bed. After a minute she said, "The gun was empty. You weren't going to shoot anybody, were you, Dr. Brand?"

Emily's hand went numb; the spoon dropped onto the napkin and left a spot.

Jenny jumped up and retrieved the spoon. "It's okay," she murmured. She put the spoon back into Emily's hand and wrapped her fingers around it.

Emily gripped it and looked up at the woman. She was helpless; she didn't know what was coming.

The woman's eyes were calm and kind. "I tell you it's okay. We pulled the car into the shed with Roy's old tractor. No one's been near that shed since Roy died. 'We' is me and Jesse. Jesse's my sister. The nurse I told you about. Drink that soup now."

Emily dipped the spoon.

"We know your name 'cause we looked in your purse. I thought we'd a right, under the circumstances. We'd a known soon enough anyway," Jenny said. "The police're looking for you."

Emily closed her eyes. The spoon sagged.

"Eat, now. You can sleep again in a bit."

Emily went back to the soup.

"Cops're combing the valley for you. We heard they've been asking everyone between here and Albany if anybody's seen you. Not just regular cops, either, but federal men in suits and ties. They know all about the car, except that they think it's black and has New York plates." She smiled. "We didn't enlighten them."

"Thank you."

"Well, you're welcome, I'm sure. But no need for thanks. It's been a deadly winter, and we were almost glad to see you. Now, of course, we're very glad. Hasn't been this much excitement around here since Nat Hardy shot his wife in the head, then put the shotgun in his own mouth and pulled the trigger with his toe . . . and that was . . . Oh, dear, must be twenty years since Nat did that." Jenny smiled placidly. "Dreadful winters around here. Not as bad as Lake Placid, of course. We know you live there. *Lived* there. I don't guess you know where you live now, do you?"

Emily didn't answer, and Jenny said, "The point is, we're glad you're here, and we'll be sorry to see you go. So you can stay as long as it's safe. I hope that's a long time, but the police could turn up here one day. We're a bit off the track, so they'll probably save us for last. Besides, they'd think Jesse'n I'd have a full-scale fit did we ever face an armed desperado."

Jenny laughed softly. "That's what old Mrs. Rourke called you. 'An armed desperado.' " Then Jenny stopped smiling and she looked away from Emily shyly.

"I'm making light of this, and I shouldn't. You're hurt. People with guns're after you. And we believe in you, Dr Brand. Both of us."

"Why?"

"You didn't load that gun, you unloaded it. We found the shells on the seat. You're half-starved, and hurt, the cops're after you, and you don't have five dollars to your name, but you *unloaded* the gun."

Emily looked blankly at her, and Jenny made a sound of impatience. "You unload your gun so you won't hurt anyone and the cops say you blew up six people so you could kill your boss. Doesn't wash, does it? In fact, it's downright horsefeathers. So we believe in you. Besides, even before we found the bullets and realized what you'd done and not done, I got a feeling about you. Just looking at you lying there on the floor in those ridiculous clothes, and white as a piece of Greek cheese, I got this feeling. You know how you get feelings about people?"

Emily *didn't* know. But Jenny Perth had *thought*, too, and if there'd been bullets in Mr. Starrett's gun, Emily knew that she would be in a prison hospital now, or dead, no matter what kind of feeling Jenny had gotten about her.

Emily looked out the window. The sun was setting.

"How long have I been here?"

"Three days," Jenny said. "You were burning up and

little off your head. But Jesse got some erythromycin and Sustagen from Sam Decker, the druggist in Grant Union. He's eighty, and he'll give you almost anything you ask for short of morphine. We dosed you with that. We was afraid you'd choke, but you swallowed real nice, and the fever came down this morning. Jesse and I figured you need another couple of days' rest before you go back . . . on the lam." Jenny smiled happily. "That's a gunshot wound, isn't it?" she asked.

Emily nodded.

"Where'd it happen?"

Emily told her.

"How many were there?" Jenny asked.

"Three."

"Did you get any of them?"

Emily shook her head, and Jenny looked disappointed. "Your gun was loaded then, wasn't it? I mean, you're a decent woman, but you ain't an ass."

Emily smiled. "It was loaded."

Jenny considered this for a minute; then she said, "You're a lousy shot."

"Probably," Emily said. "I haven't shot *at* anyone yet."

"Maybe you'll never have to. We'll pray for that."

Here Jenny bowed her head briefly. Her lips moved, and Emily watched the top of her sleek head and caught a whiff of Jenny's smell—harsh soap of some kind, the starch in her housedress, a hint of sweat, and another faint aroma, like fresh bread. Emily closed her eyes, and when she opened them again, the lights were on in her room and Jenny stood next to her bed with another woman, who supported herself on two canes.

"This is Jesse," Jenny said, "and we have a surprise for you."

From behind her back she produced a spectacle case and handed it to Emily. Emily opened it and saw her glasses. The lens had been replaced.

"We took them over to Kingston where no one knows us and had it done there. Only took a few minutes. Had to make both lenses the same. Hope that works okay. 'Course the geezer at the spectacle shop insisted on fitting them to my face, so they won't be perfect, but it's better than going without, and you get bad headaches just looking through one eye all the time."

Emily opened them and put them on. The women and the room around her came into clear focus for the first time. "They're fine," she said. The two women beamed at her. They were handsome and looked alike except that Jesse was older, and her eyes were green instead of blue.

They brought in a folding table and set it up so they could eat dinner with her. Then Jenny gave Emily her tray with a flourish. There was a small piece of boiled chicken, more broth, and vitamin pills, and rice pudding for dessert. Emily ate everything slowly, and it all tasted wonderful and seemed to go down easily.

They woke her up at eight the next morning and gave her soft-boiled eggs for breakfast; then Jenny made her get up and walk around the room.

"You'll get stiff as parchment if you lie still too long," she said. She was right; Emily's whole body ached, and she had to hold on to the wall to stay on her feet.

"This afternoon you'll come outside," Jenny said. "It's a fine day. You can sit in the yard—no one'll see you from the road. The sun'll do you more good than anything."

The sun felt wonderful, but there was a cool breeze and Jenny settled Emily in a lawn chair and put a blanket over her so she wouldn't get chilled. Emily soaked up the warm sun, had rice pudding for lunch, drank tea, and watched the mountains, which looked to be fifteen or twenty miles away. They were just the tame Catskills, and she thought proudly about her mountains, the Adirondacks, a hundred miles or so to the north, and then she fell asleep.

Later, Emily sat at the kitchen table in a square of sunlight watching Jenny cook. She dreamed: maybe they'd never think to come here, and she could stay. She could help them in the store this summer . . . No, she might be recognized. But she could help in the garden. She would pick berries with Jesse, and clean house for them. In winter—she yearned—in winter she could sit here near the wood stove and watch the snow fall. She would read one of the books she'd meant to read all of her life and never got around to. She'd read *Jane Eyre* at last, and shovel snow.

But even if she survived, even if she could hide out here for months, or even years—the rest of her life—in this pretty peaceful place with these two sweet people who reminded her of Marvin in a funny way, and a little of John, the machine would never be built. The old one would fall to ruins, like she thought it had when she was delirious, and there wouldn't be one to take its place.

She didn't want it to be so important; but she looked at the wood stove, then at Jenny's broad back bent over the counter, chopping celery.

"How much is your electric bill every month?" she asked.

Jenny turned around. "What an odd question."

"How much?"

Jenny didn't have to think about it. "Five hundred in the summer, over six in the winter. That's for the house and shop. It doesn't count the power for the gas pump. We keep that separate, and that's about another hundred and fifty. It comes to more than half of what we make in a year. Thank God, we don't need air conditioning. Poor Tom Dockerty does, 'cause he's got asthma and he can't stand breathing dust and pollen. I dread to think what it costs him to get through a summer." Her mouth twisted with annoyance. "They don't let you live." She went back to the celery, and Emily pulled her body gently against her left side. It ached, but the pain wasn't sharp and her fever was gone. She stood up with the blanket across her shoulders and moved across the room. She could walk pretty well. She slowly bent over, the blanket fell forward over her face, and she touched her toes, then stood up. She wasn't healed, but she was mending. She couldn't stop yet.

Jenny watched her in amazement. "What are you doing?"

"Testing. It's much better."

"Well, don't look so miserable about it. Lord be praised. We'll celebrate tonight. I'll tell Jesse to take some wine out . . ."

Emily sank down at the kitchen table.

"Bet it made you dizzy, all that testing," Jenny said. "Can I get you something?"

Emily stared blankly ahead.

"How about a bit of tapioca? Jesse hates tapioca, but I love it. It'll be wonderful to have someone to eat it with.

255

You *do* like tapioca?" Emily didn't say anything. Jenny sounded worried. "Oh, dear . . . oh, my dear. Can I get you anything at all?"

Emily nodded without looking at her. "The New York *Times* for the past three days," she said.

Jenny brought them from the library with wooden spindles still through the backs. She'd told Mrs. Morain, the librarian, that she'd had the flu, hadn't read the papers for days, and felt real left out of things. Mrs. Morain was surprised and pleased that Jenny read the *Times* at all.

"I don't," she told Emily. "But Mrs. Morain doesn't need to know that."

Jenny set up at the kitchen table with tea and tapioca, and then she left her alone. Emily went through the papers carefully. She read the articles about the plane crash, and the almost polite mention of her being wanted for questioning, but there wasn't anything about a fusion breakthrough by Emily Brand or anybody else. She knew she hadn't missed it, but she went through the papers again because she didn't know what else to do, and on page two of yesterday's paper she read: "SCIENCE EDITOR DIES IN FALL."

Paul Garner had jumped from the terrace of his apartment in New York. He left a note for his estranged wife. He had been depressed since their divorce, his children were growing away from him, his life had no meaning without his family. He'd written the note (typed, according to the story, and signed—), gone out onto his terrace, climbed the railing, and jumped. It was twenty-three floors to the ground, and in spite of herself, Emily imagined the fall: the wind would plaster his hair back against his skull; laws of momentum would take over, and he would fall faster and faster. His flesh would pull back against his bones, his organs would press upward. Maybe he screamed, but no one could hear him at the speed his body would be traveling, and then he'd hit the ground, and everything inside of him would explode and fill his skin like water fills a plastic sack. At that speed, the bones in his face would break, his nose would lose its shape, his chin and cheeks would fill with blood and smashed flesh and muscle.

She was sick. She knew they'd murdered Garner. She shut here eyes and crumpled the paper against her chest, the spindle digging into her shoulder. She didn't know what she was feeling; it was rotten, whatever it was. It made her heart pump and her hands sweat. She didn't know who these people were or what they wanted. The machine—but they couldn't kill seven people for a machine. They wanted something else that she didn't know about, and probably wouldn't understand if she did. She didn't understand what she was feeling now, either. Scraps of things came back to her: Margaret Pleasance's smooth beautiful neck, dimpled where the point of the knife touched it, and the collapsing shape of the dinosaur. She remembered black shapes tumbling out of the burning plane and Marsha Lipsky's haggard face at her husband's funeral. The pictures were making it worse, and she tried to stop them, but they kept snapping at her like lantern slides. She saw the black hole of Bledsoe's gun muzzle coming up at her in the reactor room, and that turned into Miss Iselin's eyes, teary with pity Emily didn't want; and then she saw Lucci's face.

"Oh, dear," Jenny cried from the doorway, "don't crumple the paper, Mrs. Morain will be furious."

Jenny brought the papers back to the library, and when she got home, Emily was still at the kitchen table, sitting alone in the dark. Jenny turned on the lights and started preparing their supper. "Did you find what you were looking for?" she asked.

"No."

"You could tell us what it is, you know. We'd never tell anyone."

"No."

"Don't you trust us, Emily?" she asked gently.

"Yes. But it's not a good thing to know about. Everybody who did is dead, except me."

It was Monday; the woman at Feinstein's house said he would be back on May 3. All she had to do was stay alive and free for six more days.

Feinstein soaked in a hot bath with baking soda in it to try to ease his sunburn. The trip had not been a success, and they came home a week early, and he was overjoyed.

He never wanted to go back to the Caribbean, he never wanted to drink rum again or watch grown men with eyes full of hatred cavort like children for his entertainment. He eased himself out of the tub after a while and dried himself carefully. Then he put on his pajamas, shuddering at the cool fabric against his warm skin, and he went out into the bedroom.

Ruth was on her side of the bed, trying to read. He knew she'd had a miserable time too, and he felt sorry for her. She'd wanted it to work, tried everything including making love every afternoon. But it was too hot, or he'd gotten too much sun or something, because even that wasn't much fun. She kept her eyes on her book and said, "Did the baking soda help?"

"Sure," he lied.

He sat on the edge of the bed and looked at the notepad next to the phone. He'd have to call his mother in the morning and tell her that they were home and thank her for calling to say good-bye. He looked forward to talking to the old lady. She had a strong Yiddish accent and she still lived in Brighton Beach. She'd be a good antidote to five days on Nassau. He lifted the slip of paper with her message and saw Ruth's next note: "Emily Brand . . . Lake Placid . . ."

The name was familiar. He turned to Ruth. "Did this Emily Brand say why she was calling?"

"I can't remember. It couldn't have been that important."

But her voice got high and tight.

"How do you know it wasn't important?"

"I never heard of her."

He whirled around to face her. "You've never heard of lots of important people."

She got tears in her eyes, and he turned away and tried to remember. Emily Brand . . .

Then it came to him—the meeting in Orin's office with that worm Carver, and talk about the work that didn't exist, the breakthrough that had never been made, the imaginary playmate. She was at Placid—that was it. Two women: Dr. Avery and Dr. Brand.

He picked up the phone and started to dial the number on the pad.

"It's too late to call anyone," Ruth said. He ignored her

and kept on dialing. She slapped her book down against the covers. "That's the lab," she said. "It'll be closed."

He put the phone down and turned to her. She'd never seen him look so angry. She was almost afraid of him. But she didn't move or drop her eyes. She stared right back at him.

"What did she say, Ruth?"

"I told you, I don't remember—"

"Goddammit, you knew it was the lab. What did she say?"

"You can call in the morning, like a normal—" He grabbed her upper arm so hard she cried out.

"What did you do, you stupid bitch!" he shrieked at her. Her courage deserted her, and she started to cry.

He shook her. "Tell me what she said . . . tell me what she could have said that was less important than that wonwerful trip we just took . . . tell me . . ."

She sobbed, and wiped her face, and tried to remember. "She said she was calling about that little man who was bothering you all the time. I don't remember his name."

"Marvin Lipsky."

"Yes . . . she was in the lab, she said, and you had to call, because something had happened. And that's all. She gave me the number, and I swear that's all . . ."

He let go of her and stared at her. For the first time in his life, he wanted to hit her. He took a deep breath and turned away from her. She sobbed wildly against the pillow.

"Shut up."

She didn't stop.

"Ruth, I swear to God, if you don't shut up, I'll put the pillow over your face." It sounded so ridiculous—ten years ago they would have laughed for a week over that one. But now she knew he meant it, and she leaped out of their bed and ran into the bathroom. She slammed the door, and her sobs were muffled.

He picked up the phone again to call the President. He might be asleep, but Feinstein would make them wake him up.

Stockton pulled the receiver away from his ear and had to wipe the sweat off it. He put it back and nodded into it.

"Yes, Mr. President, Mr. Feinstein is quite right, but we

259

knew it was Dr. Brand. We interviewed Dr. Avery, and it wasn't her . . . so by elimination it had to be Dr. Brand, *if* it was anybody. But we're not convinced—"

"I'm convinced," Orin said. "Find her."

Stockton thought: *This had to happen. How could I think this wouldn't happen?* He said, "We've been trying, Mr. President, but the lady's wanted for murder and she's disappeared . . . not surprising under the circumstances." Franklin didn't answer. "Mr. President?"

"Whose murder?"

"Didn't you see it in the papers? Well, it was a local thing, I suppose. Marvin Lipsky, and of course the other people on that plane."

"Why?" Franklin sounded shaken, and Stockton felt better. "No one knows, Mr. President. But the evidence is quite damning. The woman's been unstable all of her life. She was expelled from Trent School for trying to kill another student." He sounded confident, like himself again. "I'm afraid our Dr. Brand has turned out to be a crazy." It was quiet, and Stockton knew that Orin Franklin finally had the wind knocked out of him.

But then Franklin spoke and didn't sound winded. "Find her," he said. "I don't care if she blew up a Concorde. Find her now."

Stockton started to say something conciliatory, but the President hung up.

Stockton mopped at his hands and face and then looked down at the pad next to his phone. He'd doodled her name while he was talking, and now it covered the pad. Emily Brand, Emily A. Brand, EAB. He tore the page off of the pad and ripped it to pieces. He would have liked to burn them, say a prayer over them, throw a magic potion on the flames to dissolve the ashes. He grinned, but it wasn't funny.

His clever little trail was no use now. Franklin wouldn't be satisfied with anything except her corpse; but Stockton had a ready-made story. She had been shot trying to escape, shot trying to kill a federal officer . . . and died of the wound. It was true. She had tried to escape, she had pointed a gun at Martins and Levenson. They'd get away with killing her if she were still alive, and with having killed her if she were dead. They'd pin the plane crash on her, and the new reactor or whatever it was would go back into the oblivion she'd pulled it out of.

It could still all work, if they found her, or her body. He remembered the condition of Bledsoe's corpse, and Klusky with his throat shot out, and poor Levenson dabbing at the cuts on his face with a cotton swab and mumbling that he'd never go near her again.

"Please, God," Stockton prayed softly, "let it be her body."

CHAPTER

THE STATE TROOPER came in just as Joe Bowman got his container of coffee and left. The trooper had to stand aside to let Joe through the door.

Jenny and Jesse looked at each other, then turned to the man and smiled in unison.

Jenny spoke. "Can we get you something, officer?"

"Cup of coffee and one of them doughnuts would be nice."

Jesse wrapped the doughnut and Jenny poured the coffee. They were both relieved; the man just wanted a morning snack. But when they came back with his sack of food, they saw an eight-by-ten glossy photograph of Emily on the counter.

"I was wondering if you ladies had seen this woman anytime in the last few days?"

Jenny pretended to study the picture. Next to her she felt Jesse start to tremble. It wasn't her fault, Jenny knew. Since her stroke last summer, she didn't have very good control. Last December she'd wet her bed and was miserable about it for months, and she still insisted on sleeping with a rubber pad under her, even though the pad was cold or hot according to the weather.

Please, Jenny prayed, *hang on, Jess . . . hang on.* One of Jesse's canes rattled against the side of the refrigerator case, and Jenny knew the trooper had to hear the tapping. She kept her eyes on the photograph. "I don't believe I have, officer. What about you, Jess?"

She risked looking at Jesse. Poor Jesse's face had gone

white except for red dots high on her cheeks. One side of her mouth looked slack. Jesse stuttered, "N-n-no."

"She'd be four years older now," the trooper said. The sisters didn't answer. "She's driving a custom Volvo. Pretty fancy car for these parts. Maybe a car like that stopped for gas?"

Jenny asked, "What color is such a car?"

Jesse was beyond talking.

"Black," the trooper said.

Jenny pretended to consider. "I haven't serviced such a car. I'm sure I'd remember. My sister here doesn't pump gas. The canes . . ." She paused, and the trooper nodded sympathetically.

"Well, thank you, ladies. It was a long shot." He started to take the picture off the counter, then looked at Jesse, right into her eyes, and he said, "You ladies are the first people I've shown the picture to who haven't asked who she is and what we want her for."

Jenny was horrified to see a string of saliva drool out the side of Jesse's mouth and down her chin. She made a whimpering noise.

"You're upsetting my sister," Jenny said coldly. "We didn't ask because we were taught that the Lord hates a busybody."

The trooper laughed in a good-natured way, and he seemed satisfied. He took the photo and his coffee and doughnut. "Too bad more folks don't feel that way," he said. Then he went out the door. Jenny ran to the window, keeping to the side so he couldn't see her watching him. Jesse hobbled after her and kept to the shadows too. He was heading right for his car, and Jenny was sure everything was fine, but then he must've seen the shadow of the shed on the front yard, because he stopped and turned to look at it. Jenny held her breath; Jesse whimpered behind her and crept close. The trooper looked at the shed for what seemed a long time, then he took a step toward it, appeared to consider, and put his sack down on the ground. Jesse clutched Jenny's hand as they watched him move across the yard toward the shed very slowly. Something about it must have spooked him, because he took very slow, cautious steps, and a few yards from it they saw his hand come around the back of his belt and unsnap his holster.

"Fool," Jenny whispered. "Four-feathered fool. You'd think he had Adolf Hitler trapped in there." He got to the shed door and saw the padlock. He lifted it in one hand, and even from the store they could see the sun glint off the shiny new metal. He gave it an experimental pull, then let it drop, and he went around to the side of the shed, moving faster, and saw the window. He stood up on his toes to look inside; it was dirty and he wiped at the glass with his palm, but Jenny knew that wouldn't help him, because the day they'd pulled Emily's car in beside Roy's rusting old tractor, Jenny'd found a piece of painted canvas from an old awning and she tacked it over the glass on the inside.

The trooper stood down from the window and turned back toward the house. Her heart jumped. She didn't know where Emily was. She might be in the backyard, she might be in the back bedroom with the shades up. Jenny ran to the door and threw it open. "What're you looking for?" she called. She managed to sound indignant. The trooper came toward her. At least he wasn't looking at the back of the house anymore.

"What's in there?" he asked.

"My dead husband's tractor."

"That's a pretty fancy new lock you've got there."

"Some boys got in last summer, stole some of the parts."

"I see." He thought a moment, then asked, "Why did you cover the window?"

"So the kids couldn't look in and see a valuable piece of machinery in there."

"Of course."

"Of course," Jenny echoed. Her indignation was getting to be sincere.

"I'm sorry for the trouble," he said, and he went back to where he'd left the bag, and this time he made it all the way to his car and drove away.

"You were wonderful," Jesse said when Jenny came back inside.

Jenny nodded, but she knew it wasn't over. He'd remember the two ladies in the deli on old Route 4 and he'd ask someone about them and they'd tell him that Roy Perth had been dead these nine years and that that tractor of his had been a twenty-year-old hunk of junk even then. Then the trooper would really wonder why they'd put a brand-new lock on a shed that had nothing in it but an old tractor rusting in the dust. And he'd come back.

Jenny went in the back to tell Emily.

"You've got to have somewheres to go," Jenny cried. "Someone to go to."

Emily kept putting on her clothes without saying anything. Jenny and Jesse looked at each other, and Jenny came close to the bed where Emily was sitting to put on her heavy socks and boots.

"You've got an address book with names in it," Jenny said. "We saw it in your purse. Those're people you know . . . one of them . . ."

"No," Emily said.

"At least look," Jenny wailed.

"I don't have to look," Emily said.

"Then I will," Jenny said, and she went to Emily's purse and pulled out the address book. She turned to the first page. "Marjorie Arkin . . ." and she read the Princeton address and the phone.

"I don't remember."

Jenny read the next name in the book, Richard Breemer. He had a Princeton address too. Emily said, "I think he was my boyfriend. I don't know where he is now."

Jenny made a clucking sound, then read the next name.

"Rita Benson . . . parenthesis Reed, 59 Godfrey Road, Weston, Connecticut."

Emily was quiet, and Jenny looked up from the page. "Well?" she asked.

Rita Benson, Emily thought. Pretty Miss Benson with her fine skin and gentle eyes. Emily remembered because it was the day of her mother's funeral. . . .

The house was empty except for her and Harriet. Harriet had taken off her uniform and put on a wool dress, and she had taken the pins out of her hair so it fell to her shoulders, but she still looked grumpy and tired and as if she'd always

265

worked in someone else's house. She'd put out Emily's clothes and told her to dress and wait in her room, in her coat and gloves please, because there wouldn't be time for fooling around once her father got here. And Emily had done what she was told. She knew she'd never see the animals on the wallpaper again, or any other part of her room. She sat on the edge of the bed wearing her spring coat with the expensive lace collar that her mother couldn't resist buying for her, and held the dinosaur in her white-gloved hands, and waited. Harriet was down the hall in her room, listening to the TV. Emily couldn't hear the program, only waves of tinny laughter and giggles from a prerecorded audience. Then she heard her father's car, and she hugged the dinosaur to her and ran down the stairs to meet him. She forgot to look back one last time, and she never went upstairs again. They'd just come back from the interment, and Miss Benson was there . . . she had knelt down on the cold stone of the front steps so her plaid coat billowed out around her, and she had put her arms around Emily and said: "If you ever need anyone . . ."

Jenny and Jesse were waiting for her reaction to the name Rita Benson Reed, but Emily pretended that it didn't mean any more to her than any of the others.

Karl Banyan parked in the dooryard. It was empty, the cops had torn the coop apart, and the chickens were gone. Eddie must have given them away, and Banyan was ashamed. He wanted to turn around and drive back down to the road, but Eddie was at the kitchen door.

"Hi."

Banyan got out of the cruiser and went up the steps and into the kitchen.

"Got a couple of Swanson's beef pies in the oven," Beecham said. "Want one?"

Banyan didn't answer. He stood next to the kitchen door.

"What's with you?" Beecham asked.

"Eddie, they shot her."

Beecham crossed the kitchen and sat down slowly at the table. Banyan couldn't tell if he was sad or mad. He went to the cupboard and got out the bottle and two glasses. He poured them short shots and put Beecham's in front of him.

"Is she dead?" Beecham asked softly.

"No one knows. But she was hurt—blood all over the place. A kid over in Connecticut saw her the next day. It didn't look good from what he said."

"When did it happen?"

"Three days ago."

"Who shot her?"

"Two of the feds."

Banyan sat across from him in the straight-back chair and downed his shot. The smell of the baking meat pies filled the kitchen, but he wasn't hungry. He hadn't been able to get down a decent meal since he'd read about the shooting.

"I wasn't going to tell you," Banyan said, "but I had to. I'm sorry, Eddie."

"Screw sorry! What the fuck good is sorry? We gotta do something."

"That's why I'm here. I know a guy with the Bureau over in Plattsburg. Named Tulley. Decent guy, seems honest."

Beecham gulped the bourbon. "Another fed?"

"No one buys the Bureau," Banyan said staunchly, but he wasn't as sure as he sounded.

Gelb climbed over the padded barricade and went up to the target. "Nice shooting," he called back to David.

He pulled off the target and stripped in another. He didn't like the electronic targets. They added an element of a particular kind of light that was never reproduced in life. To his mind, the plain cardboard was better.

He went back to the barricade, pressed the button, and the sheet of cardboard whipped and jerked along the track. David aimed and fired. He was hitting center every time. Very good.

Gelb saw the door light go on in front of him and touched David's shoulder. David stopped firing and took off his ear covers.

"Someone at the door," Gelb said.

David nodded. Gelb went to the door, and David waited until he was outside and the door was closed. He refitted his ear covers and aimed again at the target. He squinted; the lines on the cardboard lost resolution, became fuzzy. He thought of her blue T-shirt with the bold yellow letters—

"U.S. Open"—across her breasts. He tried to see her superimposed on the target, but the image wasn't real; in fact he couldn't remember how she looked. The door slammed and the sound must have jarred something in his mind, because suddenly he did see her on the other side of the dull finished floor, in front of the cardboard target. Only it wasn't the woman in front of him; it was the little girl. He could see her sallow face and that mouth stuck in a thin, immovable line. *No, I can't do that*, his vision said. *No. It's not right.* He fired and kept firing until the vision poured blood through a hundred holes and began to sink.

Gelb touched his arm again and he jumped. He took off the ear covers. The echoes died.

"She's alive," Gelb said. "They found tire tracks from her car in an old tractor garage upstate. Let's go."

"Where?"

"Grant Union, New York. The Catskills. That's where she was."

"She isn't there now."

"Two old women took care of her. They will know where she went."

David shook his head. "She won't tell them. She probably doesn't know herself. And it'll take too long to get up there just to find out that they don't know."

He put his gun back in the shoulder holster he'd bought under Gelb's guidance. "Get some maps," he told Gelb. "Connecticut, Massachusetts, New York . . . and everything between Albany and Washington, D.C."

Gelb brought maps upstairs to the empty lounge and they spread them out on a table.

"They hid her, took care of her. They must have given her money," David said. "Were they rich?"

Gelb shook his head. "Two old ladies who own a deli and gas station in a little town. Not rich at all."

"So they couldn't give her much . . ." David looked up from the maps and out of the window. He saw the river, the park, the canal, and in the distance, Virginia. It had started to drizzle; the sky and landscape looked gray and worn-out to him, even though it was barely spring. A priest wearing a cassock crossed the sodden grass and went up the path to the bridge. His head was bowed as if he were deep in thought or prayer. David watched the priest and thought about how good he'd gotten with the gun. He liked the cold heaviness in his hand, and the kick and noise were exhilarating. Firing it at her, hitting her, watching her fall would be the most exciting thing that had ever happened to him. It would be the climax of his life, the finale of the most important game he'd ever played. But he wasn't sure about the death itself; nothing exhilarating about blood and glazed eyes, the total, final end of the body's muscle control and the explosion of excrement that went with it—or so he'd read. He had to be ready for that part.

Keeping his eyes on the priest, he asked Gelb, "Have you killed many men?"

"I never counted."

"Ever kill a woman?" David asked.

"Yes."

"How did you feel?"

"No different," Gelb said, "Women don't die harder than men. It's no big deal either way, no matter what you see in the movies." *What about the fact of it*, David was going to ask, *the pounds of dead flesh, the smell of blood and shit . . .* but Gelb kept talking, "I was in Korea when I was a kid, then in 'Nam. I saw the truth there, which is simple. You give a man a gun and tell him to kill and he does. Men, women, children . . . he'll kill anyone you tell him to. It's no big deal at all. The children bother me . . ."

David turned away from the window and looked at him. "It's the time with children," Gelb said, "the time you take away. There's too much of it, and I have a feeling that their years pile up against me. . . . Don't ask me to explain. But it bothers me to kill children." Then Gelb looked out of the window at the priest. "He wouldn't say killing was the worst sin, would he?"

"I don't know," David answered.

"He wouldn't. Loss of faith is—betrayal of the church. I've never done that." Then, in the same odd, gentle tone, Gelb said, "You want to kill her yourself, don't you?"

"Yes." It felt good to say it.

"Just you and her—some kind of duel."

"Yes."

"And the reactor—that's just an excuse."

"Partly."

Gelb stared at him for a second, then said, "That's romantic bullshit and you're a fool. It isn't a duel—it's slaughter, like a butcher kills a pig. Thinking of it any other way is dangerous."

"Why?"

"Because the outcome of a duel is always in doubt. But everybody knows how it'll turn out for the pig."

The words registered—*how it'll turn out for the pig*—and David felt his control slip. Suddenly he was scared of Gelb the way Talbot and Stockton were. Suddenly he was a little boy again, back in his room with the moonlight coming through the window, shining on the heaving black water of the Sound in the distance. He was looking in her notebook at the drawing that he would never decipher, and that cold spirit of something infinitely dangerous was in the room with him. He was terrified to move, because if he did, it would find him. All along, he had thought that the treacherous spirit was *hers*. Now he knew that if he had turned around that night to confront the monster with the icy breath, he would have seen Gelb's face with its tarnished metal eyes, and the long creases that ran down its cheeks like knife scars.

Then Gelb said, casually, "Feinstein came back early, by the way. She probably doesn't know, but it makes things tighter."

She would find out about Feinstein. She would get to him this time, and they'd give her the money, and she'd build the machine, and it would work. A clean win for her. Emily Brand, one thousand; David Lucci, zero. He saw the final machine that she would build. It was uglier, bigger, and more murderous than the one at Placid. She was the only one who could control it, like the alien and his robot in an old sci-fi movie. The machine *would* work and NARCON would be finished. It was the game again. Emily Brand was going to ruin it for everyone because she wouldn't give in.

He was thinking like himself again; everything was back to normal. Gelb wasn't the monster; Gelb was nothing. He demeaned what David was doing—calling it slaughter—

because he didn't know what she stood for, or the grandeur of David's mission to kill her. David couldn't explain; he'd sound mad if he tried and Gelb wouldn't understand anyway.

David had moved away from the table without knowing it, and Gelb looked at him with his pale eyes.

"Going to the can?" he asked.

"No," David answered. He came back to the table and leaned over the map.

"The women weren't rich," David said slowly, "so they couldn't give her much. Forty, fifty bucks maybe . . ."

Gelb nodded.

David said, "She was low on gas by the time she got to Washington Depot. We checked stations for two hundred miles and she hadn't stopped in any of them. She drove from Millbridge to Grant Union. So she was almost empty by the time she got to the old ladies. They have a pump, so they gave her gas and fifty dollars. At four and change a gallon, she could get . . . maximum four hundred miles. But then she'd be dead out. No money, no gas. She'll save some of the gas and at least half of the money. She has to eat. So she'll go a hundred and fifty miles comfortably . . . two-fifty in a pinch. I need a compass."

Gelb went downstairs and came back with the compass. Using Grant Union as the center point, David started to draw a circle just 150 miles around the town. The pencil crossed Weston, Connecticut, and he stopped and stared at the place name. He heard Rita Benson's voice as clearly as if she were in the room with them: *I told her I'd help her. I really meant it. . . . I hope she takes me up on it someday.*

PART
III

CHAPTER

DAVID GOT OUT of the car. Rita Reed was on the ground at the base of a tree fifty feet away. She looked right at him, through the branches, and he knew that she'd recognized him. He turned his back and faced the woods on the other side of the road.

He heard the shot. It was silenced and sounded like "puff." He turned and made himself walk up the path to the tree. Gelb waited for him; Kelsey put his gun away and started taking the cash out of her wallet.

"You don't have to look," Gelb said to David.

But David stood in front of the body and looked down at it. It wasn't as bad as he'd expected. The wound in her forehead was small. He made himself look at what he could see of the back of her head. That was a mess. His eyes jerked away from it and back to her face. She'd been dead only a few seconds, but she didn't look like Rita Benson anymore, or anybody else.

Kelsey stashed the money in his pocket, then laid her purse next to the body. It was cordovan leather, a soft sackish-looking thing, lying pitifully next to the woman who'd owned it. The abandoned purse was sadder than the body, and David looked away from it and at Gelb. Gelb was taking his gloves off. He didn't look like he'd satisfied some terrible, almost sexual urge to kill. If he'd enjoyed it, it didn't show on his face.

Gelb got the gloves off, folded them across, and put them in his pocket. "They need special tests to find that drug. They won't do them. So we take the money," Gelb explained, as if he were giving a lesson, "and they almost always think it's robbery, times being what they are."

David barred his way. "Where's Emily Brand?"

"Cape island," Gelb said.

Kelsey walked around them, down the path toward the car.

"Which cape island?" David said. His voice shook.

Gelb laughed. "It would be better to ask which cape. Cape Cod, probably. But maybe Cape Ann. We'll see."

"Goddammit, Reed was drugged."

"She was. But these things don't always work the way they're supposed to. They make it sound easy, but dosage should be calibrated by kilograms of body weight . . . usually impossible. So it's always tricky. In this case we under estimated, perhaps. Or she was more resistant to the drug than most. But we'll find—"

"Where's Emily Brand!" David wailed.

Gelb didn't answer. His dead eyes regarded David calmly.

"Fuck yourself," David snarled. "I'll find her myself."

He went down the path toward the car and opened the door on the driver's side. The keys were in the ignition.

Behind him Gelb said calmly, "I can't possibly let you take the car, David."

David whirled around.

"You see," Gelb explained in that same professorial tone, "it would leave us no way to get out of here. She might be found before we expect. Children might come along. Any thing could happen." He smiled. "Besides, Kelsey and I would make an odd pair of hitchhikers, wouldn't we?"

David wondered if Gelb would shoot him. He had the feeling that Gelb, like most of the other people he'd ever known, liked him . . . or whatever it was. They wanted him a little . . . wanted to look in their mirrors and see his face. Kelsey was watching them, leaning back against the fender of the car.

Gelb said, "We can go back to Georgetown."

"I'm not going back to Georgetown."

"I promise you there's time. If Dr. Brand accepted the invitation to the cape island and she's on her way there now in which case she'll stay until she thinks she can reach Fein stein. She won't get to him before we get to her. If she didn't accept the invitation, then she's got three hundred dollars and ten thousand miles of back roads at her disposal. Either way, we have a little time."

Gelb watched David with his clear empty eyes and that vaguely interested expression that made David's skin creep. Gelb would kill him, all right, no matter how much he liked him. Gelb was dangerous, like Emily. But he wasn't smart. He'd fucked up with Rita Reed, and they weren't any closer to killing Brand than they had been last week. David was better off without Gelb, or anybody.

He took his hand off the door handle and smiled at Gelb. "Okay, Kurt. At least take me somewhere where I can get a car."

"Stockton and Talbot won't like you taking off alone."

"Fuck them."

Kelsey must have decided that the crisis was over, and he got into the car.

They drove David to a car-rental office on the Post Road, where he rented a standard-shift Eldorado. He knew the Volvo would chew it up and spit it out if it came to that, but he didn't think that speed would be decisive on an island, and the Eldorado was huge and heavy.

He showed his license and credit card, even though Gelb had advised him not to, and the woman behind the counter made out the contract. She looked up at him longingly every few minutes. Suddenly he thought of Rita's body lying against the tree with its neat red hole like a sticker in the middle of the forehead.

He asked the woman for the rest room, and she directed him.

There was a small window in the room, open to the parking lot. He went to it, took a few gulps of air, then washed his face in cold water. The vision of Rita started to fade. It would be gone in a second, and it wouldn't come back, because *he* hadn't killed Rita Reed, and neither had Gelb or Kelsey. Emily was the murderer, Emily Brand, and her stubbornness.

He splashed his face with water again, ran his fingers through his hair, and then combed it carefully. He gave himself a second to look in the mirror. He looked handsomer than he ever had in his life. This time she would notice; or maybe she had all along, and just pretended not to. It was like her and he decided that was the case. He put the comb away, dried his hands, and went back to the counter to get the contract and the keys for the car.

Gelb was waiting in the parking lot. "I thought I'd try one more time, David."

"Don't bother."

"You need company."

"I don't."

Gelb took David's arm and led him away from the car and Kelsey to a willow tree at the edge of the parking lot. The willow was turning green and there was a fresh smell coming up from the earth that almost neutralized the exhaust fumes from the Post Road.

Gelb faced him.

"I'm in a hurry," David said.

Gelb nodded, then said, "I have a wife, you know—"

"Let me go," David said.

"I have a wife and three kids, David. I pay my taxes and my mortgage, and I go to church once a year, confess and receive absolution. Even for murder, this is possible. I take communion, and at that moment that I do, when I taste the wine and feel the wafer melt on my tongue, I *know* that I'll never kill again. I'm telling you this so you'll understand that I'm not a monster. . . ." The dead eyes looked into David's. "I'm not invincible or some agent of the devil with special powers. I take things as they are, and make my way at what I do most naturally. But it's never personal, David. Never. I've lasted all this time because I don't hate a soul on this earth. If it were any other way—if I hated the people I'm paid to kill—I'd have been long dead by now. Do you understand what I'm telling you?"

"Yes," David said.

"Then you understand that you shouldn't go alone. You should let us come with you."

"No," David said, then added, "thank you."

The woman behind the counter in the Weston Records Office was so fat her chair looked ready to collapse under her. Her face and fingers were fat, she was wearing a bright blue slimy polyester pantsuit, and her skin was caked with pink powder. "Excuse me . . ." David said.

She looked at him, and he smiled, but she didn't.

"I need to see the records of land-title transfers and wills for the past thirty years or so."

"I need names and dates," the woman said; then she looked away dismissively.

David leaned against the counter, feeling the gun cool and reassuring against his ribs.

"I don't have them," he said softly.

"Then I'm sorry."

He reached into his jacket, fingered the gun, then took out his wallet and flipped it open to the NCEC ID that Gelb had prepared for him.

"I think you should look at this," he said. "I can come back with a warrant, but then you'll be looking for another job. Of course, you might be arrested . . ."

"For what?" she demanded.

"Obstructing a law-enforcement officer . . . et cetera. Come and look, it'll save us both a lot of trouble."

She waddled over and examined the card. The ID looked official and was signed by Paul K. Stockton. The name sounded familiar to her, and she gave up. "Very well, but you have to come back here yourself. I'm not dragging those heavy books upstairs."

She opened the door for him and he followed her through the office and down a flight of stairs to a cool, dim basement room. She gave him the directory and showed him the metal stacks that held the land titles.

"I need wills too," he reminded her.

She gave him a black look and pointed to another group of stacks, then left him alone.

He looked in the directory under 59 Godfrey Road. He found the binder number, then went to the stacks and wrestled the binder itself to the table.

The land title had transferred from Charles Devereaux Benson to his wife, Amanda, in 1956, and then to the daughter, Rita Sharon Benson, in 1960. He put the binder back, and turned to the stacks of wills. These binders were much thinner. A lot of people had bought and sold property in Weston during the past two hundred years; not many died here.

He found Charles Devereaux Benson's will, probated in 1956. David's hands left sweat marks on the legal tissue and he lifted the pages and tucked them back of the binder. He read every word, and the tension got worse. He twisted his body to relieve it. If the island property had come from Mayo Reed's family, he was out of luck. The irony was terrible. Next-door neighbors a few miles away knew where Emily Brand had gone. Women who played bridge with Rita and went shopping with her knew where the Reeds spent their island summers.

The tension was turning to pain, and then on the third page of the will, halfway down, in faded manual type, David read that along with the house in Weston, a trust fund worth about eighty thousand dollars in 1956, and a three-family dwelling in Norwalk, Mr. Benson had left his wife a house and one acre on Squam Pond Road on Nantucket Island.

Someone had hit a dog and knocked or dragged the body to the side of the road. Emily speeded up, trying to get past without seeing it all. But she did, and it stayed with her as she drove east on Route 1. The traffic was bad all the way; outside of New Bedford it really clogged up, and she crept along. The road twisted through the blocks of old houses, painted pastel colors with scraps of lawn in the front. She kept seeing the dog. It was a retriever with long golden fur; the belly had split, entrails spilled out in strings that were more sad than sickening, and its beautiful fur was matted with blood. If they'd gotten her in Washington Depot, she would have ended up like that. So would Jenny, Jesse, Rita, if they got to them.

She pulled into an A&W, got change for a ten, went to the phone next to the ladies' room and called Jenny. Her heart pounded as the phone rang in the immaculate kitchen and at the same time in the little deli. Jenny answered on the third ring.

"We miss you," she said as soon as she heard Emily's voice.

"Are you all right?"

"Fine. But it's good you got out when you did. They came

back, okay. The state boys made me open the shed, then came back a couple of hours later with the suit-and-tie men. They're not nice men," Jenny said definitely, "and I dread to think what they'd've done to us if our own New York boys hadn't been there to witness. But they were. Phil Dockerty was one of them. We've known him all his life. He used to buy candy from us, and since he's grown and on the force, he buys his lunch here most days."

"Jenny . . ."

"Sorry. Can't help rambling. But we're fine."

She sounded fine, and Emily smiled at the receiver. "What did you tell them?"

"What we agreed on. That we rented out the shed for a garage to a traveling man a couple of months ago. He came for his car last week and we forgot the whole thing. They were on to us then. Asking questions so fast they interrupted each other and tripped over their tongues. It would've been funny . . . but it wasn't. We said we took cash and never asked names. We didn't think it was important; why should we? But poor Jesse blushed and stammered and they knew we were lying. Oh, Emily, she can't help it, you know."

"I know."

"But you were right about everything. They were snotty. They said—meanness dripping out of their mouths with the words—just supposing we *had* seen you, where would we think you'd gone. Well, you wouldn't tell us, so we truly didn't know. Jesse stopped shaking and drooling, and I was cool as can be. We told the truth and they knew it. They ain't dumb. I'll give 'em that." She hesitated. "You'll come back and see us when you can?"

"I'll try, Jenny."

She called Rita. She let the phone ring a long time, but there was no answer. Her hands shook as she put the phone back, and she tried to calm down. There was no reason for Rita to wait for Emily to call. She'd gone next door to see a friend or to the library where she had told Emily she helped out some afternoons. Emily had had a hundred teachers in her life; they wouldn't single out her fourth-grade schoolteacher from Weston. They'd start with Herb Mendel and work back. They'd question Miss Iselin before they ever thought of Rita Reed.

It was raining when she got to Woods Hole. The pavements and hauled-in boats glistened. The parking lot was almost empty, and she was afraid that she had missed the last ferry. But when she got inside the terminal, she saw a sign next to the ticket window:

STEAMER ARRIVES FROM NANTUCKET, 5:30
DEPARTS FOR NANTUCKET, 6:15

and a disclaimer:

ALL TIMES APPROXIMATE

She had an hour and she waited in the car out of sight of the terminal guard. The rain got heavier and it started to fog up. The ferry would probably be very late. But only fifteen minutes after it was supposed to arrive Emily heard a steamer horn blast out on the bay and a few minutes later the huge white prow of the steamer nosed out of the fog. A few cars and a lumber truck straggled out of the hold and disappeared up the road into the fog, and an attendant waved the waiting cars into the hold. Emily parked inches from the bulkhead, locked the car, and went up on deck. She climbed narrow metal steps to the top deck and stood under a streaming awning that must have been gay in the sunshine. The horn blasted again, moving docks clanked, and deep in the steamer the engine started up. The deck throbbed, the horn went again, and the ferry slipped along the wharf toward open water. She had never been on a boat before, and she clutched the metal awning support as the rumbling steamer moved.

The land slid away, shore lights bobbed and dwindled, and she felt a wild burst of joy as the steamer started its turn into the wind and she realized that she was leaving the mainland—the continent—behind. Then the steamer hit open water; the wind tore at her hair and skin, and she had to hold her glasses. Marvin's sweater was getting soaked. She gave up and went below.

She settled herself in a window seat across from an old woman who was knitting. The woman stared unashamedly; she must have been seventy-five or eighty; her shining eyes were set in wrinkles and her fingers were bony and crooked.

"Filthy night," she said.

Emily nodded. The old woman was wearing a cloth coat with a fur collar. The fur had gotten wet and stuck together in spikes around her face. She picked up the knitting; the knobby fingers flew with the yarn.

"You're not from the island," the woman said.

"No."

"Odd time of year for anyone to go to Nantucket."

"You're going," Emily said.

"I live there. Been in Boston visiting my son. Where're you staying?"

Emily didn't answer.

The woman looked up. "I say, where're you staying?"

"Near a place called Squam Pond," Emily said.

"Squam!" the woman cried. "You'll never find Squam in this fog. It's hard enough in daylight. All sand and bayberry out there. And a'course the ocean." She smiled at Emily. "Stay the night with me."

"I can't."

"Why not? I won't charge you. Be glad for the company on a night like this. Besides, you look peaked, if you forgive me for saying it."

"You don't know me."

"You look relatively clean. Been sick, have you?"

"Yes," Emily said.

"I thought so." The woman put out her hand. "Maida Gardner."

Emily took it. It was dry and warm and all bones. "Susan Cohen," Emily said.

They drove off the ferry three hours later and into the fog. The car jounced over cobbles, and they turned, turned again, seemed to come back on themselves until the harbor town was like a maze and Emily was lost. Finally they pulled into India Street, the narrowest street Emily had ever driven on. Then into a tiny drive.

The house had double doors painted black, and a silver knocker in the shape of a fox head. "1720" was painted over the door and the old woman saw Emily look up at it. "Our *new* house," Mrs. Gardner said. "The old one was out at Eel Point. Family's been here since 1659. All Quakers," she said proudly as she unlocked the door.

Emily followed her into the house, into a good-sized room with wide board floors, a Turkish rug, and a laid fire.

Mrs. Gardner leaned down to light the fire. "Can you walk the stairs?" she asked.

"Of course," Emily said.

"No 'of course' about it; you're limping like a wounded drunk." She creaked upright and looked sharply at Emily. "No luggage, I suppose."

"No."

The woman nodded. "Thought not." She examined Emily keenly, then said, "I like the look of you, for some reason. A lot of people would, I expect. You're lucky. Go on up the stairs, then, first door you come to. Clean sheets on the bed, clean towels in the bathroom. Take a hot bath and use the oil on the ledge—it'll help get the kinks out. I'm curious as sin, young woman, but I don't expect nothing out of you now but a tale. Still, maybe you'll come back someday—better make it soon or I'll be dead—and tell me what you were doing on Nantucket Island on a filthy night like this."

The fog was white in the daylight, but it had stopped raining. Emily followed Mrs. Gardner's directions: "The Wauwinet-Polpis road almost to the end. Squam road'll be on your right. Careful turning in, it's sand; if you see the conservation booth, you've gone too far."

She found the road, turned in, and the Volvo ground over the sand. Wild grapevines made twisting walls on either side of the road, the few mailboxes loomed out of the fog at her, and a few drives cut off into the mist. She heard the ocean but didn't know how close she was.

She almost missed number eighty, and had to back up. She pulled into a drive of ground shell and gravel, and massed bayberry and wild rose closed in around her. The sound of waves got louder and she saw the house through the fog.

It was bigger than she had expected, almost grand. It was weathered gray shingle, like every other building she'd seen on the drive out here, and Emily thought it faced the ocean but she couldn't tell. She left the car in the drive, walked around to the front door, and let herself in with the key Rita had given her. The house was cold and damp, the furniture was covered. She found the thermostat and turned up the

284

heat. She had four days to spend here. Then Feinstein would come and get her, or send someone. She laughed out loud—the National Guard, if he had to.

She found the kitchen. It was huge and empty, except for an ivy plant that had been forgotten and had died on the windowsill over the sink. There was a pantry with a heavy old-fashioned door that closed with a thick plank in a slot. On the pantry shelves she found instant coffee, powdered cream, sugar, and a few cans. She made coffee, drank some, and when it was nine, she picked up the phone.

Rita had remembered to have the phone connected; the electricity must be on too. The house was already losing its chill. She dialed Rita's number, but there was still no answer. Her heart beat faster. She went back to the pantry and found a can of corned beef. It was salty and stringy, but she was hungry and she ate all of it. There wasn't enough food for three days. She'd have to risk a grocery store.

She waited fifteen minutes and then called Rita again. The phone was in the living room near a window. The fog was burning off, and she saw breakers, whiter than the mist, rolling toward shore. The phone rang five times. She was ready to hang up again when a man answered.

"Who is this?" he asked.

"I'm a friend of Mrs. Reed's."

The man made a peculiar sound, then said, "My mother was robbed and murdered yesterday afternoon."

Her mind filled with terrible questions: *How did they find your mother? How did they know that she helped me? How did they kill her? . . . Oh, God, did she suffer?*

The man breathed quietly at the other end of the phone. She wanted to tell him that she was sorry, but she couldn't talk, and she put the phone gently back into its cradle.

She clutched the windowsill and tried to catch her breath.

They had found Rita somehow, and killed her. But they hadn't hurt Jenny or Jesse . . . why poor Miss Benson? Because Rita knew where Emily was, and they knew she knew. So they tortured her or drugged her to find out, and once she'd told them, they had to kill her to hide what they'd done to her.

Then they knew Emily was here. They were on their way, or here already. The island was small and thirty miles out to sea, but not isolated, Mrs. Gardner said. There were flights from Boston and New York, and two ferries a day.

Emily grabbed her purse and ran out the front door of the house. The fog was almost gone; only strands of it were left hugging the sand. Now she could see that the house was on a bluff on the beach. In one direction she saw a lighthouse, still half-covered in fog. They wouldn't come from there. She looked the other way, back toward town. The fog had cleared there, and she saw a man trudging along the sand toward the house. His feet broke the damp crust on the sand and sank.

She couldn't see his face, but his hair was black, and she knew it was Lucci.

She backed up to the house, opened the door, and slid inside. She locked the door, then ran to the window. He was under the bluff, climbing the old wooden steps or pulling himself up by the dune grass. Any second now she would see him crest the cliff. She couldn't wait. Her hands clutched the window frame, her nails dug into the wood. She thought she could tear this window out of the wall, batter down the walls themselves, and tear David Lucci to pieces with her bare hands. She wanted him to hurry.

She wanted to sit on the floor and rock like Marvin used to rock in front of the control panels. Her side throbbed, but she barely felt it. She wanted to raise her head and howl with rage like a dog. A sound actually came up out of her throat. It startled her and she came to.

He would have a gun, and she didn't. The gun had scared Jenny and Jesse and they had put it in the glove compartment. She had been so sure that no one would ever find Rita, she left the gun in the car when she went to Weston, and it was still there.

She raced out of the living room, through the kitchen, and out the back door.

A big car was pulled up in the drive behind the Volvo, blocking it. He'd come on the morning ferry, found the house, blocked the drive, then come around and up the beach to cut her off from the front. She opened the car door, leaned across the seat, and ripped open the glove compartment. It was empty.

She heard a window at the front of the house slide open,

and she knew he was inside the house. He'd come through the house to the back, and she'd be trapped in the car. She slid out, closed the door halfway so he wouldn't hear it, and keeping low, she ran for the garage. The side door was unlocked, and she went inside and closed it after her. She looked around the garage. There were garden tools hanging on pegs over a work table, and two pairs of heavy garden gloves. A pair of old rubber boots stood on one side. On the other were a pile of wood, a heavy long-handled maul with a tapered steel end for splitting wood, and a chain saw. She picked up the chain saw. It wasn't that heavy—she could wield it—and it looked wicked. But the gas gauge read empty. A red gas can stood next to the work bench, and she ran to it and lifted it; but she heard stones or bits or rust rattle inside. It was empty, too.

"Emily . . . oh, Emily . . ." he called. She jumped at the sound of his voice and dropped the saw. It fell with a crash, and she heard him laugh.

There was a small window above the woodpile. She climbed up, keeping to the side, and looked out. He'd opened one of the upstairs windows and was leaning out, with his arms crossed on the sill, as if they were neighbors having a chat. She didn't see the gun.

"You wouldn't stay in the car," he called. The sound of the waves was distant and his voice was clear. "And the brush is bayberry. Makes a hell of a noise if you try to walk through it. Terrible stuff," he said almost conversationally. "Like a jungle of dry thorns. You wouldn't get far in it. You're not in the brush, you're not in the car. So you're in the garage."

His hand came up to the sill, and she saw the metal catch the light. The gun he was holding was much bigger than Starrett's. Even if she made it back to the car, and even if the car had a chance of getting through the bayberry and around the other car, he could stay at his vantage point on the second floor, aim carefully, and shoot the tires out . . . or shoot her through the back window. She slumped down on the woodpile.

"Emily," he cried again. He sounded elated. "The garage is no good, Emily. You should've brought the gun into the house with you. I thought we'd shoot it out, western-style. Just the two of us face to face. You'd sort of have a chance

287

that way. Not much. But a chance. But you left the gun in the car, stupid!"

It was quiet for a minute; then he said, "If you don't come out of the garage soon, I'll set fire to it. There's a kerosene heater in the den—did you miss that?"

He seemed to wait for an answer; then he went on, "It's almost full. I can pour kerosene on the garage roof right from the next window. You see that window?"

She kept low and looked out. She could see half of the second window away from him. The rest of it was blocked by the garage roof.

"One of three things will happen." Emily listened in spite of herself. "The smoke will drive you out of the garage or you'll stay in there and the smoke will kill you. There is another possibility. Your clothes could catch fire. There's a lot of flammable stuff in the garage. . . ."

She leaped down off the woodpile and she thought she heard him laugh, as if he could see her. "You'll run out then, won't you? And I'll shoot you; I promise. I won't let you burn to death. Even demons shouldn't bear that pain."

There was another window above the work bench; it was close to the side of the house and looked out on it. She saw a black line of something through the other window, coming straight down the wall of the house. She went closer and looked out. *It was the electric line from the main service out on the road.* She tried to remember everything she could about the inside of the house.

"It's a different kind of game this time," he was saying. "Still, you had a chance; you could have won. All you had to do was pay attention. To people, Emily . . . to *me*. All you had to do was remember that David Lucci was in Miss Benson's class too and you wouldn't have gone to her, she would still be alive, and you wouldn't be trapped here."

She leaned against the garage wall and closed her eyes, trying to see the kitchen. There was the door facing the clearing and the driveway. Then there was the pantry door and the table in an alcove with another window facing out onto the moor of bayberry and wild rose. The sink was on the other side, under another window, facing another moor. She imagined that she was at the kitchen door facing the room. The kitchen sink was on the same side of the house as the wire and garage. He couldn't see the window over the kitchen sink; he was around the corner from it.

The sink . . . the sink was porcelain, but the faucets wouldn't be. Faucets were metal—chrome . . . or stainless. Good conductors, both of them.

"Do you remember me now?" he called. "I sat in the back most of the time, just like you did. But on the other side of the room."

"I don't remember," she shouted. She climbed the woodpile and opened the window so he'd hear her better. "I don't remember—"

He fired; the window broke and glass fell into the wood. She jumped down off the woodpile.

"Lucci, David Lucci. I was her favorite . . ."

Emily took off her boots with the steel shank and pulled on the old rubber gardening or fishing boots and the pair of heavy rubber garden gloves. She searched among the tools until she found a pair of pliers. She brushed the rust off as best she could.

"Do you remember the game we played?—Masters, she called it. To teach us what it was like to dominate other people and then to be dominated. Do you remember?"

Emily moved back to the woodpile. "No," she cried up toward the window. "I don't remember."

"It was just silly shit, in a way. Schoolteacher crap. But it really wasn't. . . ."

Emily took four pieces of wood off the pile, then made herself stop and think. She had the gloves, boots, pliers, wood. She went to the side door of the garage. It was on the far side; she didn't think he could see it. She opened it a little.

"Years later I realized that winning the game wasn't the point."

He couldn't see it. She opened it wider and then she saw the maul with the metal head. She stuck the pliers into her pocket, tucked the wood under her arm, and picked up the maul. It was heavy, but she could carry it all right. She went back to the door.

"The point was *not* to play." He yelled, "And you didn't play. Which really made you the winner; you don't remember any of it, do you?"

For some reason she stopped at the door and tried to remember. She remembered the classroom and she remembered Miss Benson. She remembered the dead wasps in the jar and thinking that she'd seen his eyes before. But she didn't remember the boy or the game.

"No," she called back, "I don't remember."

"Well," he said, "it's a little late now." He started to laugh and she laughed with him to keep him busy. The sound of their voices filled the little clearing and faded in the disappearing fog. She stopped laughing and slipped out into the clearing.

The bayberry came almost to the back wall of the garage, but there were a few inches of grass before the wild shrub started. She slid along with her back to the garage wall; there were a few feet of open space between the end of the garage and the corner of the house, and he might be able to see her. He stopped laughing too, and she stood with her back flat against the garage and heaved one of the pieces of wood away and to her left. It landed in the bayberry on the far side of the garage, and he fired at it. She leaped across the open space and settled against the wall of the house. Pain dug into her side, but she ignored it. She couldn't see him now without leaning around the corner of the house. He couldn't see her.

She didn't think he'd turned on any lights in the house; he wouldn't know when the power went off.

"That was a stupid trick, Emily," he cried out. "You can throw things out of that garage all day and I'll keep shooting at them and I'll still have enough ammunition to kill most of the people on this island. The fog's almost gone . . . the sun's out . . . I'll see you if you go into the bayberry."

Emily carefully put down the maul and the wood, grabbed the wire with one gloved hand, then leaned down for another piece of wood. She tucked the wood under her arm, then pulled out the pliers and fitted the wire into the wire-cutting slot. She grasped the pliers firmly and threw the wood in the same direction she had before. He fired, and she snapped the pliers closed as hard as she could. The wire came apart. If there was any crackle from released voltage the dying sound of the shot covered it.

"Maybe it would be better for you to run," he called. "Why don't you? Better that way—nobler or something. Go ahead, Emily, run out on the moor."

He waited. She carefully separated and stripped the wires. The insulation was brittle and came off easily.

"Okay." His voice came from the side and above her. "I'm going to get the kerosene. It'll take a minute, not long enough to get out of range on the moor or the beach. But you can try. It would be a good time to try."

She held the wire by the insulation and eased open the kitchen window. The sink was right under it. She heaved herself up to get her head and shoulders through the window. He could blow her head off if he came into the kitchen now. She heard him on the stairs. She touched the hot-water faucet with one wire. It sparked, then stopped. She wrapped the twisted wire under the spigot, then the other wire under the cold-water spigot. She worked as fast as she could, but the rubber gloves slowed her down. Finally she finished and moved the dead plant down behind the faucets, quickly draped the tendrils over the spigots, and turned on the water full force. The lack of power would shut down the pump, but there would be enough water in the pipes for a few minutes. The water spewed into the sink; she heard him exclaim over the sound of water; then she heard his steps coming toward the kitchen.

She dropped the wood, shut the window, and lugged the maul to the kitchen door. She stood to the side, watching through sheer curtains. He came in, carrying the gun in one hand and a cylindical kerosene heater in the other. He stopped and look around the room. His lips moved, but she couldn't make out what he said. He put the heater down and went to the sink. He would see the wires if he looked closely. But he must have thought that turning on the water was a trick to cover some kind of noise that she was making, and he reached out reflexively and touched the spigot. His mouth yawned in a scream she could barely hear. His body jerked, shuddered, and slammed backwards. She waited, then shoved the door so it swung open. Nothing happened. She risked looking around the jamb and into the room.

He was on his back, his head resting against the pantry door. His eyes were shut, his skin had turned red. She came slowly into the room. His chest heaved. He was unconscious, not dead, and she swung the maul up and over her head to smash it down on his head.

CHAPTER
20

"LINDA, put Kurt on," Stockton said.

"We're busy tonight," she whined. Stockton wondered what the nice suburban matron on the other end of the phone thought her husband did to keep her and the kids and the nice house in Arlington; someday he would tell her, just to see the look on her face.

"Just cut the crap, Linda, and put him on."

She gasped; then he heard the receiver being put down, and he waited. He was worried about Talbot. He'd been here earlier and he looked terrible. His face was pasty and swollen and Stockton could have sworn that one of his old friend's eyes was smaller than the other. The bitch was killing them; she was taking the agency apart, and if they didn't get her, she'd finish the job, then start on NARCON. One little woman, and now Talbot was going crazy because his David had disappeared. At least they knew where *he* was now. Gelb would get him back and finish the job on the bitch, and maybe this time tomorrow afternoon, God willing, Stockton would be in his beautiful bedroom in Chevy Chase with the windows open and a cool spring breeze blowing across his face while he slept off a Valium pop.

Gelb came on the line.

"Kurt, sorry about this," Stockton said.

"It's all right. We're supposed to go to a neighbor's party. The wife hired a baby-sitter," Gelb said tonelessly. As always, the flat sound of Gelb's voice set up jitters in Stockton's stomach.

"We know where David is," Stockton said. "The schoolteacher's husband did some psych studies with kids back in the sixties and the big computer knows all about him and his wife. David's on Nantucket Island, a section called Squam. Talbot told Red to warm up the Falcon, and he's waiting for you at Friendship."

"You don't know—?"

"No. Maybe he's dead, maybe she is; no way to find out."

"Very well," Gelb said. "I'll call you as soon as I know."

It was a little after seven-thirty when they landed at the small Nantucket airport. Gelb left the plane and walked into the hangar. One man was there working on a Lear. It was raining again, the hangar was cold and damp, and the man looked happy to see Gelb.

"How do I get to Squam?" Gelb asked.

The man took a grease-stained rag out of his back pocket and slowly wiped his hands. "Weelll . . ." he said, drawing out the word.

"Never mind the local color," Gelb said evenly. "Tell me how to get to Squam."

The man looked startled; then he stared into Gelb's light eyes for a second, and he shoved the rag back into his pocket. "It's at the end of Wauwinet Road. Go out the main road here from the airport, turn left. There's a sign for Wauwinet on your right. But the car rentals are closed now."

Gelb took a thick fold of bills out of his pocket and counted out two hundred dollars. The man watched.

"You've got a car, haven't you?" Gelb said.

"Sure, but . . ."

Gelb held out the money. "How far is it?" he asked.

"Don't know in miles—maybe half an hour from here. Whole island's only fourteen miles long."

"Two hundred dollars for an hour," Gelb said pleasantly. "You don't look like an asshole, take it."

The man took the money and said quickly, "It's a brown Ford with a Nantucket sticker. Parked outside the operations building." The man folded the money, stuck it away in the coveralls, and handed Gelb a set of keys.

Gelb went back to the plane. "I'll be back in about an hour," he told Red. "Be ready to go."

The sand road was slippery from the dew, the night was

293

dead black with no moon, and Gelb thought he'd have trouble finding the house. But halfway up the sand road, in the brights from the Ford, he saw the Eldorado that David had rented in Westport pulled over to the side of the road. He stopped next to it, got out, and opened the car door. The interior light came on, wispy in the blackness. The key was in the ignition; the rental contract signed by Lucci was in the glove compartment.

Gelb left the car, and using his flashlight, went to the break in the vines and bayberry and looked up the shell drive. The drive was empty; there were no lights ahead in the house.

He pulled his gun out of its holster, disengaged the safety, and walked up toward where he thought the house must be. His feet crunched on the broken shells; the sound was sharp in the wet black air, but he had a feeling that no one would hear him.

Keeping the small beam of light to the ground, he found the base of the house and then the kitchen door. It was open, and he stepped inside and tried the wall switch, but nothing happened. Then he stopped at the door and shone the light around the kitchen. It was empty. The pantry door was bolted and a heavy piece of wood was nailed across it. He flashed the light around again and saw a hammer and a box of nails on top of the kitchen counter. He looked through the drawers and found a screwdriver and started prying at the board.

He worked slowly. She was gone, David's car was on the road, and he knew he'd find David's body on the other side of the door. He shoved the bolt free and opened the door. The pantry was pitch black. He flashed the light around, saw shelves, cans, an empty crock. He stopped and took a deep breath, and the hair on his neck moved; he thought he'd smell blood and dead flesh, but he smelled sweat, and he jerked the light down to floor level.

David's eyes glittered at him.

Gelb staggered back, and David laughed softly, then said an old line he remembered from somewhere: "You were expecting maybe Frank Sinatra?" He laughed louder and heaved himself to his feet. He put his hands against one shelf and stretched his back.

"She didn't kill you," Gelb whispered.

"She nailed me up in here like a vampire. I came to while

she was doing it. Amazing woman, you know. Really strong." His voice had a mad lilting tone. "She must have grabbed me under the arms or by the ankles and dragged me in here. I weigh one-eighty—it couldn't have been easy. Amazing woman."

"She didn't kill you," Gelb said again.

David turned on him. "Don't be impressed, Gelb. She's won this way before and she thinks she'll win the same way again."

Gelb looked blank.

"By not playing," David explained patiently.

Emily was stalled by a stoplight on the only road through Falmouth. It was dark and raining again, the street was almost empty, and she didn't see any patrol cars. The town looked shut up except for a gas station across the intersection with all its lights on shining across the wet asphalt. An old school bus with large black letters printed on the side was parked to the side of the pumps. The letters stood out in the blaze of light against the gloom: HELP ORIN!

The light changed, and she drove slowly through the intersection, turned into the station, and pulled up next to the bus.

A woman was kneeling in front of the bus, draining the radiator into a bucket. She was big, with a pleasant bony face and hair tied back in a ponytail. The bucket was full of black-streaked antifreeze.

Emily got out of the Volvo and went over to her. "By Orin you mean the President?"

The woman looked up. "Sure do."

"Will he see this?" She gestured to the sign.

"Maybe."

"How?"

"We're going to Washington tonight, to the demonstration."

"What demonstration?"

"The demonstration on the Mall tomorrow. My God, woman, it's been on every radio and TV station, in all the papers. Where've you been?"

"Out of circulation," Emily said. The sides of her mouth twitched.

The woman looked sympathetic. "A boyfriend?" she asked, and Emily started to laugh. The woman looked worried, but the laughter was infectious; she giggled with Emily, then laughed too. Once they started, they couldn't stop. Tears ran out of their eyes; they rolled helplessly against the bus. The woman stopped and gasped. "What the fuck are we laughing at?" Emily couldn't answer, and the woman hiccuped and laughed again.

The gas jockey came out of the office. He saw the two women laughing helplessly and rocked on his feet and jiggled the change in his pockets. He shook his head and went back into the office.

They stopped and looked at each other, grinning and wiping their eyes. The woman gave Emily some Kleenex.

"He must be something," the woman said.

"Who?"

"The boyfriend."

"Oh, he is." She almost laughed again, but pain throbbed in her side.

The woman stuck out her hand. "Ann Curry," she said.

"Susan Cohen," Emily said. They shook hands.

Suddenly Ann said, "Come to Washington with us."

"Yes."

"No, I mean it. Give Touhey a couple of bucks and he'll keep the car till we get back. C'mon. We need everyone we can get."

"Yes," Emily said as soberly as she could, "I will."

Red called ahead, and by the time the Falcon landed at Hyannis, a car was waiting for them. A Honda this time.

They drove back toward Falmouth; it was her starting point, it would be theirs. There was only one road from Falmouth to the highway, and she had to take it. They passed Falmouth Center, slowed up for a red light, and David saw the back of the Volvo parked in the gas station.

He ran the light and yanked the car across the lane into the station driveway. It was ten-thirty. The lights were still on, but there was a "Closed" sign on the office door. David leaped out of the car and ran to the glass door; the man inside was at a desk working on a ledger and drinking coffee. David banged on the door. The man looked up, then pointed to the sign.

Gelb strolled over. "Wrong color Volvo," he said quietly.

"I saw it in Squam. It's green, it's been green all along." He banged on the glass again, and the man inside gave him the finger. David pulled his gun and pointed it at the man through the glass. The man turned white and staggered to his feet. Gelb didn't say anything; he knew it was no use. The man opened the door and put his hands over his head.

"Who left that car there?" David asked.

The man was too terrified to hear. He stammered, "The cash register's in there."

David pushed the gun hard into the man's middle. He bent double. "Who left the Volvo?" David asked again.

"Woman gave me fifty to keep it for a couple of days."

"Where did she go?"

The man didn't answer fast enough, and David jabbed him harder; the man gagged and Gelb touched David's arm. "You're wasting time, David, he'll tell you. Give him a chance."

The man got his breath back. "Demonstration tomorrow," he gasped. "They're on a bus . . . all the town jerks went."

"What route did they take?"

"Only one," the man said. "Twenty-eight to six, six to the throughway."

"When did they leave?"

"Eight."

David turned to Gelb. "Get the number, color, everything." And he walked away. Gelb nodded and said softly, "Yessir, whatever you say, sir."

David went to the Volvo and shot out the front tires; then he blasted holes in the doors and trunk and blew out another tire. Gelb touched his shoulder and he whirled around. The gun grazed Gelb's chest. They both looked down at it, and David dropped his arm and walked back to the Honda.

Emily woke up; the seat next to her was empty, and she looked around for Ann. She was sitting cross-legged in the aisle across from a huge black man. Emily got out of her seat and went up the aisle toward them. Almost everyone else was asleep.

She stood behind Ann and looked over her shoulder. The

black man had a poster board in front of him and was drawing letters with a felt marker. The bus swayed and bumped
gently, but his hand was steady.

The sign read: "LET THEM EAT . . ."

"Let them eat what?" Emily asked.

"Oil," the black man said. "Pretty snappy. But we've used
it a thousand times already, and we're running out of ideas."

Suddenly Emily's eyes fixed on him. The stare was total
and unwavering and it made him uncomfortable. He tried
to stare back, but his eyes burned. He tried smiling, but she
didn't notice. Ann wondered what was going on. Then Emily
asked softly, "Will the President see the sign?"

"It and ten million others," he said.

Emily put her hand gently on Ann's shoulder; her eyes
finally left Will's face, and she stared over his head. The look
was so concentrated that both Ann and Will turned. They
didn't see anything but the swaying head of a sleeping old
lady.

"Susan?" Ann said.

Emily didn't answer, and Ann knew that wasn't her name.
She had no idea who this woman was or why she'd trusted
her so impulsively.

"Susan?" she said again. She didn't know what else to call
her.

Emily seemed to come to; she looked down at them and
smiled. "Will you help me?"

"Do what?" Ann asked.

"Make another sign."

"What kind of sign?" Ann asked. Will didn't seem to have
any questions.

"I can't explain, and you won't understand what the sign
says. But I swear that it will further your cause." Then she
asked Will, "How tall are you?"

"Six-four," he said.

"Perfect."

It was still dark when they got to Trenton. They stopped
to use the toilets and have snacks. The bus stop sold everything: toothpaste, shampoo, doughnuts, Twinkies, and plastic
toys. Will asked the counter man for Day-Glo paint. He
didn't have it, but he brought out a small can of Red Devil

black enamel and they bought it. They brought their coffee and doughnuts outside, and Will went to work on the sign.

"What the fuck does it mean?" Ann asked.

"I'll tell you later," Emily said.

"When?"

"Later."

Will sat next to her this time. The heat was weak, and Emily shivered. Will pulled a heavy sweater out of his pack and draped it around her shoulders. "Try to sleep," he said to her. "You look like shit."

She put her head against the window and closed her eyes.

She smelled something rotting. She was in the kitchen in Nantucket, and the smell came from the pantry. She got the board off and the bolt open; then the door creaked slowly back and revealed her work. No one had ever found Lucci. The family never came back to the house, NARCON didn't know where to look for him, and he died of starvation and his corpse rotted on the pantry floor. The beautiful face had melted off the bones. Whisps of black hair clung to pieces of scalp, the lips were gone. Suddenly the bared teeth clicked at her and a putrid breath came out of the mouth and blew into her face. She staggered back. The corpse raised macerated arms and started to stand up. His hatred for her was stronger than death, and he was coming after her. . . .

Will was shaking her gently. She opened her eyes. "You weren't sleeping too peacefully," he said. She inhaled; the stink was real.

"Sweet, ain't it?" Will said.

"What is it?"

"The Du Pont plant in Wilmington. The sweet smell of money."

She looked out the window. The few city lights were far away. Then they went into a tunnel and she couldn't see them at all. Lucci would starve to death if no one found him. She would call the Nantucket police this afternoon and tell them he was locked in the pantry. She had meant to kill him; she had raised the maul, ready to crash it down on his skull, but it had a life of its own; it wavered in the air, sweat slicked the handle, and it started sliding out of her grip. She had to do it. He'd come after her again if she didn't. She got a better grip on the handle and thought of Rita, and Marvin, and the people she never knew on that plane. But Marvin and Rita and the other people would stay dead, no matter what she did to Lucci.

She tried to remember the game Lucci talked about. Maybe that would bring back the rage she'd felt when Rita's son told her that his mother was dead. Nothing came to her except a hazy picture of a jar of dead wasps, and eyes like Lucci's watching her. He didn't hate her because of a jar of dead wasps. She hadn't killed the wasps anyway; she hadn't even known that they were there. She tried to remember Miss Benson's class, and the game, one more time. She remembered Rita on the steps of her mother's house promising to help her. She didn't remember the classroom or anybody in it. As far as she knew, she'd never seen Lucci until he came into the control room with Carver. Even that was hazy now. She remembered showing him the reactor . . . she *thought* it was him. She remembered the reactor; she could close her eyes and see every detail of it, but she couldn't see Lucci there.

If she got out alive, she knew she probably would not remember his face clearly in a few weeks. In a year or two, she'd have to stop and think to remember his name.

She couldn't kill him for Marvin and Rita. She couldn't kill him for a jar of dead wasps or a game she couldn't remember playing. She was wasting time, and she lowered the maul to the kitchen floor.

Gelb leaned into the open car window. "They picked up the bus in New Jersey and they'll stay with it all the way. We'll meet Tomas and Clifton at the edge of the green."

"Too many people," David said.

"The busloads stay together. We'll find her."

"Stop the bus, pull her off."

Gelb shook his head. "Someone might try to protect her. She would certainly try to protect herself. It would be another mess. We have too many to clear up now."

A woman carrying a baby opened the door of the station wagon parked next to them in the service area. Gelb left the window, came around the car, and got into the front seat.

"Besides, it's easy to kill in a crowd, David, easier than

300

on a dark street or . . . on a bus. The person doesn't know, so there's no pleading or last-ditch fights. The crowd doesn't know either, at least not at first. The trick is not to make more noise than the mob makes, and to move back fast. The crush'll hold the body up for a few seconds. Nothing to it," Gelb said.

Emily and Ann came out of the bus stop north of Washington. Will was holding up the sign. The letters covered the board, but the paint faded in the sun. The President wouldn't see it.

"Wish you'd tell me what it means," Ann said. But Emily wasn't listening. She was staring at the chrome on the bus's side-view mirror. It caught light and shone it back into her eyes. She went to the mirror, then looked up at the sky. The rain was gone; it was clear. She didn't know where the President would be in relation to the sign, but she could control that; as long as there was light.

"Bangles," Emily said.

Will and Ann looked at each other.

"I need bangles," Emily said.

"What are you talking about?" Ann asked.

"Shiny plastic disks. My mother had them on a veil."

"Spangles!" Will said. "The lady wants spangles."

They found them at a Woolco about three miles from the Mall after the bus dropped them off in Washington. The manager said the spangles were a Christmas item and he had to go down to the basement for them. He did it cheerfully, which amazed Ann. He even helped them find the fast-drying glue Emily said they needed for the sign. When they got outside, Emily took one of the shiny disks out of the plastic tube and held it up. It caught the sun, made a circle of light on Will's cheek, and glittered in Ann's eyes.

Feinstein dropped into the chair across the desk from Orin. His face was gray. "Emily Brand was shot in Connecticut six days ago," he said.

"Is she dead?"

"There's divided opinion on that. Either way, she's gone."

"Who shot her?"

Here it comes, Feinstein thought. "A couple of guys from the NCEC and . . . really weird . . . there was a NARCON V.P. with them."

Orin turned white, and Feinstein thought he was going to see Orin Franklin—the great stone face, the man of total calm in a shitstorm—lose his temper.

"Stockton didn't mention it," Orin whispered.

"That's not all, Mr. President. The two guys who brought this to the Bureau in Plattsburg—one's a cop, by the way—claim that she was framed for blowing up Lipsky's plane."

Orin made the connection for the first time. "Talbot," he whispered.

"It's too early—"

"Talbot," Orin thundered. "Get him here. Get Stockton—"

"Take it easy, Orin."

"*Easy*," he shrieked. "In three minutes I've got to go out there and tell two hundred thousand people that they can kiss off half of the money they'll ever make . . ."

Glover tapped on the door. He'd never heard President Franklin raise his voice before.

"What?" Orin yelled.

Glover opened the door. "Everything all right, sir?"

"Fine, I'm not going to attack Mr. Feinstein."

Glover didn't care what the President did to Bruce Feinstein or anybody else, as long as he was okay. He looked okay—mad as hell, but okay. "It's almost time, sir."

"All right."

Orin stopped at the door and felt in his jacket for the speech. It was bland and weak, and he prayed that something better would come to him when he was out there. But it wouldn't. He needed George Talbot up on the podium with him; then Orin would tell the people that a woman named Emily Brand might have saved them, except that this mean, scared son of a bitch had had her shot. Now they were doomed. He'd tell them the story, then he'd shove George Talbot—screaming and clutching the podium, his nails scraping the platform lumber—he'd shove George Talbot off the dais into the mob.

"Not too close," Emily yelled over the noise of the crowd. "We'll miss his line of vision."

"Whose line of vision?" Ann cried, but Emily didn't hear. Will kept his arm around Emily, pulling her through the crowd in his wake. The other arm tilted high over their heads, carrying the sign. She couldn't see anything now but the back of the people right in front of her and the podium itself. She tugged at Will's arm. "To the right," she shouted, "more center." He complied, keeping his arm tight around her. They sidled through the press of bodies. The sun was hot, and the people's faces shone with sweat. Emily saw a thicket of signs over their heads. It would be hard to pick hers out except that Will was so tall and her sign shone like the summer sun on Placid at noon. She had a chance.

Ann tried to keep up. She wanted to grab hold of Emily and pull herself along with them. She knew Emily wouldn't mind, but Emily was limping so badly now Ann was afraid she'd pull her down. People surged around them; a few got between her and Emily, then a few more. It was hopeless. Ann saw Will's head and a little of Emily's bobbing in an odd limping rhythm. Will was half-guiding her, half-holding her up. Ann lost sight of Emily as more people closed between them, but she still saw Will and the crazy sign sailing high over his glossy black hair. Ann stopped pushing and let the crowd move her. She'd find them again when it was over.

She hoped the sign would catch the light. She hoped whoever it was meant for would get the message.

Two men pushed past her; they didn't shove, and she noticed only because one of them was the handsomest man she'd ever seen.

A woman with huge dark eyes was on the podium, singing and accompanying herself on the guitar. Emily could barely hear the music, but some of the crowd sang with her and swayed in time with the music.

"How's this?" Will yelled over the crowd.

Emily looked up at the podium. They were directly in front —not too far away, she hoped not too close. It was hard to keep the position in the swaying crowd.

The woman finished her song and the people all yelled at once. The noise rose up from the tops of their heads in a huge babble. Suddenly the noise muted a little. "What's going on?" Emily yelled.

"A shitload of limousines. Holy shit . . . must be fifty car doors opening at one time over there." He sounded excited, and Emily could feel it in the rest of the crowd.

"Holy shit," Will cried, "it looks like the President . . . it looks like the President. . . ."

People around her repeated it, took it up, and it ran through the press of bodies around her.

Looks like the President . . .

They swayed around her. In his excitement Will let her go so he could wave the sign with both hands. She clutched the side of his sweater and hung on.

"They're coming up the steps," he cried. "It's him!" She heard it repeated a thousand times from every side. *It's him . . . it's him.*

Now they were on the stand and she could see. The folk singer left the mike and crossed the stand. Emily couldn't see him clearly, men crowded around him, cut him off from her sight, but the folk singer was shaking his hand; then she moved to the back of the podium. The group of men around him parted, and Orin Franklin came up to the mike. The crowd went wild.

A big nigger with a shiny sign, Gelb's men had told them. They saw him once, then lost them. But they kept easing their way through the throng in the direction they'd seen him take. They couldn't see Emily in the mob, but Gelb's man said she was with the black, so they kept going. Then David saw him again.

"There," he shouted at Gelb, "over there."

Gelb nodded, and they started pushing to their right.

David couldn't see her, but he knew she was there and he went faster.

Gelb grabbed his arm and pulled him back. He lost his balance and fell against the bigger man, but Gelb was solid and held him up. Gelb shook his head, and blood pumped up through David's body. Gelb was going to crap out on him.

Gelb brought his mouth to David's ear. "They're too close. The mob's full of Secret Service. Wait till they move back."

"No," David cried. "He'll see that sign."

Gelb shook his head, and David thought he'd faint with rage.

"There's a hundred thousand signs here," Gelb said. "He won't read that one."

But David knew he would. The man said it was shiny, and David knew she'd find a way to make it glow like the fire of hell. The President would see it and recognize it, whatever it was. That's why she was here.

"Wait," Gelb shouted in David's ear.

"Go to hell." He pulled away from Gelb and started back into the crowd. Gelb didn't stop him. David saw the black man's gleaming hair again and wanted to shriek with joy. He couldn't see her yet, but he knew he would in a second. A few more ranks of people, and her back would be in front of him.

Gelb had coached him, and he knew what to do. The noise wasn't a problem. A full shot would be drowned in this bedlam, and even the people close to her would not hear a silenced one. Gelb told him to shoot her in the back of the head . . . at the base of the skull pointing up, so that the shot would come out the top of her head. Otherwise her face would explode all over the people in front of her. Also, he couldn't let the gun touch her, or let anyone see it. He had to hold it down under his chest, hidden by his jacket, and angled up toward the base of her skull. If his hand shook a fraction, Gelb said, he must go for a back shot. Under her shoulder, slightly left of center. The head shot was best, but his control had to be perfect, because he got only one shot. David's control *was* perfect. His hand was steady, his palm was dry, his finger wrapped around the trigger was strong and would squeeze the trigger as smoothly as a machine.

Even the crowd seemed to be on his side and parted easily to let him through. He saw the black man's head.

"Now," Emily yelled at Will, "back a little. Tilt a little more. More . . ." The sign moved back over Will's head while Emily stood on her toes, holding on to him, watching the light and the spangles and looking up to the podium at the blur of Orin Franklin's face.

Will got it right for a second, then moved.

"Forward," Emily shouted.

He tilted the stick forward slightly and she grabbed his forearm in a grip so strong it hurt, but he held the sign steady and she shouted exultantly, "That's it . . . don't move, Will, that's it! That's wonderful!" And Will held the sign unmoving, shining bravely over his head.

Someone in the crowd had a huge mirror or something; it caught the sun and shot it back into Orin's eyes. He blinked and squinted and rubbed his eyes. It moved a fraction and the glare snapped at him from over the heads of the people. Glover saw it too, and he put his hand over the mike. "You want me to get rid of that?"

Orin nodded, and Glover started to leave the mike stand, but Feinstein grabbed him and held on to him; then he grabbed Orin too. His fingers dug into the President's flesh, and Glover got ready to punch him, but Feinstein shouted, "Read it, Orin. For God's sake, read it."

The mike wasn't covered. Feinstein's shout went out over the crowd, and there was a slight hush.

Orin shaded his eyes and looked out. As if by plan, the sign moved slightly to cut the glare, and written out in brilliant silver circles glued to a huge piece of poster board, Orin saw the word "LIGHTSOURCE."

"Get me through that crowd," Orin said.

That went out over the mikes too, and the hush on the crowd deepened.

David saw dots of light hit the President's face, and he knew where they'd come from. But they couldn't get to her in time, and even if they found the three pages, she'd be dead, and David could take a full free breath for the first time in almost thirty years. Only a few more yards separated them. She wouldn't see him when he did it. But he imagined that there would be an instant of consciousness before she died, and she'd know that he had pulled the trigger and won. He only had a little way to go, and he shoved harder. Then Gelb grabbed his arm and pulled him around to face him. He struggled, but Gelb's grip locked on him like metal. He heard Gelb's voice, like a tape recording from the grave: "*No*. Franklin's coming into the crowd. Look."

He looked. Men were racing up onto the platform, fifty or so, and more coming.

"Hurry," the President said. Everybody heard it, and the cheering stopped and a loud whispering sound came up out of the crowd. The men on the platform made a flying wedge, with Franklin in the middle. They started down the platform and into the crowd.

Gelb's voice again: "Forget it, David. In a second there'll be one Secret Service man for everybody near her. It's over ... forget it."

David tried to pull away; Gelb wouldn't let him. The wedge was moving. If Franklin got to her, she'd win. Pain crashed in David's head, and he pulled the gun out in the open. A thousand people would see it if they looked down, but this was his day, and no one did. He jammed the gun against Gelb's jacket button, and Gelb let him go.

David turned back into the crowd, pulled the gun back inside the flaps of his jacket. People moved to let him by and he slid through the crowd. He saw the black man's back and shoulders, and then he saw her. His head stopped aching as suddenly as it had started, and he had that old, wonderful feeling of bottomless strength that he'd had a few times in his life—when he had thrown Donny Broome against the stone wall . . . when rich, beautiful, stupid Mary Talbot had asked him to marry her . . . and when the doctor had told him that he had a son.

Gelb knew that the Secret Service men wouldn't let an armed man within fifty feet of the President. But they couldn't just stop David now, he was too crazy. They would have to kill him. Then they'd find the ID card that Stockton had signed, and they'd think that a man from the NCEC was trying to assassinate the President. Gelb couldn't let that happen, and he was sorry because he almost liked David Lucci.

He pulled his silenced pistol out of his belt and went through the crowd after David.

The crowd yelled, welcoming the President into their midst; the Secret Service men were everywhere, and Gelb had to move fast.

He reached David, snaked out his arm and hooked it

around David's neck. David struggled, but Gelb was much stronger. The crowd yelled. Gelb yelled with them, and reached around to clip David's wrist with the butt of his gun. He heard the bone crack, and David's gun fell into his hand. David tried to scream, but Gelb mashed the gun so hard against his mouth that David bit his own lips. Gelb jammed the silencer against the base of David's skull, aiming up over the heads of the crowd in front of them, and he pulled the trigger.

The small calibre, muffled against David's head, made a pop. No one heard. Gelb shoved his gun into his belt, then reached into David's jacket pocket and pulled out his wallet. He held David up until he felt the crowd shoved tight against them, then he let go and inched sideways. A man pushed into Gelb's place; Gelb kept moving slowly and smoothly through the crowd toward the street. He was a few ranks away when he heard the first scream and saw a swirl of movement where he had been.

It was the crowd pushing to get away from the corpse as it sank to the ground.

The Secret Service men saw the commotion, tightened the circle around Franklin, and started moving back toward the platform. Lincoln's statue brooded down on the mob as the ring of men with Franklin in the middle started flowing up the steps of the monument.

Gelb paused for a second. He couldn't see the President, but he saw the sign and the black man inside the ring. They moved higher up the steps, above the heads of the crowd, and he saw her.

He'd never seen her in the flesh, and he strained to get a good look. After all, she had put him in the ridiculous position of having to save her life, and he wanted to know what she looked like. But she was too far away, her face was only a blur.

They kept Emily in Washington for two days. Then she went back to Falmouth to get the Volvo.

"I'm sorry," the gas jockey said miserably when Emily saw the damage.

"I know," Emily said.

"Look, forget the fifty dollars."

"It's all right, it wasn't your fault." She opened the hood. "No damage there. I have a friend back home who'll do the bodywork. Could you sell me three tires?"

"Oh, lady"—the man beamed—"I can't *sell* you nothing. Will Gregson—big black guy—he said he'd take me apart if I ever saw the color of your money. I'm to send him the bill."

She had called the Nantucket police from Washington . . . from the White House . . . but they had already been to the Squam house, checking an abandoned Eldorado half-blocking the sand road, and the house was empty. The NARCON people must have gotten Lucci out and told him there was no more point in chasing her. She stopped thinking about him.

She drove to the ferry terminal in Woods Hole and called Susie. Susie cried and laughed at the same time and promised that she and Steven would come to Placid as soon as the black flies were gone. The steamer horn hooted and Emily had to hang up. She would call John from Maida Gardner's house, and after an evening with the old lady, she would catch the first ferry back in the morning. She had to stop in Grant Union to see Jenny and Jesse, then in Glens Falls to see Smitty. She knew she could write or call to thank them and to explain as best she could—they weren't the sort of people to care about being thanked in person, or probably about being thanked at all—but her mother would have said that the debt was too great to be paid with a call or letter. She knew she had to go now, because once she started working, she would never take the time to do it.

POSTSCRIPT

THE DAY AFTER the demonstration, the Justice Department and the FBI started collecting material on the NCEC and the plane crash on Mount Marcy. Two days later, Miles Carver drowned on Lake Placid. A capsized canoe was found near the shore and the inquest ruled accidental death, even though his wife insisted that he hated boats and never went out on the lake.

That same day, at his son-in-law's funeral, George Talbot had a stroke that left him paralyzed and mute. He was moved from the hospital to a nursing home in Greenwich, where he was given daily therapy and had started to recover the use of his right hand when another stroke killed him in September.

Paul Stockton was indicted for conspiracy to murder. He shot himself, and Kurt Gelb left the NCEC (which was disbanded a few months later) and went to work for the CIA. He was named deputy director in 1993.

Orin Franklin decided to run for another term and was elected by a small, barely respectable plurality.

In June 1994 the first Tokamak-Brand fusion reactor went on line, supplying electricity for a power corridor three hundred miles wide between New York City and Montreal. The corridor was widened, and by the end of the next year it was bounded on the west by Cleveland and on the east by Laconia, New Hampshire.